Eliot Asinof and the
Truth of the Game

Also by William Farina
and from McFarland

Chrétien de Troyes and the Dawn of Arthurian Romance (2010)

Perpetua of Carthage: Portrait of a Third-Century Martyr (2009)

Ulysses S. Grant, 1861–1864: His Rise from Obscurity to Military Greatness (2007)

De Vere as Shakespeare: An Oxfordian Reading of the Canon (2006)

Eliot Asinof and the Truth of the Game

A Critical Study of the Baseball Writings

William Farina

McFarland & Company, Inc., Publishers
Jefferson, North Carolina, and London

LIBRARY OF CONGRESS CATALOGUING-IN-PUBLICATION DATA

Eliot Asinof and the truth of the game : a critical study of the baseball writings / William Farina.
p. cm.
Includes bibliographical references and index.

ISBN 978-0-7864-6302-2
softcover : acid free paper ∞

1. Baseball — United States. 2. Asinof, Eliot, 1919–2008 — Criticism and interpretation. 3. Baseball stories, American. I. Title.
GV863.A1E45 2012
796.357—dc23 2011043184

BRITISH LIBRARY CATALOGUING DATA ARE AVAILABLE

On the cover: (foreground) Eliot Asinof, senior captain of the baseball team at Lawrence High School in Cedarhurst, Long Island, 1936 (background photograph by William J. Mahnken)

Manufactured in the United States of America

McFarland & Company, Inc., Publishers
Box 611, Jefferson, North Carolina 28640
www.mcfarlandpub.com

To Phillip A. Farina
Brother, Coach, Friend

Acknowledgments

Thanks yet again to Marion Buckley for urging me forward in a good way. Thanks to Martin Asinof, John Sayles, and Jim Bouton for generously offering their time and valuable insights. Thanks to the staff of the Dolph Briscoe Center for American History at the University of Texas at Austin for helping me sift through Asinof's voluminous surviving papers and manuscripts. Thanks to the staff at the Marathon County Public Library in Wausau, Wisconsin, and the staff at the Hennepin County Library in Minneapolis, Minnesota—your professionalism was contagious. Thanks to Jeff Kisseloff for an important heads-up. Thanks to the Central Wisconsin Baseball Hall of Fame for giving me timely encouragement. Belated thanks to Ken Schrieber and Al Shinn for teaching me important lessons in my youth about baseball and about life.

Table of Contents

Part V: *Off-Season* (2000)

Introduction

Ask anyone who has ever really played it: baseball is the finest athletic game ever conceived.

— Eliot Asinof[1]

No one has written about baseball with more authority, conviction, and insight than the late Eliot Tager Asinof (1919–2008).[2] The key factors behind his unique accomplishment are, at minimum, threefold. First, Asinof was, simply put, a highly talented writer who, over a 50-plus-year career, produced a vast output of fiction, nonfiction, screenplays, and journalism covering the full spectrum of modern American life — of which baseball and professional sports were only one, significant aspect. Second, Asinof was — unlike almost all other gifted authors who have tackled the subject of baseball — a former minor league player who competed at a very advanced professional level before turning to writing for a livelihood. Third, and often overlooked, is that Asinof lived, by anyone's standards, an impressively long, full, and interesting life that informed all of his writings, including those about baseball, with a keen perception, broad vision, and diversity of outlook that only the best of authors seem to possess. This unusual combination of personal qualities places him within a very select and elite group of American writers. By the time he produced at age 36 his first widely acknowledged masterpiece, the baseball novel *Man on Spikes* (1955), he had acquired more experience in life and sports than most ever possess throughout a lifetime. Nevertheless, this was just the beginning in a long string of provocative works that would come to a halt only with his death 53 years later, as he worked on an unpublished memoir.

In addition to his debut novel, Asinof wrote four other major works on the subject of baseball, three of which (like his first effort) were novels. *Man on Spikes* was and still is considered extraordinary for its time, not only for being a brisk, entertaining read, but also for representing the first searing indictment of professional baseball's notorious reserve clause, some 20 years before it was finally dismantled by legal arbitration in 1975. As "fiction" it has stood the test of time, although readers are still often shocked at its vivid, rough insider's view of the game, one not at all for the faint of heart or those wishing to romanticize professional baseball into something which it is not. Asinof's next baseball work was the classic nonfiction *Eight Men Out* (1963), after 48 years still viewed by many as the definitive account of the 1919 Black Sox Scandal and a quality benchmark for all sports literature in general. Later, this book was turned into a critically acclaimed and commercially successful motion picture by the same title (1988). Although Asinof's pioneering work in this area is devoid of footnotes and bibliographies, its accuracy and hypothetical reconstruction of events has held up amazingly well over time, despite a constant discovery of new facts and information regarding the scandal itself.[3] Asinof begins *Eight Men Out* with a modest preface in which he briefly explains to readers how he went about finding and utilizing his source materials, including personal interviews with surviving participants.[4]

Asinof's last three baseball books are less well known, unjustly and undeservedly so. Each poses profound questions for the thoughtful reader, perhaps too complex to find a wide audience, but always deeply rewarding for those willing to ponder such things. *The Bedfellow* (1967) came four years after *Eight Men Out* and could not have more defeated audience expectations in terms of what Asinof would write next. Apart from being pure fiction, the novel deals not with the playing career of a major leaguer, but rather with his post-playing career in the world of advertising. Add to that the main character and narrator being African American and heavy doses of autobiography thrown in, and one gets a sense of how bold Asinof's departure was. Critics and audiences were typically, and not surprisingly, confused at best.

It would be three decades before Asinof wrote another baseball book; when he finally did, his taste for experimentation had not waned. *Strike Zone* (1994) may be one of the most unusual American novels ever written. A collaboration with former Yankee bad boy and popular commentator Jim Bouton, this story returns to the familiar gambling-corruption theme in sports, but with a twist. Asinof and Bouton take turns writing alternating chapters, Asinof from the viewpoint of a home plate umpire and Bouton from that of a pitcher. The intriguing results are manifold, including an implied questioning of baseball's ethical underpinnings and, by extension, the American way of life in general. His last baseball novel, *Off-Season* (2000), published on the eve of George W. Bush's inauguration as president, is a fitting swan song to Asinof's half century of musings on the national pastime. Its primary theme is race — the Great American Odyssey, as it has been sometimes called — long after professional sports became integrated and the issue was supposedly dead and resolved as a national debate. Not so, poignantly argues the novelist in a bracing work whose date of release could not have been timed better or worse, depending on one's point of view — better because the message was badly needed and worse because it was a highly unfashionable one.

Although Asinof's baseball writings will be the focus of this study, his voluminous non-baseball work is also worthy of close examination. His other efforts will be cited whenever appropriate to highlight and underscore important recurring themes in his five baseball books. For example, Asinof's *1919: America's Loss of Innocence* (1991) provides crucial and valuable historical backdrop to the World Series of that year, the same in which the author was born. *Bleeding Between the Lines* (1979) lays out in horrific, autobiographical detail Asinof's own defiant struggle amidst lawsuits and controversy to make any money whatsoever from his most popular and best known work. Because *Eight Men Out* is the author's most famous book, there are more extensive outside materials to draw upon, as well as the feature film by director John Sayles, in which Asinof participated. In a similar fashion, all of Asinof's baseball and non-baseball writings often interweave to form a continuous thematic narrative. To look at his five baseball volumes in a vacuum would be an interpretive mistake that shall be carefully avoided within these pages. Although more time will be spent covering *Eight Men Out*, Asinof's four baseball novels will also be given extensive and near equal amounts of treatment, including similar cross-references to his other non-baseball and non-sports work. The end result will hopefully help to elevate Asinof's stature among his generation of postwar American writers (a stellar group to be sure), as well as to encourage more critical and popular attention for this highly underrated and too often neglected literary artist.

Perhaps the biggest challenge in this project has been not to overly digress into Asinof's turbulent and endlessly fascinating personal life. Instead, I have presented only those biographical details that may shed light on his baseball writings. The addendum, however, will include a timeline intermingling his biography with his major published works. For example, Asinof's background as a Jewish, blacklisted Hollywood screenwriter during the 1950s probably had as much to do with his firebrand, rebellious style and choice of material, as did his prior collegiate and minor league baseball experience. Notably, it was learned from FBI files late in his life that Asinof's only "un–American activity" had been to sign a petition favoring racial integration of the New York Yankees — this was during the same era (the early 1950s), by which time many other professional baseball teams had already done so.[5] At his passing in 2008, Asinof was still writing about social injustices witnessed in the U.S. military during World War II while serving in the Aleutian Islands, over 60 years after the fact.[6] This was a deeply driven and passionate writer, not a syrupy or sentimental one. As he himself often humorously quipped, "I am not now nor ever have been Isaac Asimov."[7]

One thing that originally led me to this topic, one so ready for exploration, was my temporary job relocation to Wausau, Wisconsin.[8] This city was home of the former Wausau Lumberjacks, a (Philadelphia Phillies) minor league team for which Asinof played outfield in 1941.[9] Wausau would be his last gig as an active professional ballplayer. Earlier during his playing career, Asinof had fatefully befriended fellow Jewish teammate Mickey Rutner, a promising, future major league player. As readily admitted by the novelist, it was Rutner who provided inspiration for the "fictional" character Mike Kutner, tragic hero of *Man on Spikes*. By the 1941 season's end and in the aftermath of Pearl Harbor, everyone was off to war. When Asinof returned from service, he devoted himself more and more to writing, turning fully professional as an author around 1950. Although many of Asinof's friends, associates, and writer colleagues are now gone, some of those still living who knew and worked with him have enthusiastically shared their personal reminisces of his huge talent and bigger-than-life personality. In any event, the works speak for themselves. To repeat, this study will not be strict literary biography, although it might help to encourage such a worthy project in the future. Baseball fans, of course, should take interest in Asinof's playing and writing careers, but the subject matter is suggestively much bigger than baseball. Both general readers and academic specialists will hopefully find it interesting as well, especially those wanting to place the national pastime firmly within the larger context of American society and culture.

Each of the four chapters in the five parts of this study (one for each book) will follow an identical pattern.[10] The first chapter in each part will provide a publication history for the work and a synopsis, and discuss the extent to which the book ties into Asinof's biography. The second chapter in each part will deal with the book's critical and popular reception, as well as the aftermath of events — in the iconoclastic case of Asinof always a tempestuous and combative sequence. The third chapter in each part will explore the book's themes as these relate to baseball and the overlapping worlds of professional and amateur sports. The fourth and final chapter in each part will broaden these thematic horizons to include America and the world. For Asinof, baseball was always a harsh but accurate mirror of country and society. To him, this is what made it worth writing about in the first place.

Asinof authored or co-authored a total of 15 published books, produced over a lengthy writing career that spanned more than 50 years. Most of these books, however, are not about baseball. He occasionally wrote about other sports, but more frequently about non-sports topics. After quickly perusing Asinof's surviving manuscripts and papers, I would estimate that approximately one-half of his total writings were sports-related, and of these, approximately two-thirds were connected to baseball.[11] By my arithmetic, this means that approximately one-third of Asinof's life's work was about baseball. The half of his writings that are non-sports related might easily be dismissed as the overly-ambitious musings of an aspiring intellectual, were it not for the fact that some of these include extraordinary productions such as *People vs.*

Blutcher, *Craig and Joan*, *The Fox Is Crazy Too*, and *Final Judgment*. Other timeless, full-length works such as *Bleeding Between the Lines* and *1919: America's Loss of Innocence* do include significant sections about baseball, but these are presented only within the context of much broader, more universal concerns. Asinof was far more than a sportswriter, and always resisted, with good justification, any attempts by critics to pigeonhole him into that single category. He wrote about important social issues and current events; he wrote about modern history; he wrote about his own personal experiences in World War II and then afterwards, as a screenwriter for early television and Hollywood movies. His published writings on other sports topics, including football, golf, track and field, and tennis, are, like his baseball works, consistently authoritative and engaging.

To the best of my knowledge, no one has ever produced a full-length study on the works of Eliot Asinof, baseball-related or otherwise. For that matter, precious little has been written about Asinof's work from a serious literary standpoint. All of this is likely to change in the near future. The disadvantage of being first is that there are limited resources and secondary material to draw upon. Above all, I hope to drive home the important point that the best writing on any subject is always based on personal experience, which is apparent to anyone who has ever both played the game competitively *and* read Asinof's gritty, realistic meditations on it. What makes Asinof very unusual (unique, in fact, among writers), is that as a young man before World War II, he played two seasons of minor league baseball. His professional playing experience is a big part of the reason Asinof's baseball books are so different from others. Most baseball commentary is written by sportswriters who never played the game themselves beyond sandlot level, if that. Asinof, on the other hand, played with and against many great athletes who went on to the big time. And he was not a bad player himself: a switch-hitting, left-handed-throwing centerfielder with a lifetime professional batting average of .296. He was also a Jewish kid from New York City. This was during the prewar era which saw Hank Greenberg, a friend of the Asinof family, become the very first Jewish American superstar of the sports world. Writing many years later, Asinof said the main reason that he himself never made it to the majors was that he just was not quite good enough, plus the war took away his four best years. Add to this that he was a bit injury-prone and had a very short-temper which often got him into trouble. After the war, however, when Asinof decided to become a professional writer, he used his former playing experience to produce some of the most realistic baseball books that have ever been written.

Anyone who has ever played the game at high competitive levels knows what it is like to pick up a baseball book, look at it, and think, "What are they talking about? This is not real. This is fable." With Asinof's works on the subject, however, one never has that problem. For Asinof, baseball is a bruising contact sport — outfielders crash into walls while making catches, or cross signals and crash into each other; base runners smash into catchers while trying to score at home plate, teeth go flying, and players get carried away on stretchers or, less seriously, sustain painful injuries but then get bandaged up and go on playing; "chin music" is a routine part of the game; verbal abuse from the stands and from opposing dugouts is off the charts; above all, cheating and breaking the rules are fine as long as you can get away with it.[12] Asinof's ball-playing characters have winning attitudes, simply because they well know what it is like to experience success and victory. For Asinof, baseball is not Charlie Brown stuff— it is the real deal, often times barbaric and savage.

Some former professional ballplayers have written or co-written books, and some of these are quite good. Names like Jim Bouton and Jim Brosnan immediately come to mind; however, these are athletes who wrote perhaps a few works at most. Asinof, by stunning contrast, made a living solely as a professional writer for over half a century, writing about all sorts of things and getting wide recognition for it. Before that, he played in the minor leagues, which makes him an extremely rare commodity as an author, one to be treasured, in fact. As for established professional writers making occasional forays into the world of professional sports, the ubiquitous example of George Plimpton immediately comes to mind. His very special case, however, will be compared and contrasted to Asinof's legacy in the final Summation of this study. Perhaps most unusual of all, Asinof's writing and playing careers did not overlap, nor did he attempt to segue one into the other. On the contrary, his writing career seemed to grow organically out his playing experience several years after he had retired as a professional athlete. There was no premeditated, master plan to it. Because his writing talent combined with a stellar university education in the humanities, Asinof, along with his first editor, Vance Bourjaily (see Chapter 1), simply realized that he was probably far better equipped and qualified to write about baseball than any of his literary competitors.

Asinof's athletic experience was not limited to two years playing baseball in the minors. In 1939, when the Baseball Hall of Fame in Cooperstown first opened, he was one of the local New York amateurs invited to participate in ceremonial games specially organized for the grand opening.[13] Then after the war, he co-owned and managed the semipro Yonkers Indians for a couple years — this was during the era of Jackie Robinson and racial integration (see Chapter 1). Later, in 1959, while in Cuba working on a movie screenplay, he was invited by Fidel Castro to help organize new baseball leagues there, an offer which Asinof declined (see Chapter 2). During the 1960s, Asinof regularly played softball in New York City, sometimes with former Yankees like Phil Rizzuto (see Chapter 11). By the time he was in his mid–40s, Asinof began to focus on his golf game, and quickly became a sensational amateur golfer; golf was a sport at which he continued to excel well into his 80s. In addition to being a good athlete, Asinof was an accomplished piano player, once hired to interview jazz musician Lionel Hampton because of his musical knowledge (see Chapter 2). He was a skilled carpenter who built his own his house in upstate New York, the house that he lived in for last three decades of his life. He was a competent tailor who came from a successful family of New York clothiers. Recently, his friend and fellow baseball author Roger Kahn went on record to say that he was a good cook as well.[14] Truly, Eliot Asinof was a modern Renaissance man.

Students of the Chicago Black Sox may recall that no one was able to write about the scandal for a long time because no one would talk about it. All of the surviving participants were either too ashamed, too scared of retaliation from gangsters, or were just bad guys who would only talk for money, then after getting paid tell a very tall tale. Asinof was finally able to break the true story during the early 1960s mainly because he got former Black Sox Happy Felsch to open up for a truthful, candid interview shortly before Felsch died (see Chapter 5). Felsch, like Asinof, had been a centerfielder, and was also a lifelong resident of Milwaukee, Wisconsin. The fact that Asinof was a former minor league outfielder who once played in Wausau probably helped to break the ice with Felsch, as did their mutual love of telling off-color jokes. In fact, Wisconsin has a number of interesting connections to the Black Sox that one rarely hears about. For example, former White Sox Dickie Kerr, who won two games pitching in the 1919 Series, had managed the Wausau Lumberjacks during the 1937 season. Also, Sox catcher Ray Schalk, before making it to the majors and later the Hall of Fame, played minor league ball for the old Milwaukee Brewers. Eddie Cicotte is said to have played outlaw ball in Wisconsin after being banned from the game for his role in the 1919 scandal.[15] These were all former Sox players that Asinof interviewed or at least tried to interview with varying degrees of success.

For a quick summary of Asinof's intriguing biography, I refer readers to the timeline. It is worth stressing and repeating, however, that the roots for his qualitative success as an author can be found in the tremendous education he received in his youth at higher learning institutions such as Swarthmore College in Pennsylvania and Williams College in Massachusetts, where he was exposed to some of the finest teachers and intellectuals of the New Deal era. Although Asinof pulled good grades as a student, his youthful passion was for baseball, an extracurricular activity in which he excelled during both high school and college. For Asinof, good education plus baseball equaled, in the long run, great baseball books pouring forth from his typewriter. Former players' union representative Marvin Miller was among the many who recognized Asinof's outstanding achievement:

> There is no scarcity of baseball books. For almost a century publishers have marketed baseball novels, essays, commentary, biographies, "as told to" autobiographies, and much more. With rare but notable exceptions, these works have been less than literary gems for a variety of reasons. Prominent among these reasons is the failure to deal with reality — the tendency to ignore facts and instead give credence to mythology and management handouts.[16]

As to style, the editors of *Sport* magazine, in praising his illuminating 1980 interview of Willie Stargell, noted that "Asinof's writing has the same kind of qualities he found in Stargell — dignity and class."[17] Indeed, the same holds true for all of his credited output from beginning to end, even those collaborative works which he appears to have held in relatively low esteem such as *Strike Zone* and *10-Second Jailbreak*. It seems that, as a literary artist, Asinof was incapable of producing mediocrity, possibly because he had been forced to do so much of that during his early years as a screenwriter, sometimes anonymously and others as an assumed front for those who had been blacklisted.[18]

This study was undertaken because, thus far, Asinof's literary legacy has been underappreciated. It is hoped that more deliberate and comprehensive works on the same subject matter will appear in the future. The selected list of Asinof's miscellaneous baseball writings at the end of this study makes no pretense at comprehensiveness. It merely represents what I happened to encounter during the course of my research. No doubt there is more published material out there; there is certainly much more yet to be published, both sports-related and non-sports-related. Asinof's surviving papers and manuscripts are currently housed at the Dolph Briscoe Center for American History at the University of Texas at Austin, where I had the privilege and pleasure, with considerable help from staff, to go through boxes and boxes of fascinating documents. Most of these unpublished materials are undated and many are unsigned. Although Asinof's written legacy currently appears to be in good hands, I urge a systematic and disciplined reorganization of these papers be undertaken, especially since there are obviously so many unpublished works amongst these that are probably quite worthy of publication.[19] While I was able to find time and money to travel to various locales such as Austin, Chicago, Wausau, and Minneapolis, I was unable to visit (or, in some cases, revisit) many Asinof shrines such as New York City, Ancramdale, Cedarhurst, Moultrie, Swarthmore, Williamstown, and Cooperstown. Based on my previous book projects, I have found that personal travel to relevant sites usually sheds new light upon otherwise obscure literary work. This is yet another reason why this particular study should ideally represent only the beginning of a longer and more serious investigation into Asinof's eventful life and extensive, invaluable catalogue.

Despite his longevity and vast output, there is evidence that Asinof would have gone on to produce even more significant works, had he lived to do so. After his death in 2008, Asinof's son, Martin, remarked, "He [Eliot] was writing right up to the end."[20] This tends to be yet another distinctive trait of the greatest authors who, more often than not, are compelled to create by seemingly external forces, as opposed to having any personal choice in the matter. Such writers are seized by the Muses, as the ancients used to say. Among his papers are countless notes, outlines, treatments, sketches, and proposals that never apparently came to fruition. It is also obvious that Asinof frequently wrote "on spec," beginning and completing full-length works before he had been paid or even hired to do so — typically a big no-no for professional writers. This is another indication that once the inspiration got a hold of him, he had little control of himself as an artist, except to write down that which was inside of him. Published works of his that did make it to the light of day clearly demonstrate that he had valuable things to say and teach, whether it be in the official guise of fiction or nonfiction. Now all that we, the reading public, have left of him is a paper trail. Since Asinof's passing, director John Sayles spoke for many of us when he said, "We miss him a lot."[21]

Part I: *Man on Spikes* (1955)

1

An Egalitarian Battle Cry

> *As it was with Mickey Rutner, so it was in Man on Spikes, with its hero, Mike Kutner. He was used, victimized by the system that made up its own reasons to exploit his talents. He is, then, like so many of us in all walks of life, an unsung hero who never makes it. Everyone knows that life isn't fair. What remained for me, the writer, was to make sense of it. I had found a theme that dominated most of my work for years to come.*
>
> —Eliot Asinof[1]

Any serious baseball fan who came of age during the 1970s will vividly recall the raging controversy surrounding major league baseball's reviled reserve clause and the highly publicized Curt Flood litigation that forcefully ushered it into the public consciousness. Although Flood eventually lost his case before the U.S. Supreme Court in 1972, *Flood vs. Kuhn*, this proved to be a pyrrhic victory for team owners because of the negative publicity generated. Accordingly, within three years the reserve clause had been dismantled through legal arbitration between the owners and the recently-formed players' union. With this gain for the players came free agency and a new era of completely different problems and abuses. At the time, however, even many knowledgeable fans reacted to the Flood lawsuit with bewilderment. Many asked, what was a reserve clause? Simply stated, it was the long-standing rule that a professional baseball player was the exclusive property of the team originally signing him and could never play for another team unless traded or released. This entrenched system, which existed only in baseball and no other professional sport, was often and rightfully compared to serfdom or slavery. Other professional sports did not have it; only baseball. Today, a mere 35 years after the fact, in an era of pampered and overpaid athletes, it is hard to imagine such a system. Indeed, many baseball fans born after the 1960s are either unaware that it ever existed or fail to appreciate its former stranglehold on the players. In 1955, 15 years before Curt Flood sued major league baseball, a 36-year-old aspiring writer had his debut novel published, dealing head on with the exact same divisive issue. It was the very first of its kind, and a great book quite apart from its social prescience. In the words of the former players' union representative and Curt Flood lead attorney Marvin Miller, "*Man on Spikes* ... marks Mr. Asinof as one of the few writers ahead of his time ... a prophet—with honor."[2]

Despite all of Asinof's renowned intelligence and moral principles, he did not originally set out to write the definitive novel exposing the injustices of the reserve clause; quite the opposite, in fact. He started out as a professional player himself who, by his own candid admission, played for little else than adolescent passion for the game, and certainly not for the money.[3] After enjoying an outstanding baseball career at the high school, collegiate, and semipro levels, the 21-year-old Asinof signed on for consecutive years in 1940 and 1941 to play in the Philadelphia Phillies organization; first, briefly with the Moultrie (Georgia) Packers, and then the following summer for the Wausau (Wisconsin) Lumberjacks. He was a left-handed, switch-hitting outfielder, which is to say he batted left-handed most of the time.[4] In a total of 56 minor league games and 216 at bats, Asinof hit .296 with six doubles, one triple, no home runs, 17 RBIs, and six stolen bases.[5] Thirty-five years later he assessed his own baseball talent as "barely above the bottom rung.... For an outfielder, I didn't have the power. If it weren't for the war, I might have gone to Double A."[6] After his strangely abortive 1941 season in Wausau (see Part IV of this study), Asinof and millions of other

Asinof as a young boy, early 1920s, possibly at Coney Island. During his childhood, Asinof would meet his idol Babe Ruth, then at the height of his fame and living in the same neighborhood as the Asinof family (see Chapter 13). Their meeting would leave a lasting impression on the future author, who some eight decades later would bestow the name "Babe" on his faithful golden retriever.

young men were off to World War II. He never played professionally again but would continue to dabble in amateur baseball and softball as player, manager and owner until the 1960s, by which time he was writing professionally full time, eventually becoming one of America's most renowned commentators on the national pastime.[7]

Shortly before turning professional during the 1940 season, Asinof met the man who would first inspire him to write about baseball: Milton "Mickey" Rutner (1920–2007).[8] Rutner and Asinof were briefly teammates in a professionally sponsored amateur league of New York and New England college players recruited because of their promising major league potential.[9] Both were Jewish during an era in which Hank Greenberg had only recently proved, to the consternation of many, that Jews could be great baseball players. The initial association of Rutner and Asinof did not last long; when manager Bill Barrett (a former Red Sox outfielder) got wind that two Jews were on his roster, he quickly trimmed it down to one, keeping Rutner, the more baseball-talented of the two.[10] Rutner, still attending St. John's University, continued playing in amateur summer league that season, while the recently college-graduated Asinof was invited to try out with the Phillies and soon after wound up being sent to their farm team in remote Moultrie, Georgia. The following year (in 1941), Rutner signed with the "other" Philadelphia team, Connie Mack's Athletics, and was assigned to their farm team in Winston-Salem (North Carolina) where he began a long, frustrating (and war-interrupted) career later immortalized by Asinof's first novel.

As a player, Rutner's statistics do not belie Asinof's portrayal of him (via the fictional Mike Kutner) as a good, rugged, dedicated athlete. The apex of Rutner's career came at the end of the 1947 season when he was called up for 12 major league games with the A's, his proverbial baseball cup of coffee. He hit .250, including one home run (coincidentally, against the Chicago White Sox), then was sent back down to the minors, where he spent the rest of his professional playing days before retiring at age 34 after the 1953 season.[11] Apart from losing his potentially four best seasons to World War II, Rutner suffered a proliferation of bad luck that is the inevitable fate of most minor league baseball players. He was a third baseman, and the A's during that era already had an outstanding third baseman, Hank Majeski.[12] As for Rutner, he was popular in the minor league cities where he played, as well as a very good hitter (lifetime batting .295), hence profitable for the team organization to keep him right where he was.[13] And of course there was anti–Semitism, still rampant throughout the 1950s.[14] Happily, Asinof saw Rutner play one of his dozen major league games at Yankee Stadium in late 1947, in which Rutner performed very well. The two men then had a beer together afterwards.[15] Thus the long process continued in which Rutner the ballplayer would eventually become Asinof's first baseball writing muse.

In spite of all the bad breaks, a player of Rutner's caliber certainly could have spent much more time in the majors than he did, had it not been for the then extant reserve clause, which legally tied him in perpetuity to the Athletics, while other professional clubs pined for a decent third baseman. By the time Rutner and Asinof had their drink together in the fall of 1947, Rutner was in high spirits but Asinof was quite different as a person than when the two had last seen each other before the war. Though still involved with the game on an amateur and semipro level, Asinof was now searching for a more permanent place in the world. Like others, the war had certainly changed him; but what had especially changed him was his interim exposure to people like Dashiell Hammett, I. F. Stone, and Hank Greenberg.[16] In short, for him there was now much more to life than baseball. His experiences on Adak Island alone had seen to that. While Kutner's baseball career would after 1947 begin a depressing, downward slide, Asinof's upward trajectory as a writer would initiate in a tentative manner. The hated reserve clause, something the two men had most certainly never thought about previously within the contexts of their playing careers, would later become a central focus of their next conversations during the early 1950s.

Apart from his superb education, Asinof's origins as a writer (as he described it) dated back to his college years. Later he recalled with embarrassment how one of his freshman papers at Williams College had been held up to the class by the professor as a good example of bad writing, though his name went politely unmentioned.[17] The real humiliation, though, came when famed American poet Robert Frost visited Williams around that same time and invited students to submit their poems for his perusal. With typical chutzpah, Asinof entered an earnest 12-line baseball poem expressing the joy of playing, his first recorded original work. Frost read the poem, momentarily stared at the future author of *Eight Men Out*, then pronounced: "It's a pop fly, son."[18] All humor aside, the fact that a freshman jock would even bother to write a poem for Frost's review reflected, if nothing else, a certain confidence level. More important, the fact that Asinof did not permanently give up writing after receiving such a slam showed an impressive amount of determination. At university he would be exposed to the likes of noted historian Frederick Schuman, who taught at Williams, and Clair Wilcox, who taught Keynesian economics at Swarthmore College where Asinof transferred after his freshman year.[19] During Asinof's senior year (1940), Wilcox took the entire class to screen the newly released John Ford classic film adaptation of John Steinbeck's *The Grapes of Wrath*, then invited the class back to the professor's home for tea and discussion (see Chapter 4).[20] Such was the soaring caliber of idealism to which the young future author was exposed. It certainly helped to lay the groundwork for Asinof's identification of the reserve clause as a target of social critique in his first novel.

In addition to an exemplary formal education, by the time he left the service in 1946, Asinof had also received informal indoctrination into the finer points of journalism (and life) from noteworthies like I. F. Stone and Dashiell Hammett. In reference to Asinof's repeated (and sometimes humorous) indignation at social injustices within the military, Asinof was informed by a third party, "Yeah, he [Hammett] said it was too damn bad you weren't a writer." By Asinof's own admission, Hammett's remark "lingered in memory to be used when I needed it. When the war ended, I began to nurse fantasies about setting it all down." This, he added, did not come immediately to pass in part due to sheer intimidation caused by recently released postwar novels such as Norman Mailer's *The Naked and the Dead*.[21] As things turned out, Asinof's first, tentative forays as a professional writer would not be about his strange tour of duty on Adak Island during the war, but rather the national pastime. Baseball, education, social conscience, writing — the four ingredients had now been instilled into a single individual. All that remained was for these separate elements to be unified by that same writer into an enduring literary work.

During the late 1940s and early 1950s, Asinof returned to New York, lived in Yonkers, joined the family clothing business, married, had a child, and seems to have temporarily forgotten about writing. Below these conventional appearances, however, it was obviously apparent that he belonged to a different breed, both for better and for worse. For starters, he kept connections to baseball, briefly co-owning a semipro team (the Yonkers Indians) in the New York Metropolitan Baseball Association before it folded, due in large part to major League competition from the new medium of television.[22] He also stayed in touch with Mickey Rutner, whose professional playing career was by then going into decline. Most tellingly, Asinof could not pull himself away from the liberal humanist world in which he had been educated. He found himself frequenting Broadway during one of its most exciting periods, attending premier works by Tennessee Williams, Arthur Miller, Maxwell Anderson, and Elmer Rice.[23] His politics went against the grain. According to his own account, it was while attending a fund-raiser for third-party presidential candidate (and former FDR vice president) Henry Wallace in 1948 that he met his future wife, Jocelyn Brando (1919–2005), sister of Marlon Brando.[24] Instead of marrying a nice "wealthy Jewish" girl — the type "of prospective wife I'd long since learned to run away from" — Asinof first lived with, then (in 1950) wed Jocelyn, a professional stage actress and future Hollywood starlet.[25] Their only child, Martin Asinof, was born in 1952. The courtship was conducted around the same time Jocelyn performed in the hit Broadway play *Mister Roberts*, while her brother Marlon was simultaneously making an international name for himself in *A Streetcar Named Desire*. Almost needless to say, this was not the type of union calculated to win approval from, say, a conservative, orthodox Jewish viewpoint (or any other conservative viewpoint, for that matter). It would be just a short matter of time before Asinof's half-hearted façade of subdued business respectability, such as it ever was, would completely crumble, but to the permanent benefit of the future reading public.

By 1950, Asinof was, in his own words, "thirty years old with a history of failures and totally without portfolio." Then things began to happen. After a bewildered, frightened moment of traveling disorientation in Butler, Pennsylvania, he suddenly informed wife and family that he was leaving the clothing business because he did not want to become "like that dying salesman, Willie Loman." Instead, he announced, "I'm going to write"[26] The next two years were financially lean as Asinof attempted to phase into his new chosen career, and famous brother-in-law Marlon was apparently among family members who questioned the wisdom of the move.[27] Asinof's wife, on the other hand, not only approved and encouraged him, but provided ideas and contacts as well. "Jocelyn was marvelously supportive," he recalled many years later.[28] After having dozens of original spec teleplays rejected, and thanks to a tip from a poker buddy, Asinof made contact with NBC producer-director Larry Schwab, who paid him $400 to draft (in three weeks) a 30-minute horror script for the live television series *Lights Out*. The broadcast was a technical fiasco, but this was through no fault of the writer, and Asinof "began to make a decent living" churning out what he deemed occasionally insipid plays for live TV, as did many otherwise fine American writers from that period. Then in 1952, without warning, Asinof, his wife, and just about everyone else in the entertainment industry who supported liberal political causes or refused to name names, or could not financially afford to buy their way out of trouble, were blacklisted into unemployment (see Chapter 9).[29]

During this same start-up period of literary activity, Asinof touched base again with his disillusioned old teammate Mickey Rutner, and thus began the genesis of his first serious work, a baseball short story ironically titled "The Rookie"— ironic because Rutner was a 27-year-old minor league veteran when he was finally allowed to play his first big league game. Asinof's "Mike Kutner" is age 35, one year older than the real-life Rutner was when he retired from professional ball. Asinof submitted his first draft for consideration by the respected and accomplished Lebanese-American novelist, playwright and critic Vance Bourjaily (1922–2010), then editor of the New York literary journal *Discovery*. Once again, Asinof found his fledgling work in the hands of a master — this time one slightly younger than himself but far more savvy. Bourjaily invited Asinof into his apartment for a personal interview, only to deliver a withering critique and suggest that he return to the clothing business. Asinof later remarked that he would have turned to drink had he been a drinker; instead he planted himself on a bench in Central Park, watched kids play baseball, and rewrote his short story line by line.[30] Three weeks later, he resubmitted it to Bourjaily, who immediately called back, challenging him with, "All right, El, who wrote it?" After some additional minor editing, Asinof was paid $125, not long after he had been blacklisted out of television work. Thus Asinof's first "serious" literary piece, "The Rookie," was eventually published by *Discovery* in 1955, appearing alongside works in the same series by the likes of Saul Bellow, Norman Mailer, and William Styron.[31]

Fortunately for Asinof, he was still able to earn additional income after blacklisting by writing puff pieces for movie fanzines. This enabled him to continue his quest to produce more elevated works. Once again, Asinof turned to Bourjaily, who astutely suggested a novel be built around "The Rookie." The short story was itself about an aging minor leaguer allowed one short stint in the majors, but, when given a crucial chance, fails to deliver in the most frustrating and heartbreaking manner imaginable.[32] Anyone who has ever played the game at an advanced level, successfully or unsuccessfully, can recognize the emotions and thoughts of the story's tragic hero, from whose point of view the story is told.[33] Moreover, the tale is written in such a way that even non-baseball players or non-athletes can appreciate, though unlikely to appeal to any unrealistic, imaginary notions about the game that a non-player might harbor. Bourjaily the editor clearly recognized this unusual, distinctive quality in Asinof's writing style. He encouraged Asinof by correctly observing that even good novels about the sport were nothing more than "a skillful collage of baseball myths." Knowing that Asinof had first-hand experience in the minors, Bourjaily added: "Melville could never have written *Moby Dick* if he hadn't actually lived as a whaler."[34] Then came a crucial exhortation: "Baseball fiction seems to be all fluff and fable.... This could be something real. Only *you* can do this!"[35] Asinof was off to the races. It took him one year of writing and rewriting. When finished, Bourjaily passed judgment: "I can't tell you how good it is. You really caught the feel of it, El." After yet another year of editing and shopping the manuscript around, McGraw-Hill published the novel titled *Man on Spikes* in the spring of 1955.[36] A great American work of fiction, one condemning major league baseball's long-established reserve clause, had finally been produced.

Man on Spikes is still, after 55 years, a joy to read, but not in a sentimental or escapist manner. Almost any experienced ballplayer will vouch for its realism. Prior to this, the closet thing to a truly realistic baseball novel had been *The Southpaw* (1953) by Mark Harris (1922–2007), a fine work that Asinof had previously read several times, but in terms of lifelike representation of the game (and its economics) does not begin to compare with the physical grit, inherent unfairness, and psychological warfare portrayed in *Man on Spikes*.[37] This is not surprising since Harris, unlike Asinof, never played baseball at advanced competitive levels. Asinof incorporated "The Rookie" as the novel's final, climactic chapter, but tweaked it with minor revisions, adding a coda of redemption and hopefulness, whereas the original short story ended in a mood of despair.[38] Asinof's game vision consists of far more than hitting home runs; for him, baseball is a sport of vicious, bruising physicality. Not only does the bat strike the ball, players slam into each other, sometimes intentionally, and are knocked senseless in the process. Athletes put up with pain, insults, and low pay in order to pursue their dream or simply because they know of no other way of life. In *Man on Spikes*, the hero Mike Kutner ultimately fails at his single shot in the big leagues, but in the end gets back the girl — namely, his wife, whom he has been in danger of losing due to the strain baseball has put on their marriage. There is also closure with the talent scout who originally signed Kutner to professional baseball 16 years previous, who repeatedly and firmly insists, "You ain't a failure."[39]

The character of Kutner himself is drawn in dignified detail, both in appearance and personality. No mention of Jewish ethnicity is made; instead Kutner wears glasses, which is held against him throughout his career, despite his playing excellence, since good natural eyesight is widely perceived a ballplayer's most crucial asset. This becomes the novelist's symbol for anti-Semitism. Kutner, challenging a black teammate, holds up his glasses, exclaiming: "See these stinking things? ... I got troubles of my own."[40] Compounding this disadvantage, Kutner is neither tall in stature nor a prolific home run hitter during a post–Ruth era in which big sluggers dominated headlines and bolstered gate receipts.[41] It is interesting to note that both Mickey Rutner and Asinof were less than physically imposing, although Rutner — like his fictional counterpart — was well-built and quite capable of hitting home runs.[42] In the revamped story, Kutner declares to himself, "Frig 'em all, big and small," an egalitarian battle cry that would continue to reappear in Asinof's later work.[43] This was also the personal mantra of Mickey Rutner.[44] Indeed, during the course of the tale, Kutner admirably takes on just about everyone regardless of standing or class, from the lowest, drunkenly obnoxious fan to the highest executives of a venal team ownership. Regarding Kutner's irrepressible, combative scrappiness, one is more reminded of his literary creator than of the real-life Mickey Rutner, who apart from possessing a ferociously competitive spirit on the playing field, appears to have otherwise been a relatively mild-mannered person.[45]

From a technical writing standpoint, *Man on Spikes* is as impressive as its complicated and previously unexplored subject matter. Fourteen total chapters are each written from a different character's point of view. This journalistic device of multiple viewpoints had been used by other novelists in the past, but to utilize it for a sports book was unprecedented. This mosaic, *Rashomon*-like effect creates a kind of hyper-reality.[46] The reader sees the big picture in a way that individuals normally cannot. Three chapters are written from the viewpoints of women — the hero's wife, sister, and mother; all convincingly, another sure sign of the novelist's talent. Another chapter is bracingly written from the standpoint of an African American player ("The Negro"), during an era in which African American players were grudgingly being allowed into major league baseball. The first of Asinof's many troubled father-son relationships ("The Father") is vividly portrayed in yet another chapter. The central theme of the novel, however, is graphically laid out in the chapter titled "The Commissioner," as the gross injustice of the reserve clause, a descriptor used sparingly by Asinof, becomes painfully clear as it gradually victimizes the novel's hero. The scenario shows not only a thorough knowledge of the game, but of the business world behind the game as well. A mere baseball fan or good writer alone could not have created it.

The chapter which most foreshadows Asinof's future work, however, is "The Negro." Baseball literary critic Richard Peterson observed that in *Man on Spikes* "the issue of race does become a crucial part of a remarkably balanced and intimate study of the various forces at play in the life of a professional baseball player."[47] After *Eight Men Out* (1963), the theme of race, both in and out of baseball, moves front and center for the remainder of his writing career. This aspect will be more fully discussed in Parts III–V of this study. Many years later (in 2001), and nearly half a century after he had written "The Negro," Asinof would still write in exasperation, "Nor have race problems in professional ball, even after integration, been explored. Why haven't these horrors been written about from a black player's point of view?"[48] Social issues aside, "The Negro" is also of special interest because of its disturbing biographical allusions to Asinof's own playing career. It contains no fewer than two full episodes of an outfielder's worst nightmare — colliding with a teammate while both try to catch a fly ball.[49] On June 25, 1941, while playing right field for the Wausau Lumberjacks, Asinof's professional baseball career came to an abrupt and mysterious end after he smashed into a centerfielder teammate while pursuing a catch. Similar to *Man on Spikes,* in which Kutner crosses signals with his African American teammate, the ball was dropped by the newly installed centerfielder after the collision. This in turn sparked an opposing rally that eventually lost the game for Wausau.[50] After that fateful game, Asinof, despite having a good season (batting .296), was never seen again on the team roster (see Chapter 15). Reading these wrenching, frightening passages, it is clear that they came from the writer's personal experience.[51]

As the year 1955 progressed, though blacklisted and impoverished, Eliot Asinof had finally arrived as an American author of exciting note. While his blacklisted status would soon be lifted (in rather bizarre manner), the next five years would see an entirely new phase in his career, one producing little of long-lasting literary note, but much in terms of skill and acumen, particularly on the business end of writing. It would also lay the foundation for his next masterpiece, *Eight Men Out*, as well as all other works that followed. This next phase, however, required a major relocation. In 1955, like so many other artists of his generation, Asinof and his family pulled up their New York roots and moved west to Hollywood. There, the commercial prospects for both Asinof and his wife appeared more promising.

2

No One Ever Got Rich

In the immediate aftermath of *Man on Spikes* being published in 1955, its author learned what he may have already long suspected, that writing great American novels does not necessarily pay the bills; in fact, more often than not, it does not. Artistically, the work was an auspicious beginning for its creator. Financially, however, it was certainly not enough to support a wife and child. To accomplish this (barely), Asinof found himself chasing down reluctant celebrities and churning out fluff for movie fanzines. On top of this, he (along with his actress wife) had been blacklisted, ruling out television — during that particular era the best career opportunity for writers — as a source of revenue. If he wanted to go on producing serious works — and if there was ever a writer with serious ambitions it was Eliot Asinof— he would have to go to wherever the grass was green, as often phrased in the world of business. Such an approach was needed simply to bring home the "bacon" rather than sitting around "picking" his nose, as Asinof's famous brother-in-law Marlon Brando crudely put it to him around the same time.[1] Controversial and hard-hitting as its subject matter may have been, Asinof's groundbreaking and barely fictionalized story did not put the plight of the professional baseball player on the map of popular awareness. In this respect, suing major league baseball, as did Curt Flood 15 years later, proved a much better way to get the public's attention, than to write a great American novel on the same topic.

The good news was that book reviewers adored *Man on Spikes*, as well they should have. Accolades were plentiful and criticism practically nil. John Lardner, son of Ring Lardner who had covered the Black Sox Scandal a generation earlier, writing for *The New York Times* gushed that Asinof's debut effort was "a plain and honest book, the first realistic novel I can remember having read."[2] Lardner added that the narrative was "an eloquent, moving account."[3] Writing for the *New York Post*, respected American novelist James T. Farrell noted that the book "conveys a genuine love for the game."[4] Farrell expressed his "hope that all baseball fans who like to read books will read *Man on Spikes*."[5] Pausing here, it is noteworthy that Farrell's words of approval came from a writer who had himself entertained the idea of doing a book on the Black Sox Scandal, but voluntarily stepped aside, allowing Asinof to do the same, plus magnanimously gave his younger colleague extensive, helpful notes and a list of contacts (see Chapter 5). Awed by the unprecedented realism for a baseball novel, John Hutchens of the *New York Herald Tribune* wrote: "This is the way it must be down there."[6] Such critical praise has been steady throughout the years. Roger Kahn, author of the nostalgic masterpiece *The Boys of Summer* (1972) and often himself named among the very best writers on the national pastime, listed *Man on Spikes* as among the top "Golden Dozen" baseball literary works ever written.[7] More recently, academics specializing in baseball literature such as Richard Peterson still rank Asinof's first novel as among the very best of its genre, noting "its balance ... and insight," as well as its "its accurately detailed and comprehensive vision of the life and career of a baseball player."[8] Attorney Marvin Miller, who probably did more than any single individual to destroy the reserve clause, observed that *Man on Spikes*, as "a work of fiction, is infinitely more true than the vast bulk of nonfictional books that have been published."[9] As gratifying as such approval must have been, Asinof, in typical fashion for him, most relished positive feedback received from former professional players, especially the story's real-life hero, Mickey Rutner, who exclaimed, "Wow, El, it's a damn good book!"[10] Future Hall of Famer Ralph Kiner, retiring as a player the same year that *Man on Spikes* was published, wrote a personal letter of commendation, found among Asinof's papers after his death.[11]

To this outside reader, though, perhaps the most dramatic testament to the book's outstanding quality came from none other than "Yankee Clipper" Joe DiMaggio, long since retired as player (in 1951). DiMaggio was inducted into Cooperstown the same year (1955) that Asinof's debut novel was released, a period witnessing DiMaggio's short, stormy marriage to Marilyn Monroe publicly disintegrate. A few years later, by which time Asinof's own marriage to Jocelyn Brando had crumbled as well, the two men were introduced at a hotel by one of DiMaggio's hanger-on sportswriter acquaintances. According to Asinof's son, Martin, while making introductions the sportswriter completely botched pronunciation of the still relatively unknown author's name with something akin to "Joe, this is Mr. 'Assneff,' who would like to meet you," then walked away. DiMaggio, however, extended his huge hand and gracefully responded, "It's nice to meet you, Eliot." DiMaggio informed the thrilled novelist that he had read and admired *Man on Spikes*, then proceeded to sincerely commiserate with him on what it was like (for both of them) to have been formerly married to Hollywood starlets.[12] This was the beginning of a friendship between the two that lasted the rest of DiMaggio's life. Arguably the most remarkable aspect of this story is that DiMaggio, one of the greatest baseball players in history, had read Asinof's tale of a perceived failed career and admitted to liking it quite a bit. Even Joe DiMaggio, despite all of his peerless accomplishments, and like any other experienced athlete, occasionally knew the taste of defeat; moreover, he recognized and fully appreciated an honest, accurate portrayal of this feeling when he saw it on the printed page.

About the same time that *Man on Spikes* was being received by a startled or indifferent baseball reading public, his blacklisted status in the television industry was lifted through a series of circumstances that could not have been more improbable or laced with irony. At a New York social gathering, Asinof was approached by a producer of the CBS Sunday morning religious show, "Look Up and Live." The producer urgently explained that someone competent was needed on short notice to interview Jazz musician Lionel Hampton, just returning from concert tour in the Holy Land.[13] Asinof explained that he would love to do the interview but had been blacklisted. The impatient producer responded that the sponsoring NCCC (National Council of Churches of Christ) would intervene with the network and "go to bat" for him. A few days later, Asinof was allowed to conduct the interview and received full credit. Whether this reversal occurred solely through pure benevolence of the NCCC, or greed simply trumped stupidity, we are not prepared to say. For certain, however, is that is that within a few short months, Asinof's writing career for both television and film had been reactivated. On July 17, 1955, NBC's Goodyear Television Playhouse broadcast a one-hour live dramatization of *Man on Spikes*, with an ad hoc cast featuring Ned Glass, Robert Morse, Warren Stevens, Janet Ward, and Bill Zuckert.[14] Asinof received credit for the screenplay, and about this same time, with family in tow, he was flying out to Hollywood to work on a projected feature film adaptation of the novel.[15] He would spend the next four years working as a mostly uncredited screenwriter in the Southern California film industry, during the late 1950s still a prosperous enterprise and good graduating step for aspiring writers with accumulated television credentials.

As things turned out, Asinof made a temporary living in Hollywood, but not by writing baseball scripts. A feature film version of *Man on Spikes* never happened because soon after its author arrived in California, industry executives decided that baseball films, especially those with themes grounded in reality, were sure money losers.[16] The most notorious precedent was *Fear Strikes Out* (1957), starring Anthony Perkins (before his stardom in Hitchcock's *Psycho*), portraying the real-life Jimmy Piersall and his heroic struggle against bipolar disorder while playing for the Boston Red Sox.[17] In an age during which the Dodgers were preparing to leave Brooklyn and the Giants, upper Manhattan, it seems movie-going baseball fans were in no mood for this sort of thing. Years later, other attempts would be made to update *Man on Spikes* either for television or the big screen. In 1963–1964, in the immediate wake of his critical success with *Eight Men Out*, Asinof prepared a dramatization for NBC's short-lived *Richard Boone Show* but the production never materialized, probably due to the series being cancelled after one season.[18] Thirty years later, in 1994, Asinof also prepared another screenplay for a movie version starring Vincent Spano, veteran of John Sayles' films, but this project too was shelved.[19] Asinof himself consistently never expressed anything but disdain for the film industry, quoting the Hollywood proverb that screenwriters were "schmucks with typewriters," and that "movies were not works of literary quality but manipulations of adolescent images." He quickly added, however, that "it was no great strain to be a whore when the pay was so good."[20]

A footnote to the long, strange journey of *Man on Spikes* as an adapted stage dramatization came on January 15, 1964, when an uncredited teleplay titled "Channing: Swing for the Moon" was broadcast as an episode in ABC's popular TV series *The Best Years*.[21] It was written by Asinof, and told the story of college baseball player Eddie Martin, whose professional playing aspirations are discouraged by his older brother Frank, a successful businessman.[22] In the last, crucial game of the season, Eddie strikes out like Mike Kutner in *Man on Spikes*, but is signed to a big league contract nonetheless by a scout for the Chicago White Sox (named Durkin Fain, as in the novel) who still perceptively recognizes Eddie's talent and drive. Also of interest is the coach's name, Wally Gilbert (portrayed as a 40-something ex-big leaguer), who was the real-life coach of Asinof in Wausau, Wisconsin, and who receives praise from Asinof in his writings. Though not a dramatic masterpiece by anyone's standards, *Swing for the Moon* reflects Asinof's continuing interest in the same themes that he first explored with *Man on Spikes*. It was probably written to help pay bills during the strenuous period in which he was researching and drafting *Eight Men Out*.[23]

Asinof's four-year adventure in Hollywood during the late 1950s had little direct bearing on his baseball writing, but did pave the way in many respects for his seminal literary output the following decade. Most of his work, a good portion consisting of uncredited treatments and outlines, was reportedly completed for stock Westerns and crime thrillers, at that time the two reigning commercial genres, both for television and movies. For a person who had just written the finest novel about the American national pastime, the transition would have been a big artistic step down, but understandable given economic realities, combined with Asinof's favorite theme of the little guy trying to buck the system, one so profoundly explored in *Man on Spikes*. It would also allow him as a writer to get his feet wet with broad themes touching on genuine or mislabeled outlaws in society, as well as complex, dysfunctional familial relations, both of which would feature prominently in his later works. Perhaps most importantly, these Hollywood years gave Asinof his first close encounter with the lucrative commercial end of writing for video, along with all of its pleasant and not-so-pleasant aspects. While never reputed for great business acumen, Asinof seems to have left California with a firm appreciation for both the advantages and pitfalls of attempting to turn any serious literary work into mass movie entertainment. The pay may have been good, but his desire to produce something of lasting quality appears to have become stronger than ever.

Asinof's tenure in Hollywood came to an abrupt end in early 1959, not by choice, but rather through necessity and circumstance.[24] First, his employment was terminated by Harry Cohn at Columbia Pictures for writer insubordination, i.e., not writing exactly what he was told to write all of the time.[25] Then, while working on a Warner Brothers team to concoct a screenplay for the Western *Yellowstone Kelly* (1959)—a vehicle originally intended for John Wayne and director John Ford—Asinof proposed a scene in which a furious Wayne character punches out a villainous Indian's horse (!) after recognizing a friend's scalp decorating the same mount. This identical scenario had in fact been earlier suggested to him by writer Burt Kennedy, who eventually received screenwriting credit for the film. Three days later, Asinof was summoned to the front office, where he was personally fired by Jack Warner for having dared to suggest that the Duke would strike an animal.[26] In a final, ironic twist of events, both Wayne and Ford bowed out of the project before the film was made.[27] Unlike Asinof's first book editor Vance Bourjaily, men like Jack Warner and Harry Cohn were not interested in nurturing literary talent, let alone indulging experimentation by their hired hands.

Concurrent with Asinof's demise as a full-time Hollywood writer during the late 1950s came the final dissolution of his marriage with Jocelyn Brando. Although Jocelyn (despite the shadow of brother Marlon) went on to enjoy a long career in the movies and television, this did not appear to be the cause of the breakup ("I would not blame Hollywood for that," Asinof emphasized many years later).[28] Rather than try to analyze the details of personal lives for those now departed, it seems more constructive for purposes of this study to look at how Asinof the writer viewed marriage within the context of his works. How much of this thematic treatment reflected his own views and feelings we can only guess; however, it is safe bet that a significant element of personal experience was injected. Such analysis is not for the purpose of passing judgment, but rather for possible benefit of future readers, as the author himself no doubt intended. In *Man on Spikes*, written some five years before the couple broke up, Chapter 11 ("The Wife") is written convincingly from the viewpoint of the ballplayer's Griselda-like spouse. Briefly summarized, the player's wife attends a crucial minor league game in which her husband's performance will supposedly determine his promotion to the majors, endures the insufferable company of rival player's wives, and watches her husband play magnificently. She then discovers that the team owner's nephew, who is supposed to be scouting the game, was not even in the ball park, but rather out carousing on the town. As things transpire, the owner's by now repulsive nephew is interested in her, not her husband. The chapter ends with the wife weighing various options and consequences — a true analogy for Hollywood and big business in general. Asinof's astringent 1967 novel *The Bedfellow* would dwell upon similar disturbing themes and the potential destructive overlap between marriage and career (see Part III of this study).

With the simultaneous breakdown of his marriage and employment with Warner Brothers, Asinof made his way back home to New York, lured by, among other things, the prospect at creating teleplays for up-and-coming David Susskind's Talent Associates (see Chapter 5).[29] Before settling into a new lifestyle, however, Asinof experienced yet another strange interlude in his professional writing career. At the urging of an agent friend, Asinof flew on short notice from New York to Havana to assist in rehabilitating a poorly written screenplay about the recently triumphant Cuban Revolution. To his astonishment and terror, he was upon arrival ushered into the presence of dictator Fidel Castro, who, over strenuous objections from his advisors, surprisingly allowed Asinof to work solo. Later it came to Asinof's attention, from the dictator himself no less, that Castro the baseball enthusiast had somehow been well aware of Asinof's status as a former player.[30] Quickly ascertaining that he was the only person involved in the project with any competency whatsoever, Asinof did his part, stayed on for a while as tourist, then prudently returned home. When the film was finally released in 1961 (eventually titled *Rebellion in Cuba*, starring Lon Chaney, Jr.), it had been retooled into "a grotesque counterrevolutionary piece of trash," with Asinof's name thankfully omitted from the credits.[31] While this bizarre episode surely did nothing to improve Asinof's confidence in the movie industry, it did demonstrate that, even before writing *Eight Men Out*, he had achieved a notable degree of credibility both as a writer and former athlete.

Perhaps one way to better understanding how a writer like Asinof fit into public perceptions of that time is to compare the aesthetic of his first novel to popular baseball art around the same period. Recently, this author attended several thought-provoking exhibits at the highly regarded Leigh Yawkey Woodson Art Museum in Wausau, Wisconsin, the city where Asinof happened to play minor league baseball in 1941, about a decade before he switched careers to become an author. Most recently featured was the work of cartoonist Charles Schultz (1922–2000), an exact contemporary of Asinof's whose comic strip series *Peanuts* was immeasurably successful and widely appreciated. Produced over the course of a half century, almost identically the same period (1950–2000) in which Asinof wrote about baseball, the *Peanuts* franchise also mirrored populist attitudes towards the game via the endless but charming misadventures of Schultz's characters. Schultz's artistic vision of baseball is fondly sentimental, whimsical, and poignant, overlaid with comedic delusions of grandeur — in short, the antithesis of Asinof's view of the game from *Man on Spikes* and later works. For Asinof the former minor leaguer, grandeur was no illusion; he knew and remembered all too well what it was like to play, excel, and win, as well as to lose. For him, this was reality. For the hapless characters in *Peanuts*, reality is imagining success but never possessing the ability to achieve it (the spirit is willing, but the body says no, as athletes sometimes joke). All of us can relate to these feelings in many endeavors, but it is much harder to relate for anyone who ever competed and won baseball games at advanced levels. Schultz, by his own candid admission, never played ball beyond the sandlot level, and he drew what he was familiar with — that is why it is great art, but not very informative about the game itself. To give just one example, readers will search the *Peanuts* strip in vain looking for left-handed players, an otherwise ever-present factor in more competitive stages of the sport.

Another traveling exhibit at the Woodson featured the work of the prolific, but often underrated American painter Norman Rockwell (1894–1978), perhaps best known for his cover art in the *Saturday Evening Post*, executed over the course of 47 years (1916–1963), more or less the same period leading up to Asinof's creation of *Eight Men Out*.[32] Although this particular exhibit did not feature any of Rockwell's delightful baseball-themed work, these images have become iconic in the American consciousness, and for good reason. Like Asinof, Rockwell was born in New York City (but a generation earlier), and eventually settled in Stockbridge, Massachusetts, not far from Asinof's beloved Ancramdale in upstate New York, nor from Asinof's freshman alma mater, Williams College. Unlike Asinof, the gangly, un-athletic Rockwell was never a ballplayer, but shared the younger man's combative, restless spirit. His versatile (and often misunderstood) work as a commercial artist, well-exemplified by his baseball paintings, show a similar, unromantic realist's view of the sport, although Rockwell (again, unlike Asinof) always added a surface overlay of popular appeal that made him very successful, as well as widely misinterpreted or worse, dismissed by snobbish critics. Looking beyond this surface, however, one discovers a shrewd appreciation for the same subtle contradictions and absurdities in baseball that Asinof would put into book form about the same time that an elderly Rockwell was winding down his output.

Curiously, one of Rockwell's later and possibly most famous baseball painting for the *Post* bears the same title of Asinof's first short story, "The Rookie," which in turn evolved into the climatic chapter of *Man on Spikes*. Rockwell's *The Rookie* (1957), also known as *Red Sox Locker Room*, portrays what many believe to be the arrival of 19-year-old pitcher Mickey McDermott at Fenway Park on April 24, 1948, as dubious old veteran teammates, including a sinister-looking Ted Williams, examine him like a newly delivered piece of fresh meat.[33] Both players and non-players have been understandably entranced by the image ever since it was unveiled. Asinof's "Rookie" Mike Kutner is of course much older, more experienced, and not a pitcher, but the dog-eat-dog foreboding mood of skepticism is identical.

The same parallels apply with Rockwell's other baseball masterpieces: the raw amateur passion of *Gramps at the Plate* (1916) and *Son and Father: Baseball Dispute* (1962); the elasticity of game rules in *Choosin' Up* (1951); the behind-the-scenes shenanigans of 1949's *The Three Umpires* (also known as *Game Called Because of Rain* or *Bottom of the Sixth*); the Don Quixote-like intensity from *100th Year of Baseball* (1939). This latter work, created to commemorate the dedication ceremony for the Baseball Hall of Fame, calls to mind Asinof's recruited participation as an amateur player in organized festivities held that season at Doubleday Field in Cooperstown.[34] Arguably the most riveting of all Rockwell's baseball images, however, and one surely appreciated by Asinof (along with all fans of the game), is *The Dugout* (1948), freezing for all time a humiliating rout of the Chicago Cubs by the hosting Boston Braves on May 23 of that same year. The dejected bat boy, the embarrassed coaching staff, the vulgar heckler from the stands — Rockwell perfectly captures it all. The painting is a miraculous achievement for someone who never played, and yet had a sharp eye for revealing character detail in sport with plenty of such details to offer. Unlike Asinof, however, Rockwell found a mass audience by pretending to be cute and harmless, which in the case of the prickly and personally elusive Rockwell could not have been further from the real truth.

Returning to baseball as described by the written word, Asinof's ambiguous, critical view of game as portrayed in *Man on Spikes*, as in all of his later work, has always been rejected by the masses but embraced by a discerning few, especially those readers who have played baseball at a professional or semiprofessional level. Thirty years after being kicked out of Hollywood, and 60 years after having been recruited to play on Doubleday Field as part of the original dedication ceremonies, Asinof was honored by the Baseball Hall of Fame in 1999 by being invited as the keynote speaker during the 11th Annual Cooperstown Symposium. Anticipating this event, *Man on Spikes* was re-released the previous year (1998) in a compelling new edition by Southern Illinois University Press (with a Foreword by Marvin Miller), in what can only be described as a public service.[35] SIU Press would also release Asinof's compelling last baseball novel, *Off-Season*, the following year in 2000 (see Part V of this study). No one may have ever gotten rich off Asinof's first major work of fiction (at least, in the financial sense), but its extensive fan base remains devoted, extending all the way to Cooperstown and beyond.

The latest, somewhat revealing chapter in the long journey of Asinof's baseball "rookie" theme came in 2002, with the commercially successful Disney film release of *The Rookie*— no relation to the 1953 short story by Asinof, or to Norman Rockwell, for that matter. Disney's *Rookie* (starring Dennis Quaid) tells the true-life story of left-handed pitcher Jim Morris, a Texas high school baseball coach who, at aged 35, began a two-year major league career with the Tampa Bay Devil Rays in 1999–2000, the same period in which Asinof was being honored at Cooperstown and his last baseball novel being released to a mostly indifferent or snide public reception. The Morris story made good, uplifting Hollywood material. Victimized by bad breaks in his younger days, a much more mature athlete was compelled by his player-students and encouraged by his wife to try out for the big leagues. To the surprise of many (and notwithstanding financial hardship), he pulled it off. Morris was (and is) a baseball Cinderella Man and inspirational role model for us all. The problem is that his journey was highly exceptional, and not very informative for aspiring young athletes interested in what really is likely to happen to them in the world of professional baseball, both on and off the playing field. For that kind of all too real story, one must turn to a different kind of inspirational story, that of Mickey Rutner and his "fictional" counterpart Mike Kutner, a story yet to be given feature film treatment, and possibly never. What the elderly Rutner or Asinof thought of the Disney film is unknown. With his return to New York City in 1959, however, Asinof began his own journey, a trek eventually leading to the creation of *Eight Men Out*, a work that did ultimately end up on the big screen in quality form for everyone to see and discuss, deny or embrace.

Thus ended the 1950s for Eliot Asinof. *Man on Spikes*, despite its success among critics and former athletes who liked to read, languished, temporarily went out of print, and was for some time nearly forgotten. During the late 1970s, a quarter century after having pioneered the subject matter, Asinof would return to the theme of the aging rookie who would give anything for a shot at the majors. His nonfiction story, or rather exposé, "The Secret Life of Rocky Perone" (see Chapter 3), would, like his profile of Mickey Rutner's career, draw upon strange-but-true material for its inspiration. The reserve clause that had wreaked havoc with Rutner's major league ambitions, however, had by 1979 been permanently discarded. By then, much different (and in some ways, much bigger) issues had arisen, not only with major league baseball, but with all of professional sports. The same problems had in fact been inherent in the game from its very beginnings and, looking beyond the fictional veneer, were strongly hinted at within Asinof's first novel. With *Rocky Perone*, these previously implied questions would begin to move to the forefront of public visibility. Once again, though, unfortunately, there seemed to be a limited number of readers willing or able at the time to fully appreciate the dilemma.

3

A Purist Baseball Outlook

If one had never read any of Asinof's works, it might be easy in hindsight to dismiss *Man on Spikes* as a fictional relic of its period, an interesting though quaint condemnation of professional baseball's reserve clause before its looming abolishment and little more than that. Reading the novel over three decades after the reserve clause was eliminated, however, belies this oversimplification. For one, the exact term "reserve clause" is used sparingly by the novelist, although its grave ramifications are spelled out a number of times, including by the hero's unapologetic team owner and a helpless commissioner of major league baseball ("The Commissioner"). The latter tries unsuccessfully to reign in owner greed, which unfortunately has continued in full force long after Free agency was established. The 1950s omnipresence of team owner dominance over the players certainly drives the plot, but it does not completely define the story. Much, much more is at work in the tale of Mike Kutner than mere legalisms; Kutner is as much a victim of his own insatiable ambitions as of externally imposed injustices. For these reasons, the book holds up stronger than ever when read today. No wonder then, that general appreciation for *Man on Spikes* has slowly but steadily increased since its original publication in 1955, perhaps even more so after the official demise of the reserve clause in 1975.

During the mid–1970s came the true beginnings of unfettered Free agency in professional baseball, within various grades and categories. The long-term economic effects on the game have been well-documented, are obviously apparent to any casual fan, and need little additional commentary here. Bottom line: teams that can afford to pay high salaries to the best players tend to win, while those which cannot tend to lose. Moreover, this dynamic is never a static one; it changes from year to year. Oftentimes, a club will field a World Series champion, but cannot afford to sustain the championship for more than a year or two, especially if athletes demand raises or bonuses for their outstanding performances. Such has long been true for all professional team sports in general (especially football and basketball); but baseball, one of the oldest, and in many ways, most conservative of American pastimes,

Asinof, seated fourth from left, possibly age 19, as a member of the Swarthmore College baseball team, circa 1939. As a senior he would become a team captain. A 1940 yearbook reads: "The powerful hitting of Ellie Asinof marks him as a certainty at either the outfield or first base." Upon graduation, Asinof would sign with the Philadelphia Phillies and play briefly for the Moultrie (Georgia) Packers (courtesy Friends Historical Library of Swarthmore College).

was the last to give in to inevitable pressures of the marketplace. Usually (but not always), profitability depends on fan attendance, which often depends of winning, which typically depends on high salaries, which in the end can destroy profitability, not to mention fan loyalty if star players continuously switch clubs with every passing season. Worse, some fans eventually have the resentful realization that their erstwhile heroes earn more in one year than they will ever earn in a lifetime.[1] Those who excuse this disparity by arguing that a professional athlete's window of marketability is only a few years seem to forget that wealth accumulated early in adulthood, unless squandered, is often sustainable throughout a lifetime. Even when not sustainable, these salaries are quite high and seem out of proportion to the fans paying for tickets. The players may be like any other young entrepreneurs trying to make a fortune, but the big question remains: what is their true value to society? Are these athletes really worth what they are paid by the owners? All of this, of course, seems a long way from the Mickey Rutner story which inspired Asinof to write his first novel; yet, given that Rutner was certainly worth far more than what he was paid, then the next hard question naturally becomes, what exactly *was* he worth as a player, both comparatively as a professional athlete and in relation to the rest of us?

It is noteworthy that since the advent of free agency in major league baseball, there have been no teams to win the World Series more than two consecutive years.[2] The last franchise to win three consecutive titles was the Oakland Athletics of 1972–1974 (the last three years of the reserve clause), and by coincidence, the direct descendent of the very same franchise for which Mickey Rutner played most of his professional career. Admittedly, Asinof's beloved New York Yankees have dominated post-season play during the Free agency era, thanks mainly to the uninhibited spending of late owner George Steinbrenner, but even this dominance has come in cycles, without more than two consecutive World Series championships at a time.[3] The Oakland team of the early 1970s, on the other hand, was the last of the true great baseball dynasties, bound together forcibly by still-extant official policies and despite a shared loathing of their owner (the late Charles O. Finley), not unlike the animosity felt by the 1919 Black Sox towards their owner, Charles A. Comiskey. Had it not been for Free agency, the Oakland team would have surely gone on to win more titles; indeed, the Yankees immediately took advantage by raiding the Oakland roster for stars like Catfish Hunter and Reggie Jackson, luring them away with bigger paychecks. Thus Hunter and Jackson traded Finley for Steinbrenner as their boss. There is a personal connection here. Charles O. Finley lived in my home town of LaPorte, Indiana, where I played high school baseball at the time. In nearby Comiskey Park in Chicago, I witnessed the Athletics play (and dominate) during their heyday; then I saw them, practically overnight, scatter to the winds when no longer slavishly bound to lower pay and abhorred management. It was a stark lesson for an 18-year-old player and fan to observe.

With the demise of the reserve clause in 1975, one would have thought that Asinof was finished with the aging baseball rookie theme as a writer. Instead, within four years he produced a short piece titled "The Secret Life of Rocky Perone," published by *Sports Illustrated* on June 18, 1979. Based on the thought-provoking, true-to-life case of Richard Pohle, "Rocky Perone" tells the story of a marginal player who in 1974 successfully masqueraded his advanced age and true identity to obtain a single-day successful shot, not in the majors, but rather, in the minor leagues. Pohle is no Mickey Rutner being oppressed by the injustices of the reserve clause or the inequities of racial integration. "Rocky Perone" is instead Asinof's sober meditation on the foibles and moral frailties of professional baseball players — and by extension, all professional athletes. In typical, controversial style for Asinof, he reports a factual story in a journalistic manner by utilizing a first person narrative voice (that of Pohle-Perone), thus creating a true sense of author (and reader) empathy for the protagonist, despite that person's willful deceptions against almost everyone he encounters. In short, the 36-year-old Pohle (one year older than Asinof's "fictional" rookie Mike Kutner), after a long but very unlucky career playing amateur ball, with help from his shrink, modern cosmetics (including a wig) to conceal his age, and a more exotic, marketable identity (that of an Australian import), momentarily earns a playing spot in the San Diego farm system with the Walla Walla (Washington) Padres.[4] In addition to his solid playing ability, Pohle-Perone, before trying out, diligently scouts the scouts beforehand, carefully avoiding the "smart ones," which proves not too difficult in the mindless world of sports. During his professional debut with Walla Walla, Pohle is immediately found out and once again sent packing, but not before getting a base hit, a walk, stealing a base, and making some good plays in the field. In effect, "Rocky Perone" plays too well, draws attention to himself, and is busted for it.

Like most of Asinof's previous heroes or antiheroes (most notably, Garret Brock Trapnell from his 1976 nonfiction work, *The Fox Is Crazy Too*), Pohle is profiled by Asinof the writer as a sympathetic, even at times, likeable con artist. Ultimately, Pohle is a "cheater cheating cheaters," to borrow the Asinof's oft-quoted phrase from Abe Attell, the man who helped organize the 1919 World Series fix.[5] Like some of the Black Sox — indeed, as Asinof himself once did as a young ballplayer — Pohle assumes a completely new identity in order to continue playing the game. Like the "fictional" Mike Kutner from *Man on Spikes*, Pohle is too old, too small in stature, and too lacking in long-ball power to get a fair shot at the pros. Unlike Kutner, however, Pohle does not battle an entrenched reserve clause or, for that matter, ever entertain much hope to play in the majors. Instead, he combats old-fashioned age discrimination in the job market, combined with the insatiable greed of owners and publicists who have little regard for true playing talent. Above all, it becomes painfully apparent that Pohle is all too eager to compromise any would be ideals in order to obtain his stated objective, to "go into the record books" as a professional ballplayer. He feels no guilt whatsoever in deceiving fans, teammates, and team management, because his talent justifies his presence on a professional playing field, which otherwise would be denied if he played it straight. Asinof's conscience-rattling account ends with a (by then) 41-year-old Pohle plotting his next professional comeback, while solemnly pledging, "This time I'm not going to get caught."[6] As a literary work, Asinof's "Rocky Perone" is pure delight, containing all of the author's trademark verve, sass, and wit.

At the time of writing "Rocky Perone" Asinof was almost 60 years old, temporarily worn out by his debilitating legal struggles with David Susskind, and probably beginning to feel like time was unfairly passing him by. At first glance, one might view the Richard Pohle story as a lark, a one-time detour, or a coda on this particular subject matter for Asinof, but closer examination reveals that the aging rookie theme was near and dear to his heart throughout his writing career. The talented but ambitious and overaged rookie up against an entrenched, unjust system, reserve clause or no reserve clause, would continue to fascinate him. It also seemed to easily go hand in hand with Asinof's consistent hostility towards the negative influence of capital and marketing on the integrity of the professional game, as sourly noted in *Man on Spikes* by the old scout Durkin Fain:

> So here he was again, with the familiar assignment that insulted his love for the game. Baseball was getting to be big business these days, not like it used to be when he played ball. Gradually, it was moving into the hands of the big-money syndicates, the promoters. Anybody could run a ball club ... all you needed was a couple million bucks, and a flare for publicity stunts.... The old scout felt a growing antagonism for the new philosophy, the new baseball; and it jarred his relationship with the great game.[7]

At the very center of the Mike Kutner or Rocky Perone stories lies not the reserve clause, but rather a professional enterprise dominated by "the big-money syndicates," "the promoters," and a "new philosophy," as summarized by Asinof in his first novel, all comparatively alien to the national pastime in its earlier, pre–1919 incarnations. Also at the center of these stories, however, lies the professional athlete's irrepressible ambition and competitive spirit, typically willing to make any sacrifice or compromise whatsoever in order to achieve its goals.

As for feature film adaptations and possible mass audience exposure, neither "Rocky Perone" nor *Man on Spikes* has yet to make it to the big screen in the true sense. On July 27, 2010, a seven-minute entry titled *The Secret Life of Rocky Perone* was made at the L.A. Short Film Festival, but Asinof received no writing credit, unlike his credited 1955 television adaptation of *Man on Spikes* for the Goodyear Playhouse.[8] The closest Hollywood has ever come touching this kind of subject matter was in 2002 with the far more benign and conventionally inspirational treatment of the Jim Morris story as dramatized in *The Rookie* (see Chapter 2). Hollywood executives may be right about one thing, though: general audiences are probably not quite ready to face the grim realities of a more typical and far more widespread minor league experience, one so faithfully depicted in Asinof's "fiction"—stories in which the lines between reality and imagination are blurred and barely distinguishable.

The new baseball "philosophy" coined by Asinof—that money trumps all—one so demonized in his works, did not of course have its beginnings in the post–World War II era or even the post–World War I era of 1919. It was, in the author's view, a gradual process, rapidly accelerating at intervals including the two postwar periods of the 20th century. It had its true roots deep in the American psyche and American way of life, and was reflected by values of the players and fans, as much as the values of owners whom they often secretly envied. Perhaps one better way to try and understand Asinof's view of the system is to examine the state of baseball during and leading up to the era in which he himself played professionally in 1940–1941. The between-wars period into which he was born and came of age (1919–1941) reflected a very interesting historical interlude for baseball in which the game quickly went from being a disreputable gambler's racket to a mythological national pastime symbolic of America's strengths and virtues as it entered World War II. In addition to being dominated by the Ruth-Gehrig-DiMaggio triumvirate of Asinof's beloved New York Yankees, the most striking new feature of professional baseball during that time period was the invention and development of the minor league farm system. Thanks to the creative genius and unfettered foresight of Branch Rickey, baseball's first general manager in the modern sense of the job title, the St. Louis Cardinals became the National League's premier franchise.[9] Other major league teams, including the Yankees, followed suit, and those that did not found themselves quickly reduced to second division status. This was the same milieu in which Asinof developed as a player and played professionally, experiencing first hand, for better and for worse, the clumsy and still evolving start-up farm system of the Philadelphia Phillies organization, via the Moultrie Packers and Wausau Lumberjacks.

In a pivotal chapter titled "The Commissioner" from *Man on Spikes*, Asinof dramatizes the anticlimactic showdown between Mike Kutner's unscrupulous team owner, Jim Mellon, and a nameless, pawn-like commissioner of baseball. The commissioner tries to go to bat for Kutner's career, only to find himself alternatively laughed and sneered at by one of the men who pay his salary:

> [Commissioner] "It's bad for the players — like Kutner. It's bad for the other clubs — like Philly."
>
> [Mellon] "But it's damn good for me!" Mellon laughed. "Like I said, it wins pennants."
>
> [Commissioner] "And it's bad for baseball!" The Commissioner's voice was louder than he wished.
>
> [Mellon] "That's the sour grapes department, Commissioner. Everybody wants to win pennants and they all got farm organizations. It's a good system. Anyone can win in it. That's America, Commissioner, free enterprise and all that. But, then, maybe you got some suggestions in mind?"
>
> [Commissioner] "I've stated them: a freer interchange of ballplayers, especially to the clubs that need them the most."
>
> [Mellon] "You wouldn't attack the reserve clause, would you? Even the ballplayers don't do that. Take away the reserve clause and the players become free agents. It'd be like anarchy. The rich clubs would gobble up all the good ones."
>
> The Commissioner almost rose from his chair.
>
> [Commissioner] "Who's got them now, Jim?" he shouted. "The poor clubs?"[10]

Big money had of course always ruled professional baseball from the beginning. Even with the reserve clause still in existence, deep-pocketed owners could out bonus their competitors with respect to signing new talent; then after a contract had been signed, the new player was more or less owned by the team, lock, stock, and barrel. By the late 1970s, with the reserve clause officially dismantled, wealthy clubs still enjoyed huge bidding advantages on free agents, but now had less long-term control over players unless their contracts specified otherwise.

In one sense, the new Free agency system was more up front and less apologetic about the power of money. After all, by the 1980s, greed had become good. Free-spending franchises were now capable of building championship teams overnight, and athletes with potentially strong box office appeal could now earn paychecks far beyond the capabilities and wildest dreams of most Americans. These guiding principles applied forcefully to all professional sports, not only baseball. Lost in the transition were team stability, owners' patience in building franchises, players' patience in working their way up the ranks, and, some would say, overall fan loyalty. Money now had to be made fast by everyone involved. Branch Rickey, the general manager who built, player by player, some of the most legendary baseball clubs in history, the visionary who created the minor league farm system into which a young Eliot Asinof and Mickey Rutner were signed, would barely recognize today's business model for the game. In retrospect, Asinof's "Rocky Perone," written in 1979 but describing events on the eve of Free agency in 1974, anticipated today's situation by making unfettered athlete ambition and ownership drive for fast profits the two prime motivators of human behavior in the professional version of the game. His two post-reserve clause baseball novels (*Strike Zone* and *Off-Season*) would also later touch upon this same theme to some degree.

The situation had been considerably different when Asinof was a minor league player, as surely was his perception of the system. The 1941 season in particular, the last before World War II broke out, would have been especially influential on any baseball player who participated in it, as did Asinof in Wausau, his last year in the minors. In 1941, the year in which the Brooklyn Dodgers finally made it to the World Series for the first time (as the Dodgers), they were only to be beaten in frustrating manner by their crosstown rivals, the near invincible New York Yankees.[11] Interestingly 1941 was also the year that saw Joe DiMaggio's exciting 56-game hitting streak and Ted Williams' incredible .406 batting average, both still seemingly unapproachable records for the modern books. In brief, it was a good year for hitters, and the 21-year-old Asinof, himself a pretty good minor league hitter, would have likely been inspired by their examples. Asinof also had the uplifting example of his personal acquaintance with future Hall of Famer Hank Greenberg, by that time firmly established as the first Jewish superstar of major league baseball. It was a heady time to be a ballplayer, especially a Jewish one; moreover, it is tempting to speculate that many of Asinof's fictional characters have elements of actual people that he knew from this period. For example, his favorable portrayal in *Man on Spikes* of "The Old Ballplayer" Herman Cruller may partially represent his 1941 Wausau veteran coach, player-manager Wally Gilbert, a former major leaguer with whom he seems to have had a good relationship.[12] Likewise, the novelist's highly unflattering characterization of "The Manager" Lou Phipps might have a bit of Asinof's Moultrie skipper George Jacobs, with whom he had a short, stormy association in 1940.[13]

Just as historical people and events from the pre–World War II era (in addition to Mickey Rutner himself) are likely represented in Asinof's *Man on Spikes*, within those pages are found Asinof's philosophy of the game, his view of the ideal player or baseball credo, if you will. To the great delight of discerning baseball enthusiasts everywhere, Asinof—despite his boyhood idol worship of Babe Ruth—was not a proponent of the modern long ball power game. Instead, from his first short story to his very last baseball novel, Asinof lauded the proverbial inside game or "scientific baseball," as it is described by "The Scout" in his first novel.[14] In this approach to baseball, speed, stealth, consistency, character and intelligence—not home runs—are a winning team's best friends. It is not unlike the baseball philosophy of Branch Rickey himself. Such a view should not be surprising coming from one who as a player seems to have possessed similar qualities and did not tend to hit home runs.[15] It may well have also been the view of former Philadelphia Athletics star pitcher George Earnshaw, like Asinof, a Swarthmore College alumnus, who, while fire chief of Swarthmore after his retirement from the pros, recruited the recently graduated Asinof to join the Phillies' farm system.[16] Readers of *Man on Spikes* may be catching a glimpse of Earnshaw's crusty personality and purist baseball outlook as "The Scout" Durkin Fain who signs Mike Kutner to his first professional contract. Fain has little regard for the new-style, Babe Ruth wannabes, even as his boss, team owner Jim Mellon, berates him:

> Look, Fain. Baseball has changed since you played it. It's the goddamn long ball they want now. If a man can belt 'em that far, he goes up. The clever boys can only wave at the damn apple as it disappears over the wall. That's baseball today. It just ain't a little man's game.[17]

Fain's visceral response to his boss's directive is one that he dare not vocalize:

> One trouble was that the big hitters were everybody's meat. Find any rawboned kid who could blast the apple a mile and you'd wait in line with the other scouts to get him, dangling the ever-increasing checks before him, promising him the world if he'd come to papa. It was no longer scouting; it was a crazy kind of supersalesmanship.[18]

As for the owner Mellon's justification of giving the customers what they want, Fain expresses (at least in his thoughts), even more contempt:

> Sure, they blamed it all on the public. The public wants the long ball! It recently had its taste of the great Babe Ruth and his sixty home runs in a season. It seemed

so easy to win games that way. There was a dramatic finality to it that any child-mind could understand. There it goes, up and out, sailing over the outfielders, miles out of reach, into the bleacher bedlam and that hysterical adulation! It doesn't matter that Babe Ruth could have won more games with a timely, well-placed bunt or tap through that crazy, unbalanced infield. Fain often argued that the great Babe would execute such a simple maneuver only to show how clever he actually was. Baseball had become less a question of winning games than the way you won them.[19]

Asinof's invocation of his childhood hero Babe Ruth (through the voice of Fain) has a special poignancy within this context.[20] Given the great tragedy of the Bambino not being allowed to coach after his playing days were over, despite his obvious capacity and desire to do so, makes even Ruth himself appear to be the ultimate victim of the very system that he arguably saved single-handedly in wake of the Black Sox Scandal.[21] As becomes apparent in the very first chapter of *Man on Spikes*, true connoisseurs of the game must always make heavy allowance for the far less idealistic (and more realistic) version of the sport — one driven first and foremost by the marketing efforts and "supersalesmenship" of promoters and owners.

This element of baseball idealism was present in Asinof's writing from the moment he first sat down to his typewriter. In the original published version of his short story "The Rookie," Mike Kutner kneels in the on-deck circle during his major league debut and watches with growing disgust a younger rookie batting ahead of him:

And this was a bonus baby. Red Schalk, the new-type ballplayer. They had handed him sixty thousand dollars for being a high-school hero, for hitting .400 against seventeen-year-old pitchers. Sixty Gs for merely signing his name![22]

Schalk, after being completely fooled with two strikes, is fortuitously hit by a pitch, setting the stage for Kutner's subsequent, bitter failure at the plate. In the end, the less worthy ballplayer makes it to the big leagues and stays, while the more deserving is sent packing because of bad breaks, a corrupt system, and one bad swing. The Mike Kutner story thus becomes a baseball morality tale for the aspiring professional player: talent and hard work are not always enough — in fact, more often than not, talent and hard work are simply not enough, through no fault of the player. Most minor leaguers, no matter how deserving, never make it to the majors; conversely, many undeserving ones do often make it, however briefly.

If Asinof's sports message in *Man on Spikes* seems like a total downer, most former professional players, even the unassailable likes of Joe DiMaggio (see Chapter 2), have recognized the hard and profound truth of this theme. As for the "scientific baseball" most appreciated by true lovers of the game, it can never be taken for granted because neither the owners nor the fans demand it. If a truly great player does happen to make it to the big time, and does happen to play very well without hitting home runs, then it should be appreciated all the more, because it has come to pass in spite of these things. If that player happens to be the likes of Ty Cobb, admiration of whom off the playing field is very dubious proposition, then all the more reason to fully appreciate the multifaceted skills such a person was able to display in competition. In the next chapter, we shall endeavor to show how Asinof's purist vision of the national pastime, as reflected in *Man on Spikes*, with all of its tragedies and triumphs, clearly point towards bigger unresolved issues in American society, completely outside the world of sports. At its central core (it may well be argued), *Man on Spikes* is not really about baseball, but instead, about these much larger philosophical questions.

4

A Preference for Anti-Heroes Over Heroes

But talent alone was no guarantee, for there were too many dumbheads along the way hunting for lousy reasons to smother it.

—Asinof, *Man on Spikes*[1]

During my final years as an amateur ballplayer in Michigan City, Indiana, I was most fortunate to have as coach a former minor leaguer named Al Shinn who, in addition to being a very fine player-manager, took special interest in me at a time in life when I needed such attention. As my four-year collegiate baseball career had been remunerative but far from satisfactory, my late mother advised me to keep on playing ball until my active playing days ended on a positive note.[2] It proved excellent advice. In Al, I met a person who, like myself, played strictly for fun and diversion, without any grandiose ambitions or hidden agendas. Under his tutelage, I became the best ballplayer within my capabilities, before happily hanging up my spikes at age 24, although by this point in my life I was far more concerned with surviving law school rather than playing baseball.[3] It also so happened that Al, in his own younger playing days (during the 1950s), like Asinof's friend Mickey Rutner, had his own tough experiences with the still-extant reserve clause. In a five-year minor league career, mostly in the Brooklyn Dodgers' organization, Al was a terrific hitting first baseman and outfielder (like Asinof) who, over five professional seasons (1952–1956) batted .322 lifetime, and with power (41 home runs) to boot.[4] He never got a shot at the majors, however, because the Dodgers during that era had the great Gil Hodges at first base, as well as consistently successful teams, winning the World Series in 1955, the very same year that Asinof's *Man on Spikes* was released. Had it not been for the reserve clause, Al Shinn, like Mickey Rutner, would have surely had good opportunity to play for other major league teams more urgently needing his services. But Al was never one to complain about these things, at least not in public. It occurred to me at the time (circa 1980), that under the then relatively new free agency system,

Al would probably have gotten a shot at the majors, unlike Asinof's friend Mickey Rutner, as well as his fictional counterpart, Mike Kutner, who both got to play, however briefly, in the big time.

The obvious implication here is that the fictional or real-life experiences of ballplayers portrayed by Asinof in *Man on Spikes* are far more typical than not. That is a big part of the reason why it packs such a wallop for former players who read it. Moreover, Asinof's visceral realism — one so firmly rooted in his personal career and people that he met along the way — extends way beyond the realm of archaic legalisms such as the reserve clause. At its very heart, and as conspicuously displayed in subsequent works such as "The Secret Life of Rocky Perone" (see Chapter 3), the story of Mickey Rutner delves into universal, non-sports related themes such as labor-management relations and aspirations for wealth and fame in a free society. By extension, these issues include the inherent limits of hero worship and whoever we may happen to chose as our role models in life. In this regard, baseball literary critic Richard Peterson observed that *Man on Spikes* is "an exception among conventional baseball novels, where the game of baseball is often a reflection of life, where the baseball dream routinely transforms players into heroes and legends, and where baseball's readers can indulge their romantic fantasies while picking up lessons on the value of moral conduct and the virtue of having a good heart."[5] Readers may not pick up *Man on Spikes* to be edified, but they end up being edified in spite of themselves, whether they want to or not. As in all great novels, this is achieved through entertainment, rather than preaching or sermonizing.

One is naturally inclined to ask exactly where and how Asinof acquired this tendency as a writer, one setting him so distinctly apart from most of his contemporaries. The answer probably lies in the years of his early adulthood during the 1930s and 1940s. At Swarthmore College in 1940, the year in which he both graduated with honors and captained the collegiate baseball team, Asinof had the extra good fortune to study under Clair Wilcox (1898–1970), one of the most illustrious Keynesian economists of the New Deal era.[6] Rather than get upon a soap box and pontificate on socioeconomic issues, Wilcox invited his entire class, Asinof included, out on the town in Philadelphia to screen the then newly released film adaptation of John Steinbeck's *The Grapes of Wrath*, directed by John Ford and starring Henry Fonda.[7] After the movie, Wilcox brought the class back to his home for a late night discussion about the movie while his wife served tea. Asinof later recalled, "I learned a lot about what America was like that night ... I've never forgotten"[8] According to his memoir, another key phase in his education came a couple years later during the war while stationed in the Aleutian Islands and working with Dashiell Hammett in journalism. It was here that he first learned to both think *and* write about social injustices (see Chapter 8).[9] *Man on Spikes* would pour forth from his typewriter about a decade later.

It should be stressed that Asinof was in many ways a man of his times, and this had a great impact on his writing, all of which was done during the postwar era. Between 1932, when the Asinof family moved from Manhattan to Cedarhurst, Long Island, and 1946, when Asinof was discharged from the service, he had passed from boyhood to young adulthood. In 1932, at age 12, Asinof witnessed the election of FDR as president and the inauguration of the New Deal in response to the Great Depression. Whatever generational and philosophical differences existed within the Asinof family, there can be little doubt that they were mostly united in support of Roosevelt, who hailed from and was former governor of their home state, New York. By 1941, Asinof was 22 years old, a college graduate, former minor league player and, like his mentor Hank Greenberg, enlisted in the service well before the attack on Pearl Harbor, probably in anticipation of America's struggle against German Fascism. By early 1946, he was age 26, and the war appears to have been his real-life graduate school. It was during the war that he began to write as a journalist, however tentatively, under the informal tutelage of Dashiell Hammett. It is no wonder then that Asinof's generation produced a bumper crop of great American writers. Like him, many during their formative youth had been imbued with a soaring idealism, a sense of limitless possibilities for the world, and above all, selfless devotion to country. The "Greatest Generation" (as it is sometimes referred to and to which Asinof belonged), earned that moniker not because of its unique accomplishments (winning the war, overcoming the Great Depression, etc.), but because of distinctive personality traits which set many of its members apart. These same traits are on full display in *Man on Spikes*, as well as all of Asinof's subsequent writings.

Another major factor which shaped the young Eliot Asinof's political and economic views, as with most of us, was his family background. In a recent interview, Asinof's son, Martin, offered some valuable insights on the home environment in which his own father came of age, and which later contributed decisively to his choosing a career in writing. Although grandfather Morris Asinof and his three sons (including Max, Eliot's father) were able to quickly establish a thriving men's clothier operation soon after arriving in New York City from Russia, grandson Eliot took at first little and then, finally, no interest. "Eliot," according to Martin, "did not give a hoot about men's suits or the family clothing business." Although Eliot would be voted "Best Dressed" in his 1936 graduating class at Lawrence High School in Cedarhurst, this was apparently not due any love of sartorial appearance.[10] "That story about him being voted 'Best Dressed' in high school resulted from Eliot pleading with his classmates not to let him lose face in the eyes of his clothier family. The family joke is that Eliot never saw his father without a tie and I never saw Eliot with one."[11] Eliot's rebellious attitude towards his own father in matters of business may have been attributable to other factors such as

Max's total lack of interest in Eliot's baseball career which, in the words of Jeffrey Lott, "was how he [Asinof] defined himself as a youth."[12] This facet of Asinof's ambiguous relations with his entrepreneurial father will be further explored in Part III of this study. Martin Asinof added, "As a family, the Asinofs were a semi-dysfunctional in part because of their business. The business was essentially a sweat shop, which was typical of that time and place, but Eliot was a labor guy, and he held that sort of thing in disdain."[13] Many years later, it would be this "labor guy" aspect that would help to attract a young aspiring film director by the name of John Sayles to writing a screenplay for Asinof's career-defining second book, *Eight Men Out*.[14]

The end result of this surrounding adolescent environment was a fairly unambiguous (and uncompromising) world view as an adult for the author-to-be. For Asinof, social injustices largely stemmed from egregious economic practices, and (more often than not) flowed from poor labor-management relations disproportionately skewed in favor of management. Unfettered capitalism in baseball or anything else—capitalism unregulated and uncontrolled by strong central government—was viewed as a terrible monster that would first victimize the workers it claimed to feed, before turning upon all competitors, and finally, self-destructing through implosion. In this philosophy, he was a true child of the New Deal, with the economic teachings of John Maynard Keynes (via Clair Wilcox) on full display. The Mickey Rutner story, stripped of all period trappings (including the reserve clause), was essentially a morality tale of labor with no bargaining power being unfairly manipulated and exploited by irresponsible capital. Asinof's outlook, however, is far from being Marxist. The fictional Kutner is obsessively driven by his own aspirations for baseball fame and, to a lesser degree, a fair living wage, if not outright affluence. He will make any compromise in pursuit of these goals; in this sense, Kutner is like Rocky Perone. On the other side of the table, team ownership is all too keenly aware of this insatiable ambition, and uses it to take full advantage. In Asinof's world view, workers are seen as victims, but only up to a certain point; their own weaknesses and shortcomings are what allow them to be exploited in the first place.

From moral values so forcefully projected in *Man on Spikes* (and in subsequent works) spring other characteristics making Asinof's fiction and nonfiction so compelling, especially compared to most sportswriters. Chief among these is the prevalent phenomena of hero worship or, to be more precise in the case of Asinof, lack thereof. Mike Kutner does not hero worship anyone, and neither (we suspect), did Eliot Asinof. Kutner has well-meaning mentors such as Durkin Fain and Herman Cruller. He has caring blood relatives and a loving wife, all with whom he is often emotionally distant. He has competitors, enemies, and teammates—but no heroes and few if any friends, for that matter. Kutner is essentially on his own, and keenly aware of the fact.

For that matter, he rarely offers anyone else a helping hand. The closest exceptions come in rare instances such as the one in which Kutner protects a black teammate from wrath of fellow players by admitting fault after an outfield collision between them.[15] In terms of having no role models, however, Kutner is an enigma. Perhaps it would be better to say that Kutner himself is held out by the author as a kind of role model, a man who overcomes all odds and obstacles to achieve his goal (playing in the majors), yet knows when it is finally time to let go and patch things up with his long-suffering wife. Taking this a step further, one of Asinof's main points seems to be that all heroes, especially sports heroes, are an illusion. Love, friendship, and admiration may or may not be achievable for individuals, but to idealize a fellow being or professional colleague is, for this particular writer, only to invite disappointment and disillusionment.

Asinof's preference for antiheroes over heroes would continue to manifest itself throughout his writing career. His books speak for themselves, but another way to highlight this trait is examine Asinof's attitudes towards the great ballplayers of his own time. One may begin with Ty Cobb (1886–1961), by general consensus and with good justification the greatest baseball player who ever lived, a charter member of the Baseball Hall of Fame, and one who died during the interim period between Asinof's first two published baseball books.[16] Whatever Cobb's many shortcomings as a human being may have been, a lackadaisical approach to his profession was not one of them. Asinof, being a legendary hard worker himself, surely related to this quality alone, plus many others that Cobb possessed as well.[17] Not only was Cobb the original Charlie Hustle, he brought to his game a keen intellect and sophisticated discipline that were impossible not to admire. Combined with his maniacal desire to excel and a demonic public persona used both to shield himself from critics and frighten his opponents, Cobb's unique playing style on the field seems to be one of those rare cases never forgotten by those who witnessed and later spoke or wrote of it. It also fascinated Asinof, who admired the late Al Stump's awestruck but unflattering character study of Cobb, originally published as an award-winning magazine article in 1961 (while Asinof was writing *Eight Men Out*), then later extensively expanded for 1994 publication as *Cobb: A Biography*, in conjunction with the feature film release of *Cobb*, based on Stump's earlier work.[18] Even before Stump's original article on Cobb had been published, however, there can be little argument that Mike Kutner from *Man on Spikes* displays a similar physical grit, unbridled ferocity, and aggressive, "scientific" playing style of Ty Cobb.[19]

Long before the movie *Cobb* (1994), during the winter of 1976–1977, Asinof relates in his memoir, *Bleeding Between the Lines*, that he was given opportunity to pitch a Hollywood screenplay based on Stump's unvarnished account of Cobb's last days, but that the project never moved forward.[20] The anecdote is fascinating. The movie later made by director Ron Shelton, starring Tommy Lee Jones, Robert Wuhl, and Lolita Davidovich, is an excellent and faithful production, though, like the movie version of *Eight Men Out*, did not achieve blockbuster, popular success. Neither tells an uplifting story in the conventional sense; however, both perfectly capture the hard realities of the game and, more importantly, of the world and life in general. Ditto *Man on Spikes*, which has yet to receive its deserved movie treatment. Ty Cobb in his playing days may have been a hero and role model to millions, but after the details of his personal life became public knowledge, those who previously worshipped him faced a stark choice. One was to stop admiring him completely or even attempt to deny his greatness as a player, based on his failures as a human being — a choice still made by some fans. Another was to continue idealization of his baseball skills while acknowledging his personal foibles, both inside and outside of the national pastime.[21] It is the latter approach in which Asinof usefully instructs us as a writer. Lots of people do certain things very well, a few do several things well, but even fewer (if any) do enough things well to deserve uncritical hero worship. Role models for specific activities are acceptable, anything beyond that is not. For Asinof, an unthinking type of superman idolization no doubt smacked of Fascism, the worldwide rise of which his generation fought so tenaciously for or against during their youthful, formative years of the late 1930s and early 1940s.

If the counterintuitive example of Ty Cobb underscores the near nonexistence of hero worship in Asinof's writings, then the problem of Lou Gehrig (1903–1941) raises even more disturbing questions. In contrast to Cobb, Gehrig was an integral, essential component of Asinof's favorite baseball team from childhood onwards, the New York Yankees. Unlike Cobb, personal and public scandals were not revealed during or after Gehrig's all too short life. In sum, Gehrig is and was, by the estimation of most baseball fans, a true hero among heroes, sometimes even eclipsing Babe Ruth in this respect, whose human weaknesses off the field sometimes made fans temporarily forget that he single-handed revolutionized and possibility saved the game from the public scandals of 1919. What does Asinof have to say about Lou Gehrig, idol and role model to millions of Americans, in his published writings? In short, nothing. While the legacies of Ruth, DiMaggio, Greenberg, and many others are consistently given fond, respectful nods of appreciation, readers will search Asinof's baseball musings in vain for any mention of the man whom many consider to have been the greatest Yankee of them all. Was he just being forgetful or merely pressed for space? Neither, it would appear in hindsight. Such an omission deserves some brief exploration, as well as some hard analysis.

According to a personal reminiscence by Asinof made late in his life to literary executor Jeff Kisseloff, Lou Gehrig, a German-American product of the pre–Holocaust era, had a streak of anti–Semitism in him. Asinof reported that his mentor, the incomparable Hall of Famer "Hammerin' Hank" Greenberg (1911–1986) had shared with him his own unpleasant experiences with Gehrig while the two played together in the majors.[22] The story was concisely repeated in Asinof's 2008 obituary, as reported by Jeff Kisseloff in *The Nation*: "With Eliot, there were no sacred cows. He relayed to me a story Hank Greenberg had told him about Lou Gehrig's anti–Semitism, and one more hero bit the dust."[23] To what exact extent this alleged attitude prevailed is uncertain and will likely never be proved, but it is clear that the Jewish Asinof and his Jewish baseball exemplar Hank Greenberg were both offended by it.[24] Greenberg may have in fact been the closest thing to a role model that Asinof ever had, and the very thought that Greenberg may have taken some distasteful verbal abuse from anyone, even the great Lou Gehrig, may have just been too much for him to stomach. Consequently, rather than bad-mouth an American cultural icon, Asinof chose to remain silent — completely silent. It seems as though Asinof preferred and was far less troubled by men like Cobb, Ruth, and DiMaggio, men who had many personal faults, as opposed to Gehrig, who may have had a single, yet unforgivable shortcoming.

If true, this image of Gehrig of course flies in the face of his perceived memory, today mainly kept alive by the classic inspirational movie, *Pride of the Yankees* (1942), released one year after Gehrig's premature death and starring an all-star cast, including Gary Cooper, Teresa Wright, and Walter Brennan, as well as cameos by Yankee veterans led by the venerable Babe Ruth.[25] It is indeed a very fine film in the best tradition of American mythmaking, especially during times of war.[26] Given that in 1942 the Holocaust was reaching its frenzied climax and that the movie itself was produced by a mostly Jewish-controlled Hollywood machine, the ironies of converting the Lou Gehrig story into an inspirational tale for a nation at war against Fascism are manifold. Whether Asinof was aware of this at the time is unknown, although it was Greenberg who decisively intervened in Asinof's life that same year, getting him admitted to Air Force officer's training. Samuel Goldwyn obviously had no inhibitions about taking Gehrig's beloved memory to the bank, but Asinof later did, despite his acknowledged status as a premier baseball writer. In fairness to Gehrig, and assuming there was some truth to the allegation, his extraordinary life made very good fodder for the Hollywood machine of that era; as for his alleged personal faults, most can agree that these were few and far between. Unfortunately, these seemed to have touched a sensitive nerve in Asinof's psyche, and not without reason given circumstances of those times.

It is a shame that Asinof never wrote about Gehrig. He would have surely had many insightful things to say completely apart from Gehrig's rumored politically incorrect attitudes on race and religion. The closest thing to traces of Gehrig's legend to be found in his output are in the form of fictional or semi-fictional character traits. In *Man on Spikes*, Mike Kutner certainly has the quiet intensity, consistency, and personal integrity of a Gehrig, without the benefit of Gehrig's imposing physique or ever-present long-ball threat. Kutner, like Gehrig, has noticeable leadership qualities and leads by example for those appreciate his skills. Kutner wears glasses, however, which cause many to unfavorably judge him by appearance — in retrospect, a clear metaphor for the rampant anti–Semitism faced by Mickey Rutner, Hank Greenberg, and Asinof himself, as professional ballplayers. Early in the story, perhaps unconsciously, Asinof (through the eyes of the scout Durkin Fain) compares Kutner to "a racehorse" — calling to mind the "Iron Horse" Gehrig — whose perceived iron-like indestructibility is immediately demonstrated as he crashes into a brick wall while making a sensational catch.[27] Kutner, on the other hand, and like Gehrig, is not perfect. Among other things, he is surly and standoffish towards his African American teammate, Ben Franks, who threatens his own job by playing in the outfield. In spite of this conflict, however, Kutner is also magnanimous in protecting Franks from angry teammates by admitting fault after an outfield collision between the two. It would not surprise this writer if Gehrig had a similar noble but ambiguous manner with respect to playing field diversity.

By now it should be readily apparent to readers that all of the central issues touched upon by Asinof in *Man on Spikes* are directly and easily applicable to the non-baseball, non-sports world: racial diversity and integration in the workplace, labor-management relations, personal aspirations for wealth and fame (and the prices paid for these), hero worship and role models in society, and the never ending clash between professional goals and family life. That such a tall order was achieved in a debut novel of 276 pages is quite remarkable, to say the least. The novelist, of course, gives no clear-cut answers or solutions to these universal problems, but instead presents readers with snapshot-like realism and focused vision of the big picture. Oversimplification is banished. Readers are then invited to make up their own minds. In this way, Asinof's work is similar to that of any other great novelist, poet, or playwright. By way of contrast, classic baseball novels that came before *Man on Spikes*, such as Bernard Malamud's *The Natural* (1952) — a book that Asinof had read — may make poetic statements about human nature that are entertaining and insightful, but have little if anything to do with the realties of baseball as a sport or the exploitations and crass commodity-like trading of the marketplace.[28]

Had Asinof not written another book after his first novel in 1955, he still would have been remembered for this one fabulous and singular accomplishment. As things turned out, and fortunately for the future reading public, he had beyond this point in time over half a century of writing still ahead of him. Most of these subsequent works, like his debut effort, would present audiences with dazzling, multiple layers of meaning and real-world substance, while constantly challenging any misconceptions commonly harbored about the mysteries and contradictions of human existence. More impressively, this was often done within the context of baseball as overt subject matter. The double entendre of title for *Man on Spikes* refers not only to the plight of the professional baseball player, but also to the economic and personal struggles that most of us all face during our routine daily lives. For his next serious project, to be published eight years later in 1963, Asinof would stay with professional baseball as a framework, but this time in a nonfiction mode, written from the standpoint of a historical novelist. This nonfiction novel (if we may use such a term) would zero in on the labor-management relations theme tentatively explored in his first book, only this time to astonishingly hard-hitting and unforgettable effect. Part II of this study will thus closely examine the complex set of circumstances leading up to and following Asinof's inspired creation of *Eight Men Out.*

Part II: *Eight Men Out* (1963)

5

The Unwelcome Truth, Everyman Style

> *Harry Reutlinger was moved. How much of Felsch's story was honest and accurate, he had no real idea. What evoked his admiration was the genuine remorse and lack of self-pity. Felsch was guilty, yet he had pride in himself. The entire confession was devoid of anger or bitterness. He had simply done a bad thing and was ready to take the consequences. If he admired Cicotte for his good sense in getting paid in advance, he did not really believe that Cicotte was anything but an idiot like himself. Reutlinger had seen enough of America to know that the written rules were rigid and righteous, while the real rules were often open and dirty. Such he assumed, were the rules of baseball itself. You played hard and got away with as much as you could, legal or otherwise.*
>
> —Asinof, *Eight Men Out*[1]

In October 2005 the Chicago White Sox impressively won the World Series in a four-game sweep over the Houston Astros. Among Sox fans, there were those of us (myself included) who foolishly hoped such a victory would finally help erase some of the shame from the 1919 Black Sox Scandal. It did not. Nothing will ever erase the shame of the 1919 Series; it will forever stand as a low point, not only for the sports world, but for all of American culture as well. The scandal was a human tragedy on numerous levels: a tragedy for the White Sox players who did not accept payoffs but were still denied a championship they deserved; a tragedy for the Cincinnati Reds, a very good team whose title that year will be forever tainted by their opponents having accepted bribe money to lose; a tragedy for Charles Albert Comiskey, whose long and otherwise brilliant career was horrendously marred by the understandable rebellion of his greatest team. It was also a tragedy for baseball fans, a good number of whom lost money betting on a superior, but losing team, while far worse, many were impressionable school children having their idealism instantly shattered ("Say it ain't so, Joe").[2] And of course, it was a tragedy for the eight players suspended for life, especially Buck Weaver, whose only offense had been to not expose his friends, and for Shoeless Joe Jackson, whose immeasurable abilities have been raised, not unjustifiably, to greater mythic proportions after he was officially banned from playing the game.

The overwhelming scale of the Black Sox tragedy is partly reflected by the stark reality that it took over 40 years for a talented American writer to give the subject matter extensive, detailed analysis.[3] In the immediate wake of the event, its enormity was probably just too much to swallow. As Eliot Asinof succinctly observed, revelation of the scandal "was a crushing blow at American pride."[4] Use of the term "tragedy" of course implies that the result of the 1919 Series was not a foregone conclusion; it suggests that things could have been different if other choices had been made by parties involved. In recent years, a vocal minority of commentators have put forth an opinion that Cincinnati would have won the Series in any event, with or without the cooperation of their opponents. The Black Sox, it is suggested by this school of thought, accepted bribe money for unnecessary illegal services. This issue will be briefly addressed in Chapter 6, dealing with the aftermath and reception of Asinof's seminal work.

Asinof, age 20, circa 1940, senior class photograph at Swarthmore College. The yearbook makes reference to Asinof's academic, athletic, and musical accomplishments. While attending Swarthmore and Williams colleges, Asinof was exposed to the intellectual likes of economist Clair Wilcox, historian Frederick Schumann, and poet Robert Frost. About this time he would also meet future major leaguer Mickey Rutner, inspiration for his first novel, *Man on Spikes* (courtesy Friends Historical Library of Swarthmore College).

While *Man on Spikes* (1955) had firmly established Asinof's high reputation among literary circles and serious baseball fans, it was *Eight Men Out* (1963) that finally put him on the map with the general public and cemented his permanent legacy. Published when its author was 44 years of age, the book became an instant classic and will remain such, even as more extensive and scholarly works on the same subject matter continue to appear.[5] One unfortunate residual of the book's tremendous impact is that it has overshadowed Asinof's many other interesting (and often superb) efforts written over the 45 years following its publication. *Eight Men Out* is only one brilliant, though perhaps the most dazzling, facet of a very large gemstone representing Asinof's literary oeuvre. Another problem with great cutting edge works of this type is that they tend to confront head-on great cutting edge issues which large numbers of the general public may not yet be ready to face. Their controversial nature achieves, by definition, both fame and notoriety. Worse still (for the creator, at least), notoriety does not always automatically translate into financial success — in fact, quite the opposite sometimes. Regarding Asinof's masterpiece, this was also unfortunately the case, as we shall see in the next chapter. For the moment, however, the origins of this groundbreaking and revolutionary piece of nonfiction deserve brief exploration.

At less than 300 pages, *Eight Men Out* is a brisk read — hardly tome-like or professorial in any respect. The style is journalistic, worldly, similar to Hemingway's with its economical, urgent sentences and hard-hitting realism.[6] Asinof displays a fondness for epigrams and knows how to place them effectively, quoting near-contemporary Black Sox references by F. Scott Fitzgerald, Nelson Algren, and Ring Lardner, as well as recorded quips by owners, journalists, lawyers, and gamblers. The synopsis is straightforward, divided into six sections: "The Fix," "The Series," "The Exposure," "The Impact," "The Trial," and "The Aftermath." Where there is no documentary evidence, he forgivably imagines, conjectures, and reconstructs, all in very convincingly manner. I have personally read and reread the book several times over the last quarter century, and as in all fine literature, hidden treasures continue to reveal themselves at each sitting. Nuance and depth increase in proportion to exposure. Like many notable works, it does not appear to have been the result of any master plan or lifelong ambition. Instead, a good career opportunity simply presented itself to a gifted writer who had the unique ability and wherewithal to take full advantage, not unlike the manner in which the fictional Meyer Wolfsheim (based on the real-life Arnold Rothstein) was said to have impulsively taken full advantage of the 1919 Series fix in *The Great Gatsby*.[7] The book ends on a strangely upbeat note, hinting (quite accurately, in hindsight) that the posthumous reputation of Shoeless Joe Jackson, even in the tragic waste of his career, would become more venerated as time passed.

For any single person to piece together the baffling complexities of the Black Sox tragedy was a Herculean feat by itself. Asinof, though, went further. He reported the unlikely story in all of its subtle, ironic detail for the benefit of those able to appreciate such things. Despite some modern critical qualms that Asinof's account overly mythologized and dumbed down the circumstances of the event to the point where reality was somehow distorted, quite the opposite is in fact true. Any casual reread of *Eight Men Out* will only increase the number of unanswered questions surrounding the scandal. For example, how could it be that the greatest sports fix of all time was ultimately exposed, not by the players, owners, or media, but rather by disgruntled gamblers feeling they had been short-changed?[8] How could it be that the initial conspiracy was the brainchild not of gamblers, but of the players themselves? How is it that a club like the 1919 White Sox could win any games, given the bitter, cliquish dissension running through it? Charles A. Comiskey, though rightfully portrayed as insufferably intransigent and stingy, could also (as Asinof reminds readers) be admirable — a self-made man and former player himself, one who staunchly supported the first baseball attempt at unionization, the doomed Players' League of the 1890s. Was it his own deep-rooted insecurities over money that drove him to be parsimonious? Asinof portrays in gaudy detail the 1920 meeting between attorneys representing both Comiskey and gambler Arnold Rothstein, in which it was tacitly agreed to be in everyone's best interests if the entire affair was hushed up. Rothstein, before he bankrolled the fix, was initially opposed to the scheme for sensible reasons: it would be incredibly difficult to pull off, let alone get away with. In spite of these misgivings, he was pushed relentlessly by unsavory advisors such as Abe Attell, arguing forcibly that there was no limit to sports fan gullibility. Nor did the 1919 Series represent isolated behavior by the Black Sox, or other professional players, for that matter. The Sox were also involved in throwing games during the 1917 and 1920 seasons, even as cries of foul play continued to mount. Over and over again, Asinof reminds us that the picture is not as simple or one-dimensional as some would have us believe.

Major league baseball was going through a transitional phase in the popular imagination about the same time Asinof began working on his landmark contribution to the history of sports writing. One example was that, by the late 1950s, relocated National League franchises were beginning to win the World Series for the first time. In 1957, Wisconsin's very own Milwaukee Braves, moving from Boston only four years previous, electrified the sports world by defeating the New York Yankees in a closely contested seven game series. Two years later in 1959, the Los Angeles Dodgers, forsaking a heartbroken Brooklyn only two years previous, beat the Chicago White Sox in six games, even though the Sox had compiled the best regular season record in baseball and were favored by many to win.[9] Unlike the rigged Series of 1919, the 1959 championship was, from all accounts, played on the level; outside of Southern California, however, the result left a bad feeling among many baseball fans.[10] For one, the Dodgers organization was seemingly rewarded for its perfidy to Brooklyn. Second, it appeared the White Sox were still cursed because of 1919. After impressively winning their first pennant in 40 years, the Sox dramatically fell apart in the face of Dodger unsung heroes such as Series MVP Larry Sherry, a California native who never played in Brooklyn.[11] It was during this same period (1959) that Asinof made his way back to New York from Hollywood, where he had been a screenwriter before incurring the wrath of powerful figures such as Harry Cohn and Jack Warner.[12] Additional impetus for this move came when Asinof received word there was East Coast interest in having the Black Sox story produced for television. In short, this was an era in which many old loyalties and sacred cows of 1950s American baseball (and America itself) were beginning to be questioned.

On a much broader level, American society by 1960 was starting to become publicly uncomfortable with itself. As the Eisenhower era gave way to the Kennedy administration, there seemed to be a growing consciousness of the wide disparity between the bright media image of Camelot and its unpleasant realties, culminating with President Kennedy's horrifying assassination in November 1963, only three months after *Eight Men Out* was first published. While Asinof was putting the finishing touches on his best known work, the United States was beginning to feel unrest on a host of domestic and foreign policy issues, including civil rights, organized crime, Cuban-Soviet relations, and escalating U.S. involvement in southeast Asia. The dark side of American society was becoming more readily apparent to anyone who could watch television, let alone read a newspaper. Asinof's theme seemed to directly tie into this new cultural trend. For anyone then inclined to doubt America's exclusively good intentions or good judgment, the faith-shaking (though distant) events of 1919 — until then labeled as inconvenient history and swept under the rug of public awareness — were a powerful reinforcement of that doubt. Asinof brilliantly dragged everything back into the light of day, making the Black Sox Scandal an allegory for his own times, as well as a riveting lesson in American history.

Asinof's personal background was near perfect for the task. Crucially, he had been a professional ballplayer in his younger days and was all too familiar with the plight of the Black Sox from a player's point of view.[13] As a backup minor league player, he knew what it was like to be underpaid and undervalued, recalling that his first bonus had been "a glass of beer and a cheap cigar."[14] As a Jew, especially during the pre–World War II era, he also knew, because of rampant anti–Semitism, what it was like to be treated with lack of respect or outright hostility. In addition, he seems to have experienced a personal clash with a team owner. While playing in Wausau, Wisconsin, Asinof claimed to have been ostracized by management for being Jewish and romantically involved with the team owner's daughter,[15] From his stats and other available information, it appears that he was a fine athlete of good physical ability and obvious intelligence. These qualities alone, however, were not enough for him to be treated well or paid adequately. Like several of the Black Sox after their lifetime suspensions, Asinof once played under a professional alias in order to preserve his eligibility as a collegiate athlete.[16] Like the Black Sox, he knew what it was like to play for a regular season championship team, the 1941 Wausau Lumberjacks, that nevertheless went on in post-season play to lose (presumably not on purpose) to a less favored opponent.[17] Wausau as a town would have known the 1919 Chicago White Sox club, not only from its geographic proximity (in Wisconsin), but also from having former Sox pitcher Dickie Kerr—who had not taken bribes during the Series—as its minor league team manager in 1937.[18]

Empathy of the author for the disgraced 1919 Chicago team would not have been limited to generalities, but extended to specifics as well. As a player, Asinof shared personal characteristics with each of the eight suspended Black Sox, as well as traits with other Sox players who were not. Like Chick Gandil, he occasionally played first base and was known to have a short temper when properly provoked; like Happy Felsch, he was a former centerfielder; like Fred McMullin, by his own admission, a good baseball talent but not a great one. Like Eddie Cicotte, he was a smart competitor who seems to have favored the "inside" game—strategy, stealth, and surprise—as opposed to the power hitting, long-ball approach later popularized by Babe Ruth and others.[19] Like Cicotte, he painfully appreciated how one injury could end any career regardless of talent, as could one off season or single, mediocre performance.[20] Like Buck Weaver and Swede Risberg, he was known to be fiercely loyal to his friends, especially during adversity.[21] Like Shoeless Joe Jackson and Lefty Williams, Asinof was a left-hander and understood the important intricacies of the game from a left-handed perspective. Also like Jackson and Williams, Asinof knew the isolation of the American South, having played the 1940 season with the Moultrie (Georgia) Packers.[22]

Asinof played ball in the North as well, and was an athlete who well appreciated the profound divide between Northern and Southern societies, based on first hand experience. Moreover, he had played professionally in Wisconsin, which no doubt later helped provide him entrée to Black Sox Happy Felsch, a Milwaukee native who near the end of his life shared his personal recollections with the author.[23] The 1919 Chicago team was itself somewhat split along regional lines, with the Southerners—openly looked down upon by many Northern players—taking part in the conspiracy. To complete his regional education, Asinof played in both the East and Midwest, as well as the South, then later was a screenwriter in California (from where Gandil and Risberg hailed). Like the 1919 Black Sox, who represented all parts of the country, Asinof had personally seen these different regions and fully appreciated the potential conflicts. Not surprisingly, the two Black Sox that Asinof had least in common with—Gandil and Risberg—receive least sympathetic treatment in his book.[24] Like the redoubtably honest and future Hall of Famer Eddie Collins, Asniof was a "college boy" and hence much better educated than the vast majority of his teammates.[25] As a former co-owner of the semiprofessional Yonkers Indians, he would have even empathized with Comiskey to some extent.

As a professional athlete, no matter how incorruptible, Asinof would have been highly cognizant of the gigantic sports gambling industry, including its ferocious, inescapable impact on baseball. Given that he hailed from the East — New York City, to be exact — he perfectly understood how "big" money in sports betting often originated from geographic centers of finance and corruption. As a professional athlete who competed in remote places like Wausau and Moultrie, he was likely familiar with the close regional connections between gamblers nationwide. Whatever happened in one part of the country often had a significant, immediate impact on events taking place thousands of miles away. Even in today's endlessly interconnected world, there are many, especially among sports fans, lacking appreciation for the economic and sociological aspects of sporting events, as well as the rapidity in which cause and effect can cross state or international lines. Hypothetically (and realistically), a sports injury sustained in Chicago might immediately cause a shift in wagering odds made in New York, overnight transforming favorites into underdogs, then possibly causing one side or another to be more motivated (and dangerous to their opponents) than before, and so on indefinitely. Illegality does not necessarily have to enter the picture, but of course still can, further complicating the scenario.

Asinof's professional life as a writer came into play as well, making him the ideal candidate to write about taboo subject matter which no one had previously dared explore. As he would have candidly admitted, his birth date of July 13, 1919, made the events of that same year especially fascinating to him as a writer. On top of this, Asinof was always attracted to themes of injustice and hypocrisy in American society. One might argue that, as an author, he peaked and reached the "top of his game" during the early 1960s — a time in which these particular themes began coming to the fore of public awareness. Just as Asinof had once used an alias as a ballplayer, he fronted for blacklisted Hollywood writers before being himself banned; therefore, like the Black Sox, he knew what it was like to be denied a living for dubious reasons. Amazingly, as a youth, his Jewish family lived in the same New York City tenement as Abe "the Just" Rothstein, father of Arnold Rothstein. Based on this proximity, it is tempting to think that the young writer-to-be heard a tale or two from some fairly knowledgeable sources in his own neighborhood about the 1919 Series.

Later in life (and fatefully), Asinof came to know another Jewish Abe — Abe Attell, former featherweight boxing champion of the world and one of the main movers and shakers behind the scenes under Rothstein. Immediately after the release of *Eight Men Out* in 1963, Asinof was able to use material from his extensive contact with Attell to produce a short story for the *Saturday Evening Post*, titled "A Gambler's World Series."[26] In this vignette, as is often the case with historical fiction, fact and fiction merge to become indistinguishable, a most fitting result of collaboration between the novelist-at-heart Asinof and a compulsive hustler on-the-make like Attell. Like Happy Felsch,

Attell was an insider. Unlike Felsch, he was more sophisticated, disingenuous and slippery. Nevertheless, both Attell and Felsch, despite their differences, felt comfortable opening up in personal interviews to a writer each felt they could each relate to on certain levels. Asinof not only got these individuals to talk, but had the writing and reporting skills for effectively relaying the story to a wide readership. Asinof's very persistence and ability to obtain interviews like these set him apart from most other writers who attempt (unsuccessfully, more often than not) to tell the "true story" behind controversial and complex historical events. Additionally not to be overlooked, rather to be in fact emphasized, was Asinof's superb university education at Swarthmore College, where he graduated with honors in history and studied under its famed economics professor, Clair Wilcox.[27] Very few authors could bring to the table such a diverse arsenal of qualities: playing experience plus the ability to thoroughly understand the *business* of professional sports, as well as the broader historical context within which this peculiar and unique business falls.[28]

If all of these qualifications were not enough, fate provided yet another major, motivation boost to the author for his ambitious project. New York celebrity producer David Susskind had originally hired Asinof for a pittance ($1,000) to do research and write a television screenplay about the Black Sox Scandal in 1960 for DuPont Circle Theater.[29] Original drafts of Asinof's evolving teleplay were given various working titles such as *The Witness: Shoeless Joe Jackson* and *Say It Ain't So, Joe*.[30] Then, the entire production was nixed without warning.[31] Major league baseball Commissioner Ford C. Frick, gaining wind of the project's sensitive and potentially explosive material, intervened to block it. Frick persuaded the network sponsor that reviving this incident in the public memory would be "bad for baseball" at a time (the early 1960s) during which the national pastime was beginning to suffer an image problem. Accordingly, plans for the screenplay came to a sudden and seemingly permanent halt. The entire episode appeared to be a frustrating affirmation of all the abuses and distortions that Asinof wished to expose. Fortunately, however, the unsavory affair was reported in *The New York Times* and noticed by Howard Cady, editor-in-chief at Putnam's, who then immediately offered Asinof a $2,500 book contract ($1,250 in advance) for a full-length, in-depth treatment of the same topic (working title: *The Black Sox Scandal*).[32] This, almost needless to say, was a much better opportunity than writing a television screenplay in terms of telling the entire, unvarnished story in all of its amazing detail.

After Asinof agreed to this proposal, he learned to his alarm and dismay that renowned American author James T. Farrell (*Studs Lonigan*) was working on a similar book. In yet another astounding, fortuitous twist of fate, the over-extended Farrell voluntarily ceded the project to Asinof, then went further and generously offered a seven-page list of contacts to his younger colleague.[33] Asinof spent the next two years producing his baseball masterpiece, one which, for better or worse, would define his career during his own lifetime. The project several times almost came to a grinding halt, not in the least because most surviving eyewitnesses refused to talk. At one point, Asinof also proposed a novel on the same subject (working title: *One Man Down*) to publisher Simon and Schuster, either because he despaired of ever uncovering a reliable account of events, or presumably because he wanted to further capitalize on his upcoming nonfiction release, however fragmentary it may have been.[34] Then he hit the jackpot with Happy Felsch in failing health and feeling a need to unburden his incredible story. Abe Attell proved in the end to be an enthusiastic contributor as well, although by his very nature (as the main broker behind the 1919 fix) often did not seem to have a truthful bone in his body, which made him both invaluable and unreliable as a source.

The final heart-stopping phase in the book's tortured publication history came when the finished manuscript was several times rejected. First, a surprised Asinof learned that Howard Cady had left Putnam to join Holt, Rinehart, and Winston. Then Putnam rejected his manuscript outright without comment and did not invite a rewrite. Asinof tracked down Cady at Holt, who accepted the manuscript, only then to have it nixed by Holt's legal department as being too potentially litigious. Finally, in a climatic meeting with Cady's boss Allen Edwards, not at corporate offices but rather at the Hotel Roosevelt bar over Bloody Marys, Asinof persuaded Edwards to publish the book by regaling him with a story about his embarrassing encounter with Robert Frost as a student at Williams College (see Chapter 1).[35] *Eight Men Out* went to press and would prove to be a triumph by most literary standards. It would also in time lead to expensive and time-consuming legal battles with (among others) the formidable Susskind, who tried to claim the intellectual property as his own when television and Hollywood later showed interest. Asinof's account of the book's genesis and the aftermath of its publication are found in his cautionary 1979 memoir, *Bleeding Between the Lines* (see Chapter 6).

Before proceeding to the critical and public reception of *Eight Men Out* following its release, as well as the stupefying bad luck that seemed to follow the book wherever it later traveled, it may be useful to recall an anecdote about the stormy individual who created it. During World War II, Asinof had been stationed in the bleak and desolate Adak Island in the Aleutian chain (before Alaska became a state), where he witnessed callous acts of injustice and unfairness never forgotten.[36] One of these incidents involved two fellow soldiers accidentally killed in camp by an obsolete, exploding boiler. The mishap was preventable, according to Asinof, because a new boiler intended to replace the old one had been commandeered for personal use by the commanding officer of their post. The dead soldiers' parents and families were officially told their son died a hero. Later, when an indignant Asinof sought out one of the families to share with them his truthful, eyewitness account, they reacted with disbelief, wanting to hear no more.[37] The story is indicative of Asinof's entire writing career, and provides a useful parallel to the multiple problems posed by his wonderfully nuanced, though often unpleasant and discomforting interpretation of the Black Sox Scandal.

In sum, *Eight Men Out* had neither an easy birth nor a smooth ride in the public domain. The first controversial decision made by Asinof was to choose historical subject matter that many Americans, especially within the baseball world, would much rather have forgotten. Obviously, he believed that history forgotten might be repeated. Then he took that same divisive, historical subject matter and stoutly refused to water it down or make it more palatable. For this particular writer, oversimplified, one-dimensional, black and white interpretations would not be a faithful retelling of events. He had too much training in economics and history, too much experience in baseball and in life, to see it any other way. What readers are left with is a kind of unwelcome truth, everyman style. This was a difficult story, one not coming from an ivory tower, pulpit, or soap box; it was coming from street level, or diamond level, if you will, giving new meaning to the phrase, "cutting edge." No one but Asinof could have done it, it would seem, let alone done it as well. That he accomplished this difficult task has become a perpetual benefit for the reading public, proving that painful struggles (literary or otherwise) can sometimes be a good thing in the long term. *Eight Men Out* carries a sobering message about American society that might go against our preconceived notions, but one that should never be forgotten.

6

Not Unlike the Black Sox Themselves

It seems to me, El, you may be letting yourself get sucked in. You always need a cause. That's you. It's like your books, almost all of them; they're about some poor schnook who battles impossible forces and ends up getting the shit kicked out of him. They're marvelous, but what chance does he have?

—Walter Bernstein to Eliot Asinof[1]

Eight Men Out represents Asinof's lone foray into the realm of "popular" literature in the sense that it was his only book to achieve anything resembling widespread acclaim or recognition during his own lifetime. This was in spite of the fact that his previous work, the novel *Man on Spikes*, was considered by critics and discerning readers as one of the best examples of baseball nonfiction ever produced. Moreover, after the publication of *Eight Men Out*, Asinof proceeded over the next 45 years to write or collaborate on 13 more books—several having little or nothing to do with baseball or the sports world. All of these efforts are very high quality with subject matter seemingly more and more relevant to our society with the passage of time. Particularly telling is that far more of the general public know of the Black Sox Scandal through the film adaptation of Asinof's book, rather than through the book itself. Without the movie, it would seem, the scandal and Asinof's work would be largely forgotten, if for no other reason than thoughtful, probing journalistic studies of complex, disturbing historical events struggle to find an ever-shrinking commercial audience. Nevertheless, although *Eight Men Out* succeeded in putting Asinof's name on our cultural map, it is instructive to learn that the author profited relatively little in the financial sense from his most popular creation (at least during the first 25 years of its existence), and that the movie based on the book suffered a very long, painful gestation. In retrospect, it is surprising the film was ever produced, given the bitter controversy and bad luck that seemed to follow this intellectual property wherever it traveled.

In his great 1979 memoir, *Bleeding Between the Lines*, Asinof accurately noted the near-universal (and highly unusual), coast-to-coast critical praise for *Eight Men Out* upon its first release in August 1963.[2] Perhaps the biggest endorsement came from former Black Sox Eddie Cicotte, who on his deathbed relayed a message through his wife that Asinof had written "a very fine book."[3] Asinof then ruefully recalled how the "torrent of accolades" built up false hopes that were almost immediately dashed. Following a lauded appearance on NBC's *Today Show*, there was a quick succession of fawning interviews in Chicago by the likes of Studs Terkel, Robert Cromie, and Irv Kupcinet.[4] Then the aspiring best-selling author began to notice little things going wrong. There were inexplicable distribution problems with publisher Holt, particularly in California. After realizing that *Eight Men Out* would not be prioritized by Holt with preordained mass marketing or printings, Asinof dryly noted that he was "unwillingly to spend time selling a book that could not be bought."[5] Then interviewers less skillful than a Terkel or a Cromie learned the hard way they were hosting a guest who did not suffer fools gladly.[6] In one notorious Chicago radio appearance, Asinof's response to an interviewer who forgot his name was to make up a number of assumed identities, then mischievously improvised a book synopsis that never existed.[7]

Critical praise for *Eight Men Out* has been steady and constant through the years.[8] Although the book has more or less remained in print, it has never achieved blockbuster status by industry standards. It mainly appeals to a select and knowledgeable audience, despite its fame and influence, not unlike the Black Sox Scandal itself. It has also inspired numerous other books, which generally fall into three broad category types. The first category consists of disciplined scholarly research tapping into newly available source materials to which Asinof did not have access in the early 1960s. The latest of these academic studies is well represented by the late Gene Carney's excellent *Burying the Black Sox: How Baseball's Cover-Up of the 1919 World Series Fix Almost Succeeded* (2006).[9] Carney, while adding a wealth of new knowledge and insights into our understanding of the scandal, also validated most of Asinof's original analyses of the same events, though some of these had been made through necessity in the speculative manner of a conscientious historical novelist. For example, Asinof controversially asserted that team owners reacted to exposure of the fix by aggressively trying to hide it from the public eye, hoping the storm would pass, rather than exposing misdeeds and punishing perpetrators. Carney has conclusively demonstrated this was indeed the case. As for isolated factual errors that Asinof did happen to make, subsequent investigation has tended to underscore the relative insignificance of these items, as opposed to magnifying their importance.[10]

A second, more troubling academic response to Asinof's masterpiece has appeared over the last decade, one far less flattering to his accomplishment. In short, this vocal group consists of critics who argue that *Eight Men Out* is rife with factual errors and distortions. Because this second category of writings specifically seeks to attack the book for which Asinof is currently best remembered, it deserves extended commentary within these pages. Time will tell if these are just a passing phase or inaugurate a long-term trend. Perhaps the best example is Cincinnati-native William A. Cook's *The 1919 World Series: What Really Happened* (2001). Cook's thesis is straightforward: the Reds would have beaten the Sox in 1919 with or without the fix. His argument rightfully points out that the 1919 Cincinnati Reds were an outstanding team, especially in the pitching department. The Sox offense was effectively stymied by this pitching, the honest batters perhaps more so than the ones on the take, several of whom enjoyed notable statistical performances, especially Shoeless Joe Jackson, leading all Series batters with a .375 average. In an eight-game playoff, the Reds outscored the Sox a total of 35-20, a lopsided margin calling into question whether the Sox could have won even had their own pitchers performed better. Although on the eve on game eight, it appeared the Sox were making a comeback of sorts, they had still been held to only six runs during the first five games, and shut out twice. Their paltry, cumulative average scoring of 2.50 runs per game was itself indicative that something may have been more at work than merely half of their batting lineup not trying hard enough.

Though enticing at first glance, this theory is less impressive under scrutiny. To begin with, all statistics aside, the hard fact remains that Chicago's two best pitchers accepted large amounts of bribe money to lose on purpose, then proceeded to dump five of six games they pitched, including all the ones their team lost. Lefty Williams losing three games in a single Series was only less unusual an occurrence than Eddie Cicotte's masterful, dominant performance in a third Series outing after being lit up in his first two lackluster appearances. During the five Series games lost by these two pitchers, 30 of 35 total runs scored by the Reds were conceded by the Sox defense. Even Little Leaguers understand how such barrages can affect the respective morale of opposing teams, no matter how hard a ballplayer is trying. As for the ongoing dispute over Shoeless Joe Jackson's role in his team's defeat, anyone who has ever played with or against a great player such as Jackson knows that a great player "short-legging it" still performs considerably better than a less-than-great player. The same idea applies by extension to other Chicago starters who would not have otherwise made it to the Hall of Fame like Jackson, but were still key components of the Sox lineup, including Gandil, Risberg, and Felsch. All accepted bribe money and played less than up to expectations. In sum, it would probably take an experienced ballplayer to fully appreciate how devastating it would be to a team if its 1-2 starting pitchers suddenly threw in the towel.[11] It would also probably take a ballplayer to fully understand how a game of fractional inches and split seconds could be easily thrown without everyone noticing. As for the Reds themselves not noticing (which appears to have been mostly the case), all athletes at high competitive levels know quite well that one does not tend to focus on exactly how hard an opponent is trying when in the process of defeating him. More importantly, after beating one's opponent, the news that team was not trying its hardest is never well received because the victory is obviously diminished as a result. One thing is for sure, however: Eliot Asinof, the former minor league baseball player, noticed these things as he was researching and writing *Eight Men Out.*

What is the explanation for contrarian theories such as these? Cincinnati sour grapes? Envy for Asinof's literary achievement? More likely, works of this kind simply represent writers attempting to write insightfully about topics (professional baseball and big business) with which they, unlike Asinof, had limited personal experience. It occasionally happens to the best of us. As for the audience this sort of thing may find, part of it may have to do with some folks still having trouble accepting the hard, unwelcome truths that Asinof wrote about in *Eight Men Out.* The Black Sox lost because of willful bribery? Some fans still try to deny it. Yes, Cincinnati was a fine team capable of beating anyone on any given day; yes, they had excellent pitching that probably would have held the Sox to fewer runs than they were normally used to scoring.[12] Nevertheless, common baseball sense dictates that the Series outcome would have been likely much, much different had five or six key Chicago starters not accepted money to lose. In the final analysis, the school of thought asserting the Reds would have won in any event mistakes increased factual nuance for comprehensive revisionist history.[13]

A third category of books coming in the influential wake of *Eight Men Out* are best classified as pure fiction. With a few possible exceptions, these whimsical detours tend to work very hard at softening the stark realism so brutally presented by Asinof's journalist style. The best (or some would say, worst) representative of this breed is the best-seller *Shoeless Joe* (1982) by W. P. Kinsella, adapted a few years later into a painfully sappy but hugely profitable (and Oscar-nominated) film version, *Field of Dreams* (1989). In addition to being a major star vehicle for the likes of Kevin Costner, Amy Madigan, James Earl Jones, Burt Lancaster, and Ray Liotta (the latter as Shoeless Joe Jackson), this film featured a sentimental, dreamy musical soundtrack by future *Titanic*-theme composer James Horner.[14] While later reporting gross proceeds over $84 million, the makers of this film reused the same reproduced White Sox uniforms from the 1988 set of *Eight Men Out.* With uniforms, however, meaningful comparisons between the two movies end. Neither film nor source novel has much to do with the real-life lessons of the scandal so graphically laid out in Asinof's (much) earlier book and subsequent movie version from the previous year.[15] *Field of Dreams* took *Eight Men Out* to the bank, one could say, by watering it down for mass consumption. Like the previously highlighted, second category of writings attempting to revise history with new facts and new numbers, this third category attempts to revise history with pure human imagination, which somehow seems less egregious.[15] Given this determined refusal to accept Asinof's original work on its own terms, it would appear that many of us are still trying to come fully to grips with the Black Sox Scandal as Asinof first investigated and broke the story to the general public back in 1963.

Another undisputable fact is that the process of Asinof writing *Eight Men Out* and living to see it later become a feature film was lengthy, tortuous, and nearly futile. The story of the book's painful genesis and frustrating first 15 years of existence, along with valuable and poignant snippets of autobiography, are shared by the author in *Bleeding Between the Lines*.[17] Any aspiring author or filmmaker who reads this harrowing account is likely to thing twice before attempting any such creation out of pure professional principle. The book speaks for itself, but is worthwhile, among other reasons, for recounting Asinof's long and stormy business relationship with celebrity producer David Susskind (1920–1987).[18] It was Susskind who originally presented the idea of the Black Sox Scandal to Asinof around 1960, envisioning a television play, and also Susskind who in 1976 unsuccessfully sued Asinof to the tune of $1,750,000 over production rights for *Eight Men Out*. Not only were there issues as to who exactly owned the rights (Susskind, Asinof, or third party options), Asinof felt morally and professionally obligated to protect the artistic integrity of the project, which he felt was being compromised by very poor script writing containing gross historical distortions.[19] It was probably due mainly to this last item — artistic differences between author and producer — that the suit was initiated. Although eventually dropped by Susskind in 1977, the action all but wiped out meager book profits enjoyed by Asinof until that point and distracted him from creative activity for several years. The lawsuit also probably did more than anything to earn the project (and Asinof) a tarnished reputation within the film industry, not unlike the Black Sox themselves.[20] Fittingly (and perfectly in character for its feisty author), the memoir ends with Asinof receiving a threat from Susskind's attorney not to publish the memoir.[21]

That was in 1979. Some critics are still taking shots at Asinof. Appearing in print conveniently one year after Asinof's death when he was no longer able to respond, *Chicago Lawyer* magazine published a rather silly article on the Black Sox Scandal by attorneys Daniel Voelker and Paul Duffy.[22] Focusing on Asinof's inescapable legacy on the topic, the piece not only takes to task Asinof's interpretation of events, but questions his very competence to have written *Eight Men Out* in the first place, given that many legal transcripts and other primary sources were not used or not made available to him at the time. This is like saying Copernicus was not qualified to write about heliocentric theory because he lacked direct access to more modern scientific research and data. The alleged impetus for this latest attack came when a portion of Asinof's notes and papers became available after his death. These apparently shocked some quarters with the revelation that he had not used the strictest or most conventional regimen when compiling his source material. Asinof often approached his topics as a historical or journalistic novelist, sometimes relying on anonymous or confidential accounts of events and, if necessary (by his own admission), using his imagination to fill in the blanks.[23] One might as well criticize the late Civil War historian and novelist Shelby Foote for not using footnotes. Recent criticism thus seems to reveal not so much about Asinof's occasionally haphazard research methods as about the apparent narrow range of reading experience by some of his critics. Many, we strongly suspect, have spent far more time waxing sentimental over *Field of Dreams* than actually playing baseball at any sort of advanced competitive level.[24]

Particularly troubling is the article's attempted whitewash of Shoeless Joe Jackson. Rather than present the immortal slugger as a good man but fallible, less-than-perfect human being (i.e., the Asinof approach), the article seeks in lawyer-like black and white fashion to exonerate Jackson of any wrongdoing whatsoever.[25] Never mind that Jackson accepted money, made a confession to the grand jury, was named by other conspirators, (possibly) asked to be benched before the Series, expressed fear of retaliation from Swede Risberg, and like Buck Weaver, knew of the plot but said nothing.[26] It should be emphasized here that none of this in any way makes Jackson unworthy to be in the Baseball Hall of Fame, but to argue or suggest the whole thing was a frame-up imagined by Asinof to further his writing career is much too extreme, if not repulsive. Since 1919, no single individual has done more than Eliot Asinof to keep alive fan hopes that Jackson, Weaver, and Cicotte may one day assume their rightful places in Cooperstown.[27]

Mostly ignored by both critics and fans of *Eight Men Out* is the startling truth that it took a quarter of century to make a film version of the book after it had been written, despite its popularity and notoriety. Strong Hollywood interest had been present from the moment the work was first published, when Asinof met with executives from Twentieth Century–Fox shortly after his first book tour.[28] Things seemed to be proceeding apace, despite growing and justified concerns by the author that movie would not be faithful to the book, when fate or inevitable backlash intervened to halt the project.[29] Specifically, Asinof and his publisher Holt were sued in short order by both Chick Gandil and Dutch Ruether for character defamation. Gandil was upset about his unflattering and unsympathetic (though truthful) portrayal as ringleader and instigator of the fix among the players. Ruether was miffed ostensibly because of a careless allusion to his legendary drinking prowess. More probably, like all members of the 1919 Cincinnati team, he was unhappy that the Reds' tainted championship had been exposed by Asinof for all the world to see.

According to Asinof, he asked mutual friend Bill Veeck to intervene with Ruether, but a bemused Veeck could only report back that Ruether (by then about age 73) was drinking harder than ever in public while the suit was still pending.[30] Although charges were eventually dropped by both Ruether and Gandil, initial interest in filming the book was effectively snuffed out by this flurry of lawsuits, as was enthusiasm by publisher Holt to further market the book.[31]

Despite these disappointments, by the mid–1960s Asinof had indisputably established a notable career as writer. Had he lain down his pen forever at that point, he would still be remembered as the creator of a classic American novel on baseball (*Man on Spikes*), as well as the first and definitive nonfiction work on the Black Sox Scandal. In addition, he had by then accumulated excellent credentials as a screenwriter both for television and Hollywood, as well as a reputation for being an articulate, lively interviewee. Over the next five decades he would return again and again to the themes of baseball and professional sports in his books, plus a wide variety of controversial social topics that few (if any) other writers were willing to tackle. His new publisher, the prestigious Simon & Schuster, would release his next three books over the next three years. These included the 1967 experimental novel, *The Bedfellow* (see Part III of this study), followed in quick order the 1968 insider documentary, *Seven Days to Sunday: Crisis Week with the New York Giants* (see Chapter 13), and its companion piece, the 1969 football-themed, farcical mystery, *The Name of the Game Is Murder* (see Chapter 17). None of these enjoyed a fraction of the critical or commercial success of *Eight Men Out*, with the possible exception of *Seven Days*, recognized by a few perceptive observers as a stellar exponent of its genre. All of Asinof's books, from this point forward, would reflect varying degrees of fascination with the complexities and contradictions of the criminal mind, or to what extent those committing criminal acts should be considered "guilty" by society, as opposed to being inevitably driven to commit those acts. This sophisticated approach had been on conspicuous display in *Eight Men Out*, including its gripping trial scenes. Lengthy, provocative courtroom scenes would also be featured in Asinof's later works, such as *People vs. Blutcher* (1970), and *The Fox Is Crazy Too* (1976), both discussed in Chapter 10. Asinof's most outlandish return to the sports gambling theme occurred in 1977 (as the Susskind litigation wound down) with publication of *Say It Ain't So, Gordon Littlefield*, a comical, self-lacerating parody of himself as a fictional popular author who attempts to fix the Super Bowl, an act of revenge against one of the competing teams' owners. This compelling, little-known novelette will be examined at length in the next chapter.[32]

Interest in making a movie adaptation of *Eight Men Out* continued on and off over the next two decades as Asinof's writing career steadily progressed, especially during the post–Watergate era. The low point of frustration and futility came with the Susskind lawsuit of the late 1970s, when it truly seemed as if a feature film on this subject would never be made. Options were repeatedly bought, sold and shelved. Prospective companies and producers, especially prudent ones, were immediately scared off by risks of litigation and larger-than-life personalities involved in ongoing struggles. Sometimes it appeared just as well that a movie had not been made. In 1975, *Breakout*, a loose action film adaptation of Asinof's 1973 collaborative reporting venture, *The 10-Second Jailbreak* (see Chapter 17) was theatrically released. Despite daunting star power (Charles Bronson, Robert Duvall, Jill Ireland, John Huston) and a musical soundtrack by the redoubtable Jerry Goldsmith, the finished product was a money-losing embarrassment, though now something of a cult classic "tanker."[33] Its critical and financial failure probably helped to strengthen Asinof's resolve for artistic integrity during his dispute with Susskind, which came immediately afterwards. Better not to make a movie adaptation at all than to make a bad one, he reasoned.[34]

At the very same moment in time (1977) in which a quality film project on *Eight Men Out* looked deader than a proverbial doornail, a strange confluence of events was beginning to take shape, leading to that dream becoming a splendid reality during the next decade. In 1977, John Sayles, then a little-known novelist who had yet to make his first feature film as a director, decided on his own initiative to write an original screenplay adaptation of *Eight Men Out*.[35] It appears to have been done on a lark, strictly as a labor of love, combined with Sayles' desire to segue his career from novel writing into filmmaking, while simultaneously filling a practical need to have a sample screenplay.[36] Sayles did not own the rights to the book; in fact, this was during the height of Susskind's legal dispute with Asinof. Shortly thereafter, Sayles made his first feature, the successful and critically acclaimed art house movie, *The Return of the Secaucus Seven* (1979). Thus, a very long and distinguished American independent filmmaking career began. By the time Sayles first film was released, litigation over Asinof's book had subsided. Also about this same time, Sayles learned that a partial option had been acquired on the rights to *Eight Men Out* by fledgling movie producers Midge Sanford and Sarah Pillsbury. Soon, the three became partners in the venture, acquiring an option in perpetuity.[37] Jettisoning the latest poor script attached to the option, one in a long line that had plagued the project from the very beginning, Sayles' original prototype script was immediately adopted instead. By the early 1980s, a time in which Asinof's writing career was on temporary hiatus due to exhaustion and exasperation, *Eight Men Out* suddenly had a good director, good script, and settled ownership status. Financial backing was still needed, but talent and enthusiasm were now firmly in place.

Concurrent with these events, the never-too-financially stable Orion Pictures was going through its most profitable (and independent phase) during the 1980s. Within the space of three years, it managed to release a succession of award-winning, high-quality theatrical releases. Some of the more outstanding ones included a movie adaptation of the Peter Shaffer stage drama, *Amadeus* (1984), Woody Allen's *Hannah and Her Sisters* (1986), and Oliver Stone's first feature film, *Platoon* (1987). In this midst of these Orion successes came the company's profitable production of *Hoosiers* (1986), a basketball epic likely encouraging their management to equate sports movies with dollars. After several initial rejections of *Eight Men Out*, Orion executives changed their mind when, first, Sanford and Pillsbury produced the hit movie *Desperately Seeking Susan* (1985), and second, a galaxy of matinee idols signed on at union scale wages for a chance to portray the Black Sox, including Charlie Sheen, John Cusack, and D. B. Sweeney.[38] Orion purchased the rights for $125,000, rights Asinof had earlier optioned for $30,000.[39]

Production began in late 1987 at Bush Stadium (for baseball scenes) in Indianapolis, Indiana, with Sayles bringing in the eminent cinematographer Robert Richardson. The lightning eight-week shoot reportedly cost about $6,000,000—an extremely modest figure for a major film project.[40] Asinof was, however, invited onto the set as consultant and acted a bit part as National League President John Heydler.[41] A distinctive jazz age soundtrack was contributed by Mason Daring. The result, released in 1988, was superlative and today is considered by many to be the best baseball movie ever made. It was also one of the last films produced by Orion before the company was forced to go through yet another financial reorganization. In anticipation of the movie's release, Holt published a tasteful new edition of *Eight Men Out*, which Asinof dedicated to Sayles and his creative partner Maggie Renzi.[42] Asinof had nothing but praise for the project in his unpublished writings, pleased that "the first serious unsentimental movie about baseball was honestly made—meticulously, in fact." Noting that "Sayles stayed with the tough complex intensity of my book," Asinof added, "Where most movie adaptations are corny, sometimes insulting versions of a book, this movie gave *Eight Men Out* a special dignity."[43] In retrospect, the film's compelling realism is partially attributable to most of the hired actors themselves having been former ballplayers and athletes, just as the original book's realism partially stemmed from Asinof's own minor league playing experience before he became a writer.[44]

Thanks to the enduring popularity of *Eight Men Out*'s unlikely film adaptation, Asinof was able to resume his career as a writer, producing a spate of notable works during the last two decades of his life, plus making periodic guest appearances on television specials covering the Black Sox Scandal. He would also act a small but poignant part as "Silent Sam" in Sayles' 2002 feature release, *Sunshine State*.[45] Another positive residual of this success was that Asinof's literary work now received a degree of recognition that had been previously and sadly lacking. With this recognition came the grudging realization by many that Asinof was far more than a mere sportswriter—he also had important things to say on wide spectrum of social and political issues. The next two chapters will delve into how *Eight Men Out* became its author's springboard for writing thoughtfully about more sweeping, universal subject matter, both within and without the context of American professional sports.

7

Nothing Left to Prove in Terms of Winning

[Ayers] "Man, you got no idea the things that can happen out there!"
[Littlefield] "Agreed. But the man with the money is taking the risks."
[Ayers] "Sure. Sure. But he'll end up with the money no matter what. The jock, he end up shoveling shit!"
[Littlefield] I had to admit the truth of it. In fact, he had summed up the entire 1919 Black Sox Scandal in a dozen words.
—Asinof, *Say It Ain't So, Gordon Littlefield*[1]

Major league baseball has changed in countless ways since *Eight Men Out* was first published in 1963, let alone since the Black Sox Scandal of 1919. Rules, equipment, players, fans, stadiums, media coverage—all are now quite different; nevertheless, baseball, both in amateur and professional incarnations, is essentially the same game played a century ago. More remarkably, the same issues and controversies connected with the national pastime seem to reappear at regular intervals: gambling, substance abuse, labor-management relations, influence of money, bending and breaking rules of the game, the very moral character of its heroes and participants, etc. The Black Sox Scandal and Eliot Asinof's interpretation of the event seem more relevant than ever to baseball, as well as to all amateur and professional sports in general. The baseball connection is especially provocative, given this sport's older, revered tradition in American history. In many respects, baseball has been long eclipsed in popularity by football, basketball, and other distinctively American pastimes.[2] In spite of this, however, baseball remains hugely popular both in America and other places abroad. It still cuts deep into the collective national consciousness and psyche. Baseball as a pastime was struggling with ongoing societal questions long before other major American sports. As aficionados are well aware, baseball gambling scandals reached back deep into the 19th century, some long before any of the Black Sox were born, and continue tragically into the present day.[3] This was the great American theme that Asinof saw fit to immortalize for the benefit of future reading generations.

The best place to begin a close analysis of Asinof's moral universe within the context of sporting events is with the Black Sox themselves. Often overlooked is the fact that the 1919 Chicago White Sox had nothing left to prove in terms of winning baseball games. The very same eight Sox players later banned for life had already by 1917 been members of a World Series championship team.[4] By 1919, in contemporary jargon, they already had their rings. After an off year in 1918 due to injuries and the wartime draft, the Sox came roaring back in 1919 to win the pennant and seemed better than ever to knowledgeable observers.[5] What mattered now to some players more than winning, however, was financial security, especially to aging stars such as Eddie Cicotte and Chick Gandil. Even to those few who believe the 1919 Cincinnati Reds were the better team, there can be no denying that the Sox were obscenely underpaid, especially in comparison to the Reds, and hence far less motivated to win, at least in terms of salary (even after Series bonuses). Other unlucky developments in 1919 made for ominous timing of circumstances to encourage the fix, such as injury to incorruptible Sox star pitcher Urban "Red" Faber, who was subsequently forced to sit out the Series.[6] In many ways, the 1919 Chicago White Sox were perfect targets for gamblers — an ideal combination of underpaid and under-motivated champion athletes. These, combined with all other factors identified by Asinof in his book, set the stage in 1919 for a perfect storm of team corruption, betrayals, and sell-outs.

For this reader, the most outstanding aspect of *Eight Men Out* has always been its complicated and widely varied portrayal of criminal guilt. The eight players banned for their roles in the scandal cannot be lumped together in any respect after two seconds of thoughtful review. All readers of this work automatically become jurors, one could say. Although the players may not receive acquittal as they did from a real Chicago jury in 1921, they are never going to be found more guilty than the hypocritical system of which they were an integral part. Asinof the writer has magnificently seen to this. Team owners, fans, gamblers, reporters, and even players who were not banned, all are as likely to receive our censor as the eight men eventually singled out for punishment. The book presents a vivid spectrum of human behavior, with eight different shades of guilt for the individual Black Sox themselves, ranging from the blackest black of unrepentant guilt to the whitest white of unjustly condemned virtue. Thus the very colors of the 1919 Chicago team — White Sox and Black Sox — assume mythic, symbolic proportions which Asinof the writer-journalist-novelist was able to skillfully exploit to the fullest.

Another terrific quality of Asinof's presentation is that no human being is viewed as being all bad or all good; instead, everyone, to varying degrees, is situated somewhere in-between. Even the arch-player-villain of the story, Chick Gandil, is a man whose boundless anger and resentment we are allowed to share. He may have done bad things, but not without provocation; moreover, there can be no denying that Gandil came out ahead in the end, albeit at the expense of others. Ditto Gandil's teammate and co-conspirator, Swede Risberg, who whatever unsympathetic qualities he may have possessed ("Swede is a hard guy"), still can be rightfully admired for the relentless solidarity he displayed with other Black Sox both during and after the scandal.[7] Utility infield Fred McMullin may have been little more than an all-too-willing errand boy, yet there are few who cannot relate somewhat to a marginal outsider's anxiety at being left out of big plans made by admired insider buddies. Lefty Williams may have intentionally blown three games (including the Series finale) for pay, but instead of getting the balance due of money owed, received a brutal threat from gangsters against the life of his cherished wife if he dared to do otherwise.

The other four Black Sox come across as outright sympathetic, if not innocent of serious wrongdoing. All later show remorse at what they did or did not do, with the exception of Buck Weaver, who arguably had nothing to be remorseful about. Happy Felsch falls from grace only because of his good-natured gullibility and lack of business acumen. There is nothing spiteful or evil about Felsch, as Asinof saw and heard for himself while interviewing a most willing and cooperative subject late in Felsch's life. Felsch is a likeable person in spite of throwing ballgames to make what he thinks will be an easy extra buck.[8] Eddie Cicotte, Shoeless Joe Jackson, and Buck Weaver assume proportions of tragic heroes. Cicotte is a good man whose temporary corruption brings others into the fix and, in the end, causes everything to go down. He becomes a personification of that era's unfairly treated ballplayer — a responsible family man; a talented, proven, and dedicated professional athlete who is nonetheless ridiculously under-compensated by Comiskey and treated like an aging piece of meat despite his great intelligence, savvy and worth.[9] Yes, he sells out friends and teammates, but for the sake of his family, and only after he has been pushed into a corner. In Shoeless Joe Jackson, readers meet one of the greatest players of all time, as well as one of the most guileless and put upon, and certainly the one Black Sox who has most captured the popular imagination since. The illiterate Jackson accepts payoff money but does not know exactly what to do with it, then proceeds to hit .375 in the Series. Sports fans will forever debate to what extent, if any, he did not give a one hundred percent effort. This writer's own experience in the game has been that racking up numbers is only one small part of winning a championship playoff. More often than not, intangibles decide such contests; a Jackson hitting a hundred points less but nevertheless determined to win may have been twice as dangerous in the clutch as the confused and demoralized Jackson who showed up to play in the 1919 World Series.[10] We will never know for sure.

And then there is Buck Weaver, whom Asinof labeled as "the ultimate victim" of the scandal.[11] Weaver stands totally apart from the other seven Black Sox because no one has ever doubted or questioned that he played his heart out, never took a dime, and was opposed to the entire scheme of fixing the Series. His only crime, as Commissioner Landis and a few other higher ups saw it, was that he knew exactly what was going on, but remained silent. Other participants not on the take also knew, including Charles Comiskey himself early on in the Series — this is a documented fact — and yet it was Weaver who was labeled an outlaw and banned for life. One could argue that Weaver's inside knowledge was special in that it was acquired during pre–Series meetings with the other participants; therefore, it was in his power to expose the fraud before it began. For Weaver, however, loyalty to friends was a high priority, and he understandably blanched at helping men like Comiskey at the expense of his friends. He surely believed that through his own example results on the playing field may have been different, both by performing well (which he did) and perhaps by changing the hearts of his corrupt teammates (which he did not). The moral dilemma of Buck Weaver and the bitter injustice suffered for the rest of his life goes to the very ethical core of professional sports and well beyond, as we shall see in Chapter 8. Almost every professional trade in our society has a code of ethics which encourages, or even demands "whistle-blowing" in some situations — surely one of the most complex and difficult decisions ever made by parties confronted with such choices, as well as by the disciplinary panels that review these decisions. Part of the greatness of *Eight Men Out* is that readers are allowed to fully appreciate these questions. While Asinof clearly sympathizes with Weaver and believes in the final analysis that he received a grossly unfair sentence of punishment in relation to the extent of his transgression, the ethical conundrum that ensnared the likeable and admirable Chicago third baseman is still graphically laid out in all of its daunting, maze-like difficulty.

Asinof's long-term view of the scandal was neither static nor rigid. It gained depth and sophistication as time passed. From 1963 (when *Eight Men Out* first appeared), fast forward to 1977, a time in which Asinof was defensively embroiled in his emotional dispute with the powerful David Susskind over television rights to the story. In the midst or immediate aftermath of this controversy appeared Asinof's unsettling, comedic novelette, *Say It Ain't So, Gordon Littlefield*, published by E. P. Dutton, a minor masterpiece of self-parody and sports satire, though remaining relatively obscure since its release. The novelette tells the succinct, fictional story of Gordon Littlefield, a celebrated New York writer who decides to try and fix the Super Bowl by paying off star players of the heavily favored team.[12] He is motivated by a justified hatred for the team's owner, Lester Stillson, as well as the writer's own unmitigated ego. Littlefield is a thinly disguised representation of Asinof himself, and the fictional New York Bulls football team is a thinly disguised substitute for Asinof's beloved New York Giants, with whom he spent the 1967 season while producing his highly regarded narrative, *Seven Days to Sunday* (1968). Asinof had also used the fictional New York Bulls in a companion book to *Seven Days*, the absurdist and cleverly-titled crime mystery, *The Name of the Game is Murder* (1969). In addition to revisiting the football and sports gambling-corruption themes that Asinof had memorably addressed in the 1960s, *Gordon Littlefield* represents a searing self-indictment of both the author and his critics. In wake of his failure to earn a living, much less accumulate wealth, from his most famous work, Asinof focuses his formidable journalistic lens back upon himself to wrenching, disconcerting effect. Along the way he also manages to lampoon legions of sports fans and sportswriters failing to fully comprehend or appreciate the important issues so painstakingly identified by Asinof 14 years earlier in *Eight Men Out*.

The character of Gordon Littlefield is vividly drawn, but with nothing resembling affection. Asinof pretty much distills all of his personal vanity and perceived negative qualities into a nasty caricature, possibly representing everything unworthy that he ever wanted to be both as a writer and as a person. Writing in the first-person narrative, Asinof presents Littlefield as the toast of his elitist Upper East Side literary circle, self-described as "not one who generally suffers fits of nervousness. A placid man, educated in the finest traditions of dispassion and poise. Furthermore, a man with experience of an exceptionally varied nature, frequently not without a flare for high drama."[13] Asinof was known for his volatile temperament, but also less well-known for his surprising ability remain calm in the middle of a firestorm, a quality for which former professional athletes such as himself are in fact quite often noted.[14] Littlefield describes himself as aged 40, the age of Asinof in 1960 when he embarked on writing *Eight Men Out*.[15] Littlefield also claims Mayflower descent, an overblown distinction certainly not possessed by the second-generation American Asinof, but one which he may have been sick of hearing from less talented countrymen, and one which he may have even secretly fantasized.[16] Apart from these inherited qualities, Littlefield is portrayed as an amoral, adulterous, and vindictive schemer with huge regard for his own reputation and tiny regard for the feelings of others. Not surprisingly, the reader feels little or no sympathy for Asinof's detailed portrait of this character, in spite knowing all too well whom the character is supposed to represent.

Few other characters portrayed in the book are impressed with Littlefield either. His nemesis, the bombastic and ruthless Bulls team owner, Lester Stillson, after beating Littlefield at squash and winning a huge bet in the process, is far from being a gracious winner. On the contrary, he rubs Littlefield's nose in the defeat and uncorks perhaps one too many hard truths about the celebrity-writer in the process:

> You know something Littlefield? You're a cream puff. Guys like you, you don't know how to win. You've had life so easy, you think the world will roll over every time you show your pretty face.... Shit, you can't even look a man in the eye, Littlefield. I bet you never had to fight for anything in your life. It's all there in your goddamn books. Huh, those books! I don't believe a word of them. They're all fake, just like you're a fake. There ain't a real thing in them, all that bullshit about how you "tested your mettle." What fucking drive!![17]

As club bystanders howl with laughter, the humiliated celebrity-writer plots revenge. He sees an opportunity with Stillson's talented but long-abused Super Bowl contending team, as well as with Stillson's disaffected and long-suffering wife. Asinof's over-the-top introduction of the Bulls reads like an exaggerated and cartoonish version of the Black Sox — in short, everything that Asinof tried to avoid doing in *Eight Men Out*, yet was still perceived that way by thousands who never bothered to read the book or were not capable of fathoming the truth even after they read it:

> For the most part, the Bulls were a motley collection of social misfits, a complete violation of the straight-square-respectable image that the official world of professional football wished of its players, principally out of deference to TV sponsors intent on selling products. The Bulls were more like jackals, a bunch of undisciplined, contumacious rowdies who seemed to delight in breaking rules both on and off the field. Much to Commissioner Pete Rozelle's horror, it was revealed that there were four ex-cons on the squad, one of whom had actually robbed a bank. Another was a rapist. The quarterback was once an active member of the Ku Klux Klan. Still another was prominently known to have been a sexual aberrant. Two others were waived from other clubs because of alleged homosexuality.[18]

Throughout the story, overt references are made to the Black Sox Scandal, the 1919 World Series, and to Shoeless Joe Jackson.[19] The connections are nearly impossible for sports fans to miss; nevertheless, *Gordon Littlefield* failed to find an audience, possibly because of the author's black humor style, and possibly in part because no one likes to see their misconceptions being made fun of. Nevertheless, Asinof does not spare himself either, and the work is particularly interesting in this regard.

Arguably Asinof's most fascinating creation in this outlandish cast of characters (besides Littlefield himself) is Jake Kolacka, the convicted bank robber referred to in the team roster. Obviously based in part on the real-life Garrett Brock Trapnell, earlier portrayed in unforgettable fashion by Asinof in *The Fox Is Crazy Too* (1976), Kolacka (in the story) was found not guilty of criminal conduct by reason of insanity, although it is somewhat unclear to what extent this insanity is feigned.[20] Like Trapnell, Kolacka has a very high IQ and is a "man of action," but (in the eyes of a corrupt Littlefield) "without a proper hunger for money."[21] Kolacka does a have a high opinion of himself, though, and before Littlefield decides to aim his crooked pitch at others, has

Kolacka convinced that he wants to write a book about his colorful, wayward personality.[22] Finally, "Kolacka" is a name prominently resurfacing years later for Asinof in his collaborative baseball novel *Strike Zone* (1994), as discussed in Part IV of this study. In *Strike Zone*, "Ernie" Kolacka is an aging major league umpire faced with the moral dilemma (not unlike the Black Sox) of whether to throw a crucial game in favor of one team, both for the sake of money and friendship. This latter-day Kolacka clearly represents the voice of the author, and shows a straight trajectory from Asinof's original character study of the volatile skyjacker and social misfit Trapnell, to the raucous parody and comic overkill of football star Jake Kolacka, then lastly, to the serious, melancholy introspection of veteran baseball umpire Ernie Kolacka.[23] But more of this later.

In the end, the wild and untamed New York Bulls prove too much for even the clever, devious Gordon Littlefield to handle. Not only do bribed players decide (during halftime) not to throw the Super Bowl, crocked and straight alike later make an unpleasant house call on Littlefield after the game. In the end, Littlefield gets mob vigilante justice, rather than legal justice. As for the players, they learn, if they learn anything, that their burning competitive desire to win trumps all, including an unquenchable hatred for their owner-employer — and this emotion, too, is at one point physically indulged during the course of Asinof's comedic tale. Unlike the tragic Black Sox, the Bulls, who have little else morally redeeming about them, do the right thing at the end of the day: they play to win regardless of money. The paradox, of course, is that the despicable Lester Stillson and other magnates like him are able to capitalize on this desire to their great financial gain at the expense of their employees. As for the puffed-up pride of the narrator, not much of this is left by the end. *Gordon Littlefield* often reads as if its author were exorcising personal demons built up with years of frustration over *Eight Men Out*'s limited commercial success and widespread misinterpretation.

It is interesting to contemplate that Asinof's long and productive literary journey with sports-gambling subject matter may or may not have begun with *Eight Men Out*. On September 28, 1959, CBS televised a 90-minute live broadcast for the David Susskind-produced "DuPont Show of the Month" in which Asinof is officially credited as screenwriter.[24] The episode was titled "Body and Soul," a television remake of the classic 1947 film starring John Garfield, and dealing with the all-pervasive and inescapable influence of gambling money on professional boxing.[25] Later well-known actors Ben Gazzara and Martin Balsam both performed in the piece, although the video for this telecast is not known to have survived. It has also been questioned whether the screenwriter for this piece was in fact Asinof or Walter Bernstein, for whom Asinof had sometimes fronted after Bernstein was blacklisted.[26] If Asinof did indeed write it, then "Body and Soul" marked his first tentative step in that direction as a professional writer. It may have additionally set the stage for his disturbing but highly productive association with Abe Attell, in his day the undisputed featherweight boxing champion of the world, major protagonist-dealmaker in the Black Sox Scandal, and professional fighter himself rumored to have occasionally thrown bouts intentionally.[27] Asinof attribution to "Body and Soul" would also mean that he wrote about gambling corruption within the context of three different professional sports — baseball, football, and boxing, further highlighting its unending fascination to him.

Perhaps the biggest issue raised in *Eight Men Out*, at least with respect to professional sports, is whether any of the condemned Black Sox belong in the Baseball Hall of Fame, or more specifically, to what degree should Hall of Fame stature be dependent on perceived moral uprightness? To sever this connection completely of course risks merging Halls of Fame with proverbial "Halls of Shame" as these apply to most anything, sports-related and otherwise. With respect to the Black Sox, there can be no doubt that Shoeless Joe Jackson, Buck Weaver, and probably Eddie Cicotte as well, would have all been elected members long ago had it not been for their involvement in the scandal. Asinof himself would have supported their membership regardless, as would this commentator. There are also many observers, including this one, who believe that Buck Weaver's punishment in particular was tremendously out of proportion to the miniscule infraction he committed. Many would say Weaver committed no infraction at all. Assuming that he did — namely, he was somewhat tardy in reporting what he knew — Weaver, along with Jackson and Cicotte, all become the greatest representatives in baseball (and perhaps all sports) of athletes unjustly denied honors deserved. The injustice stems not from their pure innocence, but rather from the grotesque disproportion of their penalty in relation to whatever personal foibles and shortcomings were exposed to the public of their time. Their continuing exclusion from the Hall of Fame seems to blare out that Cooperstown justice can only be administered with a bludgeon, unable to make any distinctions between the very guilty and the marginally guilty.

The ongoing banishment of the "less guilty" or "slightly guilty" Black Sox from Cooperstown is doubly galling when the unapologetic admission of their more dubious contemporaries is considered. Charter Hall of Fame member Ty Cobb was unquestionably the greatest baseball player who ever lived in terms of numbers, and yet the less said about his personal life the better. In terms of moral character, Cobb certainly compares unfavorably with most of the Black Sox. Worse, it is well known that Cobb was probably involved in sordid gambling activities (as well as throwing ballgames) years after the Black Sox Scandal had been exposed; yet, he was (and would still be) admitted to Hall, presumably because he had been conveniently acquitted of all charges, not unlike the Black Sox being found "innocent" by a home town Chicago jury.[28] If Cobb is too extreme of an example, one may look no further than the immortal Babe Ruth, surely the most popular and influential baseball player of all time, but also a man who (at best) could be described as a good role model off the playing field only part of the time.[29] The opposite extreme (and a very contemporary one) is the demoralizing case of Pete Rose, one of the greatest modern athletes in terms of competitive accomplishments, but one very hard to admire beyond these narrow achievements.[30] If a brutal anti-role model like Ty Cobb can be in the Hall of Fame, then why not Pete Rose as well? Thanks in large part to Eliot Asinof and *Eight Men Out*, difficult questions such as these are now posed with far more frequency than only half a century ago — surely a healthier state of affairs for all sports fans.

As stated at the beginning of this chapter, sports betting, along with its corrosive effects on society, go back a long ways, in fact, to the very beginnings of civilization. *Eight Men Out* is arguably the finest literary work to ever address this timeless, borderless theme. The narrative's unsettling effectiveness at highlighting the many thorny problems surrounding, not only the Black Sox Scandal, but the entire universe of gambling in relation to sports, is due to the same unique qualities that give Asinof's work pointed relevance even if one is not a baseball fan. For example, was Charles A. Comiskey any better than the "corrupt" players he consistently mistreated and exploited? Was Kenesaw Landis an even-handed judge of these fallen athletes, or merely a politically-correct showboat? To what extent was the enigmatic Eddie Cicotte a "criminal," and was his ultimate punishment too severe?[31] One could meaningfully debate all of these questions (and many, many more), plus do it indefinitely without knowing a much about baseball. These abundant non-athletic points of interest in *Eight Men Out* shall be explored in the final chapter of this section.

8

"More Than a Game"

Well, well, who got screwed today?

— Dashiell Hammett to Eliot Asinof[1]

Ever since childhood, I have been fascinated by the Black Sox. To lose on purpose for money — this may have been my very first introduction to the shameless, bare knuckled world of American commerce, via what I loved most as a boy, baseball. I knew before and quite early on that major leaguers were paid for their services, but to compromise the integrity of the game for extra compensation — that was an entirely new concept. I believe that I was around 11 years old at the time. While my reaction was not "Say it ain't so" — I had been quite aware that such things existed (outside of baseball, at least) — this was possibly my first moment of true disillusionment with sports hero worship, just as portrayed for the (possibly mythic) young boy who confronted Shoeless Joe Jackson on that dreary Chicago day back in 1921. The hard truth had been broken to me by my older brother, who was trying to fully disclose the dire consequences of being a Chicago White Sox fan (which both of us were). As we cheered on the likes of Sox Golden Glove star Ken Berry (who years later became a consultant and actor on the movie set of *Eight Men Out*), it occurred to my young mind that baseball was far more than a game, not only for those who played it, but to anyone caring for their country.[2] Heady stuff for an 11-year-old, to be sure.

Eliot Asinof was never a White Sox fan, nor was he from a small Midwestern town like myself; he was a Yankee fan to the core, born and reared in Manhattan. Although the money movers and shakers behind the fix came from Asinof's mega-metropolis world of New York City, it would eventually be played out and decided in the Middle America urban centers of Chicago and Cincinnati, not all that far from where he had once played minor league baseball in Wausau, Wisconsin. Moreover, the idea itself would be initiated by a group of disgruntled athletes whose geographical roots were as diverse as the country itself: Wisconsin, California, South Carolina, Missouri, Michigan, Kansas, and Pennsylvania.[3] In spite of Asinof's uniquely broad personal background in athletics, education, commerce, and culture, one is tempted, at the risk of oversimplification, to try and pinpoint one single factor that led him to devote his unique talents to this particular subject matter. Some have suggested that he was drawn to outlaws, being somewhat an outsider himself, while others say that exposure of injustice was a unifying theme in all of his writings. These were of course important factors. Specifically regarding *Eight Men Out*, however, this observer would postulate that Asinof was likely drawn, above all, to the universality of the Black Sox story. You do not have to be a baseball fan to appreciate it; in fact, one could make a good case that the book is about far more than baseball or sports in general. Viewed in retrospective, Asinof seems to be writing about contradictions in everyday things that Americans take for granted, and the ethical conflicts flowing from these competing, conflicting values as a result.

In his Preface to *Eight Men Out*, Asinof states a straightforward journalistic purpose, asking: "Why did they do it? What were the pressures of the baseball world, of America in 1919 itself, that would turn decent, normal, talented men to engage in such a betrayal?"[4] The question "why?" has a very familiar ring to it within the trajectory of Asinof's career. Some 20 years before the book's publication, during the midst of World War II, a young Army Air Corps Second Lieutenant Eliot Asinof found himself stationed on Adak Island in the Aleutian chain, working shoulder-to-shoulder with 55-year-old Corporal (and popular crime novelist) Dashiell Hammett (1894–1961), then editor of the base newspaper, congenially titled *The Adakian*. Asinof later reminisced: "I was twenty-four years old, and I sat at his [Hammett's] feet. In the process I was thrown together with others who were infinitely better informed than I. For the first time in my life I began to think seriously about something other than myself."[5] This moment, according to the

U.S. Army Air Corps Second Lieutenant Eliot Asinof, circa 1943. During the last two years of World War II, Asinof was stationed at Adak Island in the Alaskan Aleutian chain, where he worked with Dashiell Hammett as a journalist. It was here, according to Asinof, that he first entertained the idea of writing professionally and first learned as a writer to ask the question, "Why?"

author, represented his genesis as a writer, although at the time (he added), "Baseball seemed too distant to contemplate."[6] Hammett's writing advice to Asinof?—"Everybody knows *what*," he said. "The real question is *why*?"[7] In typical, hardboiled Hammett fashion, he would ridicule Asinof's indignation at news of latest moral outrages committed on base, while simultaneously offering him sound guidance that years later would bear spectacular fruit with *Eight Men Out* and a host of other bracing literary works.

Asinof's transcendence of the game itself in his baseball books follows a familiar pattern for anyone who has ever experienced excelling at a sport while young, but then later embracing non-sporting activities as an older adult. First (usually beginning in childhood), a young athlete discovers enjoyment of a sport through excellence or achievement, then becomes a fan of older athletes who are admired and emulated for their own exceptional abilities. The next stage comes when the athlete or fan becomes immersed in a favorite sport to the exclusion of other things, often leading to criticism of that person's preoccupation at the expense of other more important matters, such as politics, religion, family life, etc. Then comes the alternative view or realization, that such preoccupation, for many fans, athletes, or former athletes, might be the best thing for their own personal well-being, both mentally and physically, especially if they are not considered capable or able enough to cope with other more "important" matters. Lastly comes the epiphany, reached by only a few (and typically by former athletes), that spectator sports are themselves symbolic of the societies which patronize them, and are a powerful, potential unifying force for members of that society who would otherwise have absolutely nothing in common with each other. This idea is an ancient one, running through the Renaissance to the present day, with the Greek philosopher Plato advising old men, for their own psychological good and that of the body politic, to watch young men competing in the games.[8] There can be little doubt that Asinof saw baseball in similar terms, both as a mirror of American society and as potential benefit (or detriment) to all members of that society—that is, for better or worse—and therefore worth our serious contemplation beyond mere statistical box scores.

A good recent cinematic example of this same evolutionary process can be found in the award-nominated 2009 film *Invictus*, directed by Clint Eastwood and starring Morgan Freeman and Matt Damon.[9] On its surface, the movie is about World Cup Rugby in South Africa during the Nelson Mandela era. Its overarching theme, however, concerns the manner in which a country's professional sports tradition can progress (in a rather short time frame) from a highly divisive topic to one commonly celebrated by diverse elements of society, given proper nurturing and guidance by political leaders in partnership with the athletes. Thus, in a very real sense, *Invictus* is the historical opposite of *Eight Men Out* in terms of professional sports; whereas the Black Sox took a too lofty, falsely idealized image and brought it crashing down to bitter, unwelcome reality, the South African Springboks transformed an unnecessary scandal into something that almost everyone could be proud of. John Carlin (author of the book inspiring *Invictus* the movie) shared Asinof's intensely appreciative view of popular sport's potential importance in relation to national politics.[10]

This brings us back to the 1919 Chicago White Sox, and Asinof's sophisticated take on why things went sour. As noted in the previous chapter, this was a team that had already won the World Series two years earlier in 1917. Asinof accepts as a basic law of commerce that those who achieve the top of their profession, baseball or otherwise, as did the eight Black Sox who had been members of the 1917 club, and are not properly compensated for their achievements, will then focus on becoming properly compensated, either by honest or dishonest means. Otherwise, the allure of being a professional champion is considerably diminished (if not stigmatized) as a result. Anyone who has ever been an underappreciated or under-compensated champion at anything knows the feeling. Asinof could surely relate as a writer, having never during his lifetime received proper due for his literary output. That he produced an outstanding American novel, *Man on Spikes* (see Part I of this study) only a few years before embarking on the Black Sox Scandal, yet received little more than a pat on the back for it, would suggest that he could empathize with his controversial subject matter on a very basic compensatory level. He clearly understood their underlying motivation, which is worth remembering since, to this day, there appear many unable to fathom it. The unhappy result of this dynamic, as acerbically put by Asinof's unsavory but indispensable source, Abe Attell, is "cheaters cheating cheaters"—in effect, the law of the jungle reigning supreme—with the strong continually exploiting and prevailing over the weak.[11] The bigger tragedies were its implications for society at large: hard work, talent, and achievement are not enough to ensure fair reward. Men like Eddie Cicotte were living proof of that.

Economic issues aside, Asinof makes reference to another major factor that not only spawned and sustained the fix, but prevented participants from talking about it in depth for so long, even after public exposure. This was plain, simple fear. The players were lowest on the food chain in relation to owners, lawyers, politicians, gamblers, and gangsters, and all parties were keenly aware of this pecking order. This is why the Black Sox, with the bare exception of Happy Felsch, remained more or less silent to the grave; or, when they chose to speak, said nothing revealing or significant. Asinof related his telling conversation with straight-laced White Sox pitcher Red Faber, who was in a good position to know these things. "Faber believed that some of the ball players were simply too frightened not to comply. And nothing was ever said. It was a lot easier to accept dirty money in silence if you were apt to get butchered for turning it down."[12] Felsch, who spoke candidly near the end of his life, made it clear what he learned early on, that it was much healthier to comply with the demands of violent men than do otherwise.[13] By extension, one could argue that all people, not just corrupt baseball players, often do bad things because they are afraid of the consequences for noncompliance.

Three years after release of the film *Eight Men Out*, Asinof tried his hand at writing unvarnished, big-picture American history, producing an unsettling snapshot of the irresistible political forces surrounding the Black Sox Scandal and its aftermath. The book *1919: America's Loss of Innocence* was published by Donald I. Fine in 1991 and dedicated by the author to the memory of firebrand American journalist, I. F. Stone (1907–1989), with whom a dispirited, 22-year-old Asinof had an impressionable encounter in 1941 before joining the service, but before the attack on Pearl Harbor.[14] The book opens with a quote from distinguished historian Frederick L. Schuman, who taught at Williams College when Asinof was a freshman student there in 1936–1937.[15] *America's Loss* is divided into four separate, gripping sections: (1) the League of Nations being rejected by the United States, (2) the inauguration of the Red Scare, (3) prohibition, and (4) the Black Sox Scandal. To Asinof, the horrors experienced by Europe during the Great War paled in comparison to what happened to America in the immediate aftermath of that conflict. Furthermore, and to him at least, each of these distinctly American fiascos in the long run likely had more devastating worldwide effects, repercussions of which are still being felt today. The Black Sox Scandal was the greatest symbolic exponent of events which all occurred in the epochal year of Asinof's birth.[16] He aptly concludes: "There is no more telling incident in America's loss of innocence than the fixing of the 1919 World Series."[17]

Asinof clearly lays out his moral objective in the Foreword to *America's Loss*, "It is the premise of this book that the vitality of our history lies in confronting the essence of what we are as a people, otherwise we cannot deal with what we ought to be."[18] In summation, the Black Sox are presented as being the inevitable result of rampant national xenophobia, greed, fear and hypocrisy, or, as he distilled it, "false values and impossible hopes."[19] Stemming from a collective lack of self-knowledge and artificially inflated sense of superiority, America's inability to cope with, let alone manage, its place in the modern world of the 20th century quickly manifested itself in 1919 with a proliferation of moral outrages. Asinof's evaluation of the United States in the immediate wake of World War I is indeed a harsh indictment, but one that he strongly felt was still relevant, a tough but truthful assessment that all Americans could benefit from. There is nothing self-congratulatory about it. On the contrary, Asinof's scathing judgment of the society into which he was born seems to suggest that he viewed his own turbulent life as having little value beyond a designated role to call public attention to these ongoing problems.

As presented in *America's Loss*, the overriding cause, or at least triggering event, for the Black Sox Scandal (plus all of the bad things that happened in America for the rest of the century) was the Great War of 1914–1918. This is not a controversial proposition. Any of the fortunate few who receive a humanist education in their youth are taught pretty much the same thing. Whether Asinof was first instilled with the idea by Frederick Schuman, Clair Wilcox, or any of the other outstanding teachers he may have had while attending university, is impossible to say. For certain is that by age 70, he was writing non-pandering, ringing sentences such as these:

> If Europe was suffering as it crawled out from under the war, it might be said that America was dancing its way out from over. For us, the war had been much less than horrific. No nation in history ever walked away from so much devastation so enriched, so unscathed, so empowered. And no nation ever felt so worthy or believed more in its God-blessed righteousness. Did we not have all these blessings because we deserved them? Was this not spoken from the pulpits, the halls of government, the great journals of opinion? Did we not deserve our prosperity for our sacrifices?[20]

With the Armistice of 1918 and subsequent Paris Peace Treaty, maintained Asinof, the groundwork had been laid for amplification of America's ongoing internal strife. The negative effects were considerably more far-reaching than merely the White Sox losing Shoeless Joe Jackson to the draft in 1918. The first repercussion came when the nation and its congress unequivocally rejected President Woodrow Wilson's cherished League of Nations, a repudiation to which Asinof devotes the first section of *America's Loss*. For the United States, pride and arrogance came before the fall, as its electorate sent a clear message that they believed themselves better than the rest of the world, and were therefore unwilling to work with the rest of the world on equal terms.

Next, in quick order, came the Red Scare. Russia had gone Marxist during the war and Soviet revolution appeared to terrify Western civilization more than war itself. This, in Asinof's view, was particularly relevant to the Black Sox because it decisively warped labor relations with American industry, forcefully tilting the balance of negotiating strength in favor of management to the hideous extreme. By the summer of 1919, there was essentially no bargaining power left for baseball players or anyone else not connected with ownership. Take it or leave it prevailed. Despair at the prospect of never being properly compensated, particularly for key, aging players in the scandal such as Chick Gandil and Eddie Cicotte, surely helped to ignite and propel the conspiracy, just as sure as the unsatisfactory conclusion of World War I caused ugly political demons to be released throughout Europe and America. The Red Scare effectively crushed labor union solidarity in this country until the advent of the New Deal, some 14 years later in 1932. By then, however, permanent damage had been done; the seeds for the Cold War had been sown. This latter item would have a direct, personal impact on Asinof and most of his friends, all whom were blacklisted at various times during the 1950s.[21] During the second half of the century, this self-inflicted struggle would consume countless lives and immeasurable resources, both at home and abroad. Asinof the historian firmly believed that it had its origins in the same hysteria that had in large part driven the 1919 Black Sox to desperation, and to eventually sell out the national pastime.

The third section of *America's Loss*, in some respects the most hard-hitting, deals with prohibition, the sinister twin corollary to the Red Scare. Because of America's self-righteous need to be a moral beacon for inferior, less divinely favored nations, alcoholic beverages were criminalized. Today, it seems too incredible to contemplate. The predictable, swift result was that the United States became world-famous for organized crime and gangster violence. One could argue, and the book strongly implies, that prohibition gave organized crime a foothold in this country that did not previously exist and has not since relinquished. Illicit activities prominently extended to sports gambling, where it collided head on with the tragedy of the Black Sox. Asinof is particularly fascinated and repelled by the disreputable figure of Arnold Rothstein, bankroller of the fix, whose family came from the same Manhattan Jewish neighborhood as the Asinofs. *America's Loss* dwells upon incongruities. Arnold's father, "Abe the Just," was a "devout and righteous man" widely admired for his integrity; but the son rebelled big time, and was rewarded by society for it. Arnold the son was about the same age as Eddie Cicotte, the pivotal player in the fix, but the two men could not have otherwise had less in common with each other. By the year of the fateful World Series, Rothstein was wealthy enough to never bet on anything ever again, "But," observed Asinof, "asking him to quit, of course, would have been like asking Woodrow Wilson to put away his Bible."[22]

In the fourth and final section of *America's Loss* (over the course of four short chapters), Asinof offers a condensed recap of the Black Sox Scandal, some three decades after writing *Eight Men Out*. The impression of simple human decency possessed by most of the Black Sox, especially Happy Felsch, as recalled by Asinof, remained constant. He remembered how he had challenged Felsch during their fateful interview: "Why did you do it? How could you be so stupid? He [Felsch] smiled and shrugged, shook his head, palms up."[23] Chicago reporter Harry Reutlinger had a similar sympathetic reaction to Felsch some 40 years earlier while covering the scandal:

> What struck Reutlinger was that Happy Felsch was completely without basic evil. He wasn't even a dishonest type. He would never steal a dime from you, even if you left him alone with an unlocked safe. He would probably stake you with his

last five dollars. He had merely been sucked into a plot for some easy money in a society that thrived on the worship of it. The cruel irony was that the unseen men who used him — the gamblers — had gotten rich on his broken back.

"The joke," as Felsch so artfully put it, "seems to be on us."[24]

Felsch and his fellow Black Sox did what they did for money; on the other hand, most never received full payment. Felsch, even in his guilt, expressed admiration for Cicotte, who got fully paid, and, more outrageously, a degree of sympathy for team owner Comiskey, viewed as a sort of fellow-hustler whom he was forced to double-cross.[25] In the final analysis, Felsch and most of his player co-conspirators are seen by Asinof as victims of unbridled American capitalism, and far more sinned against than sinning.

The broader, more disturbing implications of Asinof's philosophical insights include the very real possibility of similar circumstances overtaking any American worker at any given time and place. He has readers empathizing with the Black Sox to such a great extent that we finally realize there but for the Grace of God could go any of us. Indisputably honest members of that same team such as Dickie Kerr, Red Faber, Ray Shalk, and Eddie Collins may have just said no; but then again, they were never offered, cajoled, or threatened. Assuming they still would have said no (and there is no good reason to believe otherwise), were they truly any more ignorant of the fix, and hence less "guilty," than say, Buck Weaver? Had Eddie Collins not had a college degree and been earning three times as most of his teammates, would he have still been bypassed by the gamblers, or was it the hatred between Collins and ringleader Chick Gandil that kept him excluded? Regarding Dickie Kerr, his subsequent punishment by Landis and Comiskey for merely daring to consort with former teammates may be the most troubling aspect of the scandal highlighted by Asinof. If Kerr — a man who had absolutely nothing held against him and was widely admired — could be penalized solely for interacting with those who were blacklisted, then whom among us is really safe from a similar fate in the workplace? These are the kind of difficult questions that readers find themselves asking after reading Asinof's masterpiece. In short, great books have a tendency to shatter stereotypes. Citing similar observations made by F. Scott Fitzgerald and Walt Whitman, Asinof concludes: "Baseball, then, was more than a game."[26] While *America's Loss*, the author's in-depth supplement for *Eight Men Out*, has never achieved wide circulation, the book has been praised by almost everyone who takes trouble to read it. After reading it, one can only query whether the same cycle of disunities are repeating themselves nowadays in different forms and shapes.[27] Is baseball now, as it used to be, more than just a game?

Thus *America's Loss* is Asinof's essential, explanatory guidebook to *Eight Men Out*, especially for readers who did not "get it" the first time around. Whereas *Bleeding Between the Lines* tells the harrowing true story of an author trying to first write, then survive writing, a great book, *America's Loss* is the same author's admirable effort to give his own work historical perspective. It is particularly useful for the baseball fan who may know something about the Black Sox but absolutely nothing about the Paris Peace Treaty. The connection may first appear tenuous, but Asinof's convincing linkage between the two is a testament to his skill as an unabashed historian. In his introduction to *Eight Men Out*, Stephen Jay Gould quotes the French intellectual Jacques Barzun, who famously wrote, "Whoever wants to know the heart and mind of America had better learn baseball." Gould wittily adds, "We must also understand the Black Sox if we ever hope to comprehend baseball."[28] Asinof reportedly confronted Barzun to ask for clarification of this dictum, but was only told that Barzun did not understand the meaning of his own words.[29] In *America's Loss*, one passage might be Asinof's response:

> Baseball was a reliable key to the way Americans like to see themselves. It reflected the pride, the honesty, the skills of American men. The national pastime transcended ethnic, class, and social lines; it was a team game that perpetuated democratic values through waves of immigrants.[30]

If we are to assign this greater meaning to baseball in relation to America and the world, then the Black Sox Scandal is a warning signal for all of us to heed. It becomes far more than a sports tragedy, pointing to potential cracks at the very core of our values system, pitfalls that we must remain alert to, lest the unhappy lessons of the past be repeated.[31]

As fate would have it, Eliot Asinof became one of our most perceptive chroniclers of this crucial period in American and world history. After writing *Eight Men Out*, Asinof could have spent the rest of his career writing baseball sequels and seeking talk-show guest appearances. Fortunately, he immediately branched out instead. In the next section of this study, we shall examine his return to the straight novel format, combined with a bold dose of experimentation, late 1960s style. A professional baseball point of reference would be retained, but not in the thematic forefront. *Eight Men Out* may have been the finest book of its kind ever written, but it lacked specific subject matter that goes to the very heart of the American character: namely, Race. *Eight Men Out* also strongly hinted at another obvious but often-ignored problem: what does a professional athlete do in the world after having been a professional athlete?

Part III: *The Bedfellow* (1967)

9

"A Big Free Bubbly Show"

My love life was a potential tempest that had to make too many waves.
—Asinof, *The Bedfellow*[1]

The writings of Eliot Asinof, especially his baseball-themed works, often tend to be unfairly pigeonholed or dismissively oversimplified as socially conscious, pro-labor manifestos advocating the rights of workers in the face of corporate, capitalist greed. His little-guy heroes (or, to be more precise, anti-heroes) are victimized, exploited, and taken advantage of—supposedly through no fault of their own—and yet, close reading belies this narrow interpretation. More often than not, the proverbial common man in Asinof's fiction and nonfiction compounds his own misfortune with irrational decisions, destructive passions, and hopelessly naïve perceptions of the new and strange environments into which he is suddenly thrust. After the widely lauded publication of *Eight Men Out* in 1963, its author often found himself pegged as baseball's leading apologist for players' rights—not without some justification, since his first two books had made this such a prominent theme. It would be a great mistake, however, to end the discussion with this single aspect of his work, especially given Asinof's prolific literary production over the next 45 years, including three more full-length baseball-related books. In 1967, three years after *Eight Men Out*, came *The Bedfellow*, released by Asinof's prestigious new publisher, Simon and Schuster, as part of a New York trilogy, along with *Seven Days to Sunday* (1968) and *The Name of the Game Is Murder* (1969).[2] *The Bedfellow* represented Asinof's return to the straight novel form, as well as a bold departure coming from one who could have easily spent the rest of his career regurgitating the same sports gambling-corruption motif that he so effectively pioneered. While retaining a strong connection to the game of baseball, *The Bedfellow* also attempts to explore the game of life outside of professional sports, particularly with respect to the often unfathomable vicissitudes of love and commerce. More precisely, *The Bedfellow* probes the treacherous overlap between the worlds of sports and commerce for any professional athlete attempting to make the difficult transition from active sports partic-

Asinof (*left*) with Clarence "Cito" Gaston in Batavia, New York, circa 1966. By this time, Asinof had made a name for himself as a writer (*Man on Spikes*, *Eight Men Out*) and was working on a feature article for the *New York Times Magazine*. During this same period, the novelist was revising *The Bedfellow*, deciding to give his main character, Mike Sorrell, an African American identity.

ipation to a successful business career. The book portrays one man's attempt to come to terms with his family, his employers, and his own ambitions, after realizing that his former perceptions of all these things had been grievously mistaken.

In some respects, *The Bedfellow* is a relic of its time (the late 1960s), in which old taboos and stereotypes were being rapidly dismantled to the simultaneous delight and consternation of the general public (Asinof's multifaceted thematic concerns in this highly experimental work will be examined in Chapters 11 and 12). The novel is prominently dedicated "to my son, Marty," then about 15 years old and coming of age during an era of great social upheaval. It is clear from the opening pages that the 48-year-old novelist had been reading works of the recently deceased Albert Camus (1913–1960), Franco-Algerian Nobel Laureate and approximate contemporary of Asinof's postwar generation of writers. *The Bedfellow* begins with a double quotation, first from Camus' 1956 Existential-Absurdist masterpiece *La Chute* ("The Fall"), in which "modern man" is dismissed by future historians as a bore ("he fornicated and he read the papers").[3] Asinof's novel is indeed filled with fairly graphic, drawn-out sex scenes — by then a standard feature of popular fiction. True to Asinof's unflinching style, sex is portrayed in all of its realistic ambiguity, alternatively sensual and clumsy, complete with extreme mood swings and double-edged pillow talk. Wild passion arrives when least expected, but so does unwelcome frigidity and impotence. Like a good baseball umpire, Asinof calls it as he sees it. Regarding these vignettes, the overall lesson is not a bad one for any hormone-challenged adolescent reader. It may well represent a father trying to tell his son about the birds and bees the best way that he knew how, through storytelling.

The second opening quote in *The Bedfellow*, one from which the novel takes its title and thematic cue, is Shakespeare's *The Tempest*. In Act II of this play, the clown Trinculo, before unwittingly sharing a confined, makeshift shelter with the monster Caliban while storms gather, apologizes to audiences with "misery acquaints a man with strange bedfellows." In Asinof's novel, the "bedfellow" is retired African American major league baseball star, Mike Sorrell, a man in bed not only his wife, but also (figuratively speaking) with her entire white Jewish liberal family and high society of Manhattan's Upper East Side. This cast includes his spoiled, princess wife, Janet Carr; her father, a successful and respected men's clothier, Matthew Carr (formerly Matthew Katz); and Janet's cousin, the provocatively named psychiatrist, Dr. Allen Fuchs, who earnestly advises Sorrell that he has "all the ingredients necessary to become a successful man — in other walks of life [besides baseball]."[4] One antagonist (among several) is Sorrell's boss, Public Relations magnate, D. J. Biddle (lauded author of *Truth Is What You Make of It*), who first persuades Sorrell to abandon his dream of becoming a lawyer by hiring him as a PR rep for big bucks, then attempts to seduce Sorrell's somewhat less than reluctant wife.[5] Finally, all roads lead back to Sorrell's hated, estranged father, whom he has spent his entire adult life trying to escape and forget. Like Shakespeare's Trinculo, Sorrell is truly a miserable person caught in the middle of a tempest, particularly with respect to his marriage. In addition to the novelist's concerns with the plight of the retired professional athlete in the modern business world, Asinof uses *The Bedfellow* to expand upon his continuing favorite themes of race relations and marital infidelity, both of which were originally introduced, and tentatively explored, in his debut novel from the previous decade, *Man on Spikes*.

In *The Bedfellow*, Sorrell becomes Asinof's fictional vehicle for the rapid, systematic deconstruction of a prototypical hero-athlete. As a prematurely retired star outfielder for an unnamed National League franchise (presumably the New York Mets since the team's home park is old Shea Stadium), Sorrell is torn on whether he should return to baseball, finish law school, or stay with his currently lucrative but morally bankrupt job position.[6] It is worth recalling that the New York Mets of the mid–1960s were a recent expansion club having yet to display any capacity for a winning season, let alone a pennant, and with no mention of such a possibility in the story.[7] The novelist appears to have needed a New York franchise because Asinof knew the city quite well enough to write convincingly about it, plus he needed a National League team because the African American Sorrell's retirement is motivated by his trade to a Southern city (Atlanta), which did not exist in the American League at that time.[8]

In addition to being a good ballplayer, Sorrell is a thinking man. He socializes with the black intelligentsia of New York.[9] He reads F. Scott Fitzgerald.[10] Moreover, he seriously aspires to be a civil rights lawyer ("a Negro Darrow"), but instead finds himself lured into the lucrative world of Madison Avenue advertising.[11] In this respect, he resembles the real-life Conrad Lynn, noted New York African American activist-attorney (and friend of the novelist), who would later become the focal point of Asinof's remarkably in-depth profile of inner city race relations and police brutality in 1970's *People vs. Blutcher* (see Chapter 10). Sorrell is not a stereotypical, dumb jock; on the contrary, he is intelligent almost to a fault, making his character very relatable to most readers, despite his ever-present and often uncontrollable inner demons. Indeed, as a businessman (when not being portrayed on the playing field), Sorrell could easily represent almost any talented white-collar American worker trying to survive the ever-shifting pitfalls of the affluent service sector economy.

In terms of literary structure and technique, *The Bedfellow* is daringly experimental, to the say the least, and very representative of its era. Playing it safe never seems to have been part of Asinof's artistic credo, and this entry in his catalogue, if it can be faulted for anything, could be said to attempt too many unprecedented things simultaneously. To begin with, the reader is presented with a rare situation in which a white novelist attempts to write from the viewpoint of a black main character. The sincere but startling effect is not unlike that of New York-bred, Jewish American popular vocalist Al Jolson performing blackface in *The Jazz Singer* (1927), and not unlike the manner in which Mike Kutner from *Man on Spikes* wears glasses as a metaphor for being Jewish.[12] In effect, blackness in *The Bedfellow* is substituted for Jewishness. At one point in the story, Sorrell's Jewish wife Janice exclaims, "Sometimes you seem so white! ... I don't think of you as colored any more."[13] Truly, it is often easy to forget that Asinof's character Sorrell is black. At one point, Sorrell's African American teammate Ed Kroll mocks him as "Mr. Integration.... The Sammy Davis of Sutton Place."[14] Radical black intellectual Eric Lopert disdainfully challenges Sorrell by calling him "a white man's nigger."[15] For his part, Sorrell labels 1960s-era professional baseball "An integrated-segregated split-screen colorvision show" in reference to the continuing and profound separateness of black athletes within the system even after being allowed to participate within it.[16] Throughout the story, Sorrell is a man constantly moving between two distinct worlds of black and white in society, not really at home in either, however hard he may try belonging to one or the other.

The genesis of *The Bedfellow* went back to the early 1960s, long before *Eight Men Out* was published, as Asinof tried to come to grips as an artist with the failure of his marriage.[17] Asinof's unpublished papers provide intriguing clues to the process; these include an early but undated short story titled *Like Love* and a longer version of the same, both touching upon the suspicions, deceptions, and mistrust that plague Mike Sorrell's marriage in *The Bedfellow*. The most surprising document, however, is a fully completed, bound manuscript dated December 1, 1964, and titled *Like Married*, clearly an early version of the 1967 novel. This work, though containing most basic elements of the later version, had at least two notable exceptions. The first is that there is no indication that Mike Sorrell is African American; the second is that Sorrell's volatile history with his biological father is absent. It therefore appears that both the racial overlay and father-son conflict in *The Bedfellow* were added sometime during 1965–1966, perhaps in the aftermath of racial turmoil then sweeping the country or Asinof's acquaintance with an African American professional baseball player (see below). Another clue is provided by manuscripts of an unpublished historical espionage-thriller novel (variously titled *Thundercloud* and *The Crash at Ndola*). Here the main character is named Paul Sorrell, a man whose heterosexual love life seems to be the unhappy antithesis of James Bond-like confidence and ease. An outline for this novel is dated September 10, 1961; at some point (probably around 1964), Asinof shifted the slightly renamed Sorrell character, along with his personal demons, into the plot of *Like Married*, which later became *The Bedfellow*.[18]

Stylistically, *The Bedfellow* is laced throughout with musical references, images, and figures of speech, reflecting Asinof's reputation as a knowledgeable working musician, among his many other accomplishments. Classical and popular music allusions abound. Many of these involve famous composers and performers. Examples include Billie Holiday and Bessie Smith (p. 38), Ginger Rogers and Fred Astaire (p. 44), Frank Sinatra and Barbra Streisand (p. 160), Duke Ellington (p. 12), Brahms (p. 133), and Beethoven (p. 14). Asinof's musical touchstones, however, go far beyond name-dropping; typically they are used to underscore situations in the plot. For example, classical symphonic dissonance is used to represent Sorrell's ambivalent status within the Madison Avenue advertising world (p. 139), as well as his own hostile and antagonistic relationship with his father (p. 167). Early in the story, Sorrell forebodingly describes his unsustainable lifestyle as "Cloud Nine," seemingly anticipating the powerful 1968 song of the same title by the Temptations (p. 12).[19] The storyline as a whole is similar to a lengthy jazz improvisation, in which Sorrell (and readers) can barely guess at what twists are coming next. Rather disconcertingly, in the opening pages of the novel, a party entertainer segues the iconic "Take Me Out to the Ballgame" into a mock dirge lamenting Sorrell's once thriving baseball career that is, by then, a thing of the past.[20] In fact, any reader lacking musical appreciation is likely to have a difficult time understanding some of Asinof's reference points.

In addition to music, Sorrell's language is (as one would fully expect) teeming with baseball colloquialisms. Sorrell, either consciously or unconsciously, uses terminology of the sport to describe marital relations (pp. 48, 59, 83–84, 87), interaction with his psychiatrist (p. 98), long-term retirement (p. 104), brushes with law enforcement (pp. 191, 200), and life in general (p. 177). Long after Sorrell quits baseball, boss Biddle addresses him as "Slugger" (p. 20). At home he likes to fondle his old bat while watching TV (p. 151) or while contemplating its use as a weapon against his hated father (p. 154). As revenge against his materialistic wife, he uses the same bat to destroy their luxurious apartment as he compares his precision mayhem to the pin-point control of Sandy Koufax (pp. 194–195). Beyond physical trappings and figures of speech, Asinof (through Sorrell's flashbacks) repeatedly demonstrates his trademark close familiarity with the advanced competitive levels of the game. Some of this inside knowledge (so clearly based on Asinof's own playing experience) includes an episode in which Sorrell's fielding error compounds into a hitless performance and game loss for his team (p. 32); the peculiar but typical dugout etiquette of silence towards teammates following a called third strike at the plate (p. 59); and the oftentimes ugly post-game locker room racism of Southern whites against integrated black teammates (pp. 144–147). Above all, Asinof accurately portrays how love and sex can affect a player's performance for better and for worse, or, in some instances, abruptly end a professional playing career altogether.

As a novel, *The Bedfellow* is at best nominally tied to real-life events in Asinof's life (somewhat unusual for him), and yet, in many ways, is also the novelist's most autobiographical statement. Aside from becoming a successful author during the late 1950s and early 1960s, three major events in Asinof's earlier life laid the essential groundwork for his creative impulse. These three groups of occurrences included his minor league playing career, personal impressions of race relations, and his own failed marriage. In particular, Asinof's brief, unhappy stint in Georgia with the Moultrie Packers during the summer of 1940 seems to have provided the future novelist with his first hard glimpse of segregated America prior to the Civil Rights Movement.[21] In the novel, Sorrell's thoroughly Southern-bred teammate, Tex Munson, tries to compliment him with a jolting slur: "You're a good nigger, Mike."[22] In Munson, readers may be catching an unpleasant glimpse of the type of ballplayer Asinof suddenly found himself shoulder-to-shoulder with in Moultrie for the first time in his life. Issues of race aside, bits and pieces of Sorrell's recollected baseball memories call to mind those documented in Asinof's own playing career. For example, at one point Sorrell nostalgically recalls hitting his first home run in a sandlot game as a life-changing event; in *Off-Season* (2000), Jack Cagle remembers the true start of his baseball career being a home run he hits at age 10.[23] Asinof recorded a very similar occurrence during his own boyhood stay at summer camp in Massachusetts.[24] Another parallel example occurs when the retired Sorrell is willingly drafted into a pick-up softball game in Central Park; Asinof noted a similar detour for himself in Central Park during the early 1960s, one in which he encountered a friendly old opponent of his, former Yankee Phil Rizzuto, by then long-retired as a professional player.[25] In *The Bedfellow*, after Sorrell hits a home run to win the meaningless softball game, he mocks the overblown reaction generated among bystanders as "a big free bubbly show with celebrities and folklore and a happy ending, all wrapped into one lusty climax." His bemused contempt is nearly identical to that expressed by Asinof's perceptive scout Durkin Fain from *Man on Spikes*, who sourly notes, "There was a dramatic finality to it [a home run] that any child-mind could understand."[26] Clearly, on the basis of these baseball references alone, a good part of Asinof's own biography and philosophy can be found in his fictional counterpart, Mike Sorrell.

Asinof's very brief, notorious career with the Class D Moultrie Packers of the Georgia-Florida League in 1940 may be easily summarized in a few sentences. As the 20-year-old minor league rookie stepped off the train in Moultrie — which appears to have been Asinof's very first trip south of Mason-Dixon — he encountered a black woman holding a bag of groceries while leading her child down the sidewalk. In a reflexive act of chivalry, Asinof yielded the sidewalk to the woman and child, then was promptly arrested and detained by a police office witnessing this alleged violation of Jim Crow protocol. After being bailed out of jail and vouched for by the Packers, Asinof proceeded to play very good baseball for a short while, but within a matter of days proved himself a repeat offender. After landing on third following an extra-base hit, Asinof was given an ovation by the segregated black portion of the spectators on that side of the stands, they having learned of his previous altercation with local law enforcement. Asinof tipped his hat in acknowledgment of the applause and, accordingly, was immediately sent packing by Packers' team management.[27] Records show that he played in a total of 15 games and batted a solid .296 in 54 turns at the plate.[28] Thus ended Asinof's first misadventure as a professional ballplayer. It was an episode that for him probably became forever linked with America's troubled history in matters of race.

The novelist's repeated close encounters with America's volatile race conflict seem to span an entire lifetime, both in and out of baseball. The very year of Asinof's birth witnessed some of the most brutal white-on-black urban violence during the Jim Crow era, as noted several times in Asinof's scathing 1991 historical tract, *1919: America's Loss of Innocence.*[29] After World War II, Asinof became owner-manager of a semipro team in the New York Metropolitan Baseball Association (the Yonkers Indians), one which often found itself competing against some of the best African American talent at a time (1946–1947) when Branch Rickey was launching his great experiment with Jackie Robinson in Brooklyn.[30] Then around 1949, Asinof found himself among audience members harassed by the American Legion after a Paul Robeson concert in Peekskill, New York.[31] Finally, in 1951, Asinof was blacklisted as a television screenwriter. Many years later, perusal of his declassified FBI file showed that his lone alleged un–American activity had been to sign a petition outside Yankee Stadium, urging the team to integrate, as had recently the Brooklyn Dodgers, Cleveland Indians, and other major league franchises.[32] In retrospect, it seems ridiculous that an unrepentant political liberal such as Asinof, one who supported so many progressive and controversial causes at various times throughout his life, should have been singled out for this particular item. One suspects the action was merely a ruse or pretense used by industry employers to punish him for more serious, unnamed offenses. In any event, within four years of being blacklisted, Asinof was reinstated as a writer through an unlikely series of events (see Chapter 1). About the same time, Elston Howard became the first African American to play for the New York Yankees in 1955; that same year, Asinof's *Man on Spikes* debuted on bookstands. In lieu of all these occurrences, it should come as no surprise that race relations, especially in connection with baseball, intensely interested Asinof as a novelist and began to move to the forefront of his thematic concerns, beginning in earnest with *The Bedfellow.*

During the mid–1960s, Asinof made another acquaintance that likely had a significant impact on his next book in terms of race relations, especially within the sphere of professional baseball. In 1966, while working on a story for *The New York Times* on minor league baseball in Batavia, New York, Asinof met Clarence "Cito" Gaston, then a 22-year-old outfielder playing Class A ball for the Batavia Trojans in the New York-Pennsylvania League.[33] Gaston, baseball fans may recall, in addition to later having a notable playing career with several major league teams, went on to become the first African American coach to win a World Series championship with the Toronto Blue Jays in back-to-back years, 1992–1993. In 1966, Gaston's star as an athlete was beginning to rise, and the following year (1967) would find him a rookie with the Atlanta Braves, rooming with none other than Henry Aaron. During this same period, Asinof was no doubt revising and rewriting *The Bedfellow*. While most of Mike Sorrell's personality traits in the novel appear based on Asinof himself, several aspects of Sorrell's character also suggest Gaston.[34] Sorrell's name has a French ring to it, with accent on the last syllable, somewhat like Gaston.[35] "Cito" was a self-adopted name like Sorrell in the book. Like Gaston as a player, Sorrell is physically big and a long-ball threat, but also has speed and range — more a rare combination at that time.[36] In the book, the early-retired Sorrell is 27 years old, and would have been in his early twenties as an active player; Gaston was a 23-year-old rookie with the Braves in 1967.

Sorrell, in the novel, like Gaston in actual life, is a standout (and somewhat of a misfit) among professional athletes black or white, because of his intelligence. In the story, Sorrell's premature retirement is triggered by his pending trade to Atlanta, a team for which Gaston played briefly during his first season, 1967 — the same year of the novel's publication. Sorrell's statement, "Baseball is what made me a man," (p. 65) is reminiscent of Gaston's later widely quoted remark that Henry Aaron taught him "how to be a man." Gaston once went on record to say that professional baseball caused the breakup of his first marriage, just as baseball is a source of bitter ongoing conflict between Sorrell and his wife.[37] Sorrell comes from a dysfunctional, impoverished background in Watts, while Gaston, though originally from San Antonio, appears to have experienced considerable childhood upheaval as well, with a father, stepfather, and extended families all in the picture.[38] It may well be that, given then-recent urban racial unrest sweeping across the country (prominently including Watts), plus Asinof's previous residence in the Los Angeles area, it made more sense for his lead character to hail from a neighborhood with which he was far more familiar than, say, San Antonio.

Lastly, Asinof's nearly decade-long failed marriage to actress Jocelyn Brando surely played a significant role in his depiction of the tortuous, back-and-forth relationship in the novel between the fictional Mike Sorrell and his wife, Janet Carr. In the book, ethnic tables are turned with the Jewish voice of Asinof the author assuming an African American identity, while a difficult spouse and in-laws are depicted as Jewish; in real-life the Brandos were of mixed Dutch descent. Other major differences between the story and Asinof's biography are readily apparent. For one, Janet does not have a famous, successful brother like Marlon Brando, but rather a respected, successful father who is, interestingly enough, a prosperous clothier similar to Asinof's own father. Overall, the tale contains significant elements of autobiography while nevertheless falling far short of being strictly autobiographical. Surely this was by design. The novelist could certainly not be expected to lay out, in overt detail, the heartaches and failures of his private life for the whole world to see. All that readers are allowed to glimpse is the turbulent relationship between a young and professionally ambitious couple. For both of them, career advancement must come at the expense of walking a fine line between harmless flirtation and adulterous betrayal with those who hold the keys to power.[39] Perhaps Asinof wanted to show open-minded readers, as well as his teenage son, a true representation of a doomed marriage in the aftermath of a sports career, complete with elements common to most troubled marriages that he could personally attest to as a witness in his own unhappy case.

Sorrell's story ends on a downer, with him appearing to abandon all hope of resurrecting his baseball playing career or pursuing the law, while staying in his unhealthy and compromising relationship with the Carr family and, as a result, establishing close business ties with his evil father — in effect, selling out. He clings to his bad marriage and can no longer bear to look at himself in the mirror. It may have been Asinof's way of telling the world, including his teenage son who had possibly reached an age where he might be able to understand, one reason he had left his own marriage. In effect, Asinof may have been trying to keep his self respect, which Sorrell has obviously lost by the end of the novel. For the sake of a short-term secure monetary career and extravagant life-style maintenance, Sorrell relinquishes his nobler ambitions. In the words of his psychiatrist, Fuchs, he becomes a "successful man" outside of baseball, but pays a terrible price for it. In effect, Sorrell allows himself to be integrated into the "great big bubbly show" that he so despises, except on a much larger and more destructive scale than the benign softball game he encounters while strolling through Central Park.

In hindsight, *The Bedfellow* comes across as Asinof's most boldly ambitious, though not necessarily most successful, novel. It also represents an important artistic bridge for the novelist into the world of non-sports fiction and nonfiction, which in turn later yielded such seminal Asinof works as *People vs. Blutcher*, *Craig and Joan*, *The Fox Is Crazy Too*, and *Final Judgment*. Given its ambitious, multiple departures from familiar thematic patterns established by Asinof in *Man on Spikes* and *Eight Men Out*, it is not surprising that this mid–1960s artifact has since been mostly ignored, or met with puzzled bewilderment. This is unfortunate because *The Bedfellow* has much to offer the baseball fan and non-baseball fan alike. Indeed, a comprehensive understanding of Asinof's baseball writings must both begin and end with *The Bedfellow.* If nothing else, this probing, fictional character study of a post-athletic professional career in crisis set the stage for later explorations of the same subject matter in Asinof's last two full-length works of baseball fiction. For the moment, however, it is useful, if not essential, to examine how *The Bedfellow* fits squarely within the context of Asinof's extensive and fascinating nonfictional output over the subsequent decade.

10

"The Quintessence of All Our Self-Destructive Tendencies"

The late-1960s literary output of Eliot Asinof, represented in the baseball category by *The Bedfellow*, is a sobering case study in what can happen to good, previously successful writers attempting to go against the grain of audience expectations. If the circumstances leading up to the creation of this work make perfect sense in terms of what was eventually produced, then the aftermath of publication demonstrated how massively uncomprehending readers and critics can be in spite of this progression. With the rapid release of three Asinof books—*The Bedfellow*, *Seven Days to Sunday*, and *The Name of the Game Is Murder*—all within the space of approximately three years (1967–1969), the market became suddenly saturated with same-author choices for any consumer who happened to like *Eight Men Out*. The problem was that none of the three new books overtly resembled *Eight Men Out* (or, for that matter, *Man on Spikes*) in the slightest. *The Bedfellow* has a strong baseball atmosphere, but only as a backdrop for a lead character trying to make it in the non-baseball world. *Seven Days to Sunday* was sports-related, but as a pro football documentary rather than baseball. *Name of the Game* was a murder mystery nominally placed within a pro football landscape. All three works were set in New York City. Almost needless to say, Asinof was trying to expand his horizons; and his new publisher, Simon & Schuster had decided to indulge him, without necessarily providing support in terms of marketing and publicity. The resulting commercial failure of Asinof's New York trilogy predictably led to a break with the same publishing house, probably a good thing for him in the long run. With commercial failure came creative freedom for an artist who knew exactly how to make use of it. These events in turn set the stage for Asinof's later production of several non-baseball-related masterpieces during the 1970s.

A brief word is in order at this point regarding the two other works in Asinof's New York trilogy, and their respective relationships to *The Bedfellow*. By far the best received of the three was 1968's *Seven Days to Sunday* (see

Chapter 13), a straightforward, documentary account of one week Asinof spent in close quarters with the New York Giants of the National Football League. Despite not being about baseball, and despite its Big Apple bias, *Seven Days* had the most in common of the three with *Eight Men Out* in that it represented realistic and off-beat professional sports journalism at its best, written by someone who well understood what it was like to be a professional athlete. *The Name of the Game Is Murder* from 1969 was Asinof's lone venture as a novelist into the crime thriller genre, written as homage to his old wartime mentor, Dashiell Hammett (see Chapter 17).[1] Though, like *Seven Days*, utilizing a New York professional football setting (albeit fictional), *Name of the Game* was perhaps the oddest entry of the three.[2] Unlike *The Bedfellow*, it appears to have been written a bit tongue-in-cheek, occasionally burlesque in tone, and possibly under the colossal false assumption that significant numbers of football fans also liked to read murder mysteries.[3] Like *The Bedfellow*, it immediately sank into oblivion and is today a very hard volume to find on any library shelf. Despite their obscurity, however, both *Name of the Game* and *Bedfellow* still make worthwhile reading, particularly the latter. Both have enjoyable quantities of Asinof's trademark wit and depth. Moreover, reading all three works of the trilogy provides an impressive and vivid portrait of late-1960s New York society, especially in the often hidden private realms where professional sports and big business overlap, although each of the three are separate, autonomous entities with no common or continuous narrative.[4]

Despite their obvious differences and points of departure, the other two books in Asinof's New York trilogy have significant resemblances to *The Bedfellow. Seven Days to Sunday* covers a similar, real-life time frame (approximately one week) in which complicated, interpersonal relationships first clash and maneuver with each other, then forever impact professional careers, both in and outside of sports. *Name of The Game* offers surprising commonalities as well. Asinof's cynical narrator-detective, Lieutenant Mike Ogden, like Mike Sorrell in *The Bedfellow*, is emotionally unstable almost to the point of being cartoonish.[5] His adolescent son is 14 years old when the mother is killed by a senseless hit-and-run driver, much like a 15-year-old Sorrell when his mother dies a violent death. Father and son have a distant, uncommunicative relationship, similar to Sorrell and his father in the opening chapters of *The Bedfellow*. Both are high school dropouts and runaways. Although both novels are set in New York City, *Name of the Game*, like *The Bedfellow*, comments upon the grinding ghetto poverty of Watts and South Central Los Angeles during the late 1950s, a time and place that Asinof would have been quite familiar with via his Hollywood writing tenure.[6] The novelist interjects that "Los Angeles has produced a special kind of bitterness," writing at that time in specific reference to urban racial unrest sweeping through Watts during the summer of 1965.[7] *Name of the Game* relates a much different story than *The Bedfellow*, both in style and tone, but uses a number of touchstones common to both novels while telling its tale.

Baseball literary critic Richard Peterson, one of the few serious writers to have recently commented on Asinof's category-defying novel, judged that "*The Bedfellow* ... has little to offer about baseball."[8] This is true only in the sense that comparatively few pages are devoted to the playing field or the locker room. In terms of the professional baseball athlete's frequent struggle to function in society apart from the sports world, the novel has tons of insights to offer, and has been unjustly neglected in this regard. Asinof's Mike Sorrell is a ballplayer to the mental core, even during self-imposed retirement. Whether at home or in the office, at a social gathering, or on the street, Sorrell is physical, competitive, and team-oriented, as well as intelligent and perceptive; moreover, he thinks in baseball terms, that is, when not reminiscing about his former playing career or contemplating a comeback. The prospect of life without baseball troubles him, and his life outside of sports becomes increasingly ludicrous and painful as the story progresses. Apart from its free-form, avant-garde spirit, the book surely failed to find any kind of commercial audience in part because it seemed to intentionally defy established marketing niches. Literati and devotees of cutting edge fiction likely had a hard time with the baseball stuff. They would have also deplored a supposed perceived "sportswriter" like Asinof trying to produce a serious work of fiction. As for diehard baseball and sports fans, they too found themselves in unfamiliar and confusing territory, being all-too-often completely oblivious to the omnipotent world of public and media relations. These are possibly some of the reasons why *The Bedfellow* was generally ignored or dismissed upon its release.

Those critics who condescended to review *The Bedfellow* at the time of its release tended to be, at best, uncomprehending. For the most part, it was ignored.[9] *Publishers Weekly* was impressed by the biracial sex scenes, but little else: "Readers attracted to this novel by the thought on inter-racial sex won't be disappointed. There's lots of it, although it's really no different from any other kind." The reviewer seemed on one hand to recognize a certain depth in Sorrell's character, but then did an about-face and dismissed him as being too shallow: "Mr. Asinof is dealing with a man whose personal problems affect him more than those of race, but unfortunately his major character, Mike Sorrell, seems lifeless and one-dimensional."[10] A snide review written for *Kirkus* tries to be witty but only demonstrates the reviewer's own incapacity to focus on anything beyond the prurient.[11] Even more bizarre was a review from *Library Journal*, which recommended the novel, but for unfathomable reasons. Here, too, the reviewer focused on sex, drawing some startling messages from the text:

> Despite flaws and typed characters, the main characterization is believable and sympathetically delineated. This novel by a beginning writer of power with ability to go places should be considered by all libraries attempting representation of sincere fiction in the current mode of sex and violence, and could be considered by young adult librarians who work with sexually precocious youth. Values include learning to live with *one* mate, and understanding a gangster father dedicated to ghetto violence.[12]

Apart from some curious wording (plus the reviewer's apparent unfamiliarity with Asinof's well-known past work), the emphasis on "values" is a good example of reading whatever one wants to read into a book, regardless of what the book actually says. If *The Bedfellow* preaches monogamy, it does so in odd fashion by condemning Sorrell's decision to stay with his unhappy and morally-bankrupt marriage. As for parental relations, Sorrell understands his father no better than he understands himself, although it should be added that George Sr. seems to have a very good understanding of his corruptible son. Asinof, if he read this notice, no doubt cringed.

If his later work is any indication, the only review that seems to have made an impression on Asinof came in the form of a blistering notice by Margot Siegel, writing independently for the *Minneapolis Tribune*, who complained that "Asinof's Negro is no Negro at all. None of his thoughts or deeds are motivated by his race or background." After accusing Asinof of using his subject matter to chase a movie deal, the Jewish Siegel admonishes Asinof to write about things that he really knows about, such as being Jewish.[13] Apart from the movie-deal accusation, this was the only review of the book that resembled valid criticism. Asinof must have taken it to heart, because his next work on race, 1970's *People vs. Blutcher*, is an unforgettable and exemplary exercise in nonfiction investigative reporting. Notices for *The Bedfellow*, however, were not all negative or obtuse. Positive, thoughtful reviews appeared in the *Fayetteville* (North Carolina) *Observer* (January 28, 1968), the *Kansas City Star* (January 21, 1968), the *American Statesman* in Austin, Texas (January 14, 1968), the *Cleveland Press* (February 2, 1968), and the *Springfield* (Massachusetts) *Daily News* (January 30, 1968). These were all carefully preserved in a scrapbook by Asinof.[14]

In terms of baseball, Asinof would many years later return magnificently to the race motif with *Off-Season* (2000).[15] Unlike *The Bedfellow*, this novel would examine similar issues of racial conflict from the spoiled viewpoint of young, white superstar pitcher, Black Jack Cagle (see Part V of this study). Over the course of the tale, Cagle becomes inadvertently educated in a manner that he never anticipated, but grows as a person into a far greater awareness and appreciation of America's deep racial divide, both within and without the sports world. As in *The Bedfellow*, the time frame of the protagonist's educational process in *Off-Season* is very short (a matter of days), but develops for readers in far more convincing and compelling manner. It is clear that in the 33 years separating the two novels, Asinof had given considerably more thought to the problem, and had much more to add on the subject as a novelist, even as he had undoubtedly learned much during his formative years, spanning from Jim Crow segregation in Moultrie, Georgia, all the way to incidental encounters with urban racial tensions in Watts neighborhood of Los Angeles. It is also clear that by the final decade of his writing career, Asinof had grown considerably in his artistic craft as well. One reason that race relations portrayed in *Off-Season* seem more credible and believable than in *The Bedfellow* is that the novelist was obviously writing to a greater degree from personal, first-hand experience in the later work, that is, from the outside vantage point of a cocky and overindulged white baseball player.

Asinof's true sequel on the theme of America's race problem, however, came three years after *The Bedfellow* with *People vs. Blutcher* (1970), a searing piece of on-the-beat journalism based entirely on documented, real-life events. Around the same time that *The Bedfellow* was going to press in 1967, Laurence Blutcher, an African American shopkeeper in the Bedford-Stuyvesant district of Brooklyn, was being harassed, beaten, and framed on various charges by white policeman acting in concert with a corrupt New York City criminal justice system. Asinof was invited to write about the case by Blutcher's defense attorney, noted New York civil rights activist Conrad Lynn, a friend of the novelist.[16] Thus, before 1970, Asinof was a popular author writing in depth about urban racial conflict in the U.S., as well as American cultural stigmatization of the ghetto, making him one of the pioneers in this genre.[17] Unlike the fictional Mike Sorrell from *The Bedfellow*, who is rather politely pursued by New York detectives for infractions actually committed, Asinof's documentary portrait of Laurence Blutcher focuses on the true victimization of an innocent man because of his skin color. Blutcher is presented by the writer as a man with more than his share of personal faults, but these have nothing to do with the alleged crimes that he is falsely accused of. After being forced to accept an unfavorable plea bargain, Blutcher's fate calls to mind a disturbing exchange in the *The Bedfellow* between Sorrell and a white neighbor after hearing a white boy admit to stealing a bicycle from two black kids. In reference to the black children, the white neighbor defensively mumbles, "They stole that bike from *someone*.... You just gotta believe *that*."[18] The incident becomes a foreshadowing of Sorrell's own enraged criminal conduct near the end of the story.

In contrast to *The Bedfellow*, *People vs. Blutcher* is purely a document of on-the-beat journalism (similar to *Eight Men Out*), in which genuine and typical black experiences in urban American are portrayed. The work opens a searing quotation from *The Autobiography of Malcolm X* (1965): "We didn't land on Plymouth Rock, Plymouth Rock landed on us."[19] By this time, the life and writings of the murdered Malcolm X had become an obvious influence on Asinof, as well as most other impressionable readers during the latter part of the 20th century. Like Malcolm before him, Laurence Blutcher had been a recent convert to the Nation of Islam, and recurring themes of black alienation within American society are repeatedly expounded upon by Asinof.[20] Blutcher is somewhat similar to the fictional Sorrell in this respect, except that Blutcher is far more sympathetic, being an ordinary man just trying to get by in life, as opposed to a pampered and overpaid ex-professional athlete; moreover, Blutcher's story is obviously unvarnished nonfiction, which gives it additional resonance. While *The Bedfellow* certainly remains an engaging and instructive read, one can often forget during the course of the narrative that its celebrated and affluent main character is African American; frequently, we instead seem to reading about the novelist himself. No such ambiguities or dichotomies are to be found in *People vs. Blutcher*. Even Conrad Lynn, the closest thing to a black role model presented in the book, is modest and unpretentious almost to a fault as he attempts to secure justice and dignity for his abused client.

Perhaps the biggest change in worldviews between *The Bedfellow* and *People vs. Blutcher* has to do with black attitudes toward law enforcement. The fictional Sorrell has nothing but contempt for the detectives who track, capture, and eventually incarcerate him. His disdain is partially justified by their occasional resemblance to the Keystone Cops and often thuggish, shallow demeanor.[21] Three years later, Asinof views the police in a far more sinister light, particularly with respect to white policeman interacting with black civilians in black neighborhoods. At the very outset of *Blutcher*, like a good reporter breaking news, Asinof bluntly states his then-controversial thesis:

> In the black ghettoes of America, law and order is a farce. The relationship of police and civilians is akin to an undeclared war wherein the "occupied" citizens have never known it any other way. It is a war that touches them all, some brutally, as all wars do, leaving scars that cut deeply into the mores of their lives; and the resulting chaos appears to have become as absolute and irrevocable as death and taxes.[22]

This assertion certainly applied to Blutcher, but not to the fictional Mike Sorrell. Sorrell feels a slight sting of racism in his various episodes with police, but on a much more benign level; if anything, they are more deferential and careful with him as a celebrity former pro-athlete. Sorrell receives physical bruises — but not from his captors — rather from an ugly scuffle with his gangster-hustler father who has recently re-entered the picture. Sorrell's experiences with the law as an African American, almost needless to say, are far less typical than those of Laurence Blutcher in real life.

A more universal issue (in the context of racial conflict) grappled with by Asinof in these two works touches upon the antihero's response to unfair adversity in life, and whether that person is a rare individual capable of reacting to these in a non-self-destructive manner. More often than not, they react as most of us would, with frustration, blind rage, and occasional violence. In *Blutcher*, Asinof summarizes the dilemma faced by all those who grow up amidst urban poverty, including the fictional Mike Sorrell: "The quest for manhood is not a simple thing in any community, but in such areas as Bedford-Stuyvesant in Brooklyn it is as difficult as an escape from prison. At thirty, a black man is defeated and a black woman is an unloved mother."[23] Asinof then elaborates on what may be the most common mistake by anyone, black or otherwise, who attempts to break out of the poverty cycle: "the action is what happens on the streets, and when a youth graduates from them, he has his diploma into adulthood but he is not necessarily a man."[24] This comment once again calls to mind Sorrell's defensive remark in *The Bedfellow* to his unhelpful psychiatrist, in which Sorrell credits baseball with helping him to achieve manhood.[25] It also stands in contrast to a quote from Cito Gaston (a possible inspiration for Sorrell's character), who credited Henry Aaron with teaching him how to accomplish the same goal by handling adversity and racism while playing professional ball in a Southern city (see Chapter 9).

If *People vs. Blutcher* well represents Asinof's progressive thinking on race relations after having initially broached the topic in earlier novels, 1976's *The Fox Is Crazy Too* explores similar humanist issues, but well beyond the confines of race and in a far more trans-ethnic fashion. As such, it makes a neat compendium to those prominent aspects of *The Bedfellow* which do not relate strictly to the plight of African Americans, but to all former professional athletes. *The Fox* is another one of Asinof's unforgettable nonfiction character studies, this time of the infamous Garrett Brock Trapnell (1938–1993), convicted bank robber and skyjacker. Trapnell was also an incredibly daring, brilliant, and innovative con man, ironically descended from one of the nation's most illustrious military families. Trapnell's two main lasting claims to fame were that his successful skyjacking escapades led to the first major revamp of commercial air travel security, and, before eventually dying in prison, more than once beat his rap through creative use of the insanity plea in court.

During the Nixon-Watergate era, his disturbing life story offered perfect material for Asinof's adroitness at producing socially-conscious exposé both expedient and offbeat. It also offered Asinof a convenient opportunity to expand upon his favorite themes of personal disaffection, rebellion, and moral responsibility — all crucial topics touched upon in his two baseball books of the 1960s, *Eight Men Out* and *The Bedfellow*. Mike Sorrell, when baseball is no longer an option in his life, does not seem to fit in anywhere else, much like Trapnell after leaving the U.S. military as a young man. Fittingly, *The Fox* prominently quotes the Canadian poet Robert Service (1874–1958), whose popular works such as "The Men That Don't Fit In" seem to glorify misanthropy in modern man, or at least view positive qualities in this otherwise negative trait.[26] For Asinof, the same idea applied to Trapnell, as well as to Mike Sorrell, the Black Sox, and many of his other antiheroes, both real and fictional.

The Fox Is Crazy Too ranks as one of Asinof's most compelling works. Unfortunately, the biggest public notoriety garnered by the book came in 1981 when John Hinckley, Jr., attempted to assassinate President Ronald Reagan. After his arrest, a copy of *The Fox* was found among his possessions.[27] Subsequently at trial, Hinckley was found not guilty by reason of insanity and has since remained institutionalized. Like Garrett Brock Trapnell, Hinckley evaded prison through the insanity plea, but unlike Trapnell, no would ever accuse Hinckley of being clever or fox-like. Asinof, for his part, detested the insanity defense (as so eloquently argued in his book), and had no great love for psychiatrists: "It seemed as though psychiatrists could be found to say in court whatever they were paid to say."[28] This express loathing first manifested itself in Asinof's writings a decade earlier with *The Bedfellow*. Fuchs is self-described as "a headshrinker who never cured anyone." Calculatingly (to gain Sorrell's trust), he refers to his own "promising" baseball career terminated by polio at age 14, the age at which genuine athletic talent often becomes first recognizable.[29] Finally, Sorrell learns that Fuchs is prominently on his own family's payroll, for which the psychiatrist makes absolutely no professional apologies.[30] The final irony with respect to the Hinckley incident came in the aftermath of his incarceration when Hinckley's attorney reportedly offered Asinof a large sum to write his client's story as well, which Asinof, true to his character, firmly refused to do.[31]

Consistent with Asinof's philosophy throughout his writing career, society bears a significant share of the blame for these misdeeds, as does the individual. In certain passages from *The Fox*, one could easily substitute the fictional name of Mike Sorrell for Garrett Trapnell, or perhaps even the name of the author himself. Asinof offers his own critical take on society's view of the controversial issue:

> The career of Garrett Trapnell represents the quintessence of all our self-destructive tendencies, from the folly of the insanity ruling to the hypocrisy of what is euphemistically called law and order. His life becomes a showcase for our follies, especially those of his prosecutors who blind us to our failures and deficiencies, forcing us to look the wrong way, nurturing a false sense of security. Trapnell is the epitome of what "mental illness" has come to represent, that flip side of the coin of respectability. He defied all the acceptable notions of societal conduct, so the psychiatrists called him sick. (Indeed, if there were no such thing as mental illness, we would have to create it.) Sick, yes. But only so long as he kept his aberrations within certain bounds—which, of course, turned the whole scheme of things into a farce, for once he stepped beyond it, we said he wasn't sick at all, in fact *never* was. This was, as Trapnell protested, "breaking the rules."[32]

In *The Bedfellow*, Sorrell does not plea temporary insanity for his destructive actions, but he might as well. Upon news of his younger brother's death in Vietnam, a death that Sorrell arguably caused by encouraging his brother to enlist, he goes berserk. Then, after all his theft and mayhem are finished, he returns to "normal" by selling himself out to the advertising world. The questions are naturally raised: when was Sorrell crazy and when was he sane, or, was is always one or the other to varying degrees? In the final analysis, much of Asinof's writings inject a healthy dose of psychological self-exploration — a quality found in most great writing — and probably does so in a far more effective manner than most psychiatrists would ever accomplish. The true beginnings of this distinctive trait (at least on an extensive basis) can be traced to *The Bedfellow*, since Asinof's first two books had external, rather than internal emphases.

Both *The Fox Is Crazy Too* and *People vs. Blutcher*, like *Eight Men Out* before them, culminate in factual, highly-publicized public trials, exposing numerous shortcomings in the American justice system. In a very real way, these two nonfiction books (*The Fox* and *Blutcher*) are a set pair on the theme of provoked, individual rage against the injustices of society (one white, one black), both initially probed in fictional manner with *The Bedfellow*. It appears to have been a topic that Asinof could relate to well on a personal level. One easily recalls film director John Sayles teasing Asinof with "everybody in the movie business thinks you're a troublemaker," (see Chapter 6, note 39). Nevertheless, it was this same reputation for troublemaking that suggested Asinof's special status as an American writer. He was among the few always willing to explore his own psyche, and *The Bedfellow* becomes Exhibit A this regard. Asinof may have been perceived by others as "God's angry man," but his anger was usually justified, and could be aimed at himself as well as others. Those who knew him on a more personal basis considered him cheerful.[33] Whether cheerful or angry, there can be little doubt that Asinof created one of the more boldly daring novels of the late 1960s when he wrote *The Bedfellow*. Its non-acceptance by the fiction-reading public of the time comes as no surprise in retrospect. As for baseball and sports fans, the work essentially told them frank and candid truths that they probably did not care to hear, namely, that the post-playing professional career of a star athlete can be even trickier business than making it to the big leagues as a player in the first place.

11
In Need of a Pick-Me-Up

As every former professional or collegiate baseball player knows, for every talented, hard-working athlete who makes it to the majors there are dozens of talented, hard-working ones who do not, either through bad luck, injuries, or other forces totally beyond their control. With a few oddball exceptions such as Rocky Perone (see Chapter 3), Eliot Asinof always wrote about ballplayers, real or fictional, who do in fact make it to the big time, even if for only a brief moment.[1] Even the semi-fictional Mike Kutner from *Man on Spikes* eventually gets his "cup of coffee" in the majors, but is disappointed by his short stint there. In *The Bedfellow*, the completely fictional Mike Sorrell first successfully escapes from the Watts ghetto of Los Angeles to Shea Stadium of New York City, then abandons his professional baseball career for romantic love and social respectability, neither of which turn out to be quite what he expected. In fact, Asinof's baseball antiheroes tend to always get what they want, but are rarely satisfied by their achievements. The old proverb, "Be careful what you wish for," appears to have been one of Asinof's favorite recurring themes in all of his baseball and sports writings.

As a professional writer and a former professional ballplayer, Asinof was no doubt frustrated by *The Bedfellow*'s lack of commercial and critical acceptance; yet, he seems to have written exactly the kind of challenging, personal novel that he set out to produce in the first place. Accordingly, many decades after its publication, the fictional tale of Mike Sorrell still offers plenty of useful (and entertaining) lessons to offer for any young, ambitious athlete willing to take these in. In retrospect, the novel still holds up well on its own terms, whether read strictly within the context of sports or on a broader sociological level (see Chapter 12).

When *The Bedfellow* was published in 1967, major league baseball's reserve clause, a focal point of Asinof's first great novel *Man on Spikes*, was still in full force. It would be another two years before the trade of Curt Flood would initiate a six-year chain of legal events eventually leading to the reserve clause's official demise in 1975. In the novel, however, it is the still-extant rule binding players to their teams for life that once again propels events in Asinof's

Asinof on the links at Noyac Golf Club in Sag Harbor, Long Island, New York, date unknown. Note the right-handed swing, although Asinof spent most of his baseball career batting left-handed as a switch hitter. In 1998, at 79 years of age, Asinof was able to shoot his age on the golf course. This same swing was later immortalized in the John Sayles film *Sunshine State* (2002).

storyline. Sorrell is quite content with his playing career in New York until, without warning, he is traded to Atlanta. Sorrell's horrified Jewish fiancé exclaims, "Tell them to trade you back.... How can we possibly get married and live in Georgia[?]"[2] Sorrell is more philosophical, but also acknowledges his helplessness in lieu of professional baseball's then-perfectly legal status quo:

> As any professional ballplayer knows, this can happen to the best of us, and there is little a man can do about it. He is neither consulted nor given a choice. When a man is owned outright, he can be sold outright. He can bargain over his salary at contract time in January, but his only weapon if he doesn't like the terms is to quit — which means he doesn't play ball again, unless he can make a deal for himself in Japan or Venezuela or wherever, a threat that usually amuses club owners.[3]

Rather than beg for a trade (as does Mike Kutner in *Man on Spikes*), Mike Sorrell in *The Bedfellow* gets a trade that he detests, much like Curt Flood would two years later. Instead of hanging in there just for the opportunity to play ball in the majors (like Kutner), Sorrell takes what he considers to be the high road (as Curt Flood did), and retires from baseball in his prime. This choice is especially feasible given a lucrative job offer from Madison Avenue. In addition to Asinof's loathing of the reserve clause, the plot reflects the novelist's trademark abhorrence for the racist heritage of the American South. This attitude was based on a number of Asinof's own personal experiences, particularly his very brief and highly unpleasant minor league playing tour in Moultrie, Georgia, during the summer of 1940 (see Chapter 9).[4]

Although Asinof would soon afterwards address race issues in a far more direct and compelling manner with *People vs. Blutcher* (1970), this nonfiction work also would often employ the same baseball language which permeates *The Bedfellow*.[5] For example, Blutcher's beleaguered defense attorney, Conrad Lynn, utilizes a brilliant baseball analogy after key witnesses fail to appear following an unfair ruling by the judge: "I felt like a pitcher who had just thrown his best pitch and the umpire had called it a ball, only to turn around then and discover that the outfielders had disappeared."[6] Lynn, as a friend of the writer, probably well knew that Asinof was a former outfielder when making this comparison. It also presents a powerful image to any reader who happens to have played the game at advanced levels, reflecting Asinof's own first-hand knowledge in this regard. I, for one, well remember as a pitcher being once cheated by an umpire out of a perfectly thrown strike down the middle of the zone, and the fury that it provoked both from myself and my catcher. I was nearly thrown out of the game; only though the intervention of my catcher (who threw an even bigger fit) was it prevented. On the very next pitch, the batter (as so often happens in the game), drove a tremendous live drive towards the center field fence — this was with potentially scoring men on base. Rather than having deserted me, as in Lynn's analogy, our team's centerfielder made a spectacular, Willie Mays-style over-the-shoulder running catch some 400 plus feet out to end the inning. In baseball lingo, such a rescue is often referred to as a "pick me up."[7] Asinof the former pro centerfielder well understood and appreciated the demoralizing significance of Lynn's chosen images, as the renowned attorney tried to describe to him helpless feelings of futility while trying to defend his client during the Blutcher trial.

One of the most unattractive features of Sorrell's circle of family and friends in *The Bedfellow* is that none of them, to a man or woman, appear to enjoy baseball. Psychiatrist Fuchs claims to like the sport while reeling Sorrell into his trust, but comes across more as being deeply envious of Sorrell's celebrity or, worse, outright obstructionist as Sorrell gravitates towards attempting a comeback. Everyone else, including Sorrell's gangster father, views baseball as a juvenile, naïve, and unproductive activity at best. The same motif would crop up again three years later in *People vs. Blutcher*, as if a sincere enthusiasm for baseball underscored one's racial alienation in modern society. Judge Joseph R. Corso in the Blutcher trial was a Brooklyn native who still lived in the borough but, "when the Dodgers left, a big piece of what was Brooklyn went with them. And I [Corso] stopped being a baseball fan."[8] Readers almost get the impression in Asinof's baseball writings that to have an unconditional love of the game is to be doomed, whether it be within the context of race relations, sports gambling, or the desire to be a major league ballplayer. This fatalistic attitude towards anyone emotionally attached to the sport would only relent somewhat with Asinof's very last baseball novel, *Off-Season* (2000), another work closely examining America's great racial divide, and discussed in Part V of this study.

When addressing the issue of race in a professional baseball setting, whether it be in *The Bedfellow* or any of Asinof's later works, it is of course impossible to ignore the peerless and noble legacy of Jackie Robinson. It should be recalled that Asinof's 1967 novel was published a mere 20 years after Brooklyn Dodger General Manager Branch Rickey had made his visionary and controversial decision to forcibly integrate major league baseball.[9] Asinof's friend Bill Veeck also deserves some credit in this area as he showed solidarity with Rickey at the time by bringing Larry Doby on board with the American League Cleveland Indians. During that same period, Asinof was witnessing first-hand the interaction, if not integration of black and white ballplayers at the semipro level while himself co-owning and managing the Yonkers Indians of the New York Metropolitan Baseball Association. *The Bedfellow* is hardly a boring treatise or monograph on these important historical events, but the precedent, along with its multiple aftershocks, would have been in back of the novelist's mind as he wrote. In the book, as Sorrell makes his premature escape from police, he describes the speed of his fleet-footed evasive maneuver as being "faster than you can say Jackie Robinson."[10]

On a more serious level, it is sobering to note that the same Bedford-

Stuyvesant neighborhood in Brooklyn which had so enthusiastically cheered Jackie Robinson's integration into the majors during the 1947 season, was also by the 1960s (only 20 years later) witness to bitter rioting and the racially divisive Blutcher incident occurring within its confines. For Asinof, the relatively short time span between 1947 and 1967 represented both progression and regression in terms of civil rights. With legalized integration came ongoing social strife, economic upheavals, and new kinds of segregation, some more insidious and secretive than their older counterparts. As these applied to professional baseball, *The Bedfellow* perhaps best encapsulates the novelist's open ambivalence. To him, African American ballplayers, like the fictional Mike Sorrell, had come an impressively long way in just two decades, yet still faced daunting hurdles both within their sports and in society at large, in addition to their own inner demons. Many, by the late 1960s, were fairly well-paid, idolized by fans, and lionized by the media; nevertheless, there were still many pitfalls, and one did not necessarily have to be African American to fall into them. Nonfiction events in the real world of professional sports over the next several decades would amply demonstrate the extent of these vexing problems, once again proving Asinof as a writer to be a kind of prophet, in the words of attorney and reserve clause foe, Marvin Miller (see Chapter 1).

As emphasized in the previous chapter, *The Bedfellow* is not about race alone; it is also about the plight of all professional athletes after retirement from sports. The solution that most former athletes find to this problem is simple: complete withdrawal from sports after retirement is unhealthy, if not destructive, and the substitution of a new physical activity for the old sport, a new pastime more fitting to one's age and inclinations, becomes an absolute necessity. For Asinof, as with many other former professional ballplayers and athletes, this substitution eventually became golf. Though presented as an innocent throw-aside in the novel, Sorrell's "I don't play golf" comment (as events in story spiral out of control for him), can, in the bigger scheme of things, come across as a key, revelatory moment in the plot.[11] Amateur golf proved to be Asinof's answer for staying athletically active into old age, and one which his fictional creation, the 27-year-old Sorrell had not yet discovered for himself. In the novel, readers can always sense Sorrell's constant craving for diversion and need to blow off steam. Clearly, he would not be such an unhappy person if he only knew how to escape from his problems to the links. To the non-athlete it may sound funny or ridiculous, but to anyone who has ever walked away from competitive sports in the prime of life knows exactly what Asinof was (figuratively speaking) driving at. Golf may have not solved any of his other personal problems, but it might have made him less angry a person.

The golf aspect of Asinof's sports philosophy may seem a light-hearted, frivolous detour until one contemplates some of the future events that came to pass in decades following release of *The Bedfellow*. For one, an African American, Tiger Woods, became the greatest golfer anyone has ever seen, as well as a paragon of controlled concentration under competitive pressure, among all professional athletes in general. Then, seemingly overnight, his enviable career (and biracial marriage) unraveled as sports fans and non-sports fans alike were media force-fed a highly unpleasant close-up of the personal life that lay behind the façade of his carefully crafted public image. Many are still trying to come to grips with how such a fantastic athlete can simultaneously be such a frail, fallible human being. Such contradictions, however, would have come as no surprise to Asinof. Many of his characters, such as Mike Sorrell, are walking contradictions. A more disturbing example of how Asinof's fictional thematic concerns came to pass in real-life within a few short decades was the lurid and sinister case of O. J. Simpson. At the time *The Bedfellow* was being written, Simpson had yet to even make his mark as a college football player with the University of Southern California, an institution coincidentally located in the same South Central Los Angeles area from which hailed Asinof's fictional Mike Sorrell. Like Sorrell, though on a far more felonious level, Simpson, after his retirement from football and subsequent, temporary employment by the advertising industry, became synonymous in the popular imagination with the prototypical, maladjusted ex-professional star athlete, including an ill-fated, biracial marriage ending in tragedy and murder. What Asinof himself thought of these later unsettling developments is not recorded.

One thing is indisputable, however; Asinof was himself able to successfully make the bumpy transition as a young man from professional athlete to professional writer. It is also beyond question that, after Asinof became a successful writer, he developed into a sensational amateur golfer. The well-known simple fact that in 1998, at age 79, he successfully shot his then age as a total score at the 18-hole Taconic Golf Club adjacent to Williams College in Williamstown, Massachusetts, is testament to his prowess.[12] As an aside, Williams College had been one of Asinof's alma maters (before he transferred to Swarthmore College) during the late 1930s, as well as the alma mater of John Sayles, later film director for the movie version of *Eight Men Out*. Anyone doubting Asinof's formidable skills on the links can view his golf swing as later immortalized in Sayles' 2002 film *Sunshine State*, in which Asinof was invited to play the bit part of Silent Sam, and who dryly laments the fate of Florida Native Americans in the last line of the movie. Asinof was then 83 years old. Also of interest in this sequence is Asinof's perfect right-handed golf swing, despite the fact that he had spent most of his baseball career batting left-handed as a switch hitter. Asinof had opted in his youth to learn golf right-handed, since this gave him an arguably similar advantage to the one he previously enjoyed batting left-handed against primarily right-handed pitching, providing further proof of his not inconsiderable, ambidextrous athletic ability.[13] He also enthusiastically wrote golf-related articles for various sports publications throughout his literary career.[14] Above all, we suspect that Asinof took to the Scottish-invented sport because of its absolute demand that successful participants be in total control of their emotions while on the course. As a well-known volatile personality, Asinof no doubt saw a chance to kill two birds with one stone by learning golf, which he proceeded to do with aplomb. Who knows, perhaps the origins of his later-achieved excellence in the sport lay in his earlier creation of the short-tempered and emphatically non-golf-playing Mike Sorrell from *The Bedfellow*.

This is not to say that Asinof, or for that matter, his former baseball-playing characters, ever lost their love or nostalgia for the game. In *The Bedfellow*, this nostalgic longing for a return to the playing field is ever present. "I still like it [baseball]," Sorrell insists to his disapproving psychiatrist Fuchs.[15] After becoming the hero of the moment in a meaningless, bush league game of softball in Central Park, Sorrell realizes the absurdity of his self-satisfaction and apologetically reflects on his own feelings:

> Sure, that's my trouble. At such moments, the loneliness of the ex-athlete can be brutal. I want to bathe in the glory, but they've pulled the plug on me. But then, it's always been that way. An accolade, after all, is a temporary thing, and I always went home to the same loneliness. The exquisite difference, though, was in knowing it would be there for me again, the next day and the one after, a constant challenge that exhilarated me. It was a part of being young and hungry, and life had an upward thrust that kept me jumping.[16]

For Sorrell, baseball obviously satisfies an important psychological need that his new lifestyle fails to provide for, one that his psychiatrist, interestingly enough, refuses to acknowledge. He longs to somehow regain it, perhaps by trying to resurrect his playing career, but is not sure about that either. At age 27, his is already beginning to feel over the hill as a player. Perhaps for the first time in his life, he finds himself living off of memories, rather than the "constant challenge" of "the next day and the one after."

Sorrell's nostalgic longing for his playing days parallels that repeatedly expressed by Asinof in his 1979 memoir *Bleeding Between the Lines*. Reminiscing on the high points of his playing days in Wausau, Wisconsin, during the summer of 1941 (see Chapter 14), he writes as if these were the happiest moments in his life.[17] Returning home from the war in 1946, Asinof's abortive tryout in Montpelier, Vermont, with the Phillies organization was justified with his telling comment, "I had no prospect of making a comeback, but merely sought the pleasure of one more season on spikes."[18] Many years later (in 1959), Asinof found himself in post–Revolutionary Cuba working on a movie screenplay (see Chapter 2); more congenial to him, however, was an invitation by locals to play outfield during their baseball games. Those moments, as he later blissfully recalled, "were ten days full of friendliness and fun, the most enjoyable time I'd ever spent on foreign soil."[19] By the time Asinof was in his 40s, he was still, like Mike Sorrell in *The Bedfellow*, playing softball in Central Park. One day, retired Yankee Phil Rizutto, on the opposing field, saw Asinof come to the plate and, though they had not played against each other in three decades, had the defense shift positions to meet a familiar threat. Asinof was flattered: "It was a marvelous moment, and it carried me through the day, another reminder of what baseball had meant to me."[20] Reading these passages from both *Bleeding* and *Bedfellow* underscore the novelist's unabated passion for the national pastime and its personal significance to him, long after he had become too old to play the sport himself, although he did boast to Rizutto that "a man can hit until he goes blind."[21] Asinof, like Sorrell, could never let go of baseball completely, and found that he had to keeping returning to it in some form or another at regular intervals.[22]

Getting back to the novel, *The Bedfellow* is perhaps, at its central core, a cautionary tale for former professional athletes, regardless of race or temperament. By the end of the story, Sorrell appears to have surrendered to all of the external forces which conspired to prematurely end his professional playing career. These evil forces include his ambitious wife's wealthy, self-serving family and the blood-relative psychiatrist they pay to help keep Sorrell's disaffection in check, the sleazy and exhibitionist world of Madison Avenue advertising, and above all, Sorrell's despised hoodlum-turned-entrepreneur father. The book is designed for the reader to put down after finishing and hope that post-professional athletic life offers more choices than the ones Sorrell is able to glean. Asinof the novelist may well have been groping towards a solution for himself at the time, having by then carved a niche in the literary world, but still longing for recreational outlets, not to mention more satisfying personal relationships in his life. In the novel, no solutions are expressly offered, but several are implied. For one, Sorrell's uncontrolled temper and impulsive, rash choices only seem to dig a deeper hole out of which he must climb; once the digging stops, it is suggested, only then he can begin to climb out. As for his disinclination to play golf, Asinof is certainly not preaching that all ex-athletes should buy a set of clubs; rather, he seems to be encouraging everyone to stay as physically active as they are able to, even in retirement. Back in 1967, this would have been more an unusual idea in the popular realm than today. In this broader sense, everyone — not just the fictional Mike Sorrell — is in need of a pick-me-up.

Most former ballplayers know quite well what it is like to have deep dreams at night of playing the game, not merely in the past, but in the vivid present as well. We relive our past successes and failures through this present medium, even after we are no longer physically capable of sprinting around the bases. After the dream is over, however, all of us must return to our careers, our families, and, if we are very fortunate, to other physical recreation less challenging than the bruising contact sports of our youth. Asinof's *The Bedfellow*, as a skilled work of fiction, seems to occupy that same eerie no-man's-land situated somewhere between reality and fantasy, one that every aging athlete must one day cross. As such, it presents readers with a far more comprehensive view of the big picture in sports life than most readers are used to seeing. Then again, all of Asinof's baseball writings, in the final analysis, are concerned with much more than merely the game itself. For this particular unique entry into the Asinof catalogue, the all too infrequently remarked upon overlap between professional sports and the insistent demands of commerce are exposed, dissected, and critiqued. To these less popular, but in many respects, more profound aspects of the novel, ones which point accusingly in non-baseball directions, we shall now turn our attention.

12

Like an Ancient Chinese Curse

The problem begins with race and dates back to slavery.... "If you're white you're right, if you're black go back." This is our heritage and the ghetto is its outgrowth. To the blacks, the basic meaning of race is poverty. Poverty is the key that locks the black man in, and the culture of the ghetto is the struggle to surmount it. It is a relentless struggle that few can win, made all the more gruesome by the colossal titillation of television, exacerbating the black man's frustrations with its enticements of glamorous possessions and a life of affluence. In the end, it leads to confusion and crime and violence, and, above all, keeps him from being a man.

—Asinof, *People vs. Blutcher*[1]

Not long ago this writer, along with a few other former ballplayers, attended a Chicago White Sox game at U.S. Cellular Field.[2] We were fortunate that day, through the connections of one in our group, to have expensive box seats situated directly behind the third base home dugout. Here we enjoyed the afternoon with a genuine, close-up view of the contest. As most Chicagoans will agree (even Cub fans), Sox fans have a reputation for being more knowledgeable and discerning about the game than their north side counterparts. Here, situated amongst the most dedicated and committed of the "pale hose" partisans, I expected to eavesdrop on sophisticated, perceptive baseball commentary. Instead, all we heard was nonsense, some of it outright delusional, ignoring reality a few feet away in front of our eyes. People seated next to us could not distinguish breaking pitches from fast balls; routine pop flies were thought to be home runs as they left the bat; some fans around us seemed genuinely surprised when foul balls from left-handed hitters sharply sliced in our direction over the dugout; amazingly, most seemed oblivious to the perpetual psychological battle between pitchers and batters, or at best, complained impatiently for players to stop stalling and get on with the game. The super-sized flat-screen monitor near the centerfield scoreboard often commanded more rapt spectator attention than simultaneous events occurring on the playing field. As for the quantity of alcohol and junk food consumed, the less said the better.

I was appalled. How could people who spend most of their time and a substantial portion of their incomes attending these ballgames still know next to nothing about the sport? The only answer, to my mind, is that few if any of these fans ever played baseball themselves beyond sandlot level of competition. Then I had a more troubling thought: is it that way with everything? For example, how does a former professional star athlete, say, the fictional Mike Sorrell from Asinof's *The Bedfellow*, cope with a new career environment having little or nothing to do with sports? Can long familiarity with a single, highly specialized field then fool us into believing that we are experts in other specialized fields as well? Is personal experience the true foundation for reliable expertise in everything? If so, then we can only conclude that there are many people in society today thinking they are quite qualified to do many other things, when in fact they are not in the least qualified or able.[3] Has the modern world made all of us so hyper-specialized in our little niches that we have become in all other things, as the classical economist Adam Smith once warned could happen under these conditions, as stupid as it is possible for human beings to become?

This brings us straight back to Asinof's fictional character Mike Sorrell in *The Bedfellow*. He is a fabulous athlete *and* possesses a keen intellect—a rare combination in any time or place. He is also African American, which normally would be a disadvantage in white upper-class society, but Sorrell has seemingly found a way to turn this to advantage as well, both in his professional and personal life; in fact, for him the two frequently overlap and often appear to be one and the same. For example, to stay in good graces with his employer, Sorrell must allow him, at minimum, to make a public pass at his wife. This compromise is also necessary to advance her career ambitions as a model.[4] Things seem to be smoothing out until Sorrell's younger brother is killed in Vietnam, having enlisted upon his older brother's advice. The death is concealed from Sorrell by his wife so as not to interfere with their imminent social engagements. When he discovers the deception, he goes on a rampage and is only saved from the police by his powerful white in-law connections. At a glance, Sorrell appears to have the modern world completely figured out. Below the surface, however, he is a miserably unhappy "Bedfellow" careening from one crisis to the next until his psyche finally breaks. His beloved jet set lifestyle is unsustainable, although by the end of the story that is exactly what he resolves to try and maintain. As a result, something inside of him dies; he can no longer bear looking at himself in the mirror.

Sorrell, now a retired professional black athlete in the advertising world, is a proverbial fish out of water. As in Shakespeare's play *The Tempest* (from which the novel takes its title), Sorrell transmutes into a kind of Caliban, a hideous monster lacking moral compass, a land-roving creature with a very fishy smell. After Trinculo shares a bed with Caliban (as Sorrell does with his dubious Madison Avenue cohorts), he too smells fish-like and, by the end of the play, is lumped together with Caliban by the playwright as a dangerous conspirator and threat to society at large. In a broader, more disturbing sense, readers may well ask by the end of Asinof's novel if all of us are faced with similar choices in our everyday lives. Do we sell out our principles (assuming we possess these to begin with) in order to maintain a certain materialistic standard of living, or dare we risk taking a more upright but much harder, less traveled path? Analyzed from this vantage point, *The Bedfellow*'s astringent message represents quite a statement coming from an author whose previous work (*Eight Men Out*, published only four years earlier) eventually became one of America's most well-known baseball books. Whatever shortcomings the novel may have as a work of fiction, no one could accuse its author of artistic complacency or not trying to push the envelope of public acceptance. Asinof was certainly the not the first postwar American writer to attempt such an about-face, but he does not receive nearly enough credit for having done so either.[5]

This is not to say that Asinof does not present Sorrell's chosen career path as being quite difficult to negotiate on its own terms. Sorrell is made an honorary member of the ruthless, insular world of 1960s Madison Avenue marketing and public relations. Anyone doubting the treacherous, cross-fire rivalries and duplicitous, obfuscating insincerities of this landscape should watch a few episodes of the award-winning AMC television series *Mad Men*, in which the industry of that time and place is depicted with a fair amount of historical accuracy.[6] Asinof would have been quite familiar with the Madison Avenue world as the lauded New York author of 1963's *Eight Men Out*. It was a world for which he had a relentlessly low opinion, not only based on the way in which it is portrayed in *The Bedfellow*, but also for Asinof's failure to commercially capitalize on his writing celebrity in the immediate wake of *Eight Men Out*'s publication. The odious depiction of Madison Avenue advertising, including by extension the entire sphere of capitalist marketing and public relations apparatus, remained a constant throughout Asinof's works. In his gripping last novel, *Final Judgment* (2008), the martyr-like Anne Miner has a villainous brother, Robert Miner, an account executive for a large advertising agency in Washington, D.C. Main protagonist Kenneth Flear, a professional writer clearly representing the voice of the novelist, is outright contemptuous of everything this evil sibling stands for: "I did not ask him what he advertised or who his clients were. Perhaps I was afraid to know."[7] For that matter, Sorrell's fictional employer in *The Bedfellow*, D. J. Biddle Associates, a firm owned and managed by its Mephistopheles-like namesake and his younger, subservient brother, Walter, is a very mysterious entity when it comes to specifics. We are never quite sure what Biddle Associates is trying to sell at any given moment, but it hardly matters. The important thing is that they are willing to sell anything for a price, and are apparently very good at their trade, based on their lofty status within the industry. Sorrell's role in the company is strictly as a face man, running humiliating errands while giving cheery public credibility to whatever venture the firm happens to be pursuing at any given moment.

In the moral universe of Eliot Asinof, media for profit consistently represents the lowest of the low. This message became increasingly urgent as his writing career progressed, and remained his mantra right up to and including his last novel. In *Final Judgment*, a disillusioned (and slightly tipsy) Anne Miner vents her anger at the self-satisfied Kenneth Flear, who is in imminent danger of turning into an updated, white version of Mike Sorrell because of his inner complacency:

> We are all living a lie. We allow the most monstrous assaults on our way of life to go by without so much as a comment. No one wants to deal with the truth. "Give 'em what they want!" say those captains of the media who seek to control their viewers. They give us fake news as entertainment, movies, and TV shows of candy-coated nonsense or pornographic evisceration. All the citizens are gone. Now there are only consumers. They tell us to relax, enjoy, be titillated — anything but *think*! America is sick with its need to escape from the truth.[8]

Miner is obviously railing in this passage against the burgeoning media empire of Rupert Murdoch, along with its numerous aspiring imitators. This perceived monstrosity is, for Asinof the novelist, a horrendous but logical outgrowth of 1960s Madison Avenue culture with its over-the-top pandering to mass audience prejudices, stubborn misconceptions, and insatiable appetites. Her line, "Now there are only consumers," comes down with the force of a hammer blow. It could have easily been spoken by Sorrell's opportunistic boss, D. J. Biddle, without a trace of Miner's despair. Before the novel is over, Flear must make a stark choice between materialistic profit and personal integrity, just as Sorrell is eventually forced to do in *The Bedfellow*.

Sorrell's ethical decline during the course of events is hastened by his unique vulnerabilities in society as an African American. First, he quits the professional game that he loves in part due to his fear of playing for a Southern-based franchise (in Atlanta). Next, he is encouraged into a bad marriage because of his Jewish father-in-law's strange, guilt-ridden need to be accepting towards blacks.[9] Finally, Sorrell is hired by Biddle specifically because his blackness will allow the firm to reach into untapped minority markets, although this obvious motive goes tactfully unspoken.[10] In addition to these external forces, Sorrell is sorely tempted into giving up his higher ideals by his own personal need to live extravagantly. The same advertising industry that allows him to do this by paying his generous salary simultaneously ensures that he is addicted to the pleasures that it can buy. The header quote of this chapter, taken from Asinof's *People vs. Blutcher*, coming three years after *The Bedfellow*, speaks directly to this interdependent relationship between consumers and advertisers. Marketing via television has effectively conditioned Sorrell to yearn for the "glamorous possessions" (beginning with his trophy wife) and "life of affluence," which, in the final end, "keeps him from being a man." About the only thing that can be said in his defense is that such "enticements" are typically aimed at both blacks and whites alike, although targeted in sophisticated and specialized manners that require, in the case of impoverished blacks, a carefully selected pitchman or spokesperson such as a perceived African American role model in the person of Mike Sorrell.

In effect, Sorrell is lured into a high-salary advertising position because he is black, rather than in spite of it. This was not the case in his professional baseball career, where (it is heavily implied) he clawed his way into the Majors on the basis of sheer playing talent and desire. While Asinof does not use the precise term, he repeatedly touches upon the concept of affirmative action based on race, which began to exert itself as an economic force in both public and private sectors of the American economy during the 1960s. Interestingly, affirmative action seems to have interested Asinof well before it became a legal federal mandate. Not surprisingly, his interest came within the context of professional baseball. In 1955's *Man on Spikes* (see Chapter 3), Mike Kutner fulminates that African American prospect Ben Franks will get a shot at the Majors before him because of his skin color: "Ben Franks was labeled to go up *because* he was black."[11] Many years later, Asinof looked back on the transitional pre–civil rights era in professional baseball coming after Jackie Robinson had first broken the color barrier in 1947. He wrote with firm conviction that a prime motivator in the opposition to these developments from white athletes was the harsh specter of increased economic competition: "White ballplayers battled all attempts to integrate, not only for the usual reasons of racial bigotry but out of fear of losing their jobs."[12] In 1955, Asinof was yet again writing way ahead of the times, in anticipation of what would soon become a fiercely debated political issue, and one that remains controversial into the present day. It is even more remarkable that such a hard-headed viewpoint repeatedly came from the pen of a dyed-in-the-wool political liberal like Asinof. In his baseball fiction, he keenly appreciated the potential negative ramifications of affirmative action, whether these applied to Mike Kutner or Mike Sorrell, while at the same time fully supporting economic racial integration in all things, including baseball. This highly complex, duality of attitude on matters of racial integration is readily apparent in Asinof's baseball novels, including *Man on Spikes*, *The Bedfellow*, and *Off-Season*.[13]

In light of Asinof's career-long fascination with American race relations, a preoccupation that produced so many prescient insights on the subject, it is a remarkable coincidence that this writer died less than five months before the United States elected its first African American President in 2008.[14] Here, too, Asinof, the writer seems to have had intuitive foresight.[15] In the climactic sequence to his last novel, *Final Judgment*, the flawed and fallible hero, writer Kenneth Flear, while secretly preparing to make amends on national television for recent commercial compromises in his work, meets then-Senator Barack Obama in the green room, who urges Flear to "do the right thing."[16] The time setting is the year 2005, following George W. Bush's 2004 reelection as President. The novel was published posthumously on September 1, 2008, less than three months after Asinof's death on June 10 of that same year. This was also some two weeks before the downfall of Wall Street investment banking firm Lehman Brothers (on September 15), which began an accelerated economic downtown and chain of events eventually leading to Obama's surprising election victory in November. Some three weeks after the novel was published (on September 22), Asinof's beloved old Yankee Stadium, "the House that Ruth Built," was demolished in favor of a newer, bigger model. Taken as a whole, these combined events seemed to represent the passing of a bygone era, both in terms of baseball and American history in a wider sense. *Final Judgment*, like *The Bedfellow*, opens with a sardonic, religious-like quote from Albert Camus, reminding readers that "Final Judgment" comes on a daily basis and not merely at the end of time. In other words, with individual passing comes a higher moral evaluation of the manner in which individual lives have been led, both for better and for worse.

As discussed in the previous chapter, and with all matters of race set aside, *The Bedfellow* has much say about human psychology and, in particular, plenty of negative things to say about the profession of psychiatry. Sorrell's startling, violent outbursts of what can best be described as temporary insanity increase in frequency and ferocity towards the end of the novel, until finally, in the end, he calmly and unattractively resigns himself to a morally compromised life and career. Sorrell's in-law-provided and paid-for shrink, Allen Fuchs (his wife's cousin), is no help whatsoever throughout the story as his patient descends into despair and apathy. Indeed, Fuchs slyly facilitates the degenerative process by consistently giving Sorrell bad, self-serving advice. One strongly suspects that Asinof, who was himself known to have occasional anger management issues, must have had his own bad experiences with psychiatrists at some point, although this has not yet come to light. Initially, Sorrell is lured into misplacing his trust with Fuchs through the latter's ingratiating manner and enviable worldly possessions.[17] Sorrell's climatic decision to stay with his job and his marriage, and which also entails reconciliation with his hoodlum father for business purposes, is influenced in no small part by Fuch's active, uninvited guidance. On other hand, Sorrell is a more than willing subject; even Fuch's admission of doing what he his paid to do by the family makes little or no impression on Sorrell. He is too wrapped up in his own ego and desires to notice that these things are being used to manipulate him.

Sorrell's criminal behavior towards the end of the novel is benign compared to acts committed by some of Asinof's more lawless characters in his other books.[18] He steals a coat, he resists arrest, he beats up his father, he trashes his wife's personal possessions, he tells lies — at the same time, readers hardly feel sympathy for his victims, all of whom provoke Sorrell and are curiously forgiving so long as he agrees to remain within their corrupt fold. Although Asinof does not at any point overtly label Sorrell as insane or temporarily insane, *The Bedfellow* lays important groundwork for his subsequent nonfiction work during the 1970s, including his notoriously sympathetic portrayal of convicted skyjacker Garrett Brock Trapnell in *The Fox Is Crazy Too* (see Chapter 10). Given Asinof's well-known contempt for the insanity plea as a legal defense (successfully utilized by Trapnell on more than one occasion), including his generally unfavorable view of psychiatrists as mere hired guns for any proposed agenda, it is not surprising that Sorrell is no way defended by the novelist on this basis. Instead, Sorrell is a tragic victim of his hostile surrounding environment, as well as his own uncontrollable passions — but not of any inherent mental aberrations.[19] Ironically, punishment for his various misdeeds comes not in form of incarceration, ghetto poverty, or social ostracism; on the contrary, Sorrell is rewarded with the paradoxical, ancient Chinese curse of getting exactly what he wishes for, only to lose in the process everything in him that was originally good.

To make matters even worse for Sorrell, he ends up regaining perhaps the worst aspect of his younger life, namely, a working daily association with a biological father, George Henry Johnson, whom he not too inaccurately describes as "a rat in a sewer, reeking with slime.... Even the other sewer rats stay away from him."[20] Born George Henry Johnson, Jr., Sorrell changes his name as a teenager and abruptly severs his unhappy, abusive relationship with the father upon the death of his mother, itself caused in part by George, Sr.'s callous and sordid street activities. After becoming first a baseball and then a PR idol, Sorrell thinks he has successfully freed himself from George, Sr., until the latter reappears in his life, skillfully persuading Sorrell's amoral boss and in-laws that he (the father) is not such a bad guy after all. In anger, Sorrell beats his dad to a pulp, only to hear him sneer back, "You ain't changed a motherfucking thing!"[21] In the end, George, Sr., is proven correct when his son agrees to tow the company line and renew working with his father as part of his employment. Sorrell's bitter reuniting with George, Sr., becomes the symbolic epitome of his ethical backsliding or, to be more precise, the illusion of his previous ethical progress.

It is worth noticing at this point that the hostile father-son relationship so vividly portrayed in *The Bedfellow* hardly represents an isolated example of this phenomenon in Asinof's overall literary output. In his very first novel,

Man on Spikes, hero Mike Kutner has a totally non-communicative rapport with his father, who openly opposes his son's love of baseball, tries to burn his glove, and refuses to attend any of his son's games, even after the son turns professional. In return, Kutner would rather play in a professional ballgame than attend his father's funeral, to the understandable fury of his mother. In Asinof's other New York trilogy novel, *The Name of the Game Is Murder* (see Chapter 17), Mike Ogden's teenage delinquent son has little if anything to do with his father after the mother is killed, although this incident, unlike the death of Sorrell's mother in *The Bedfellow*, is in no way connected to the father's deviant behavior. The son, within three years of his mother's demise, drops out of high school and, like Sorrell, runs away from home.[22] Unlike Sorrell, however, he never suffers physical abuse.[23] The last line in *Name of the Game* has Ogden longingly confiding, "I want to fine my son."[24] For 1994's *Strike Zone*, Ernie Kolacka, perhaps Asinof's most autobiographical creation, becomes distant and argumentative with both of his children. In Asinof's last baseball novel, *Off-Season*, hero Jack Cagle has a terrible relationship with his authoritarian father, who is literally the home town sheriff, and who by the end of the story proves to be a true villain. In *Final Judgment*, Kenneth Flear loses the respect of his college-age son and can only regain it with a dramatically public act of contrition, almost along the lines of a *deus-ex-machina*. In the same story, and in a similar manner, the hyper-idealistic college student Anne Miner completely turns against her establishment-friendly senator-father. After her death, his diminished self-respect is redeemed only by Flear's incredible moral courage as well. In Asinof's nonfiction works, troubled parent-child dynamics are portrayed in *People vs. Blutcher*, *The Fox Is Crazy Too*, and *Craig and Joan*. In fact, it is not too far off the mark to say that warm, smooth parental relations are almost totally absent in Asinof's catalogue.[25] It was obviously a theme that deeply resonated with him.

In his published work, Asinof had little if anything to say about closeness or lack thereof with his own father, Max Asinof, who, along with his grandfather and two uncles, had immigrated to New York City through Ellis Island from Pskov, Russia (near Kiev and the Ukrainian border) in the early 20th century.[26] Thanks to Eliot's son Martin Asinof, however, some interesting details concerning the family history have been revealed. When asked if his father Eliot had a turbulent history with his own father Max, Martin reminisced at length:

> I don't believe so, but they were quite different personalities. Unlike Eliot, his father had a very reserved manner, and he did not participate in Eliot's life. For example, not once did he see Eliot play baseball. In return, Eliot did not give a hoot about men's suits or the family clothing business. That story about him being voted "Best Dressed" in high school resulted from Eliot pleading with his classmates not to let him to lose face in the eyes of his clothier family. The family joke is that

> Eliot never saw his father without a tie and I never saw Eliot with one. As a family, the Asinofs were semi-dysfunctional in part because of their business. The business was essentially a sweat shop, which was typical for that time and place, but Eliot was a labor guy, and he held that sort of thing in disdain.[27]

It would of course be going too far to assert that Asinof's writings, baseball or otherwise, represent a mirror image of real-life associations with his own father. It would be just as inaccurate, however, to claim that there was no influence whatsoever, or that the influence was only slight. With respect to Eliot's post-marital relations with his son Martin, it speaks for itself that many of his books are dedicated to Martin, and that *Final Judgment*, his last novel (also one of his finest), ends with reconciliation and mutual respect between the father-writer Kenneth Flear and his disaffected son, Ted. Thus it appears that Eliot Asinof, even after his divorce, was determined to do better in this regard than his own father, and apparently succeeded.

Although Asinof shifted into high gear with his writing after publication of *The Bedfellow* in 1967, it would be another 27 years before he wrote another baseball book. By that time he had, not surprisingly, developed a different kind of viewpoint in his style, which shall be explored in the next section of this study. As to his motives in producing such a complex and daunting novel in the immediate aftermath of *Eight Men Out*'s critical (if not commercial) success, readers must constantly bear in mind that this was not a writer who wrote strictly for fame and fortune. On the contrary, he was a driven natural artist with a profound sense of moral obligation to the public, one who probably would have written even without financial or limelight incentives. Admittedly, *The Bedfellow* does not directly address racial discrimination and injustice, as do later works such as *People vs. Blutcher*, *Off-Season*, and others. Perhaps his motives can be best understood by once again turning to a passage from *Blutcher*. When challenged by Laurence Blutcher's reticent family and friends, Asinof provided an explanation that was simple enough: "'Why do you want to write about this?' I was asked.... If the reader can benefit but a fraction of what I experienced in pursuing this account, my efforts will have been amply justified."[28] Regardless of whatever the novelist's motivations may have been, it is the firm premise of this survey that *The Bedfellow* is a very good book, written by an occasionally great writer, and one rather unjustly ignored up until the present.

Part IV: *Strike Zone* (1994)

13

A Kind of Belated Redemption

Some umpires played ball, most didn't. Those who didn't, say it doesn't matter. Baseball writers say the same thing. I say, bullshit.

—Asinof, *Strike Zone*

During the pre-game locker room banter between umpires in Asinof's co-written 1994 novel *Strike Zone*, one of them launches into a mock-lyric rendition of "Take Me Out to the Ballgame." The basic message is that everyone hates umpires and wants to see them dead. This is immediately preceded by Asinof's autobiographical antihero, home plate umpire Ernie Kolacka, taking some cutting verbal abuse from his despised arch-rival, Ben Sirotta, who ironically (or possibly not ironically) predicts that before the contest is over, Kolacka will "invent a whole new strike zone."[2] The moment recalls an episode from Asinof's 1967 baseball novel, *The Bedfellow*, in which a party pianist segues from playing a dirge-like version of "Take Me Out" into an ironic (or possibly not ironic) lament for the bygone baseball career of antihero Mike Sorrell (see Chapter 9). Although Asinof's creation of these two works was separated by more than a quarter of a century, this similarity represents but one example of a clear thematic continuum. Among other things, both novels present vivid reflections of (and on) the novelist's long life and past works. Although Asinof only wrote half of *Strike Zone*, and was far from being pleased with the end result, the portions that he did write contain some of his most intensely personal thoughts on the national pastime, as well as his own small but indispensable place in that pastime's long, colorful history.

The three-decade interim separating *The Bedfellow* and *Strike Zone* saw, not surprisingly, many important changes in both the world at large and Asinof's career. In-between, Asinof produced nine full-length books (including *The 10-Second Jailbreak*, co-written like *Strike Zone*), numerous articles, interviews, withstood a hellacious legal struggle with producer David Susskind (see Chapter 6), and, perhaps most crucially, lived to see a very fine film adaptation in 1988 of *Eight Men Out*. This last item finally brought to Asinof, after years of involuntary exile in the literary wilderness, a long-overdue degree of recognition and supplemental income. It also rekindled his interest in writing, which had laid comparatively dormant during the early 1980s, after a period of manic productivity in the previous decade of the 1970s.[3] For one, it emboldened him to write a no-holds-barred account of 20th century American history, *1919: America's Loss of Innocence* (1991), a highly respected volume in the nonconformist tradition of dissident commentators such as Noam Chomsky and Asinof's old mentor, I. F. Stone. By the early 1990s, Asinof had definitely caught the writing bug again, and the final years of his long career would see a resurgent Indian summer of productivity, resulting in a significant number of important books and various shorter pieces. Baseball, which had always been near and dear to him, would remain so. The two baseball works dating from this later period, *Strike Zone* and *Off-Season* (see Part V of this study), would, in many ways, summarize and encapsulate his philosophy, thoughts fermenting in his imagination ever since he had first met a more-than-friendly Babe Ruth as a star-struck, seven-year-old child in New York City during Ruth's heyday of the mid–1920s.[4]

Asinof was about 75 years old when *Strike Zone* was published. In style, it represented another complete departure for him. The novel's diary-like, professional sports-insider realism had literary precedents going back to the 1950s with other works that had, as one might expect, been influenced in turn by Asinof's early books. The two granddaddies of all candid baseball diaries were *The Long Season* (1960) and *Pennant Race* (1962), both personally written (without a ghost author) by journeyman pitcher Jim Brosnan, respectively detailing his nomadic, roller coaster stints in 1959 and 1961 with the St. Louis Cardinals and Cincinnati Reds.[5] The stage for Brosnan's frank revelations about the professional game had been set in part by Asinof's groundbreaking novel, *Man on Spikes*, in 1955 (see Chapter 1).[6] After Asinof's sensational *Eight Men Out* appeared in 1963, this new trend in sports literature seemed to accelerate. Several noteworthy insider books about professional football appeared during the late 1960s, including, in 1968, Asinof's own *Seven Days Before Sunday* (see below). Then, in 1970, came the baseball tell-all to end all baseball tell-alls. Its rousing, unexpected commercial success came at a time when Asinof's own very fine New York trilogy of books, with the possible exception of *Seven Days*, was failing to make much of an impression on critics or the general reading public. Asinof was, understandably, among the tens of thousands of readers for whom the new release likely made a lasting impression.

The first edition of Jim Bouton's *Ball Four* detailed his initial, tumultuous comeback season in 1969 as a reinvented knuckleball hurler with the Seattle Pilots and Houston Astros. The book was presented in the form of an unvarnished, un-expunged diary-memoir. Its release provoked widespread fury and produced brisk sales, particularly when Bouton refused to retract a word of it under pressure. I well remember first reading the book as a sickly, emaciated 14-year-old while convalescing in a hospital bed. It had been given to me as a get-well gift from my older brother, helping me both to feel better and, strangely enough, have a sunnier outlook on life. The work also influenced my own then-germinating baseball philosophy (along with that of countless others), as a moderately successful amateur player over the next 10 years. *Ball Four* also taught the important lesson in baseball (and life) that one does not have to be a lock-step conformist or unthinking member of the herd in order to excel or win ballgames. In fact, in a tight competitive situation, non-conformism can sometimes be a tremendous asset. As for Jim Bouton, his long, tenacious, and much written about career as a player, sportscaster, and sportswriter needs little elaboration here.[7]

When asking how such two strong personalities as Eliot Asinof and Jim Bouton first came into contact with each other, it might be useful to keep a few things in mind. For one, Asinof was that most heinous of baseball species, a New York Yankee fan, and Bouton's glory years as a Major League pitcher had begun as a rookie with the Yankees in 1963.[8] This was the same year that Asinof's *Eight Men Out* first appeared in print. By the 1970s, both men were under heavy fire — Bouton from his former playing colleagues for revealing their off-field behavior in an unfiltered light, and Asinof for having previously exposed professional baseball's most shameful historical incident. At the nadir of Asinof's writing career during the late 1970s, he saw fit to give Bouton an honorable mention is his own memoir as the latter successfully struggled to achieve another brief Major League comeback as a player:

> As I write this, a thirty-nine-year-old ex-Big-League pitcher named Jim Bouton has given up a relatively lucrative broadcasting career, mortgaged his home, and destabilized his family for the unlikely but exquisite challenge of trying to make it back to the biggies. *He* knows where the beauty is.[9]

That is to say, Asinof recognized in Bouton something of a kindred spirit whose love of baseball trumped any love of money or prospect of short-term gain. This was a quality that the novelist could certainly admire and relate to, having made a few past sacrifices himself. It was also a quality that tended to alienate those less idealistic. Thus Asinof and Bouton were both, in a very real sense, outsiders to the baseball establishment, despite their unimpeachable professional playing résumés.

Asinof's previous works, both before and after the appearance Bouton's *Ball Four* franchise, had also laid the essential groundwork for the *Strike Zone* collaboration. The sports-gambling corruption motif pioneered by Asinof in *Eight Men Out* is, quite understandably, handled with ease. Direct reference to the Black Sox is made repeatedly in *Strike Zone*, as umpire-on-the-take Ernie Kolacka cites their precedent and scoffs at his own behavior with "Say it ain't so, Ernie."[10] In 1979, Asinof returned to the very same theme, but in a humorous, fictional context of professional football's Super Bowl with *Say It Ain't So, Gordon Littlefield* (see Chapter 6). In this novelette, Asinof assumes the first-person voice of a petty, corruptible and often absurdly grandiose narrator, a similar technique later employed with subtle effectiveness in *Strike Zone. Gordon Littlefield* also introduces the memorable character of Jake Kolacka, a colorful but mentally unstable defensive cornerback extraordinaire with the fictional world champion New York Bulls football club. Kolacka shares the fictional last name of Asinof's umpire-narrator in *Strike Zone*, and (as a character) is obviously based on the notorious real-life personality of Garrett Brock Trapnell, convicted skyjacker and subject of Asinof's controversial 1976 nonfiction masterpiece, *The Fox Is Crazy Too*. In *Strike Zone*, umpire Ernie Kolacka seems to gradually metamorphose into a more redemptive version of his earlier character prototypes, the reliably dishonest Jake Kolacka of *Gordon Littlefield* and criminally insane G. B. Trapnell from the *The Fox*. Something about this personality type obviously appealed to Asinof, as he used it as a vehicle to make some of his most personal and distinctive statements as a writer.

The Asinof book that perhaps best prepared the author for the *Strike Zone* project, however, was also one that had helped pave the way for Bouton's *Ball Four*. *Seven Days Before Sunday* was the second (and best) entry in Asinof's New York trilogy of the late 1960s, and documented in pure journalistic style one chaotic week in the life of Asinof's beloved New York Giants football club late during the 1967 season. The work was dedicated to Giants' team management who gave him both unrestricted locker room and sidelines access.[11] Asinof had successfully pitched the idea to them as a publicity perk, posing the same questions articulated in the book's introduction: "How was a club run? What were their lives like? How did they get along? What was it like in a training camp? What did they really go through on game days? A million questions that no one could answer except a man who had lived with them."[12] We would add that no one could answer these questions effectively except one who, like Asinof, was capable of empathizing with the players as athletes. This same insider's view of the rowdy side to professional sports, one running like a constant thread through all of Asinof's baseball writings, would be taken to a new, heightened level in *Strike Zone*. Somewhat predictably (because of its more familiar, popular layout), *Seven Days* was the only Asinof book in the late 1960s to receive anything resembling consistent praise. Robert Cromie of the *Chicago Tribune*, admittedly an Asinof fan to begin with, unabashedly called it "one of the finest sports books ever written." The more critical *New York Magazine* reported that "as a good battle painting gives us the smell of gunpowder, the author ... gives us that just-out-of-the-huddle feeling when everything — from triumph to tragedy — is imminent and possible."[13] Asinof himself perhaps gave the best assessment of *Seven Days*: "If this be childish, then let all good children make the most of it."[14] The same judgment could also well apply to *Strike Zone* (see Chapter 14), where boyish enthusiasm for baseball still abounds amidst some very adult-like problems.

Before examining at length the plot, structure, and thematic content of *Strike Zone*, it is appropriate to study the book's origins, particularly the well-known but infrequently discussed disputes developing between Asinof and Bouton soon after the novel was started, and intensifying as it progressed. Both Bouton and Asinof's son, Martin, were kind enough to share their versions of events during personal interviews, and I came away struck by their complete agreement on all main points of alleged contention. When asked how *Strike Zone* came into being, Bouton answered unequivocally: "It was all Eliot's idea. He called me."[15] The sports-gambling corruption theme, which always fascinated Asinof, would be used to tell a story in which an umpire is approached to throw a crucial year-end game. The story would be told in alternating chapters from the different viewpoints of the umpire and an opposing pitcher against whom the game will be fixed, with both having flashbacks of their lives in-between. It is very likely that Asinof had recently taken notice of Daniel Okrent's engaging *Nine Innings: The Anatomy of a Baseball Game* (1989), a blow-by-blow account of a 1982 contest between the Baltimore Orioles and Milwaukee Brewers.[16] No doubt Asinof felt he could up the ante with this kind of genre, and at some point hit upon the idea of recruiting Major League Baseball's best-known memoirist as co-author and marketing tool. Bouton recalled that he and Asinof had previously met at baseball-sports dinners: "I had always liked *Eight Men Out*, although I believe that it was the movie I saw first. We also lived not too far from each other, Eliot in upstate New York, and me in western Massachusetts."[17] It is unknown whether Asinof ever witnessed Bouton pitching in person, although it is more than likely that Asinof saw Bouton on television during the mid–1960s, given his unswerving, lifelong fan loyalty to the Yankees.[18]

When asked how the two of them got along while collaborating, Bouton was his usual candid self: "The truth? Not that well. I have to say, however, that since Eliot cannot answer for himself, it would not be fair to comment about it beyond a few general observations." Viking Press editor Al Silverman was quoted in the *New York Times* as saying, "As we went along, I wasn't an editor anymore ... I was a referee."[19] Bouton acknowledged that part of Asinof's anger resulted from Silverman's impartiality, which tended to rule in favor of Bouton during their disputes:

> Al was a saint. Originally, Eliot planned to write the first chapter, but Al wanted to lead with my chapter. Then, Eliot wanted to edit my writing, which he thought we had both agreed to, but in fact had not. Al took sides with me and allowed my original work to stand. By Chapter 6 (the sixth "inning"), Eliot and I were no

> longer speaking to each other. The final insult came with the book jacket. Viking gave my name top billing over Eliot's for marketing purposes. Eliot was not pleased.[20]

Martin Asinof's recall of events was essentially the same:

> Eliot knew the sportswriter who worked as Bouton's editor on *Ball Four*, and through him approached Bouton with the idea. Bouton had a large ego, though, and tried to take too much control of the project after it began. Eliot received a large advance for the book, but was so mad at one point that he tried to give it back to the publisher. The publisher told him, "Eliot, finish the book."[21]

Asinof's fury over ceding absolute control of the project after being paid a hefty retainer is reminiscent of his legal feud with David Susskind during the late 1970s, one proving nearly fatal to his writing career (see Chapter 6).[22] There too, Asinof was offered considerable money to let others have their way with *Eight Men Out*, but staunchly refused; in the process he seemingly alienated half of the people in the entertainment industry. For the *Strike Zone* project, at least insofar as the book went, he gave in after making loud protestations. The big difference, however, is that the end result in *Strike Zone* became much more worthwhile than any reconfigured and distorted television broadcast of *Eight Men Out* would have likely been.

The plot and structure of *Strike Zone* are deceptively simple. Sam Ward, a 35-year-old rookie pitcher (a character voice assumed by Bouton), gets his Major League debut start with the Chicago Cubs against the Philadelphia Phillies at Wrigley Field in the last game of the regular season. It is a crucial contest that will determine if the Cubs make the playoffs. Only Cub fans can perhaps fully appreciate the rarity of such an opportunity. Umpiring behind home plate is Ernie Kolacka (whose narration is assumed by Asinof), a 60-year-old veteran working the very last Major League game of his professional career. Kolacka, for reasons of personal friendship and financial insecurity, is on the take; he has been paid a handsome sum ($100,000) by gamblers to assist in throwing the game in favor of Philadelphia. The novel is structured as an inning-by-inning account, told alternatively from the opposing viewpoints of Ward (Bouton) and Kolacka (Asinof), plus repeated flashbacks from each of their dissatisfied, unfulfilled lives. The result may not be *War and Peace*, and far from what Asinof originally hoped for, but any baseball fan with a working knowledge and appreciation of the game — especially a former player — is likely to find numerous delights in this brisk, entertaining, and suspenseful read. Bouton is often a good writer while Asinof is usually a great writer, even when allegedly operating on auto-remote and under protest — not unlike Shoeless Joe Jackson still being a great ballplayer even when he was supposedly not trying his hardest. Bouton's writing by comparison is usually engaging but occasionally tedious — for example, his prolonged analogy of building a sturdy yard wall to effective pitching, successful marriage, and living the good life in general. The analogy is absolutely true, of course, but still can make slow going for the reader as pure sports fiction.[23] The novel is dedicated by Bouton to his wife Paula, and by Asinof, once again, "For my son, Martin."[24]

Both Asinof and Bouton perfectly capture the distinctive psychological warfare between pitcher and batter that lies at the heart of the game, albeit from opposing points of view. Both narrators clearly know from hard experience what it is like to stand on the playing field (see Chapter 15) This includes catching a ton of verbal abuse from the stands and opposing dugouts — another unique aspect of the sport. The old rookie getting "a cup of coffee" in the big time was a motif that appealed to both writers. Asinof set the standard in literature with his novel *Man on Spikes*, based on his friendship with Mickey Rutner. Bouton wrote autobiographically from his repeated attempted comebacks in the Majors lasting well into his late 30s. The choice of Cubs versus Phillies is also highly suggestive on several levels. Asinof had played in the Phillies farm system a generation earlier. He would have been well attune to the Philadelphia National League franchise's ancient reputation for being resistant to racial integration. In the novel, as far as one can tell, the Phillies' lineup is all white, whereas the Cubs are thoroughly (if somewhat uncomfortably) integrated as a team. Significantly, it was the rumored fixed match-up of these very two same clubs at Wrigley Field in the last game of the fated 1920 season which sparked an official investigation, one in turn leading to public exposure of the Black Sox Scandal from the previous year's World Series.[25]

Not surprisingly, the shadow of the 1919 Series hangs over the plot in *Strike Zone*, but in subtle ways only to be recognized by those versed in history. For example, when Kolacka's subcontracting father is caught ripping off a general contractor, he makes no apologies to his thunderstruck son: "He's a crook. I'm a crook. That's the building trades kiddo."[26] The remark strongly recalls Abe Attell's justification of the 1919 fix as "cheaters cheating cheaters."[27] Kolacka reassures himself with a reminder that umpires can appear foolish without necessarily being crooked, citing the 1919 Series as an example.[28] His offhand comment that "catchers are likely to be hotheads" immediately calls to mind the upright but volatile White Sox catcher from 1919, Ray Schalk, famous for his short temper.[29] In *Strike Zone*, Asinof repeats the same off-color joke about porcupines that helped break the ice with former Black Sox Happy Felsch while researching *Eight Men Out*.[30] Resolution at the end of the novel, i.e., a dramatic Cub game victory and playoff birth, ultimately comes across as a kind of belated redemption for Major League Baseball following the distant tragic events of 1919. This runs parallel to the unlikely personal redemptions achieved by Kolacka and Ward in the final chapters.

The equation of Kolacka with Asinof is unmistakable. Kolacka, like Asinof, has Long Island roots (p. 98), is a former, promising minor league ballplayer (p. 75), maintains a similar, lean athletic physique throughout life, is abstemious when it comes to drinking and smoking, and later turns to golf as a personal pastime (p. 11).[31] Kolacka is recruited into professional umpiring by a former Phillies player, just as Asinof had been recruited into the Phillies farm system as a young man (p. 101).[32] Early in his umpiring career, Kolacka shows strong labor sympathies and is labeled as a troublemaker by the baseball establishment, calling to mind Asinof's pro-labor, combative reputation and early blacklisting as a writer. First, Kolacka gets into hot water by sticking to a controversial call made against a popular local player in Moultrie, Georgia, the same town and league (Georgia-Florida) where Asinof first played professional ball in 1940 (p. 113). Then, to the chagrin of his materialistic wife, he shows solidarity with other umpires during their strike (pp. 86–87). Like Asinof's Mike Kutner from *Man on Spikes*, Kolacka's dedication to baseball causes him to miss being at his father's deathbed and suffer odium from his family as a result (p. 145). Kolacka also reiterates Kutner's famous battle cry and slogan recurring reoccurring throughout Asinof's literary work (see Chapter 1), "Fuck 'em all, big and small." (p. 142) As with Asinof at the time of the novel's writing, Kolacka is advanced in age and nearing the end of a long career.[33] Above all, Kolacka strongly believes that good professional umpires should be former professional players (see chapter header quote), as both he and his real-life creator, Asinof, had previously been.[34]

Asinof, despite all objections and misgivings, completed his reluctant collaboration with Bouton, and *Strike Zone* went to press in 1994. Although it failed to achieve anything remotely resembling blockbuster sales, the finished product revealed a bevy of fascinating details and valuable insights into Asinof's baseball mentality. Those who now read it generally found themselves entertained without necessarily having to know anything special about its unusual co-authors; moreover, none of the details from Asinof would have likely ever come to light otherwise. It had been a very long time since he had mused at length about the team sport which he loved the most; since then, both the game and the world, including his personal and professional life, had seen countless changes. Among these was the legal dismantlement of Major League Baseball's hated reserve clause, which had been at the center of his first three books produced between 1955 and 1967. It would be another six years before he produced his next full-length work on the national pastime. In the mean time, Asinof's literary career (and notoriety) would proceed apace. Within five years of *Strike Zone*'s appearance, he would be fittingly invited to Cooperstown, New York, as a keynote speaker at the Baseball Hall of Fame. By the time the 20th century had ended, it would become apparent that beneath the surface of novel's somewhat frivolous, gimmicky veneer, lay some of Asinof's most heartfelt baseball observations and feelings since those recorded for *Bleeding Between the Lines* in 1979. Part of Asinof's frustrations, many unfathomable at the time, are now evident in that he originally envisioned a much bolder and more grandiose project than eventually released to the public.[35] His greater, unfulfilled ambition, however, only becomes more apparent in the aftermath of the novel's lukewarm sales. On a brighter note, and for possibly the first time in his writing career, Asinof appears to have made more money on a project than his publishers. This was in spite of this prickly and one-of-kind artist attempting to offer them a refund.

14

"A Routine Complimentary Nod from One Pro to Another"

Strike Zone would be the last project in which Eliot Asinof worked with a major publishing house.[1] As he saw it, he had come to Viking with a good idea, grand ambitions, and a marketable co-author, only see the final product comprised and then commercially tank. For him, it was a depressingly familiar pattern observed over a long career, and one not to be repeated in the relatively short time that he had left to write. Nearly two decades in hindsight, however, the offsets of his disappointment are that Asinof was (for a change) reasonably paid for his services, and, more remarkably perhaps, *Strike Zone* holds up fairly well both as pure entertainment and as personal statements by the co-authors, especially as sports novels go. Asinof at his worst was still a better novelist than many others at their best. Regarding the precise reasons why Viking was unable to recoup its investment in sales, we suspect these had more to do with the declining reading habits of the general public, especially among sports fans, than for any lack of trying on the part of those involved in the book's production. Asinof, even at his most commercially successful (i.e., *Eight Men Out*) was never a marquee name attraction like Jim Bouton, that is, big enough to automatically place itself within the *New York Times* best seller list. As to the failure of Bouton's celebrity to achieve that for Asinof, it is possible that Bouton fans failed to get exactly what they were looking for in *Strike Zone* either. For one, they were getting fiction, as opposed to the controversial nonfiction that they had come to expect from the Bouton brand name. Perhaps the two would have been better off in terms of sales by collaborating on nonfiction, at which they both excelled. Then again, it is possible that Asinof's distinctive style and content were too incompatible with any broad market appeal to ever reach a wide audience. He was often just too dark, too knowledgeable, and completely incapable of pandering to ignorance, superstition, and prejudice. As such, he would have made a lousy newscaster or ad man — distasteful skills which all consistently best-selling authors must cultivate to some degree, whether they want to or not.[2]

One cannot blame book reviewers for *Strike Zone*'s lackluster sales at the time of its release. They paid attention, and in general, they liked it. *Publishers Weekly* gushed: "This inspired collaboration melds the humor of Bouton's *Ball Four* and the darkness of Asinof's *Eight Men Out*. It's an exciting read with an ending that will make fans cheer."[3] *Library Journal* concurred: "This is a terrific story about two men who love and need baseball as well as a suspenseful story about one important game. Strongly recommended."[4] *Booklist* was slightly more circumspect, but still positive: "As drama this is as predictable as *Rocky*; as a thoughtful study of two men facing a personal crossroad, though, it works well.... This is a readable and reasonably entertaining baseball thriller that will profit from the Bouton name on the title page."[5] Most other reviews were in a similar vein: a few quibbles expressed, but by far and away these were outweighed by superlatives. To this day, and in spite of all the hurdles that the novel presents, those who take the trouble to read *Strike Zone* usually come away satisfied customers, often knowing little if anything about its famous co-authors. Any quick read of the artless reviews posted on Amazon or other internet sources will confirm this. My own opinion is pretty much the same, if for no other reason because Asinof was probably incapable of writing a truly bad book. Some works are naturally better than others, and some have their undeniable problems, but all are well worth the paper they are printed on. Not very many writers can boast this.

The sad irony of this positive critical reception is that Asinof himself expressed a very low personal opinion of *Strike Zone*; and in the final analysis, it must be admitted that this novel, in spite of its many virtues, also represents the weakest entry in his baseball catalogue. One simple reason for this comparative weakness is that, because of the very nature of its co-authorship, it is the shortest of his five baseball books. In a 251-page novel, Asinof writes approximately 115 pages, or less than half of the total. That which he does write is splendid, but there is just not enough of it to rank next to the masterpieces coming both before and after. Even his last baseball novel, *Off-Season*, at 149 pages has larger pages, smaller font sizes, more words, more gravitas, and, above all, a calculated compression and thoroughness in exposition not to be found in *Strike Zone*. Asinof's own assessment was brutal, telling at least one stunned admirer that he hated *Strike Zone*, "thought it was garbage" and sneered at anyone who liked it.[6] Bouton's critical view in distant retrospect was more balanced and philosophical—a view that I happen to share. When asked if he was personally satisfied with the result, Bouton replied, "Yes, even though the writing experience was not as enjoyable as I thought it might be."[7] In spite of Asinof's undisguised loathing, *Strike Zone* remains a fine baseball novel, as well as one of the most unusual ones that readers are likely to ever encounter. Perhaps it is fitting for this uncompromising author that critical praise and proper financial remuneration should exclude his own approval of the endeavor. His most-disliked baseball book coming from his own typewriter was in fact the slightest one that he ever produced, and a money loser for his high-profile publisher thrown into the bargain.

Fast forward five years from the publication of *Strike Zone* to 1999. For its end-of-the-20th century (and 60th anniversary) celebration, the Baseball Hall of Fame invited Asinof to be keynote speaker for its annual Cooperstown Symposium on Baseball and American Culture.[8] A more appropriate guest could not have been selected.[9] No writer before or since has better understood the game from both a literary and playing perspective than Asinof; no writer has better understood the larger societal context into which fits the national pastime. The main content of the speech is summarized in "Asinof: A Baseball Life" by Tim Wiles.[10] Although neither article nor, presumably, the speech mentioned *Strike Zone*, it touched upon several commonalities with the novel, while shedding new light on more than one of these shared points of interest. For example, Asinof recounted his wave-making, one-month tour as a minor league player in Moultrie, Georgia, a town and league repeatedly referenced by Kolacka in *Strike Zone* (see Chapter 13). As one would expect, Asinof commented upon the sports-gambling theme which he had introduced with the nonfiction *Eight Men Out* and later continued with fictional works such as *Strike Zone*. Referring to himself, Wiles commented, "This columnist sat in the audience thinking that there are no stories better than our true life stories, at least if we have lived lives as full as Asinof's."[11] If nothing else, the comment underscores how the power and realism of Asinof's fiction is routinely buttressed by events from his personal life; moreover, as noted throughout this study, the line dividing Asinof's fiction and nonfiction works was sometimes blurred by his novelistic style and journalistic approach to subject matter.

With Asinof's speech at Cooperstown came another revelation. He spoke of his 1941 playing experience in Wausau, Wisconsin, which was also his last season as a minor leaguer. On this basis alone, the summer Asinof spent in Wausau — the last one before world war broke out — would have likely made a big impression on his psyche as a 21-year-old, future baseball writer of note; however, there was more. In an almost jocular vein, Asinof (according to Wiles) related how he played well for the team but was fired, not only for being Jewish, but, more egregiously, for having an unrequited, potential romance with "the team owner's teenage daughter."[12] For a man who, at various times in his young adulthood, was reportedly involved with the likes of Kim Hunter, Rito Moreno, and Jocelyn Brando, the rumor of a forbidden platonic affair with an anonymous Midwestern girl while playing minor league ball would normally be of little or no interest. Indifference, however, changes to fascination when one realizes that in *Strike Zone* (Asinof's latest novel at that moment in time), the semi-autobiographical character of Ernie Kolacka has an unhappy, nagging wife of some 40 years who hails from Wausau, Wisconsin. If this aspect of the novel is indeed based on fact, as were so many other of Asinof's fictional conceits, then the prominent character of Enid Wynant Kolacka from *Strike Zone* deserves some additional commentary, which shall be provided to the best of our ability in Chapter 16 of this section. If true, it would then also throw Asinof's 1999 Cooperstown address into a new perspective, a Shakespearean "What's past is prologue" aspect to Asinof's work (including *Strike Zone*), as it must have been indelibly shaped by the baseball and non-baseball experiences of his youth.[13]

Before delving into these sensitive biographical aspects, however, it is important to emphasize that the young Eliot Asinof came to Wausau to play professional baseball, not to get into trouble with the locals. In his own writings, this is the focus, and should also receive priority in this study. Almost four decades after the fact, Asinof wistfully wrote of his time spent in the minors: "It was a time of learning and self-appraisal. I came to understand my limitations as well as my talents, especially in the presence of ballplayers better equipped than I."[14] He was particularly nostalgic about Wausau, where on a very competitive field he had once played his best. The pinnacle moment of his success as a ballplayer was recalled by Asinof the memoirist with obvious relish, and deserves extensive quotation:

> One summer the Phillies sent me to their Class-C farm club in Wausau, Wisconsin. The playing manager was an ex-Big League third baseman named Wally Gilbert, broken down at forty with an expanding waistline and a propensity for too much whiskey. In the late innings of a close game, I was on first with one out when Wally came to bat and gave me the hit-and-run sign. The third baseman was playing deep, protecting the line against a sharply pulled extra-base hit that might permit me to score. I took off on the pitch as Wally laid down a perfect bunt, and as the third baseman made a desperate try to throw him out, I rounded second on high, for third was being left unguarded. At it turned out, it was perfect, absolutely perfect. I stood on the base like a king of the hill, smiling across the diamond at Wally, safely on first, breathing heavily from his sprint, hands on hips, cap down low over his eyes. He met my eye and nodded, a routine complimentary nod from one pro to another. He was over twice my age, but he did not patronize. Though we had never practiced the play — nor even discussed trying it — he knew I would get there. And that's what made it so perfect.[15]

Readers should take note that Asinof is not writing about hitting a home run, or scoring a winning run, or even getting on base. He is writing about his beloved "inside" game (see Chapter 3), in which teammates cleverly work together with improvised skill to achieve a desired result. Only a former player would cherish such a memory; non-players are far less likely to understand such things, let alone write about them.

Asinof does not stop there. He goes on to assert that this represented not merely a bucolic moment during his bygone playing days, but also one that encapsulated his personal reasons for playing baseball in the first place. In short, it was one of the happiest moments in his life:

> I'd been accustomed to hearing people at home say that I was a fool to play ball. I'd never make it to the Big Leagues, they'd tell me. My college education, the cum-laude degree, all that high-cultured energy was being wasted. I should be pursuing a real career, settling down, making money. Baseball was for farm boys, etc., etc. At the time, I didn't know how to answer them. It wasn't until I joined them, years later, that I realized how wrong they were. What did they ever do that was more beautiful than that moment in Wausau?[16]

The author who wrote these words was an unusual combination of athletic and literary ability, the latter shaped in large part by an enviable humanist education in formal institutions well-known for producing outstanding intellectual talent. That Asinof graduated with simultaneous academic and athletic honors was by itself exceptional.[17] That upon graduation he more than willingly threw himself into the world of professional baseball for starvation wages and a ton of abuse more than speaks for itself. The *Strike Zone* collaboration of the early 1990s may have been Asinof's first and only attempt to come to grips with his unique sojourn in the form of popular fiction. It was a novelist's way of looking back at his own life, in some respects far more effective and revealing than any tell-all memoir or autobiography.

Though it may seem counterintuitive, perhaps the best way to fully understand Asinof's dismissive attitude towards *Strike Zone* is to take a brief detour into the novelist's baseball past; specifically, his final season as a player in Wausau deserves additional scrutiny. To put it euphemistically, a search for ghosts may be in order here. Fortunately for baseball biographers, the documentary record of that summer is there for everyone to see in the sports sections and box scores of the local newspaper. Wausau, Wisconsin, has always been a baseball town. Although no longer home to a minor league franchise, Wausau baseball fans today still enthusiastically support the semiprofessional Wisconsin Woodchucks of the Northwoods League, a convenient summer outlet for collegiate and aspiring professional players, many of whom are Major League draft picks.[18] Having attended several games during the 2010 season, I can attest that the overall quality of play is very high. The Woodchucks play their home games at Athletic Park, the exact same venue in Wausau that a young Eliot Asinof played in during the 1941 season. Originally built (like many other ballparks) as a Works Administration Project in 1936, the stadium that Asinof frequented would have been relatively new at the time (five years old), and somewhat different in appearance.[19] Since 1941 numerous additions and renovations have been made to expand seating capacity and amenities, but the park is still ringed by an original, distinctive wall made of red granite (indigenous to the region), more or less retains its original dimensions, and is still surrounded by a working-class neighborhood. The feel of the stadium is intimate (expanded seating still holds less than 4,000 spectators); the outfield fencing retains a multi-colored polyglot of billboard advertisements, reminiscent of the Depression era in which it was first constructed. Asinof would surely still recognize the place. It was here that he achieved the apex of his baseball playing skills during the summer of 1941, before suddenly and mysteriously vanishing from the official record as a professional athlete.

The Wausau Lumberjacks of the Northern League in 1941 were a Class C affiliate of the Philadelphia Phillies. Though featuring some fine talent and distinguished personnel (including former 1919 White Sox Dickie Kerr as manager in 1937), the Lumberjacks had never dominated their league, which historically was very competitive.[20] Different, however, would be 1941 with Wausau fielding a team that would go on to win the regular season league title, the only time in fact this distinction would ever be achieved by a Wausau-based Northern League club. It was for this unusually stellar outfit on an opening day road game in La Crosse, Wisconsin, on May 6, 1941, that Eliot Asinof was chosen to be the starting centerfielder and second hitter in the batting order. He went 1-3 at the plate, including a "sharp hit to right, scoring two more runners" during a 5th inning rally which tied the game at 3-3, before the contest was called after seven innings on account of rain. The next day (May 7), the Wausau newspaper carried a group photograph of the Lumberjacks' opening day starting lineup in full uniforms and warm-up jackets, including Asinof, then not yet 22 years old and standing second from the left.[21] It was an auspicious beginning, but for him the season would come to a discouraging halt less than two months later.

For the next 41 days (until June 17), Asinof played centerfield and hit at a torrid .328 clip, peaking at .337 on June 6, as the Lumberjacks got off to an unusually fast start.[22] In *Strike Zone*, Kolacka happily recalls himself as a very young minor leaguer hitting well over .300 before the war came and ended his playing career.[23] The details between the fictional Kolacka and the real-life Asinof vary, but the sentiment was likely much the same. His most impressive game came on June 2, in which he made the news byline with "Asinof Has Perfect Day at Bat with Four Hits" and was a defensive standout in centerfield. The local "Sports Chatter" reported that "the flashy play in last night's ball game was the catch of a fly ball by Asinof within a few inches of the right field fence."[24] This feat brings to mind Mike Kutner's spectacular centerfield catch made near the wall in the opening chapter from *Man on Spikes*.[25] Even as Asinof was hitting the cover off the ball, however, he was still willing to successfully execute a sacrifice bunt when called to do so, or continue playing while suffering from a charley horse.[26] It is no wonder that he reportedly had a good relationship with Lumberjacks manager and ex-big leaguer Wally Gilbert, who was probably more than pleased to have a newcomer who could hit, field, bunt, run, and think. Such players are rare commodities at any competitive level, but especially in the professional ranks.[27]

From this high point of accomplishment in mid–June came what was probably inevitable, at least in terms of Asinof's playing performance. He fell victim to a malaise far worse (if you ask any ballplayer) than physical injury or intimidating opponents—he entered into a prolonged, incurable batting slump. Beginning on June 17 and extending nine days and six games to June 25, Asinof's batting average fell from .328 to .296. He barely hit his own weight during this time frame. There were also disruptions on the playing field. On June 19, he was switched from batting second in the order to the leadoff slot, a much more difficult assignment, especially for someone like Asinof who had a swinging mentality at the plate and did not take very many base on balls.[28] Asinof once remarked that some umpires aware of his being Jewish liked to expand the strike zone whenever he came to the plate; pitch selectivity for hitting therefore became almost impossible.[29] The anecdote immediately summons forth the very title of *Strike Zone*, as well as Kolacka's repeated cynical musings on the topic (see Chapter 15). The problem occurs in other Asinof works as well, such as *The Bedfellow*, in which an incredulous Mike Sorrell must endure the absurd called strikes of an unfriendly umpire.[30] Then on June 23, Asinof was shifted from playing centerfield to right field, ostensibly to make room for more productive hitters in the lineup.[31] Here, *Man on Spikes* is again recalled, as an angry Mike Kutner is ordered by management to move from his accustomed centerfield position to left field so that the team's promising new African American recruit, Ben Franks, can feel more comfortable.[32]

For Asinof, the unhappy and unexpected end finally came on June 25. According to the brief newspaper account, Asinof, while playing right field, crossed signals with his centerfielder teammate and the two collided, causing a fly ball to be dropped. This mishap in turn sparked an opposing team rally and Wausau went on to lose the game.[33] This factual episode in Asinof's playing career is almost identical to repeated incidents from *Man on Spikes* in which Kutner and Franks have trouble communicating with each other in the outfield, causing errors, bruised bodies, and team dissent (see Chapter 1).[34] It also calls to mind a lengthy passage from *The Bedfellow*, in which Mike Sorrell's committing an outfield error compounds into a hitless performance, with his team losing the game in the process (see Chapter 9).[35] In *Strike Zone*, there is nothing directly comparable, although Kolacka's on-field clash with despised umpire-rival Ben Sirotta over a controversial interference call comes across in many ways as a metaphor or allegory for the same kind of conflict. In the story, the interference play, which favors the home team, is initially ruled not to be interference by Sirotta, whom Kolacka considers to be a "homer" (an umpire always favoring the home team from fear of the crowd) and ignorant of the rules besides. Kolacka overrules Sirotta, calls interference, and in the process incurs the wrath of everyone in the stadium except for the visiting team. When a nearby Cubs fan shouts out, "*Kolacka, you're dead! You are dead*," the beleaguered home plate umpire has stadium security remove him. Kolacka's unpopular decision stands.[36] The most interesting aspect of this scene is that Kolacka, though on the take, is able in this instance to makes things work in his favor by being honest, even to the point of taking abuse for it. Taken in isolation, this unusual passage in *Strike Zone* seems to reinforce the hard lesson that popular notions of justice and fairness can be as skewed in baseball as in all other things. Asinof was surely well acquainted with the feeling, based on experiences such as colliding with an outfielder teammate.

Remarkably, after the June 26 newspaper account of the previous day's game, Asinof's name never again appeared in a Wausau box score nor was ever mentioned again by the Wausau sports press. He presumably left the team at that point or, more likely, was "fired" (as he put it). He had played in a total of 41 games, batted 162 times, and gotten on base 54 times with 48 hits, including four doubles and one triple. The Lumberjacks went on to win the league regular season title, but were defeated by an interleague rival during the post-season playoffs.[37] Sometime soon after this, but before Pearl Harbor was bombed on December 7, Asinof enlisted in the military, and thus began a brand new chapter in his unsettled life. He was still only 22 years old, but was permanently finished playing professional baseball, although he would continue to dabble in the sport right into middle age, long after he had become established as a professional writer. Notwithstanding Asinof's own explanation during his 1999 Cooperstown address, the sudden unfavorable turn of events that summer in Wausau is puzzling. Those of us who have played the game of baseball beyond sandlot level know the consequences of a batting slump combined with making a bad play in the field, if indeed Asinof made a bad play in the field during the game in question. One is booed, yelled at, or benched — but rarely let go from a team unless there are other external factors at work. Often mediocre performance is used as an excuse to cashier a player for other unspoken reasons, when other athletes far less productive are kept on. As for Asinof, his explosive temper was legendary. Perhaps words were exchanged with the wrong people. This difficult but essential topic will be further explored in Chapters 15 and 16 of this study.

Kolacka's salvation in *Strike Zone* comes on the final pitch of the game, when he decides to call a strike a strike, even though this will allow the wrong team (the Cubs) to win the game, thus thwarting the gamblers already having paid him off. At crunch time, Kolacka just cannot bring himself to go through with the dishonest scheme, which otherwise would be a betrayal of his entire, unblemished career. Unlike Mike Sorrell in the final chapter from *The Bedfellow*, Kolacka is, in the end, able to look at himself in the mirror: "My ugly face is beautiful. It's a face that says 'Fuck you' to the world but not to itself."[38] At the end of the day, Asinof and his alter-ego Kolacka choose to remember the things about baseball that they cherished, rather than the disappointments and missteps, such as the "routine complimentary nod" that Asinof once received from an appreciative Wausau coach during happier times. If *Strike Zone* failed as a novel to achieve what Asinof had originally set out to do, which appears to have been obtaining a sort of closure and peace in his long, up-and-down relationship with the national pastime, then his final baseball book, *Off-Season*, would seem to successfully accomplish that only a few years later (see Part V of this study). In the mean time, however, Asinof and his collaborator Jim Bouton managed, either intentionally or not, to raise some provocative, deeper questions about the game and American professional sports in general. To these more subtle issues we now shall turn our attention in the next chapter.

15

The Anatomy of a Slump

Question: When is a ball not a ball? Answer: When the umpire says it's a strike.

—Asinof, *Strike Zone*[1]

Any typical baseball fan who picks up *Strike Zone* for a casual read is likely to come away a bit unsettled by Asinof's contribution to the novel. Although readers who have taken trouble to go through the volume generally come away satisfied, they will also tend to miss, ignore, or downplay some very disturbing undercurrents running throughout the text. Critics and reviewers who superficially praised the book were uniformly silent on these deeper implications as well. If Asinof were alive and here to comment, no doubt he would deny that any such subtleties exist; he would probably assert that he was simply churning out pulp to fulfill a contract obligation when he wrote it. Be that as it may, Asinof the writer on autopilot still tends to be far more engaging and provocative than most other authors. In-between the lines of his least-artistically successful baseball book can be found some vexing questions rarely posed elsewhere in the world of sports literature. Whether these more thoughtful aspects of the work were manifested in a conscious manner by the novelist, we are not prepared to say—more likely, these were unconsciously or instinctively brought forth. In either event, the questions are certainly worth further exploration. When Asinof grudgingly forced himself to complete *Strike Zone*, he did all sports readers a big favor, and in the process managed to put his finger (yet once more) on some of the most unique and distinctive qualities of the national pastime, setting it quite apart from other sports.

That Asinof was able to accomplish such an unusual feat—create something profound when he was just trying to put an unpleasant task behind him—can be attributed mainly to two factors. The first and rather obvious component is that he was a prodigiously talented and vastly experienced writer, placing him within a very small group of people on this basis alone. The second was that he also happened to be a former professional ballplayer. When

I spoke with Jim Bouton on this topic and asked him to comment, Bouton was his usual articulate self— not too surprisingly, since the same two factors applied to him as a former professional athlete turned writer:

> Number one, personal experience gives any writer an emotional edge. Through the experience, a writer actually feels all of the ups and downs, the worries and doubts, which make the descriptions more believable and credible. Secondly, experience allows a writer to see the full picture. If you play baseball, you not only know what it is like to play the game, you also know what it's like before and after the game — the long bus rides, the players hanging out at some bar at 2 AM, etc. It gives you a certain perspective that non-playing writers can only guess at.[2]

Bouton, like Asinof, is a baseball writer who also played the game professionally, albeit at a much higher competitive level. Both Asinof and Bouton have demonstrated that the best writing on any subject, baseball or otherwise, is crucially informed by personal experience. One could easily go further and assert that attempted writing on any subject matter in the absence of personal experience on that topic will have inherent and severe limitations, at least in terms of realism and insight.

WEDNESDAY EVENING, MAY 7, 1941

BATTING ORDER FOR OPENING GAME—Manager Wally Gilbert today announced the batting order for the opening Northern league game at Athletic park between the Wausau Lumberjacks and Superior Blues, which starts at 4:30 o'clock Thursday afternoon. They are shown

Asinof, age 21, second from left, batting second in the lineup and playing centerfield for the Wausau Lumberjacks on opening day, May 6, 1941, in La Crosse, Wisconsin. The summer of 1941, Asinof's last professional playing season in the Philadelphia Phillies organization, was an eventful one, and later that year (before Pearl Harbor) he would enlist.

In the case of Asinof, we dealing with a writer of outstanding ability and education to begin with, one who repeatedly demonstrated a facility for writing memorably on a wide variety of subject matter. Additionally, this high quality level was consistently achieved over a very long period of time, over half a century to be precise. In the case of his baseball writings, the excellence of these works were also bolstered by his two summers of playing experience in the minor leagues, in addition to a notable athletic career in college and high school before that time. One can add to all of this Asinof's continued attachment to the game on an amateur and semiprofessional level after he hung up his spikes as a player. It is no wonder then that his baseball writings, taken as a whole, stand thoroughly apart in a vast and highly competitive field. For the attentive and appreciative reader, there can be no mistaking Asinof's baseball books for those of any other writer.

Nowhere is Asinof's intimate knowledge (and Bouton's as well, for that matter) of baseball more apparent than in *Strike Zone*'s jaundiced view of official, written game rules, rules that (as the reader is constantly reminded) set baseball completely in a class by itself and distinct from other American sports. The nebulously worded rulebook for the game, ever-open to varying interpretations, is explored at regular intervals, including slippery concepts such as base-running interference, pitching balks, and (of course) the imprecise notion of a strike zone itself. Above all, in baseball cheating is tolerated as long as you can get away it. Like the ancient Spartans, one is punished in baseball not for cheating, but for getting caught cheating. The novelty of *Strike Zone* is that the only dishonest people on the diamond are two of the umpires — Kolacka, who knows fully well that he is being dishonest, and Kolacka's foil-antagonist, Sirotta, who is ignorant, greedy, petty, and hypocritical, but does not even realize it, let alone admit it. The corollary to allowed cheating (if effectively disguised) is that vigorous argument with umpires by players and coaches is always allowed, and is vividly presented by Asinof the novelist in all of its cantankerous glory. The fans get into the act as well — another unique aspect of baseball culture — and often there are loud exchanges between the stands and the playing field.[3] After Kolacka makes a series of damaging, crooked calls against the home team, a woman in the front rows heckles him: "Damn you, umpire. If you were my husband, I'd poison your coffee!" Kolacka shoots back: "Lady, if you were my wife, I'd drink it!"[4] The irrepressible torrent of verbal abuse, the ragging and heckling from the stands, opposing dugouts, players and umpires are unforgettably portrayed from the unfortunate recipient's viewpoint on the playing field. Kolacka reflects that "baseball is the only game where managers can come out on the field to humiliate you. It's the only game where fans believe in their right to abuse you."[5] Only a former player or perhaps umpire would truly know what this barrage was like; moreover, in the case of Asinof, he usually knew how to write humorously about it.

And then there is the definition of the strike zone. Kolacka bitterly recalls one of his early umpiring experiences in the Georgia-Florida League (where Asinof actually played in 1940) in which making an honest call ended up costing him both reputation and money. For him, the lesson was simple: "If you want to survive, pal, you've got to know the real difference between a ball and a strike."[6] In another passage, Kolacka has it broken down into mathematical terms:

> The plate is 17 inches wide with a black beveled edge, and the ball is 2½ inches in diameter, any part of which nicks a corner, it's a strike, stretching the strike zone to 22 inches if you have a mind to. Stretch it for Greene. Squeeze it for Ward. Baseball is a game of inches.[7]

Readers looking for contested calls on borderline pitches (both arbitrary and intentional) in *Strike Zone* are not to be disappointed. A climatic moment comes at the end of the seventh inning when Kolacka calls a third strike that should have been a ball on fictionalized Chicago Cub Leon Banks. The intended result, at the expense of Banks, is that a potential Cubs rally is snuffed out. Bank's outspoken fury at the injustice of Kolacka's decision provokes a near donnybrook on the field until, as so often happens in baseball, the team manager physically intervenes to save one of his key players from being ejected.[8] Earlier, Kolacka had boasted to himself how no fewer than three Philadelphia runs were, in effect, manufactured by his own biased umpiring efforts: "Three runs created by me. I gave Kruk, the leadoff man, two balls that should have been strikes and walked him. That's all it took."[9] Disturbingly, the home crowd, though it hates Kolacka and hurls endless insults at him, never seems to suspect his crookedness because of the baseball veteran's subtle knowledge of the game.

Kolacka's mistreatment of Banks, as well as the fallout, both have racial overtones, since the latter is an African American player. Though there is no indication that Kolacka is an overt racist, his thoughts leading up to making the call are cavalier and callous. He resents Banks' elaborate batting rituals and "equipment-adjustment dance" before Kolacka decides to "let him [Banks] hear the bad news with a shriek and a vicious strike thrust of my right fist to punch him out."[10] Earlier, Kolacka mocks Banks as "the Cubs' multi-million-dollar hot-shit left-handed cleanup hitter" who "comes up swinging four bats ... over and under like he's a giant baton twirler."[11] Kolacka's animosity is foreshadowed several innings earlier as he angrily recalls once having to eject an African American batter for throwing his bat. This occurred after the batter had first endured racist taunts from the catcher, then struck out swinging in frustration. The end result was that Kolacka was unfairly—at least in this instance—labeled a racist by fans, media, and even the league president.[12] If Asinof's later memories about suddenly expanding strike zones for Jewish American batters such as himself during the pre–World War II era were at all accurate (and they probably were), then he would have been writing from hard personal experience in this instance. The question is also naturally raised whether this type of double standard, combined with the obligatory race baiting typical of the era, contributed to Asinof's sudden batting slump during the month of June, 1941, while playing for the Wausau Lumberjacks.[13] Did a tantrum or outburst similar to the one displayed by Banks in *Strike Zone* help set the stage for Asinof's eventual downfall as a professional ballplayer?

Another example of Asinof's casual, first-hand knowledge of the game comes in *Strike Zone*'s repetitive, satirical musings on the balk rule. If Kolacka's strict, by-the-book interpretation of runner interference against Sammy Sosa during the fifth inning makes him the most unpopular person in Wrigley Field, then his back-to-back balk rulings against both team pitchers causes mainly bewilderment among all concerned. Kolacka loves the balk rule, and rightly so since it empowers him to decisively affect a game's outcome without having to justify himself:

> Who knows what a balk is? Every year there's a different interpretation. Every umpire makes his own judgment. Sometimes I see games on TV, the pitcher makes moves, you'd think there was no such thing as a balk. A balk is anything an umpire claims he saw.[14]

First he calls a balk against the Phillies' pitcher Greene (p. 166), then against the Cubs' pitcher Ward (p. 182). In-between, he recalls almost with pride how one his past balk rulings in the minor leagues "set off a twenty-minute rhubarb" (p. 141). With less fondness, Kolacka also remembers one of his angry wife's parting shots against him: "You're gonna die a loser, Ernie. Your last words will be 'Balk! Balk!'" (p. 145). Thus the traditional arbitrary nature of the balk rule's selective enforcement casts suspicion on its very use, whether it be appropriate or not in any given case.[15] Kolacka's flippant view of the concept as a sort of all-purpose escape hatch in any situation might easily, as his wife bitterly reminds him, prove one day to be his final undoing.

Some creative things are done by the players in *Strike Zone* which do not involve breaking or bending any rules, but are actions that only former players would likely be familiar with nonetheless. During the third inning, Ward (as described in detail by Bouton) fends off a Philadelphia rally by fielding an intended sacrifice bunt and quickly throwing to third base (being covered by the Cubs shortstop, a prearranged play without coaching consent) for a crucial force out.[16] Kolacka is impressed, "I've got to admit. Ward's play on that bunt was masterful."[17] As a baseball story plot device, the thwarted sacrifice bunt is both surprising and reminiscent of Asinof's experiences playing minor league ball in Wausau (see Chapter 14). There, according to his memoir, the 21-year-old Asinof rushed from first base to third on his player-coach's sacrifice when the third and first basemen rushed in to field the bunt while the shortstop and second baseman covered second and first, respectively, leaving third base uncovered. Asinof wistfully wrote of this moment as if it were the high point of his playing career.[18] In *Strike Zone*, however, the tables are turned in a very similar situation; the shortstop covers third (instead of second) and base runner is thrown out. To make the action more plausible, runners are placed on first and second base, rather than just first, thereby making the prearranged movement more justifiable, although Ward and his shortstop still must defy their more cautious-minded coaches in doing so. Accordingly, after a secret huddle on the mound between the pitcher and shortstop, they do not dare make their intentions known to anyone else. Coaching criticism is blunted only by the play's sensational success. The sophisticated dynamic of the strategy is perhaps best described in military terms: a flanking maneuver (the sacrifice bunt) was thwarted by a counter-flanking maneuver (the throw to third), not unlike the manner in which Caesar defeated Pompey at the battle of Pharsalia. Only experienced and savvy former ballplayers would be able to think of such tactical handsprings to begin with, let alone put them into fictional writing form.

Strike Zone contains a treasure trove of similar back-and-forth devices that most baseball fans and, for that matter, most baseball writers, would be completely oblivious to. The baseball connoisseur and the former player, however, will take delight in these intricacies and not likely find them in any other authors besides the likes of Asinof and Bouton. To give one additional example, during the bottom of the fifth inning, Kolacka takes uneasy note of Chicago Wrigley Field's notorious Lake Michigan wind picking up and blowing towards the outfield, as indicated by the motion on top of the flagpoles. Normally, this outward lake breeze would favor batters on both sides but, as Kolacka correctly observes, it also favors a knuckleball hurler like Ward, because his specialty pitch will break sharper and more unpredictably when thrown into an oncoming wind. Therefore, Cub batters are helped decisively by the noted change in weather, while Phillies batters are somewhat stymied and neutralized.[19] This development is (for Kolacka) an ominous prelude to Sosa's game-winning home run for the Cubs a few innings later, while the Phillies offense is more or less held in check by Ward during the second half of the game. This short but significant passage in the novel is indicative because while some supposedly knowledgeable fans are aware that Wrigley Field's Lake Michigan wind generally means more home runs, few if any are aware of the special advantage it also presents to junk ball pitchers like Ward. It takes a former player like Asinof to notice and articulate such crucial subtleties.

The key hit in the contest is Sammy Sosa's dramatic eighth inning, three-run homer, giving the Cubs an exciting come-from-behind victory, and forebodingly described from Kolacka's viewpoint behind home plate. The unlikely turn of events is interesting on several different levels, and brings us back to the subject of hitting, which was never too far from the forefront of the novelist's thoughts. Sosa's fictional long-ball heroics in the story immediately call to mind his media-promoted home run derby race with Mark McGuire during the 1998 season. *Strike Zone*, however, was conceived and written at least five years earlier when Sosa was still, in the words of Kolacka, "one of the best eighth hitters in the National League."[20] In 1993, Sosa was no more than a promising recent acquisition by the Cubs; he had yet to become the ballplayer that posterity will remember him by. The novel was also written long before Sosa's playing legacy was tainted by accusations of performance-enhancing drug use, or his being caught red-handed in the act of using a corked bat. Sosa was of course not the only prolific home run hitter from that era discovered breaking the rules. While Asinof's benign portrayal of Sosa (and the players in general) do not directly anticipate any of these future controversies, Asinof does imply some very troubling possibilities with umpire Kolacka's initial disregard of both personal honesty and the impartial spirit of the written rules. He makes it look so easy, and it is clear that he could have gotten away with much more had he cared to. As for the spectators, they have little if any conception as to what is taking place. In real life, it is noteworthy that neither the fans nor media could immediately face up to the multiple scandals obviously brewing in Major League Baseball by the late 1990s. Public reluctance to let go of its favorite illusions, combined with an overeager quickness to condemn individuals once these illusions had been exposed, represents one the latest examples of deep cultural contradictions existing within the American sports world, both at the professional and amateur levels.

Getting back to hitting, though, Kolacka's (and Asinof's) deep pro-batter and anti-pitcher biases manifests themselves throughout the story — not too surprisingly, since the fictional Kolacka and the real-life Asinof were both former hitters themselves. In anticipation of Sosa's game-winning shot, Kolacka becomes euphoric at the distant memory of his own batting heroics:

> I remember the unforgettable joy of hitting when a game came down to me. Never be a man to end an inning. Never let a third strike get by. Never, ever so much as think there's a pitcher on God's green earth who is better than me. I remember the beautiful feel of the bat in my hands. No batting gloves when I was a kid, there was no such thing. I'd twist my bare hands lovingly around the bat handle, move the barrel out over the plate, once, twice; then I'd wait for the pitch, my bat high over my shoulder as I felt the power building in my legs. The first sight of the ball would trigger instant responses for the perfect timing of my stride, the driving power of the bat swing as I made that sweet solid contact.[21]

The above passage is similar in tone and content to one that Asinof had written three decades earlier for *The Bedfellow*. In that 1967 novel, a prematurely retired Mike Sorrell remembers with satisfaction what it was like to be hitting the ball well:

> As any ballplayer can tell you, there is no joy like a hot streak. Your body begins to move with a rhythm that sends you gliding through the day. You even brush your teeth with a special grace. You can't get the shower water cold enough to chill you, and your appetite is ravenous. Day after day, you feel your power in the tips of your fingers, and when you pick up a bat, it feels like a toothpick. You do everything right, everything; all you have to do is take a cut at the ball and everyone in the ball park knows it's going to drop in for a base hit.[22]

Words common to both descriptions like "joy" and "power" are used to convey feelings of invincibility and dominance as hitters grip and swing a bat. It is a familiar feeling to anyone who has ever experienced success at the plate—a delusion perhaps, but one essential to the winning athlete's positive mindset as competitive levels of the game become more advanced and intense. Asinof knew the positive mindset quite well, as do his fictional baseball characters.

The nostalgia of Kolacka for the joy of hitting naturally calls to mind his creator's various ups and downs at the plate in Wausau during the months of May and June, 1941. First he was hot, then he was not. Curiously, nowhere in *Strike Zone*, or for that matter, nowhere in *any* of Asinof's baseball writings, is the agony of a batting slump described, analyzed, or even dwelled upon. Failures on and off the playing for individuals are relayed or recounted in painful detail, but batters striking out are never attributed to them being in any sort of negative mental rut or bad luck streak. In *Bleeding Between the Lines*, Asinof gives a revealing encapsulation of his own hitting philosophy as a minor league player before the war: "I'd hear stories about great hitters who needed to hate pitchers in order to hit them.... I never felt that way. I always came to the plate smiling. I think I loved it all so much, the pitcher was out there just to give me a chance to hit."[23] As for his mental approach to the science of hitting, Asinof wrote: "Hitting became like a chess game, every pitcher representing a different rival. Years later, Yogi Berra would say, 'I can't think and hit at the same time,' but my own style was the opposite. I relied on thinking."[24] That someone like Asinof should have tried to compensate his good but admittedly limited physical abilities with intelligence and cunning as he faced other professional prospects in grueling competition should not come as a surprise.[25] Although he was a devoted fan of the Yankees and Yogi Berra, one could not expect him to emulate Berra's inimitable style, let alone his instinctive unflappability. Berra's own clumsy acknowledgment of the game's cerebral aspects came in the form of his famously botched remark that baseball was ninety percent mental and fifty percent physical.[26] Berra was of course referring to both intelligence and attitude, qualities that Asinof the player seems to have possessed in abundance.

The very same scientific, methodical qualities that can make a hitter formidable, however, can also (as any coach will affirm) unnecessarily cause a batter to fail, sometimes repeatedly. Worse, a crisis in confidence or stubborn unwillingness to make adjustments, combined with external forces beyond any hitter's personal control, can sometimes coalesce into a plummeting batting average. These factors may have formed the anatomy of Asinof's dismal batting slump in mid–June, 1941, which formed the prelude to the termination of his professional playing career. In *Strike Zone*, Kolacka's open disdain for Banks' cockiness and bravado at the plate may have in fact represented the novelist's projecting more than a little bit of his younger self onto the frustrated African American star.

Asinof, after all, had done a similar thing many years before in *The Bedfellow*. In that novel, Sorrell makes an error in the outfield then goes hitless. He strikes out after upbraiding himself for engaging in "dumb superstitions" at the plate, including "the inane ritual of pocketing a pebble, then hitching up my pants and securing my hat." After his "concession to witchcraft" and inability to "stay loose," Sorrell swings at a "terrible pitch" for strike three.[27] *Man on Spikes* has a similar sequence. African American player Ben Franks steps to the plate thinking, "The thing to do was to be loose up there, to think only of hitting."[28] Franks then takes a called third strike on an obvious ball from a racist umpire, then only manages to compound his shame by making a series of misplays in outfield.[29] Asinof's incredible writer's empathy for wronged black outfielder-hitters such as Franks, Sorrell, and Banks hits a little too close to home, especially considering these three novels were written over the course of almost 40 years. Once again, visions of the young Asinof in Wausau slumping as a batter and making an unpopular play in the outfield come to mind.

As deep and rich as the combined baseball wisdom of Asinof and Bouton is in *Strike Zone*, the non-baseball flashbacks and the manner in which these overlap with the obligatory baseball sequences, are even more telling. In the case of Asinof, who was becoming considerably advanced in years at the time of the novel's production, the action transpiring outside of the baseball stadium is especially revealing. While Asinof, whatever his reasons may have been, chose not to write directly about the plight of batters struggling to get their timing back, he did elect to do something more valuable. He perceptively wrote about the difficult phases of life in general, outside of sports. In this regard, *Strike Zone* rather surprisingly seems to offer as much, if not more, commentary of matters of love, marriage, family, finance, and personal fulfillment, as it does about the ethical quandaries of baseball. As in hitting, life usually presents all of us with both slumps and hot streaks, along with a lot of in-betweens.

16

Outside the Bounds of Respectability

Being a native of New York City and living in the Big Apple until he was age 65, Eliot Asinof did not appear to have much attraction to or interest in small town American life during the years in which he made a name for himself as a writer. Up until that point, his works have little say on the subject, and when they do so, express a mostly negative view of the type found in 1979's *Bleeding Between the Lines*. In his memoir, obscure places on the American map like Moultrie, Georgia (where Asinof played in the minor leagues), and Brandon Mill, South Carolina (home of Shoeless Joe Jackson), are given less than, shall we say, glowing reviews. Then in 1985, with little warning to anyone except his closet intimates, Asinof cashed out of his Manhattan co-op unit, moved upstate to the Hudson Valley hamlet of Ancramdale, and there, with the help of his son, Martin, built a house in which he lived the remaining 23 years of his life. During this final golden period, Asinof would witness the successful adaptation of *Eight Men Out* into a feature film and resume his literary career, producing (among other works) four new books of note, including two novels about baseball, *Strike Zone* and *Off-Season* (see Part V of this study). Both, particularly the latter, are informed by the novelist's first extended close encounter with day-to-day life outside of the big city. Just as Asinof had previously written about baseball with authority in large part because he was a former professional ballplayer, he now wrote perceptively about isolated living environments with small populations and (one could say) smaller ambitions. In the case of *Strike Zone*, these passages take the form of occasional flashbacks examining the foibles and joys of everyday small town life in the American South and Midwest.

Although only mentioned expressly on one page in the novel, the shadow of Wausau, Wisconsin (in the form of his bitter, permanently estranged wife), seems to hang over Ernie Kolacka's life story as it plays out in the final baseball game of the season at Chicago's Wrigley Field. Whereas pitcher Sam Ward (the voice of Jim Bouton) obtains reconciliation and forgiveness from his alienated family by the end of the tale, for Kolacka (represented by Asinof) there is no such resolution, or rather, there is resolution of an opposite sort.

Asinof relaxing on the front porch of his home still under construction in Ancramdale, New York, circa 1985–1986. Asinof did the carpentry himself, with help from his son Martin. It was here that *Strike Zone* would be written, as well as late masterpieces such as *1919: America's Loss of Innocence*, *Off-Season*, and *Final Judgment*.

After calling a crooked game for eight innings, with two outs and two strikes in the top of the ninth, Kolacka decides to play it straight on the final pitch, thus giving victory to Ward, as well as the more deserving team (the Cubs). Then, regarding his longstanding dysfunctional and unhappy family, Kolacka elects to cut his losses, moving forward into a new communal relationship with his adoring girlfriend and her son in Hawaii. Though a native Long Islander who still domiciles there with his scolding Midwestern wife of some 40 years, Kolacka, at age 60, makes the decision to get away from it all, and heads far west for the Pacific, figuratively and literally riding off into the sunset.[1] All throughout Kolacka's numerous flashbacks before, during, and after the game, it is quite clear that the only happy moments in his long relationship with his wife came before they were married and before she became pregnant. The rest that follows is pure mutual dissatisfaction, especially on the wife's part. Accordingly, her scolding, her contradictory values, her general disapproval of her husband — all of these become indelibly associated with her geographic place of origin. Wausau, the last town in which Asinof played professional baseball in 1941, in effect is equated by the novelist with narrow personal values and futile feelings of helpless despair. This connection is never overtly stated; on the other hand, it is very hard for the reader to miss.

Today, Wausau is one impressive component of a sizable, combined metropolitan statistical area situated along the Wisconsin River in Marathon County and home to well over 100,000 souls. It is the largest MSA in central Wisconsin, roughly equidistant between Madison to the south, Green Bay to the east, and Eau Claire to the west. I had the pleasure of living there for one year during 2009–2010 in order to be close to my appointed job. Though dealing with many urban problems typical of bigger cities, Wausau retains a small town feel. Originally, during the 19th and 20th centuries, it was a city essentially built by German immigrants, and this shows, with the overall layout being a widely recognized small masterpiece of Wisconsin urban planning. The downtown area, in spite of the recent economic downturn, is well developed and remains vibrant. The modern population of Wausau, by Midwestern standards, is diverse.[2] A shrinking industrial base continues to survive against all odds, while the long-established medical and insurance industries, plus their numerous service supporting personnel, dominate the local economy. The only active synagogue in central Wisconsin is to be found in Wausau.[3] Irish, Italian, and African Americans are to be found in significant numbers as well. More recently, Hmong immigrants have made Wausau one of their geographic and cultural points of reference. While newer and bigger buildings have been built over the last half century, the city is not too much different from the one that a 21-year-old Eliot Asinof saw when he arrived to play Class C baseball for the Wausau Lumberjacks in the late spring of 1941. Athletic Park, where Asinof once played, is still in use and by far the best place in town to watch high-quality baseball being played as home to the semiprofessional Wisconsin Woodchucks (see Chapter 14).

Given Asinof's somewhat off-the-cuff assertion at Cooperstown in 1999 that anti–Semitism existed in Wausau on the eve of World War II, and that this allegedly played a role in his sudden dismissal from the Lumberjacks during mid-season, a bit of scrutiny at this point is deemed appropriate. Wausau's small but prominent Jewish community has always played a visible and active role in civic affairs, and whatever anti–Semitism that once surely existed in this proudly German-American town is now (at worst) kept under the careful wraps of political correctness. There is also possibly an element of shame in terms of what the sentiment eventually led to with the European Holocaust of World War II and subsequent postwar creation of modern Israel.[4] The official team photograph of the Northern League regular season champion Wausau Lumberjacks does not include Eliot Asinof.[5] This is not particularly surprising, since he played his last game for the Lumberjacks on June 25 and the photo was probably taken much later to commemorate the team's regular season title. Somewhat more surprising is a full-page promotional newspaper spread on May 7, 1941 (following opening day of the season), in which no fewer than 11 Lumberjack players pitch various local products and businesses. Asinof is not to be found among these photographed endorsements either. One might speculate that he had not yet arrived in camp except that, in fact, he had; moreover, Asinof is photographed among the eight batters in the starting lineup that same day in the very same newspaper.[6] The implications are suggestive. Asinof was good enough to be photographed and play in the starting lineup, but as a Jew perhaps not the best choice as a poster boy for local commercial advertisements. It is of course possible, perhaps even likely, that these ads were put together long before Asinof came to town. The truth of the matter will probably never be known. In either event, Wausau, even back in 1941, would have still certainly been a much friendlier host town to a young Jewish American athlete than was Asinof's previous minor league gig in Moultrie, Georgia (see Chapter 9).

In the novel, Ernie Kolacka recalls meeting his wife in San Francisco while she was a nurse and he was recovering from a Korean War wound. Enid Wynant Kolacka hails from Wausau, and is the daughter of an insurance man there. After her local boyfriend joins the Marines and disappears from her life, Enid takes up nursing and trains in Chicago before being stationed out West.[7] With nursing and insurance, Asinof accurately alludes to Wausau's most prominent employers. Enid likes poetry and astrology, and is roughly the same age as Kolacka.[8] At one point she unwittingly describes herself as "Enid the Crab"—an intended reference to her zodiac sign as Cancer which, interestingly enough, was also Asinof's sign. In the novel, however, Kolacka is given the birth sign of Taurus.[9] Enid is not a striking beauty, and Kolacka is a partial invalid, but in the hospital ward, the two of them become an item. News of her pregnancy (with twins) comes as a shock to the 20-year-old father—the approximate age of Asinof when he was in Wausau—but Kolacka nevertheless marries Enid to do right by her. Their relationship from that point forward goes completely downhill, but the marriage barely manages to hold together as bad marriages often do.

Enid proves to be very materialistic, in no small part the result of Kolacka's meager umpiring salary. When the umpires' union calls a strike, Enid urges her husband to scab for higher pay, which he indignantly refuses to do.[10] As Kolacka realizes her shopping sprees intentionally outpace his earnings, he laments that theirs was "the oldest story in the history of marriage: she was spending all that money *to get even with me*!"[11] The grown twin children are distant, disrespect their father, and share their mother's worship of the almighty dollar. Kolacka's relations with his daughter become strained after her car salesman husband coaxes him into buying a lemon ("I guess I didn't thank them enough").[12] As for Kolacka's son, he likes to rub in the fact that he earns more money owning a carwash business than his father does as a professional umpire, then sanctifies his superior enterprising spirit by criticizing Kolacka's lack of "family values."[13] With respect to his own immediate family, whether through his own fault or not, Ernie Kolacka can best be characterized as a total outsider.

It is interesting (though not necessarily central) that throughout Asinof's fictional works, both baseball-themed and otherwise, there are a number of troubled male characters whose unhappy wives have names beginning with the letter "E." All of these women are either deceased or of limited intelligence and homely appearance. In addition to Enid Wynant Kolacka from *Strike Zone*, there is Emily, the wife of the unstable Mike Ogden from *The Name of the Game Is Murder* (1969). Emily is a much more sketchy character than Enid, mainly because she has been killed in a senseless hit-and-run accident before action in the novel begins. She is, however, similar to Enid: a "Red Cross girl" who nurses her war-wounded husband-to-be back to health, and then later becomes the mother of his child. Her premature death, not surprisingly, inaugurates an extended phase of turbulence in the lives of both surviving father and teenage son.[14] More disturbing still is Ellen Stanley from *Off-Season*, who is married to the hero's slippery financial handler, Gordon Stanley. Ellen, who is only referred to casually by Gordon, is specifically courted by him because she is "not too smart and definitely not too good looking," which he believes will help to further his business interests.[15] Based on these examples, and taken as a composite, it is not too good or flattering a thing to be female character with an "E" first name in Asinof's novels. One can of course make way too much of this interpretatively; on the other hand, given the unpleasant prominence of Enid's character in *Strike Zone*, taken in tandem with her correlation to other fictional creations in Asinof's stories, the phenomenon at least deserves passing mention.

The easy temptation for critics at this juncture is to search for real-life models in the novelist's work. Since Asinof once told a Cooperstown audience that he was fired from the Wausau team in part because a local girl (allegedly, the team owner's daughter) was paying to much attention to him, and because Enid Kolacka expressly hails from Wausau, it would appear natural to equate the two personages. Close examination of this puzzle, however, reveals multiple complications. This should not surprise us since a skilled storyteller will rarely use cut-and-dried factual people and situations, only selective bits and pieces of facts, in order to further a specific imaginative purpose. To do otherwise is to invite trouble from potentially offended parties and, worse still, risk producing mediocre fiction. Genealogical research reveals that the owner of the Wausau Lumberjacks in 1941, Richard J. Dudley, did not have a daughter, only sons, nor was he affiliated with the insurance business (as mentioned in the novel), but rather with the meatpacking industry, that is, when not otherwise engaged in financially running a ball club.[16] One could no doubt proceed further at this point with additional examples of how Asinof's fiction, as well as his autobiography, departs from the documentary historical record.

The best thing to do, however, is to pause and consider what common sense dictates in terms of trying to develop a better appreciation for a novelist's work. Then we may ask to what extent that fictional work ties into a novelist's autobiography, whether that autobiography was strictly factual or romanticized and selectively glossed. One thing appears certain, however; the Wausau material and greater delineation of Enid's character in *Strike Zone* came in Asinof's later drafts of the work, at the urging of Viking editor Al Silverman.[17]

Was Asinof therefore deliberately lying to his Cooperstown audience in 1999? The truthful answer to this question, as in many other complicated issues in life, is probably both a yes and a no. Given the totality of strange circumstances surrounding Asinof's mysterious dismissal from the Lumberjacks team in June of 1941, it is more than likely that undisclosed external factors, possibly including anti–Semitism and/or an illicit romance, played significant roles, and that a recent batting slump combined with a bad play in field were not the sole reasons for his sudden departure (see Chapter 15).

Whether giving speeches at Cooperstown or writing books, however, it would not be in Asinof's typical style to expose living acquaintances or their relatives to public controversy — quite the opposite in fact. He was consistently known to be identity protective of anyone for whom he cared at all, and would not use real names in his novels unless given permission to do so, or use of the name was entirely dignified and complimentary, or (in rare cases) he so loathed an individual that he did not care.[18] Above all, it should be remembered that the supreme prerogative of novelist, poet, and playwright is to alter and color the unadorned facts whenever it suits their dramatic purposes. This applies even when giving public speeches concerning their own supposedly factual, past personal lives. To effectively tell the whole truth about any particular matter, they must sometimes conceal part of it from full view. Throughout literary history, greater writers than Eliot Asinof, from Dante to Shakespeare to Mark Twain, have done no less the same.

Regarding any attempted equation of Asinof's fictional characters with people that he may have known in real life, one can only speculate rather than prove. Therefore, as no proofs can be offered, such attempts would be especially inappropriate given that these individuals (as well as their immediate families) may still be alive. If for no other reason, their anonymity should be preserved, at least in the near term, out of respect for the privacy of living relatives and friends. If Asinof opted to use an unrequited romance from his youth as an imaginative springboard for his fiction, but did not want other people involved to be judged or analyzed, then we, the reader, should not be frustrated or dismayed. The same holds true for anonymous or pseudonymous personages in his nonfictional work. The dead cannot answer for themselves, and it would be wrong to emulate the bad example of those Asinof's critics who have seemingly emerged only after his recent passing. Over and beyond this, Asinof himself obviously wanted to shield certain personal identities, and this was hardly a writer adverse to stirring up controversy or exposing hard truths. During his long life, Asinof did not hesitate to take on the likes of David Susskind, Jack Warner, and Harry Cohn, often at great personal and professional cost. In the final analysis, the novelist's wish should be respected, since if he wanted readers to know these identities, he would have inserted actual names, and in fact, often did precisely this. Moreover, there appears to be little or no reason to equate Enid Kolacka in the novel to Asinof's decade-long spouse, Jocelyn Brando, whose known personality and biographical details are polar opposite to those of the fictional Enid Kolacka in *Strike Zone*. For bits and pieces of Asinof's own failed marriage (such as these are to found), one must turn to much earlier baseball fictional works such as *Man on Spikes* and *The Bedfellow*.

In absolute contrast to the highly unpleasant portrayal of Enid from *Strike Zone* is her female foil and counterpart, Trisha Harrison, Kolacka's lover with whom he chooses to live at the end of the story. Kolacka meets Trisha while umpiring in Honolulu and under fire from both the league for his unpopular calls and from his wife for his meager earnings. They meet, appropriately enough, at a Little League game in which Trisha successfully coaches her own son to hit a home run that wins the contest. She is everything that Enid is not: intelligent, transparent, encouraging, compassionate, and, above all else, she loves baseball. She is also lame in one leg, the result of a car crash caused by her drunken husband who then subsequently deserts the family. Though now four years after the fact, it is never clear whether their divorce was final. Kolacka could not care less, though, and immediately falls head over heels:

> She saw me the way I wanted to be seen. Umpiring was not show business, and neither was baseball. She could go from Little League to the World Series in one sweep of her thoughts. When that kid hit his home run that afternoon, something about his young life was on the line. Every kid who played baseball knew that. That's what she knew.[19]

Trisha not only accepts Kolacka for what he is, but admires him for it. She is not a younger model for whom Kolacka dumps his wife, nor is she physically attractive in the conventional sense. Instead, she is beautiful more in a spiritual way, which seems to animate her physical person ("Her eyes were all I could see, clear brown eyes that made me feel like the center of the universe").[20] Trisha's son adores Kolacka, quite unlike his own biological children, and Kolacka reciprocates his attention. When Kolacka is finally promoted to the Major Leagues, Trisha is the first to congratulate him, while Enid only remarks upon his salary increase. Enid is also quick to perceive that her husband has been unfaithful, albeit on a single occasion, thanks in part to his involuntary utterance of Trisha's name while asleep.[21] The subject of money, ever present in Kolacka's unhappy, loveless marriage, never seems to come up between him and Trisha. They make love once, then remain in each other's hearts and minds until reuniting in the final Asinof-written chapter of the novel.

This attractively vivacious female character type can be found throughout Asinof's work, both fictional and nonfictional. In his last baseball novel, *Off-Season*, Asinof presents the rambunctious local news reporter Hortense Foxx as the near-personification of hero Jack Cagle's conscience. Foxx simultaneously represents the positive flip side of Cagle's selfish, ruthless, and amoral girlfriend, Judith Pagonis, although Judith is portrayed more as a classic femme fatale, rather than the querulous, discontented spouse, Enid Kolacka, from *Strike Zone*. Foxx, like Trisha from *Strike Zone*, is a red head, which for Asinof the novelist clearly symbolized an attractive kind of fiery courage and spunk. Both heroines call to mind Asinof's memorable, nonfictional, live-in girlfriend identified only as "Janet" from *Bleeding Between the Lines*. Janet is described as "a lovely redheaded divorcée" who waitresses in New York while trying to make it as a professional singer. Asinof wrote that "she [Janet] was bright and funny and, I thought, not nearly as tough as she pretended to be. I liked that."[22] Trisha from *Strike Zone*, Foxx from *Off-Season*, and Janet from *Bleeding* all seem to represent different variations on a single female character type that Asinof was unapologetically attracted to during his post-marital life (more on this in Part V of this study). All of these inspiring women, like Asinof's male heroes and antiheroes, find happiness only by straying away from mainstream society and in turn are definitely perceived by that society as being outside the bounds of respectability.

Of all the insults hurled against Kolacka by his family and enemies, the one that resonates and hits the hardest is made by his wife, who accuses of him of having a martyr complex, in addition to being a loser who always finishes last.[23] Kolacka, for his part, admits (as narrator) to having suicidal tendencies early in his married life, before being invited by friends to become a baseball umpire, a move which rescues his sanity. Curiously, prior to his being saved by baseball, Kolacka's planned and preferred method of self-demise is through asphyxiation by carbon monoxide poisoning in his own automobile.[24] Those familiar with Asinof's other books cannot help but recall his 1971 journalistic masterpiece, *Craig and Joan* (see Chapter 20), first breaking the oft-suppressed story of two New Jersey teenagers who committed suicide by the exact same method as a protest to the then-raging Vietnam War. The provocative theme of suicide-martyrdom would be taken up yet again by Asinof in his swan song novel, *Final Judgment* (2008). Unlike the tragically fictional Anne Miner from *Final Judgment*, and unlike the tragically nonfictional Craig Badiali and Joan Fox, Ernie Kolacka in *Strike Zone* does not contemplate killing himself for a higher cause. He is simply a person experiencing unbearable emotional pain, one who sees no reason to go on living until rescued by a fortuitous return to the game that he loves. Not surprisingly, he receives no support in this new endeavor from his family, all of whom can think of nothing in life except what can be bought with dollars and cents.

Whatever shortcomings *Strike Zone* may have as a novel or baseball commentary or autobiographical statement, these may, in a retrospective sense, be viewed as fortunate, since Asinof would be inspired six years later produce a baseball novel of far greater depth, quality, and range. This time, however, he would write it by himself without a co-author and working with an academic publisher who gave him full artistic freedom, as opposed to a major New York publishing house. Lastly, he would accept suggestions and commentary only from those who were not primarily after short-term financial gain and were thoroughly familiar with (and admiring of) his past literary work. If *Strike Zone* failed as a novel in the eyes of its creator and did not achieve what Asinof set out to accomplish, then it nevertheless effectively laid the groundwork for what would soon follow. At the very least, it made a good warm-up for a great writer in the process of returning to the literary fold after a long quiet spell. Taken on its own terms, and without measuring it against the dauntingly high quality standards of its original conception, *Strike Zone* succeeds as a uniquely entertaining and informative baseball novel. After it was completed, however, Asinof needed to satisfy his own artistic ambitions, which he would then proceed to do with dazzling aplomb.

PART V: *OFF-SEASON* (2000)

17

A Grotesque Compilation of Lies, Corruption, and Greed

There were times when the home field advantage could really beat you.
—Asinof, *Off-Season*[1]

As a turbulent 20th century began to wind down during mid–1999, an 80-year-old Eliot Asinof found himself standing on the speaker's podium in Cooperstown, not for induction into the Hall of Fame—which would have been not inappropriate for him as a writer—but rather to address its 11th Annual Symposium on Baseball and American Culture.[2] Asinof's seminal baseball novel *Man on Spikes* was, however, quite fittingly ushered into the Cooperstown library, in conjunction with that work's re-release in a sympathetic, dignified new edition by Southern Illinois University Press. The novelist had formed a new association with this academic publisher, along with its distinguished english department chair, Professor Richard Peterson, both for the purpose of getting Asinof's first novel back on the market, and also to follow it up with the projected release of his last baseball novel, *Off-Season*, the following year in 2000.[3] This burst of activity would inaugurate the new century for Asinof, and would prove to be a far more favorable creative environment than during the early 1990s when he had co-authored his novel *Strike Zone* (see Part IV of this study) under the strict and financially constricting auspices of a major New York City publishing house (Viking).

By the time that *Off-Season* appeared in 2000, Asinof had approximately eight years left to live. As things turn out, he still had plenty meaningful left to say as a novelist, both about baseball and the world in general. In 1997, two years prior to his Baseball Hall of Fame speech, he participated as a primary commentator in the A&E History Channel's extensive documentary on the Chicago Black Sox Scandal, *World Series Fix!*[4] The following year (in 1998), along with the reappearance of *Man on Spikes* in print, the novelist had impressively shot his age (79) at the Taconic Golf Course near his freshman alma mater of Williams College. Then in 1999 came Cooperstown. When

Asinof posing outdoors with his manual typewriter and disconnected phone in Ancramdale, New York, circa 1990. Note the birch-colored paint on his desk and filing cabinet, provided to him by a neighbor friend to match the surrounding grove of birch trees. Around this time, Asinof was basking in the recent (1988) and successful John Sayles movie adaptation of *Eight Men Out*.

Off-Season was released in 2000, it would be dedicated, like so many of his other works, "For my son, Martin." It would also open with two quotes from the ever-quotable Yogi Berra, both of which, if the reader takes time to look beyond Berra's distinctively confused syntax and fast-forward thinking process, point to the absolute necessity, both in baseball and in life, for growth, progression, and avoidance of personal stagnation. This idea went to the very core and underlying moral of Asinof's distinctively offbeat, inspirational tale in *Off-Season*.[5] Later that same year, America would endure one of its most controversial and hotly contested presidential elections, the results of which would leave Asinof, like millions of others, appalled though, in his particular case, far from being surprised. These cumulative events would also spur the novelist into completing his intrepidly fierce and politically charged valedictory statement, *Final Judgment*, later to be published posthumously in 2008.

The subject matter and influences for Asinof's last baseball novel are, not unexpectedly, rich in diversity, scope, and complexity. Both *Off-Season* and his very last novel, *Final Judgment* (2008), pull out all the stops in this regard. The prominent themes are small-town homecoming, in tandem with confronting personal demons after the seemingly triumphant accomplishment of difficult career goals. Both of these motifs had been lingering in Asinof's work from the very beginning, and now came to the forefront with a vengeance. Asinof's paradoxical comment midway through the story regarding *Off-Season*'s hero having a home field disadvantage referred precisely to these unlikely types of challenges in life. Only a former ballplayer like himself could have written it. On and off the playing field, home can in fact sometimes be a huge disadvantage; moreover, the opening homage to Yogi Berra's deceptively innocent philosophizing foreshadows what is to come in the novel. As the last of Asinof's intriguing baseball antiheroes returns "home" in the literal sense, his conscience forces him to continually make difficult, unexpected choices.

Asinof more or less spells out his main literary influences in the opening acknowledgments. Missouri-born (1941) Pulitzer and Emmy-winning writer Ron Powers is given a respectful nod, specifically for his 1991 masterpiece, *Far From Home*, a forcefully unpleasant but candid examination of socioeconomic turmoil in Cairo, Illinois. Presumably, real-life Cairo is located not too far up the Mississippi River Valley from the novel's fictional setting of Gandee, Missouri, nor from Powers' own home town of Hannibal, Missouri.[5] Asinof also pays tribute to *The Visit*, a classic 1956 black comedy by the Swiss avant-garde playwright Friedrich Dürrenmatt (1905–1990), later made into a 1964 film by the same title, starring Ingrid Bergman and Anthony Quinn. Asinof added that he received coaching on the ins and outs of small town politics from a New England mayor who understandably remained anonymous, no doubt for the sake of his own personal protection and keeping his job. Other individuals thanked include Professor Peterson, who helped to edit the novel, Asinof's son and dedicatee, Martin, his literary executor Jeff Kisseloff, author and NPR sports commentator Bill Littlefield, noted copywriter Julian Koenig, and Alexis Lalli.[7] Thanks are also given to the english department at the renowned Hotchkiss School in Lakeville, Connecticut, located not too far from Asinof's familiar haunts of Ancramdale, New York, and Williamstown, Massachusetts. This was clearly a creative team that Asinof the novelist was comfortable and happy working with.

The plot construction of *Off-Season* is deceptively simple. Superstar major league pitcher "Black Jack" Cagle triumphantly returns to his podunk home town for the purpose of helping to consecrate a newly constructed baseball park named in his honor. This is Cagle's first trip back to Gandee since rising to the highest heights of fame with the Los Angeles Dodgers. Thus the story begins on a celebratory note. One by one, however, Cagle encounters painful memories and ghosts, which gradually turn into horror. First, Cyrus Coles, the local African American catcher who first taught him to pitch successfully in high school, is found murdered en route to the ceremony. Then Coles' widow, Ruby, is wrongfully imprisoned for the crime by Cagle's father, the town sheriff, with full connivance from Cagle's uncle, the town mayor. With the help of Hortense Foxx, a local reporter (and local misfit), Cagle realizes that the entire power structure of Gandee, beginning with his own family, is built upon a grotesque compilation of lies, corruption, and greed. The new baseball field bearing Cagle's name is shoddily built upon an environmentally contaminated site. The community remains as segregated and racist as it was when Cagle was growing up. Except for a secretive, tight circle of graft and extortion amongst a small, privileged minority of the populace, there is no meaningful economic growth or prosperity to speak of. Anyone left in Gandee who is honest or decent does their best to conceal their goodness lest they are singled out and punished for it. Leaders publicly perceived as being morally upright are the people most to be feared by those who really are virtuous. Cagle, because of his tremendous wealth, celebrity, and (above all) his sense of justice, is eventually able to overcome all of these obstacles, but only at a frightening personal cost. He finally leaves Gandee a changed man for the better, though painfully more conscious of his own personal limitations and shortcomings — in short, older and wiser.[8]

In a charming yet profound coda to the novel, Cagle flies back to Los Angeles and finds himself seated on the plane next to none other than an aged Mike Kutner, hero of Asinof's first novel 45 years earlier, *Man on Spikes*. As one might expect, the two characters hit it off. Kutner vents to Cagle about various unfavorable changes in the game (see Chapter 18), including the typically overlong length of players' head and facial hair, but still admits to loving the game ("Because of baseball, the old man lived").[9] Then Kutner reveals that after leaving professional baseball he became a full-time barber and made more money doing that than he ever did as a player.[10] In a symbolic act, both in respect to his elder and demonstrating rebirth as a new person, Cagle allows Kutner to shave and give him a crew cut right there on the spot, much to the excitement of passengers and crew.[11] By Cagle meeting Kutner in the final pages of *Off-Season*, Asinof's baseball heroes come full circle, simultaneously comparing notes on the game while growing exponentially as human beings.

Significantly, Cagle is portrayed as being 27 years old at the time.[12] In the baseball fiction and nonfiction of Asinof, this seems to be a crucial age of moral reckoning for many of his characters. Mike Sorrell in *The Bedfellow* is about 27 years old. Mickey Rutner, the factual model for the fictional Mike Kutner of *Man on Spikes*, was 27 years old in 1947 when he played in short stint in the major leagues. Black Sox Happy Felsch, who was Asinof's breakthrough source for *Eight Men Out*, was 27-28 years old during the fateful 1919 season. Asinof himself was 27 in 1946, the year he returned home from the war and elected not to continue his professional playing career in baseball. Kutner, in many respects Asinof's fictional counterpart, is about the same age when he returns from the war and alternatively chooses to pursue his dream as a major league baseball player, with bittersweet results.[13] For the novelist, the late twenties appears to be an important time in life in which young male athletes must fully come to terms with their consciences (or not), then live with the consequences of these difficult choices for the rest of their lives.

In the case of Jack Cagle, Jr., the first hard choice he must come to grips with upon returning to Gandee is his home town's disgraceful, ingrained traditional of racial discrimination, both overt and, much more difficult to tame, that which is hidden from view. For example, the only black person in Gandee who seems to be getting ahead in the world is a deputy sheriff who spies on Cagle's activities when not dealing drugs on the side to the area's impoverished black residents. This is all done with full, tacit approval from Cagle's evil father, Sheriff John Clyde Cagle, Sr., an embittered and prejudiced Vietnam War hero who appears to support his son's baseball career but in actuality does everything he can to undermine it out of jealousy. The biggest villain, however, is Jack Junior's uncle (by marriage), Mayor Sam Manning, who uses everyone in town, both black and white, as pawns for his own personal pleasures, financial profit, and political aggrandizement. He too is a racist, but a master at concealing it; in fact, Mayor Manning proves to be the hero's most formidable adversary after initially masquerading as his best friend. In effect, Jack Junior must vanquish both his father and uncle to achieve justice for the wronged black community of Gandee, in which he succeeds magnificently by the end of the tale.

As repeatedly noted throughout this study, American race relations both in and out of baseball are a constant recurring theme in Asinof's literary work, beginning with *Man on Spikes* in 1955. The novelist upped the ante with race topicality in 1967's *The Bedfellow*, then produced a classic nonfiction work on the subject with *People vs. Blutcher* in 1970. In 1980, Asinof conducted a masterful interview of Willie Stargell for *Sport* magazine, in which Stargell's universal celebrity in wake his team's 1979 World Series triumph was dramatically contrasted with the slugger's humiliating treatment as an African American player much earlier in his career.[14] Although 1994's *Strike Zone* had hinted at these issues within the context of baseball (see Chapter 15), Asinof returned full force to the subject of American racial strife with *Off-Season*. The very title of the novel, though literally referring to the part of the year in which the story action takes place, also has a double, if not triple meaning. In a sweeping reference to all of the social and economic problems encompassing Gandee, Cagle's high school pal and first baseman Gus Guida laments, "We're in an off-season that don't never end."[15] Later, Cagle's best friend and African American Dodgers teammate, Corky Corcoran, echoes the same sentiment: [Cagle] "Shit sure happens, Corky." [Corky] "Hey, it's the off-season, remember?"[16] *People vs. Blutcher* had particularly well prepared him for the task, in that it exposed the novelist turned journalist to the realities of white-on-black police brutality, as well as collusion of the criminal justice system in the overall process, both intentional and inadvertent. Asinof's fascination or near-obsession with the distinctively American clash between black and white cultures is fully understandable coming from a writer who was an impressionable age 27 when Brooklyn Dodger General Manager Branch Rickey introduced the great Jackie Robinson to a startled and excitable postwar nation. During this exact same time period, Asinof was seeing racial integration in baseball firsthand as co-owner of the semiprofessional Yonkers Indians. Therefore, this aspect of his work makes a fitting centerpiece to his last baseball novel.

Somewhat more surprising than Asinof's focus on small town race relations in *Off-Season* is a simultaneous return to his beloved but rarely utilized murder-mystery genre. The last time that he had delved into this area had been with 1969's *The Name of the Game Is Murder*, the final installment in his New York trilogy written during the late 1960s (see Part III of this study). *Name of the Game*, despite many fascinating aspects, including its uneasy combination of the crime thriller and professional sports (albeit, football) interests into a single novelette, had more or less sunk without a trace and made virtually no impression on the general reading public. Its hyperbolic, semi-comedic tone had foreshadowed 1977's *Say It Ain't So, Gordon Littlefield*— the narrator in both novels is presented as a bit of an idiot — but no one dies in *Gordon Littlefield*, whereas corpses multiply in *Name of the Game* and *Off-Season*. As in *Name of the Game*, the true killer identified near the end of *Off-Season* comes from a somewhat surprising direction, and much closer to the narrator than he is comfortable dealing with. One gets the sense that part of Asinof's motivation as a novelist in writing *Off-Season* was to revisit the murder mystery format, but to do so in a baseball framework that he was far more comfortable and knowledgeable working within.

Asinof's old wartime mentor and detective novelist extraordinaire, Dashiell Hammett, had been the dedicatee of *Name of the Game*, and his much of his influence presides over *Off-Season* as events unfold.[17] Jack Cagle, Jr., has more than a bit of Sam Spade in him. Cagle looks tough but has a hidden sentimental streak. He bucks the system, goes where he is not wanted, gets beaten up, gets help from a girl or buddy, dodges the femme fatale, and in the end, triumphs, but at a steep cost. The formula is timeless, and Asinof knows well how to use it. Readers who care little for baseball or socioeconomic issues are still likely to be drawn into *Off-Season*'s crime thriller facet. And the baseball banter is not too bad, either, to say the least (see Chapter 19); nor can *Name of the Game*, despite being a story about professional football, resist making baseball allusions as well. At one point narrator Mike Ogden refers directly to Shoeless Joe Jackson and the 1919 World Series, and his preliminary count of likely murder suspects is conveniently listed as eight, identical in number to the White Sox players who were eventually banned from baseball for life by Commissioner Kenesaw Mountain Landis in 1920.[18] There is also a gratuitous boxing reference thrown into the mix, calling to mind the fateful participation of former world featherweight champion Abe Attell as go-between during the Black Sox Scandal.[19]

More surprising still than Asinof's utilization of the murder mystery template in a baseball novel is his combination of these with the standard storytelling device of freeing a wrongly accused, incarcerated, but not so completely innocent party. In the case of *Off-Season*, this idea applies to Ruby Coles, troubled imprisoned widow of the murdered Cyrus Coles, a woman who has known Cagle Junior from adolescence and thus far had none too high opinion of him. For this journalistic aspect of the story there was precedent in Asinof's previous work as well. In 1973's *The 10-Second Jailbreak*, Asinof had co-authored (along with Warren Hinkle and William Turner) an account of American Joel David Kaplan's sensational rescue by helicopter from a Mexico City prison during the summer of 1971.[20] The escape had been coordinated by Kaplan's friends back home, including his well-known American defense attorney, Melvin Belli. Kaplan, wealthy heir to a Caribbean sugar fortune, though certainly no one's idea of a model citizen, seems to have been falsely convicted in Mexico of murdering a dubious former business associate, one Luis Melchor Vidal, Jr. In managing to arrange his own ingenuous escape, as noted by *Time* magazine, "Kaplan seems to have pulled off a practically non-criminal crime."[21] The appeal of the story appears to have struck a psychological chord of sorts during the Watergate era following Richard Nixon's reelection as president in 1972. The book itself represented a prime example of "team journalism" of the type then being made respectable (and bankable) by Bob Woodward and Carl Bernstein.[22] Although Ruby Coles in *Off-Season* is eventually freed by process of law rather than a forcible breakout, her unjust peril at the hands of tainted white law in Gandee lends a similar kind of tension and motivation to the characters' actions in the story.

Though hardly a masterpiece, *10-Second Jailbreak* tends to be an underrated work in Asinof's catalogue, and his return to the same kind of serious mood and tone in his final baseball novel makes sense upon some reflection. Its second-rate reputation as a book is probably mainly due to the inaccurate, silly, garbled and factually-inaccurate film version starring Charles Bronson which appeared two years later in 1975 (see Chapter 6). The book, on the other hand, which bears the unmistakable stamp of Asinof's style, is often fascinating. Asinof's favorite *Rashoman*-style of multiple and conflicting narrative viewpoints is employed to good effect, and the main players in the fast-moving action are delineated in all of their realistic ambiguity. Kaplan, like Asinof, had left the service after World War II, sympathized (in the beginning, at least) with the Cuban Revolution, and had an "ambivalent relationship" with his self-made father.[23] The last item applies equally to Jack Cagle, Jr., in *Off-Season.* Kaplan's alleged victim, Vidal, has his own checkered past, despite being blood related to some of America's most famous families.[24] Asinof's last baseball novel has no direct parallel character to Vidal but offers several others with vague similarities. These include Gandee murder victim, Cyrus Coles, who originally taught Cagle a formula for pitching success, but is rewarded for it by being killed. Another is the shifty airport escort, Alvin Algar, who smoothly introduces Cagle to the hero's own assailants soon after he is beaten senseless by them. Still another is the local Spanish-speaking thug-for-hire, Carlos Sanguellan, who, once we get to know him a little better, turns out to be one of the more transparent individuals in Gandee. It is difficult to imagine any of these highly complex and disconcerting gallery of figures that fill *Off-Season* coming from Asinof's typewriter before he produced his bracing series of nonfictional works from the 1970s. Notable examples of this fascinating period in Asinof's work, were *10-Second Jailbreak*, *People vs. Blutcher* (1970), *Craig and Joan* (1971), and *The Fox Is Crazy Too* (1976).

Cagle's closest parallel in *10-Second Jailbreak*, however, and the individual with whom Asinof as a journalist obviously related to most on a personal level at the time, is Kaplan's daring helicopter pilot rescuer, the late Roger Guy Hershner (1942–2009).[25] Hershner, like Asinof, was an Air Force war veteran who came from a respectable two-parent household but was nevertheless often attracted to dubious people such as Kaplan. Also like Asinof, Hershner was a former standout athlete and music lover who played a competent piano, and was known to be intensely loyal to those he considered friends. Tragically, Hershner was killed in a March 2009 helicopter crash during a routine cross-country flight, less than one year after Asinof's own passing in June 2008. Although having lived a very full and eventful life, Hershner's most famous adventure for which he will be long remembered was immortalized in Asinof's 1973 collaborative book.

Asinof's *Off-Season* does not have its hero facilitate any helicopter rescues from prison, but rather accomplishes this in the figurative sense. Jack Cagle pulls out all legal stops to free Ruby Coles from prison; these include spending a personal fortune, getting himself physically and verbally abused in the process, and putting his own career and reputation on the line for what he truly believes to be morally correct. In no other Asinof literary work prior to *Off-Season*, fictional or nonfictional, does this occur except in *The 10-Second Jailbreak*. It was also a good storytelling recipe that he would repeat with rousing success a few years later in *Final Judgment*.

If all of this were not enough, Asinof was able to weave yet another thematic thread straight through his inspirational baseball tale, however in a subtle and understated manner. Throughout the plot of *Off-Season* runs the constant idea of personal sacrifice for the good of the greater community. Almost all of the "good guy" characters—Cagle, Jr., Ruby, Cyrus, Foxx—

share this trait, while the "bad guys"—Cagle, Sr., Mayor Manning, Judith Pagonis, Gordon Stanley—are completely devoid of it. This dichotomy of character goes to the very moral center of Asinof's novel, and indeed to the very core of his entire corpus of writing. It deserves separate, more extensive treatment, which we will attempt to provide in the next chapter (Chapter 18). The years immediately following the appearance of *Off-Season* are perhaps the best context in which to do this because the exact same theme would immediately surge to the forefront of Asinof's concerns as a novelist in his last work. The roots of his exploration for the human ideal of self-sacrifice (or, many would say, martyrdom) went back to Asinof's sublime 1971 portrait of doomed teenage idealism, *Craig and Joan*. After nearly three decades of dormancy, it then reappeared with full force in *Off-Season*, and finally found full, articulate expression in *Final Judgment*. It should be emphasized that, in his writer's heart of hearts, Asinof was a moralist. During his final decade of activity, Asinof's fictional characters, despite their endless diversity and shades of personality, can more or less be divided into two camps: those who are selfish and those who are selfless. The latter group help to build up and nurture society, while the former tear in down in the name of progress while enriching themselves.

With the publication of *Off-Season* in 2000, Asinof had completed a cycle of five full-length baseball books interspersed over the course of some 45 years. Four of the five had been baseball novels, one of which (*Strike Zone*) was co-authored. The fifth was a nonfiction work written in the style of a historical novel (*Eight Men Out*), now generally considered a path-breaking exemplar for its difficult, elusive subject matter. Since that time, however, almost four decades had passed, and the game of baseball, along with the American society that had invented it, had changed in ways that could hardly be enumerated. Asinof's final work on his most beloved theme was, in the truest sense, his very last word on the topic. Few, if any other writers, were as well qualified to make it. Afterwards, other than giving sporadic personal interviews, Asinof had comparatively little left to say (at least in writing) on baseball, professional or otherwise. Most of his remaining energies and talents would be spent on his posthumously-published novel, a non-baseball story with a gripping political message. The scattered reviews that greeted *Off-Season*'s initial appearance, we suspect, were irrelevant to its creator. By that time, more urgent matters were occupying his time. Nevertheless, *Off-Season* proved in many ways to be a catalyst for 2008's *Final Judgment*, as well as a new virtuoso display of Asinof's ability to make sweeping social commentary with a minimal amount of words, and, perhaps most importantly, do it in entertaining fashion.

18

"Then History Turned Sour"

With the controversial election of George W. Bush as U.S. president in late 2000 and early 2001, Asinof plunged into the final phase of his long professional writing career with unapologetic vengeance. Over the remaining term of his life he would continue to produce a string of smaller-scaled, baseball-related pieces, but his primary focus would be on writing, rewriting, and then rewriting yet again his culminating fictional masterpiece. *Final Judgment*, an economically succinct but densely packed, politically-themed novel, had its creative origins in the Ronald Reagan era of the early 1980s. If Asinof disliked and distrusted opportunistic Democratic politicians, he morally and ethically despised hard-lined Republicans and anyone else who supported them. The ascendancy of conservative political orthodoxy during the 2000 and 2004 U.S. presidential elections accordingly inspired the aging literary lion to come out his den for one last great roar. While the 1990s had seen an encouraging return of Asinof to the public eye with the publication of several new bracing works and much more media visibility in general, the first decade of the new century saw him become even more uncompromising and combative. His long-held skeptical attitudes towards business and politics now pushed straight to the forefront of his literary concerns. Figuratively speaking, the candle burned brightest just before the flame went out.

Asinof's final burst in activity was not motivated by money or fame; in fact, popular and critical reception to *Off-Season* had been, at best, indifferent. Typical was a baffling, unattentive notice from *Publishers Weekly*, which seemed to be searching for qualities that Asinof, in actuality, had never really sought nor strove to achieve since becoming a published author during the 1950s:

> The novel comes to a tidy conclusion, but its sparkling, suspenseful passages about baseball are overwhelmed by Asinof's more sentimental themes.... It's admirably ambitious, but it shies away from the kind of kinetic sports descriptions Asinof is known for ... his first foray into fiction, Man on Spikes was not as successful, commercially or critically ... Asinof's new novel ... falls in between.[1]

Reference to *Man on Spikes* as not having been critically successful automatically discredits the review (see Chapter 2), but there is also the insidious, oft-repeated suggestion that Asinof was a mere sportswriter who should have stayed within those assigned boundaries. Did the reviewer even read *Eight Men Out*? That work is not about "kinetic sports descriptions"—it delves into the business of sports, and how sports business relates to its employees and society at large. That the reviewer praises "sparkling, suspenseful passages about baseball [the game?]"—passages which are scarcely to be found in *Off-Season*—calls into question whether that book was actually read either. We suspect that most reviewers have themselves never written fiction a fraction as engaging as *Off-Season*, let alone nonfiction that told us half as much about sports or the world, as did Asinof on repeated occasions.

Other reviews reiterated similar fallacies. *Library Journal* was uncomprehending: "This latest work includes too little of Asinof's fine baseball writing (Eight Men Out), and its too-easy conclusion is also disappointing."[2] If "fine baseball writing" means detailed play-action descriptions or presenting the inherent psychological drama of the sport, then readers should definitely look elsewhere than *Eight Men Out* (see Chapter 7); as for Asinof's alleged "too-easy conclusion," one would be challenged to cite any another novel in which the hero must endure a more hard-won victory at high personal cost, that is, assuming, one knows what it is like to experience such things in actuality.[3] Admittedly, it would be difficult for any reader to fully appreciate the physical and mental hardships inherent to genuine self-re-evaluation as laid out by the novelist, unless they too had some sort of past track record along these lines. This represents yet another unique aspect of Asinof's writing content and quality: he had precisely that kind of personal experience to relay to anyone who might be able to grasp it. Finally, there is a strong suspicion from perusing these reviews that non-sportswriters know well how to cite the titles of various sports-related books, but have not actually taken trouble to read any of these very carefully, if at all.

Writing for *NINE*, Peter Carino got it. His was one of the few favorable notices which seemed to fully appreciate the terrific scope and diversity of Asinof's achievement, and with a bit of humor thrown in:

> Off-Season bridges the gap between popular and literary fiction. Readers seeking only a good story and suspenseful plot will enjoy this book; readers looking for more literary sophistication will find something as well.... However readers approach the book, Off-Season will provide a few nights of good reading to warm up, well, the Off-Season.[4]

George Needham, writing for *Booklist*, was more ambivalent, but acknowledged Asinof's unique talent and grand ambitions: "This is a short novel that tends to do too much, but Cagle is an interesting character.... An unusual but successful mixture of hard-boiled mystery, coming-of-age story, and baseball yarn."[5] All in all, however, such perceptiveness was hard to find among the critics. As for the general public, comparatively few to begin with enjoyed both reading novels and contemplating the glories and pitfalls of the national pastime. Among those who did, fewer still knew what it was like to play the game of baseball successfully for money, or were capable of grasping the mostly invisible but nevertheless substantial connections between profession sports superstardom and American socioeconomic political issues. In spite of all these hurdles, and in spite of thoughtful fiction being a difficult sell under any circumstances, those readers who approach *Off-Season* with an open mind tend to be highly engaged by its one-of-a-kind morality play.

My own critical assessment of *Off-Season* should be obvious at this point. In comparison to Asinof's other four baseball novels, and indeed to all other sports fiction, the book stands magnificently apart. Asinof's only other fictional baseball work to compete in terms of sheer literary quality and visceral impact is *Man on Spikes*, which still may be rated higher if readers choose to focus more on professional baseball realism and unvarnished personality struggles within that arena. For broad social commentary and technical virtuosity, however, *Off-Season* must take the first prize — not surprisingly since it summarizes and encapsulates the novelist's long life, one full of experience inside the game as a player and outside the game as a writer. Both *The Bedfellow* and *Strike Zone*, despite their many worthwhile qualities (particularly the former), are not as fully realized or successful on a conceptual level, nor are these nearly as entertaining, although *Strike Zone* has its moments. Asinof's greatest baseball book overall must of course still be considered the nonfiction *Eight Men Out*, although part of its greatness lies in its tough investigative journalism being adorned with the outer trappings of a historical novel. On the other hand, as a pure statement about baseball within the context of American society at the turn of the 21st century, combined with its dazzling blend of fictional genres, one can do no better than Asinof's valedictory novel. Over a decade after its maiden publication, *Off-Season* continues to draw in new admirers, although it has far from reached full and proper appreciation among reading audiences. This is in no small part because many of these same readers refuse to even admit the possibility that such a high quality work can be found within the ranks of sports literature.

The last eight years of Asinof's life moved quickly. In 2000 and 2001, *Village Voice* published two riveting essays by the novelist, one on race relations in Major League Baseball (see Chapter 20), and one on the life of Joe DiMaggio (see Chapter 19). Later in 2001, he provided an attractive Foreword for Richard Peterson's book, *Extra Innings*, surely in part a thank you for Peterson's active role at SIU Press in getting Asinof's recent books published. Peterson in turn made some insightful comments on Asinof's works (see Bibliography). That same year (2001) Asinof appeared as a guest commentator for *ESPN Sports Center Flashback: The 1919 Black Sox Scandal.* Then came the 9/11 terrorist attacks, followed in short order by the U.S. invasions of Afghanistan and Iraq, a geopolitical nightmare from which the country has yet to awaken. All of this turmoil seemed to spur Asinof into completing his final, posthumous novel. Still he found time in 2002 to appear as Silent Sam, a thinly-disguised cameo of himself, in the John Sayles film *Sunshine State*, a role to which he had been invited specifically because of his fantastic golf talent, even at age 83.[6] In 2003 he wrote a short but quotable profile of former pitcher Ferguson Jenkins for *Time International* magazine (see Chapter 20). Two years later, in 2005, Asinof again appeared on cable television for ESPN's *The Top 5 Reasons You Can't Blame the 1919 Chicago White Sox for 'Throwing' the World Series*. Then in 2007, Asinof wrote another Foreword, this time for the late James T. Farrell's previously unpublished novel, *Dreaming Baseball*, a work that also had its origins in the Black Sox Scandal of 1919, no doubt given a benediction by Asinof as a sort of belated thank you for Farrell's enthusiastic and generous support of the younger writer's own classic work on the same subject matter (see Chapter 5).

In 2008, on June 10, Asinof died while hospitalized in Hudson, New York. His death was immediately followed by numerous obituaries and the posthumous release of *Final Judgment* by independent publisher Bunim & Bannigan on September 1. The remainder of that month and the year 2008 proved eventful as well. On September 15, Wall Street investment banking firm Lehman Brothers fell, and the U.S. economy went into an accelerated tail spin. In November, after an accumulation of unlikely political events, Barack Obama was elected the first African American president of the United States. Asinof would have no doubt been pleased, but did not live to see it. Perhaps most symbolic of all, however, on September 22, demolition began of the old Yankee Stadium, the "House that Ruth Built," and the physical landmark around which Asinof's long life as baseball fan had mostly revolved. It was here that he had seen Mickey Rutner and Hank Greenberg play, as well as Ruth, Gehrig, DiMaggio, and all of the other Yankee greats. What he would have thought of the new Yankee Stadium is anyone's guess. Given his repeatedly stated preference for a more intimate and less commercial version of the game, it seems likely that he would have seen it as a change for the worse. With Asinof's own passing, it seemed as though an old era was passing away as well, and, for better or worse, a being replaced by a completely new one.

Looking at Asinof's entire body of work, it becomes quite evident that he foresaw most of these trends, oftentimes many years in advance. Just as his first novel, *Man on Spikes*, had anticipated controversy over the reserve clause in Major League Baseball some 15 years before it reached the public consciousness (see Chapter 1), the predominating theme of *Off-Season*—self-sacrifice for the communal good—had been rigorously explored by Asinof almost 30 years before in his poignant nonfiction work, *Craig and Joan* (1971). This extraordinary book told the all-too-true story of Craig Badiali and Joan Fox, two high school teenage lovers from Blackwood, New Jersey, who in 1969 committed suicide together (by carbon monoxide poisoning) as a protest against the Vietnam War, then at its height. Shortly after the incident had been reported in the *New York Times*, Asinof was hired to write a piece on the same story by *Seventeen* magazine, which was then published on March 1, 1970, as "The 'Peace Suicides': Why Did They Do It?" The by-line repeated an exhortation of *Seventeen*'s editor to Asinof to "find out why; why did they do it?"[7] An identical journalistic directive had been given to a 24-year-old Asinof during World War II by Dashiell Hammett as the two worked together for the base newspaper on Adak Island (see Chapter 1). It proved to be sound advice for the budding novelist-journalist throughout his lengthy career.

Asinof's article for *Seventeen* won praise and immediately grew into a full-length book project released by Viking Press, the same publisher that commissioned Asinof's important *People vs. Blutcher* from the previous year. As a nonfictional set pair dating from 1970–1971, both *Craig and Joan* and *People vs. Blutcher*— though neither made it anywhere near the best-seller lists — represent American independent investigative journalism at its very finest, and Asinof was especially proud of these two efforts.[8] As in *People vs. Blutcher* and, for that matter, *Eight Men Out*, Asinof had to endure considerable public hostility in order to get the bottom of the story.[9] Cagle and Foxx in *Off-Season* must brave similar opposition. Both Asinof books from 1970–1971 today remain highly readable and socially relevant as ever. Like many of Asinof's works, *Craig and Joan* opens suggestively with quotes from other writers, including Camus, whose quotes also earlier opened *The Bedfellow* (see Chapter 9), and then, much later, *Final Judgment*, a novel with themes similar to those in *Off-Season* and *Craig and Joan*. Asinof additionally quotes British free-thinking psychologist Havelock Ellis (1859–1939) and, more surprisingly, the song lyrics of Bob Dylan, a popular songwriter whom the censorious Asinof had once booed for giving a disrespectful speech at the 1963 annual meeting of the National Emergency Civil Liberties Committee.[10] All three quotes hint at seismic changes then taking place in late 1960s American society.

Some 30 years later in Asinof's novel *Off-Season*, Cagle and Foxx represent more redemptive and updated (albeit fictional) versions of the historical Craig Badiali and Joan Fox memorialized by the same writer during the early 1970s. Cagle and Foxx's dangerous and seemingly futile efforts to bring a tiny bit of social justice to the small town of Gandee, Missouri, are perceived by most others as mere crazed and self-destructive gestures. The hero's assigned name of Jack Cagle, with the initials "J. C.," may represent Asinof's lone attempt at creating a literary Christ figure in his fiction.[11] The wrongly incarcerated Ruby Coles is often herself presented by the novelist in a light of martyrdom, at one point described by her own attorney as "suicidal" and mentally unstable.[12] Her husband Cyrus Coles does in fact die in an attempt to represent African Americans at Gandee's ballpark dedication ceremony, not unlike many martyred civil rights activists in the American South during the 1960s. *Craig and Joan* is the closest thing to a religious-themed book that Asinof ever produced. In it he wrestles with ideas of personal sacrifice for the collective good and the true meaning of "martyrdom" both in the religious and political sense. Joan Fox herself reportedly used similar terminology in trying to explain to friends their impending sacrifice.[13] In *Off-Season*, the hero learns about personal risk and sacrifice to a near-suicidal degree, which can in fact be perceived that way before happy resolution of events at the end of the story. For Asinof, this same difficult concept had first been explored long before in *Craig and Joan*, which represented somewhat of a breakthrough for him both as a writer and as a social critic, only then to be set aside by him for nearly three decades.

The similarities between political and religious martyrdom were not lost upon Asinof. Once again, he was way ahead of his time. In *Craig and Joan*, he noted that the young couple's deaths represented only two of 18 protest-suicides made against the Vietnam War over the course of four years. To him, these acts represented "a symbolically religious quest for martyrdom, like Christian martyrs burned at the stake, only to be condemned by the modern Christian church itself."[14] Secular institutions were no better in this regard, according to Asinof. Blackwood, New Jersey, simply wanted to forget that the suicides ever happened. One of the couple's friends observed that had they died for "super patriotic reasons," for instance, people not having enough respect for the flag or against hippies in general, then flags would have been flown at half-mast and brass band memorials would have been staged.[15] In *Off-Season*, the initial town reaction in Gandee to Cagle and Foxx's risky protests range from apathy and fear to outright hatred and active opposition. Cagle's father and uncle become his determined enemies and threaten to destroy his baseball career if he does not cease and desist. Only through a skillful combination of bribery, cunning, and public relations are the hero and heroine able to slowly win the townsfolk over to their side of the fight.

Asinof's skill as a storyteller becomes apparent in *Off-Season* as he introduces sinister character foils to his heroes and heroines. Cagle's sleazy financial manager and personal handler, Gordon Stanley, is established early in the novel as the antithesis to his multi-million dollar client's naïveté and good will. "For those of us who can't throw a baseball 106 miles an hour," Gordon chides Cagle, "we rely on the power of image-making."[16] Thus emerges once again in Asinof's writing the hated specter of public relations and mass media marketing (see Chapter 12). Later, when Cagle thinks about leaving unfinished business in his home town for quick return to a life of indulgence, Gordon encourages him with "mission accomplished"— this was over three years before the same phrase was unintentionally given ironic meaning by the 43rd president of the United States.[17] When Cagle realizes that Ruby is innocent, he toys with the idea of fighting fire with fire by hiring a Johnny Cochran-like attorney from L.A. to defend her with their own media blitz.[18] This same idea later evolves into Cagle's decision to buy the town newspaper and use it as a platform and bully pulpit to fight rampant city corruption, which lay at the root of most town problems. As for Gandee itself, innocuous airport employee and shrewd social commentator Alvin Agar mocks the "family values" held in such high esteem as little more than a hypocritical smoke screen to disguise cupidity and rapaciousness.[19] In this respect, the fictional Gandee, Missouri, is reminiscent of Asinof's nonfictional and highly unflattering portrayal of Blackwood, New Jersey, from *Craig and Joan.*[20] As most of this would suggest, there appears to be a direct creative process linking Asinof's memorable 1971 work with his last two novels, one baseball-related and the other not. All are concerned with personal sacrifice and the true meaning of martyrdom for the legitimate sake of a greater good. To this interesting topic we shall return on a more extensive scale in Chapter 20 of this study.

If 2000's *Off-Season* was a fitting conclusion to Asinof's impressive series of full-length baseball works, then his posthumous 2008 novel *Final Judgment* was a tour de force, one quite worthy of his literary legacy taken as a whole. It continued to explore serious questions first posed in *Craig and Joan* and then later further developed in a baseball context with *Off-Season. Final Judgment,* written in the first-person narrative, tells the inspirational tale of popular author Kenneth Flear (a close representation of Asinof himself) and his moral awaking that results when one of his students and former admirers, Anne Miner, publicly commits suicide by self-immolation to protest a commencement speech by President George W. Bush at the fictional Kingsley University where Flear teaches.[21] Miner considers the president to be nothing more than a war criminal and hired salesman for special interest groups, and cannot live with the thought of his presence marring her graduation. Her desperate act of protest not only brings the commencement speech to a permanent halt, but also has the effect of eventually bringing Flear to his moral senses, his own former political idealism having long since given way to comfortable middle-class complacency. Even before Miner kills herself, Flear recognizes in her one of the "few remaining saints" of "political heresy" and is ashamed of himself for flirting with and being dismissive of her.[22] Thus the theme of martyrdom in the political sense is once again taken up by Asinof, one in which the individual, unlike those in *Off-Season* (with the arguable exception of Cyrus Coles), chooses to make the ultimate sacrifice, but with positive end results for others who survive.[23] In *Final Judgment,* Flear finally succeeds in redeeming himself by orchestrating a dramatic statement to the media that both embarrasses defenders of the status quo and reflects his true inner beliefs. To do this, though, Flear must first rise above his own fear. Like Cagle and Foxx in *Off-Season*, he successfully fights fire with fire, figuratively speaking, while in turn being inspired by the more grisly and literal example of Anne Miner.

Flear's transformation is foreshadowed early in the novel as he describes with self contempt his own previous descent into moral apathy. In recapping his personal history as a professional writer, he recalls how modest financial and critical successes during the Reagan era of the early 1980s enticed him to turn his back on youthful idealism. Interestingly, he comes across as a middle-aged intelligentsia version of Jack Cagle, and would have been about Cagle's stated age (27) at the time his youthful ardor for social protest began to cool. By the 1990s and the end of the 20th century, Flear is clearly frightened both by what he has become as a person and what still may happen to him in the future as a citizen:

> Then history turned sour, and so, indeed, did my stomach, blighted by Ronald Reagan. Mockery replaced respect. A whole nation appeared to glorify ignorance. Having given up the faith, we would bend our culture to pay obeisance to the faithless. How long before Americans stopped caring, the largest sin of all, and when we did, how long before the writers who still cared began to drift into the grey areas of exclusion? There I was in 1999 ... and starting to have the sense to run scared.[24]

Flear holds himself out as being 41 years old in 1999, about the same age of Asinof in 1960, the fateful year in which he began research for his definitive *Eight Men Out* project. The new millennium signals Flear's recognition, one surely shared by the novelist, that "history turned sour" for America during the final decades of the century. Asinof, the history major cum laude from Swarthmore, had lived to see his country transformed for, what he believed, to be the worst. Also, 1999 was the year that Asinof addressed a Cooperstown audience as keynote speaker at the Baseball Hall of Fame (see Chapter 14).[25] It may well have been that, by the late 1990s, Asinof was himself feeling a bit complacent and apathetic (by his own high standards, at least), especially given that during the 1980s his own professional writing career had been resurrected, in no small part by the filming of his seminal *Eight Men Out* by John Sayles in 1987, as well as the subsequent, tangible benefits that Asinof reaped from this fortunate development.

As was usually the case for a major book release by Asinof, *Off-Season* also had plenty to say about the game of baseball, even though live play action is scarcely depicted within its pages. If contemporary readers, whether they be young adults, old, or somewhere in-between, had little interest in politics, economics, or social injustice, the novel could be enjoyably perused strictly for its sports-related commentary. An especially impressive aspect of the work was that its various baseball and non-baseball concerns are not presented by

Asinof in alternating or separate sections, but rather as a seamless, integrated whole. For example, when Cagle's buddy and African American teammate, Corky Corcoran, delivers his mock "I have a dream" speech over the phone (see Chapter 20), he is making a lively commentary on racial prejudice on several different levels—within the industry of Major League Baseball, within economically troubled communities like Gandee, and within America as a whole. Another example comes at the end of the story when Kutner complains to Cagle about how the game has changed over time for the worse. Kutner's remarks speak directly to professional baseball, but also tie into aspects of modern America that decisively influence the sport, including greedy commercialism, the mindless ignorance of grossly overpaid athletes, and, perhaps most of all, the sincerity and dedication of those involved. In short, it all ties together. Nevertheless, it usually starts with baseball, and then goes from there. For Asinof, by the end of his stories, the national pastime has become a mirror of the nation itself.

19

A Few More Parting Shots

It always intrigued me that three-quarters of the sportswriters I'd met had never played a sport more physical than stud poker.

—Asinof, *The Name of the Game Is Murder*[1]

It is difficult, if not impossible, to avoid conflation of the fictional 80-year-old Mike Kutner in *Off-Season* with the 80-year-old Eliot Asinof at the turn of the 20th century. Like Kutner, Asinof tried repeatedly in life to leave baseball behind him, first as a player, then as an owner-manager, then as a novelist (*Man on Spikes*), and then as a journalist-reporter (*Eight Men Out*). He later turned to writing about non-sports and non-baseball topics, often with great creative success. Afterwards, burdened by lawsuits, shaky finances, and (worst of all), lack of reader appreciation, he temporarily gave up writing itself. An unsatisfactory return to baseball fiction in 1994 (*Strike Zone*) seemed to be the last straw; nevertheless, he came back only few years later to produce a baseball fiction masterpiece (*Off-Season*), which appeared to represent his writer's farewell to the game, at least as a novelist. Like Mike Kutner, however, Asinof kept coming back for more, almost right up until the end. As an addled Kutner tells Cagle in the novel: "I ain't on the field but I'm still in the dugout, you get what I mean?"[2] The same might well be said for Asinof during the first decade of the new century. As things turned out, he still had urgent things to say about baseball, though not necessarily in a fictional format.

Within a year of *Off-Season*'s appearance in early 2001, New York's venerable *Village Voice* published a lengthy piece by Asinof titled "Hey Joe: The Booing of the Great DiMaggio."[3] For anyone still paying attention, the article was a make-you-squirm, set-you-straight sworn statement in the absolute finest of the Asinof writing tradition. If the happy (though hard-won) ending for a fictional Jack Cagle made Asinof at all uneasy, he more than made up for it by recapping his friendship of 40 plus years with Joe DiMaggio, who had died in 1999 at age 85 while *Off-Season* was being completed. If Jack Cagle represented the ultimate distillation of Asinof's fictional baseball heroes, then DiMaggio—even more than Babe Ruth—was the living embodiment of everything that the novelist, like millions of other fans, most admired in a professional baseball player. DiMaggio, as most true baseball fans will agree, was about as great a player as ever set foot on the playing field, as well as one of the most lionized by fans and media. Asinof believed that the whole truth had not been told in the numerous obituaries and biographies which came in the wake of the Yankee Clipper's passing, and probably felt that he owed something to DiMaggio's memory by setting the record straight, at least for those willing to entertain such hard truths. Readers may recall that Asinof, though a hero worshipping fan of DiMaggio since adolescence, had not met the great Hall of Famer until shortly after publication of *Man on Spikes* in 1955 (see Chapter 2). It was then that the notoriously reticent DiMaggio expressed unrestrained admiration for the realism contained in Asinof's first baseball novel. Asinof then recounted to the recently retired superstar an unsettling incident that they had both been witness to some 17 years previous, much to DiMaggio's surprise and pleasure, but certainly not at the time the incident occurred.

Specifically, on May 4, 1938, at Yankee Stadium, DiMaggio came to the plate for the first time at home that season and was greeted with fan chorus

A very casually-dressed Asinof delivers the keynote address at the 11th Annual Symposium of Baseball and American Culture at the Baseball Hall of Fame, Cooperstown, New York, circa 1999. During this period, the novelist was formulating his final thoughts on the national pastime, finding expression in his novel *Off-Season* and two articles written for the *Village Voice* in 2000–2001.

of thousands — booing him. It had nothing to do with his performance; during his first two seasons with the Yankees (1936–1937), DiMaggio led them to consecutive World Series championships and was already being widely recognized as one of the greatest players of all time. So far during the 1938 season, on the road, his batting average was somewhere around .600. DiMaggio's sin, however, had come during the previous "off-season" when he had the effrontery to demand a small raise from Yankees owner "Colonel" Jacob Rupert.[4] This was during the prewar era of the reserve clause and long before Free Agency. Rupert not only denied DiMaggio a raise, he launched a media campaign aimed at the great slugger that turned many, if not most fans against him. When DiMaggio realized he had no other options, he went back to work and led the Yankees to more world championships. An astonished 18-year-old Eliot Asinof happened to be in the stands that day in Yankee Stadium, and never forgot the experience, nor did DiMaggio, although almost everyone else seemed to forget or did not want to remember. Then, in 2000–2001, Asinof's intrepid typewriter dragged it all back into the light of day.

In his revelatory article, Asinof confessed that the unsettling events of that day stayed with him for the rest of his life; moreover, it was one of the factors that eventually led him to write his first book. As he put it, "For me ... the holdout experience became a source of energy. I would nurse my resentments until, 17 years later, I wrote a novel, *Man on Spikes*."[5] Because of the affable relationship between the two men, producers would try to get at DiMaggio through Asinof to portray DiMaggio's unhappy personal life on the big screen. Asinof, true to his nature, was disgusted and flatly refused to do this, often at the cost of his own writing career.[6] In regards to DiMaggio, Asinof felt compelled to give what he felt was an accurate journalistic account of the great man's demise, surrounded on his deathbed by unsavory handlers and unscrupulous media vultures: "Even Ty Cobb's loveless death seemed less sordid. Whatever lesson Joe learned in his lifetime, it was not one that brought him joy."[7] Therefore it seems fitting that *Off-Season*, which earlier had working titles of *Hero* and *Free Agent* (made in reference to Jack Cagle), was wisely later re-titled for publication. To Asinof, the ultimate baseball hero and would-be free agent, both for both better and for worse, had always been the late Joe DiMaggio.[8]

In addition to fan fickleness and the vicissitudes of stardom, the narrative of *Off-Season* continues to address one of Asinof's ongoing and longstanding favorite topics as writer, both in and out baseball, namely, race relations in America. Cagle has close personal relationships with no fewer than three African Americans in the story — Cyrus, Ruby, and Corky. In spite of these associations, however, Cagle is typical of modern sports superstars in that he is totally ignorant of the troubled history of his chosen profession with respect to race and, its close ancillary issue, labor relations. Early in the novel, Cagle's shady handler, Gordon Stanley, though himself little more than a business opportunist, finds it ludicrous that his young client has never heard of Curt Flood, and sharply upbraids him for it: "My God, you're like the black ballplayers who never heard of Jackie Robinson. Flood sacrificed his career to fight the reserve clause that kept you dumb ballplayers in virtual bondage."[9] By the end of the novel, though, Cagle's initial lack of social awareness has been heightened to a considerable degree. More importantly, his newfound knowledge comes not from textbooks or formal schooling, but from the proverbial hard-knocks university of life that his belated homecoming to Gandee has unexpectedly provided.

Another striking aspect of Asinof's last baseball book is that the profound importance of the game in his life shines as brightly as it did 45 years earlier when he produced *Man on Spikes*. The earliest childhood memory that Cagle shares with readers is one of him hitting a home run in Little League at age 10.[10] The incident is described as a life-changing event, as indeed it is for anyone who has ever lived through a similar triumph. For Asinof, the image is a recurring motif in his work. In *The Bedfellow*, Mike Sorrell's sordid ghetto life in Watts is immediately transformed when, at age 13, he blasts a homer during a sandlot game.[11] Asinof, in his own memoir, recalls hitting his first round-tripper at a tender age of seven.[12] Cagle, however, is somewhat of a completely new creation for the novelist in multiple respects. For one, Cagle becomes a pitcher, whereas Asinof's previous heroes had been outfielders, as he himself had been during his own playing days.[13] Cagle is also physically big (six feet four inches tall, 220 pounds), showing Asinof's cognizance of perhaps baseball's most distinctive new trend — pitchers well above average in height who seem to be striding half-way to home plate from the mound before they release the ball.[14] The novelist once again demonstrates his expertise by reminding readers of a pitcher's limitless importance in any baseball contest.[15] This may seem obvious to some, but not, say, to those who continue to question whether the 1919 World Series was really thrown, despite the 1-2 pitching rotation for the Black Sox accepting bribe money and then dumping five of the six games in which they pitched (see Chapter 6). More subtle aspects of the pitching game are displayed as well. Cagle's sinister father intentionally breaks the taboo of mentioning his son's perfect game before it is completed.[16] Even off the playing field, the novelist empathizes with a pitcher's plight. For example, after Cagle's evil Uncle Sam sends him packing, "like a pitcher leaving the mound after hanging one too many curve balls."[17]

While Asinof introduces numerous character innovations in *Off-Season*, he is still Asinof, the former switch-hitting lefty, to the core. Cagle, who begins playing the game as an outfielder, later becomes a left-handed fireball pitcher and, his first pitching instructor, Cyrus Coles, is (much more unusually) a left-handed catcher.[18] Thus the bias of the novelist towards left-handers is hard to miss. There might also be some political symbolism here as well. Intermittently, the novelist cannot forget to include mild doses of his trademark off-color dialogue, sometimes to hilarious effect and other times (intentionally), not at all. Asinof, as in all of his other baseball works, gives the reader plenty of the typically crude and often unfunny humor so prevalent on the playing field. For example, an obnoxious joke about baseball gloves and human anatomy from *Strike Zone* is repeated in *Off-Season*. This comes from, not surprisingly, the foul mouth of Cagle's despicable Uncle Sam as the latter unsuccessfully tries to impress his nephew.[19] On a more gut level, Asinof reminds his audiences what it is like to be in physical pain, either from injuries suffered during a game or off the playing field. After Cagle is beaten unconscious by hired assailants, he accurately remembers from his playing experience that he is going to physically hurt even more the next day."[20] Whether it be nagging injuries, dirty jokes, or left-handed playing advantages, Asinof's close, intimate familiarity with the game of baseball on its most gritty and elemental plane is apparent throughout all of his baseball works from start to finish.

Chatting with the elderly Mike Kutner on their flight back to Los Angeles, Cagle comes to the realization that twice now during his early adult life he has essentially become a new person, first with his African American battery mate from high school, and then at the end of the tale, thanks to a chance meeting with Kutner. Asinof the narrator takes us into Cagle's innermost thoughts: "And suddenly the fat black left-handed catcher behind the Shell station had become an old white man on a flight to L.A."[21] This unusual morphing of two seemingly opposite characters into one person calls to mind Asinof's own earlier efforts as a novelist, writing from the viewpoint of a retired black baseball player in *The Bedfellow* (see Part III of this study). It also movingly reminds us of "The Negro" chapter from *Man on Spikes*, in which a surly, resentful Kutner must first compete for his playing job against an African American rookie, then protect that same rookie from the racist resentments of his teammates. Cagle's final apotheosis as a new, reborn man (symbolized by the close shave and haircut that he receives from Kutner) comes immediately after he breaks the color line in his own mind's eye between Coles and Kutner, recognizing in both the profound influence that each has made in his life and career.

Perhaps Asinof's most personal (and humorous) commentary of the game comes near the end of *Off-Season* and, once again, from the running commentary of Mike Kutner. As he and Cagle compare notes on the professional aspects of the sport, it comes to the surface that the younger athlete plays primarily for money, while his older counterpart had played the game mostly out of passion and despite a meager salary. Kutner, obviously representing the voice of the novelist, vents to Cagle that this difference has affected playing skills for the worse:

> Too many third-raters getting' paid millions.... Can't bunt. Can't run the bases right. Can't get wood on the ball. I hear them sayin' how they found God, you know, but by God, they can't find the cut-off man. They can't even stay in the batter's box, always half way down the foul line after every pitch, zippin' the Velcro on their batting gloves, fussin' with their shirt, their caps, strokin' the barrel of the bat like it was their dick. All them look-at-me-TV superstitions.... Like tight pants to show your ass. Skin tight shirts. If a ballplayer wore a floppy shirt, then if a pitched ball just nicks it, it's an HB and he'd get on maybe a dozen times more.... Things like that, they add up.[22]

This amusing diatribe is essentially a half century recurring refrain for Asinof. A few years previous, in *Strike Zone*, umpire Ernie Kolacka, and again, representing the novelist's personal viewpoint, gives an almost identical critique of modern Major League ballplayers (see Chapter 15). In particular, and just like Kutner, Kolacka especially objects to tight uniforms: "Preseason, equipment managers get them [the players] measured with micrometers for the exact size of their buttocks so the ballplayers can look like ballet dancers in leotards. What kind of bullshit is that?"[23] Tight uniforms aside, and going back much further to 1955's *Man on Spikes*, the wise old scout Durkin Fain (who discovers Kutner) eschews a similar baseball philosophy, one completely at odds with the school in which Jack Cagle has been trained as a player. When Fain yells in futility at his boss, "You're just buying weight ... at fifty bucks a pound!" he is warning against the same "Big boys who can't hit their weight" that later so infuriate Kutner.[24] In this respect, the fictional Kutner is echoing the sentiments of the fictional scout (Fain) who signed him to a professional baseball contract during the era prior to World War II.

Picking up on his own suggestion, Kutner then continues to comment on what he perceives as the core problem of the professional game, as well as in most athletes aspiring to play baseball professionally: "I'm sayin' it's sad. People say, it's the same all over. Politics, celebrities, zillionaires. But with baseball, it ain't right.... You guys, you're like actors out there. Costumes and make-up, like you're givin' a damned show."[25] Because the athletes are playing mainly for money (as Cagle more or less admits), not only are they suffering from atrophy in their playing skills, but, according to Kutner, and more seriously, their sincerity and integrity (both real and perceived) as competitors are being compromised.[26] Instead, they are becoming "like actors," pretending to do something strictly for the monetary value of entertainment, rather than actually doing something they enjoy and are fully committed to. Asinof stops one sentence short of bringing up the Black Sox in this context, and leaves it to readers to make that alarming connection. In effect, baseball has become an unpleasant reflection of all undesirable qualities in contemporary American life. Rather than society being inspired by baseball's purity, baseball has been corrupted by society's lack of values or, to put it more precisely, society's overemphasis on fame and profit. Once again, this is far from being a new idea for the novelist; on the contrary, the very same notion was established in the opening pages of *Man on Spikes* in 1955: namely, that money corrupts. For Asinof, it becomes his greatest and most consistent baseball theme throughout a long, prolific writing career, probably even more so than American race relations, notions of self-sacrifice, or any other topical issue.

The sinister role of mass media in the overall process, however, never goes un-remarked upon by Asinof, and *Off-Season* is no exception in this regard. When he steps out of line, Cagle is threatened by his uncle and father (of all people) with fabricated media blackmail, and must purchase the local newspaper, along with the loyalty its employees, before he can effectively fight back. In the baseball world, Cagle's own financial marketability as a sports superstar is based, not on his real personality, but rather on a false "Black Jack" public image created by sportswriters and skillfully perpetuated by his unprincipled, Harvard-graduate agent, Gordon Stanley: "Gordon turned Jack into a satanic figure. No interviews. He never spoke to reporters in the locker room.... He was trained to ignore everything and deny nothing."[27] Cagle's manufactured persona becomes a symbol of his moral obliviousness; in fact, its blatant phoniness is possibly the only thing about Cagle that both his old antagonist-father and new girlfriend-sidekick Foxx can agree upon. The symbolic erasure of the image through a haircut and shave received from Kutner at the conclusion of the novel represents the hero's moral redemption and deliverance from the clutches of unscrupulous handlers, owners, and sportswriters.

On the subject of sportswriters and sportscasters, Asinof uses every opportunity in *Off-Season* and its *Village Voice* companion pieces to deliver a few more parting shots. He was, to put it mildly, never very fond of these two intertwined groups and deeply resentful that critics often labeled him as a sportswriter while ignoring or trashing his own numerous and quite worthy literary efforts outside of the realm of sports topicality. In his last baseball novel, before Asinof has written three pages of the first chapter, he delivers a withering opinion of television broadcasters, producers, and promoters, with whom he had long and unpleasant experience as a professional writer:

> "Mean" was a more marketable image than "gentle," so under no circumstances was he [Cagle] ever to smile, not even in the dugout lest some TV camera catch a glimpse of it. Whatever effect this may or may not have had on hitters, TV announcers reveled in it. Indeed, Gordon wrote copy for them.... Nobody wanted to admit it, but everyone knew that the devil was the more powerful of the two deities.[28]

Later, after Cagle is mugged and hospitalized, the novelist's contempt extends to all of the popular news media with the hero disgusted by his unintentional appearance in *People Magazine*. The final insult comes when the press, effectively manipulated by Mayor Sam Manning, focuses on the angle that Cagle's assailants are black, rather than the true reasons or motivations behind the attack. Foxx, who seems to be the only ethical journalist in town, sums up Cagle's PR defeat by paraphrasing Julius Caesar, "You came, you saw, you got conquered."[29]

Asinof's undisguised hostility towards the sports press and popular mass media was nothing new for him. Back in 1955, he had devoted an entire hard-hitting chapter from *Man on Spikes* to "The Reporter." Here, a much younger Mike Kutner, returning from World War II to resume his minor league playing career, must endure newspaper jibes of Houston sportswriter and columnist Orville Jenkins, who publicly criticizes the hero for holding out when the team owner tries to cut his already meager salary. Afterwards, in a masterfully written locker room confrontation, Kutner verbally dresses down and embarrasses Jenkins in front of his sympathetic teammates, then shortly thereafter re-signs with his team for undisclosed terms. As for the outraged Jenkins, the novelist scathingly labels him as "strictly a little man."[30] Some four and a half decades later, Asinof, while writing about race relations in Major League Baseball for the *Village Voice*, still found space to take a swipe at sportscasters. He opined that it was probably best watch the World Series at a crowded sports bar where fans could share the "inevitable tensions" of the contest, and to avoid being "smothered by the sugary drivel of the announcers" covering the Series.[31]

In early 2001 (following the release of *Off-Season*), Asinof was attacking the sports media again, this time in reference to his late, great friend, Joe DiMaggio. Following Yankee owner Colonel Rupert's successful media blitz and smear campaign against his reputation in 1938, DiMaggio never again opened up to sportswriters. Asinof sadly observed:

> Writers constantly invaded his privacy, filling their columns with ludicrous comments, most of them false. Athletes have always been wary of writers — so-called "jock-sniffers" in the locker room — who are fascinated by off-the-field gossip and adept at stirring up controversies to make for more exciting copy. They thrive on extremes, like great streaks or miserable slumps. They are slaves of statistics. They don't bother with the marvelous subtleties of the game. That's why ballplayers used to tell reporters, "If you could hit you wouldn't write." To a ballplayer, a writer is as suspect as a cop to an inner-city kid. DiMaggio, shy to begin with, would want no part of them, and certainly not a biographer.[32]

DiMaggio himself had little to say of the whole affair except in regards to the voluminous hate mail that he had received: "You would have thought I'd kidnapped the Lindbergh baby, the way some of those letters read."[33] The traditional hostility between athletes and sportswriters exemplified by DiMaggio's tragic case is important, because it was this same barrier that Asinof was able to successfully break down when he became the very first writer to fully and accurately lay out the true story behind the 1919 Black Sox Scandal during the early 1960s.[34] On the other hand, he could see both sides of the coin: reporters Hugh Fullerton and Ring Lardner are held up as near-heroes in *Eight Men Out* for their determined and persistent efforts to bring the scandal to public light in spite of all opposition. Make no mistake: it was Asinof's own former professional playing experience that allowed him to do this.

"Hardball is a team sport, Jack," says Foxx appropriately to Cagle as he makes his fateful decision to remain in Gandee until Ruby Coles is freed from jail and the town leaders' corruption publicly exposed.[35] Cagle especially needs the reminder because, as a baseball pitcher, he tends to think the entire ballgame revolves around him, which is true to some extent, but with crucial limitations.[36] The same principle is applicable to the hero's non-baseball, non-sports challenge in *Off-Season*; he needs the help of others to prevail, all in fact that he can muster. Raw talent and hard work are not nearly enough. Foxx knows this, and so does Cagle by the middle of the story. Contrary to Asinof's widespread reputation as an author who glorified individual heroism over and against the collective mainstream, his philosophical viewpoint, particularly towards the end of his writing career, is far more subtle and complex. By the time he had completed his last two novels, it was apparent that his dominant message — if one may use such a descriptor — involved the welfare of the community over that of the individual. By definition (for him at least), this abstract ideal included an uncompromising emphasis by society upon education of its citizenry. This highly idiosyncratic version of communal welfare often entailed, by necessity, the exercise of individual courage, savvy, intelligence, unselfish personal values, and sometimes, even personal sacrifice for a greater good. This was Asinof's idea of heroism. That he was so often able to put the idea across in the form of popular entertainment is no small cause for our wonder and amazement. In the final chapter of this study, we shall examine how these more universal notions of virtue and idealism found expression in the novelist's last major work of baseball fiction.

20

"The Heart and Soul of Racist America"

One of the most distinctive and enjoyable qualities of Asinof's baseball writing, one making him practically unique among those authors choosing to engage the subject, is that sports commentary, more often than not, segues in social commentary, sometimes within the very same sentence. A seemingly innocent and innocuous remark about hanging curve balls can instantly transform itself into sweeping political exegesis, assuming the reader is capable of making such a leap. Oftentimes this effect is accomplished by turning an aphorism on its head. For example, the oft-quoted dictum by historian Jacques Barzun, "Whoever wants to know the heart and mind of America had better learn baseball," in Asinof's more discerning view becomes, "Whoever wants to know baseball had best understand America."[1] For this former professional ballplayer turned professional writer, the so-called national pastime was a mirror reflection of the nation that invented the game, rather than a wellspring, and a highly accurate, frequently disconcerting one at that.[2] Most authors who tackle sports-related subjects are (at best) able to boringly download what little genuine information they can glean secondhand from others, while filling in the rest of their writings with fantasy and make-believe. Not only did Asinof have unimpeachable, firsthand baseball expertise, he also could casually, effortlessly employ that same expertise to make much bigger, more important statements about the world in which we live. Such rare attributes are to be found only in the very best of writers from all ages throughout history.

On its surface level, *Off-Season* persuasively argues that America at the recent turn of the last century, notwithstanding self-congratulatory assertions to the contrary, was far from coming to terms with issues of race, either within the game of baseball or without. The white hero of the novel, Black Jack Cagle, has childhood-conditioned attitudes towards African Americans that are firmly established in the first chapter: "He had grown up wary of all blacks. One way or another they bothered him."[3] Cagle's wariness is presented as being the joint product of growing up in a Missouri backwater under the stern supervision of a racist, authoritarian father. Cagle's bigotry, however, is not innate; through his adolescent discovery of baseball, he is able to form meaningful relationships, and later genuine friendships, with blacks. He has in him more than a bit of Huckleberry Finn, whose creator Mark Twain, aka Samuel Clemens, hailed from Hannibal, Missouri, which appears to be located not too far Asinof's fictional town of Gandee.[4] Thanks to his early escape from Gandee into the wider world of major league baseball stardom, Cagle, by adulthood, has as his closest friend, African American teammate Corky Corcoran. Throughout the novel, Corcoran is adroit at making pungent, controversial statements on the topic of race, much to the surprise and delight of Cagle who takes in every word and sometimes shares in the physical and verbal mistreatment that Corcoran receives from other whites. Jack and Corky thus become updated versions of Huck and Jim, figuratively navigating together the treacherous currents of professional sports and, in Jack's case, his volatile, segregated home town.

After Cagle suffers initial defeat in his quest by being beaten senseless and confined to a hospital bed, he has time to reflect on his life, his profession, and who his true friends really are. Realizing that it is Corky (rather than his family, business manager, or trophy girlfriend) who makes him laugh and feel better, Cagle recalls the time that the two of them were jailed in Texas for getting into a bar brawl provoked by slurs made by local yokels against Corky. While in the clink, to amuse his white cellmate who is quite unused to such treatment, Corky delivers a parody of Dr. Martin Luther King, Jr.'s famous "I have a dream" speech, originally delivered at the Lincoln Memorial in 1963, the same year that Asinof's *Eight Men Out* was published. It is one of the most gripping and controversial passages that Asinof ever wrote (even by his standards), and therefore deserves to be quoted here at length:

> "I have a dream," he'd announce in stentorian tones. "I have a dream that someday professional baseball will be completely segregated. No black man will play on the same team or in the same league as a white man. National League, all black. American, white.... Every game will be interleague. Stadiums will be divided.... All games then, will be a racial clash. I have a dream, Roomie, of high-flying spikes, of pitchers decking hitters, of body-crashing drama at home plate, of violence and rumors of violence. I have a dream of great rivalries spurred by racial pride. Colossal ball games that would inspire ballplayers beyond fat pay checks. Baseball will become the heart and soul of racist America, bringing in crowds beyond the greediest club owner's dream. The World Series, then, would be a modern reprise of the Civil War itself. I have a dream, Roomie, where the bullshit hypocrisy of America's quest for racial amity will once and for all be abandoned!"[5]

Though outrageous in and of itself, Corky's proposal is thought-provoking. Baseball, always viewed by Asinof as a rough-and-tumble, hurly-burly contact sport, is suddenly envisioned as a sort of futuristic, gladiatorial race riot, controlled and channeled, which (to more than a few spectators) American professional sports have always seemed to some extent. Three years previous in 1997, major league baseball had begun regular season interleague play for the first time in modern memory, thereby shattering the longstanding mystique behind American and National League separation, and this may have sparked the novelist's imagination. Bigger issues naturally present themselves. If major league baseball primarily is, and should be, a big business driven by owner-shareholder expectations of short-term profit, then why not? What, if anything, should be off-limits so long as it generates gate receipts? Does not the same debate apply to everything else in our society? Though masked in the guise of popular entertainment, *Off-Season* is a rare commodity in that it dares to pose such explosive questions.

As brilliant and brutal as Corky's speech is, and as blasé as Cagle's response to it sounds, the unusual friendship of the two characters also represents progress of a sorts for the novelist, compared to his earlier works.[6] In 1967's *The Bedfellow*, Mike Sorrell resignedly describes professional baseball as "an integrated-separated split-screen colorvision show" (see Chapter 9) in which blacks "ate separately, roomed separately, socialized separately.... Baseball had broken the color line, but it couldn't abide the Brotherhood."[7] Three years later, in Asinof's gripping 1970 nonfiction profile of racial conflict in *People vs. Blutcher*, the urban ghetto of Brooklyn's Bedford-Stuyvesant is graphically presented as a kind of hell on earth in which whites and blacks are able to interact with each other only on a hostile, confrontational basis. He wrote: "Americans tend to think of the ghetto with such shame and opprobrium, we tend to forget there are real, live people trapped in them, fighting for whatever dignity they can hope to achieve."[8] Thirty years later in *Off-Season*, the ghetto remains and racial separateness still usually prevails on and off the field, but not always. Jack and Corky are exceptions, as are Jack's guarded but productive relationships with Cyrus and Ruby Coles. Asinof used his last baseball book as a vehicle to express his most advanced thoughts on the topic of race, views that had remained largely unchanged over the course of 50 years of writing, but during the interim his work had acquired a significantly greater degree of depth and detail.

Anyone hoping that Asinof's outburst (made through Corky's speech) was an isolated occurrence or regrettable mistake made at a bad moment need search no further than the incendiary article he produced for the *Village Voice* about the same time that *Off-Season* was being released. This opinion piece, "The Dis-Integration of Baseball: A Modest Proposal for the Great Game," in addition to the devastating double-meaning within the title, more or less reiterates the content of Corky's speech from *Off-Season*, and then expands upon it to make sure there is no reader denial or mistake in meaning.[9] The article begins and ends with the same Yogi Berra humorous-serious quotes that act as a prelude to Asinof's last baseball novel. After repeating his old argument that that "national pastime" in fact has long since become a misnomer, Asinof plunges into his jarring sports bar experience during the 1999 World Series between the New York Yankees and Atlanta Braves.[10] In *Off-Season*, Cagle's attendance at this exact same event is used by the novelist to make him realize how much he enjoys the game, even as a spectator, and how little he really has in common with his consort, the team owner's self-centered daughter, Judith Pagonis.[11] In real life, Asinof bellied up to a crowded bar to watch the contest and by chance found himself standing next to an older, unnamed African American who, like Asinof, used to play the game himself.

The lengthy dialogue between the two elderly ex-players (on opposite sides of the racial divide) that Asinof proceeds to share has the ring of partial fiction to it, but larger segments and perhaps the core as well all pack as realistic a wallop as anything he ever wrote. During the televised playing of the Star-Spangled Banner, as players lined up along the foul lines, Asinof politely noted that it was "good to see all those blacks and Hispanics." His drinking companion grunted in response and then, as the camera mindlessly panned through crowd observed, "More blacks on them foul lines than in the seats." Asinof was stunned: "It was true. I did not see a single black face!" As for the reason behind this disparity, after rejecting all of the usual socioeconomic explanations, the gentleman was matter-of-fact: "White man's ballpark, mister. White man's teams. Still the white man's game." What follows in a nutshell is the gentleman's proposal to remedy the situation, which is exactly the same as Corky's suggestion in the novel, namely, encourage segregation and turn it into a box office draw. Then, maybe ordinary kids, especially black kids, will start playing the game again in large numbers as they had before World War II. Then the old man had to leave. Asinof recalled, "It was such a preposterous conversation I had to laugh."[12] This "preposterous conversation," however, immediately appeared as the centerpiece in *Off-Season*, in which a hospitalized Cagle begins to slowly come around to his senses and resolves to take a heroic stand, this time off the playing field on unfamiliar home ground.

Two years later in 2003, Asinof's final published commentary on race relations appeared in his modest but memorable profile in *Time International* of Ontario-born, former major league pitcher Ferguson Jenkins, the first Canadian to be inducted into the Baseball Hall of Fame, and a black man, though not strictly speaking, African American.[13] In typical Asinof style, he focuses on rarely commented upon aspects of Jenkins' life which he found fascinating or significant. Jenkins' father had been an outstanding pitcher in the Negro Leagues just before the color barrier was broken, and the son had been originally drafted by (and played for) the Philadelphia Phillies, the same organization for which Asinof had played as a young man.[14] After acknowledging Jenkins' extraordinary talent as an athlete, Asinof then finishes with the central point of the profile—Jenkins' career after his retirement as a professional player in 1983 and election to the Hall of Fame in 1991. Asinof reports on Jenkins being named a commissioner of the then newly formed (and now defunct) Canadian Baseball League, with an emphasis on getting kids in that country to play the game, praising Jenkins with, "From player to ambassador—this is a man who knows how to make a great pitch."[15] The Canadian connection is interesting because 37 years earlier (in 1966) Asinof had written briefly about Cito Gaston, then only a marginal minor league player, but who would go on to manage the Canadian Toronto Blue Jays to consecutive World Series titles in 1992–1993. This acquaintance, as noted earlier in this study (see Chapter 9), may have influenced his creation of the fictional Mike Sorrell in 1967's *The Bedfellow*. In any event, the appearance of the Jenkins profile marked a fitting coda in Asinof's writing career on the subject of race, one that had been so resoundingly explored in *Off-Season* three years earlier.

Another old and prominent theme in Asinof's work which finds full expression in his last baseball novel is that of finding true personal identity through self-knowledge. No character in Asinof's catalogue changes so much for the better in such a short time period as does Jack Cagle, Jr. At the beginning of story, Cagle is little more than human vacuity disguised behind a false public persona. Foxx immediately recognizes the fraud and ferociously upbraids him for it:

> You don't even look like you. That's not your face, it's a horror mask.... What are you, Jack? Just another working stiff trying to make a living? Are you kidding? Why the meanness, Jack? What for? To sell shoes? Those commercials are so insulting. Why do you do them! For more money? I don't understand, isn't a hundred million dollars enough? ... I remember that perfect game. You were so in love with what you were doing. The intensity was beautiful. Your shyness was endearing. It was you, Jack. But now it's all an act, isn't it. It's not love anymore. That's so sad.[16]

Cagle takes this destructive criticism mostly in good cheer, mainly because he has been trained not to do interviews (which is not what Foxx is after) and partly because deep down he knows what she says is true. After continuing in this same vein for several pages, and just as it seems that Foxx is winding down, she lets Cagle have it again:

> Why don't you just go, Jack. You shouldn't have come back. You don't belong here anymore. Just look at that limo! Jesus, what's it doing in Gandee? Why it's bigger than our high school! ... Tell me something, Jack: when you look in the mirror, who do you see? Do you see anyone you know, Jack?[17]

This last insult is noteworthy. Soon afterwards, Cagle unpleasantly recalls staring at himself in a mirror after a broken teenage date when he begins to develop his fearsome "Black Jack" image.[18] Foxx's challenge for him to once again take a good look into the mirror, brings to mind the closing sentences of Asinof's *The Bedfellow*, in which a morally compromised Mike Sorrell can no longer bear to see his own reflection.[19] It also recalls Ernie Kolacka's glance into a mirror with a clean conscience at the conclusion of *Strike Zone*.[20] Just as baseball becomes a mirror of American society, for Asinof the mirror becomes a literal and symbolic reflection of individual self-awareness and ethical uprightness. In the final sentences of *Off-Season*, after Cagle receives his shave and crew cut from Kutner on the airplane, he looks into a compact mirror and sees himself clearly: "Hey, I remember this guy! A good kid, but all screwed up.... What saved him, he really loved playin' ball." Cagle then shakes hands with Kutner, who responds with: "Don't you forget that sonny."[21] On this happy note, the novel ends.

Curiously absent from *Off-Season*'s otherwise graphically unflattering description of Gandee, Missouri, is any mention of education, public or otherwise. As quoted above, Foxx tears into Cagle for his overblown lifestyle, tossing in her exaggerated (?) accusation that his limousine overshadows the local high school in size. This brings us lastly to an all-important topic in Asinof's works: namely, the recent decline of the American public educational system. To achieve their goals, Cagle and Foxx must, in effect, educate themselves since there appears to be no other institutions willing or able to do this for them. Cagle goes pro right out of high school, and does not have a college degree. Foxx's background is a little more hazy; nowhere is it stated she attended university and presumably, she does not necessarily need a degree to work as a reporter for the local newspaper. As for the public high school in Gandee that Cagle and Foxx attended, it goes nearly unmentioned other than its new baseball field, which is shoddily and secretly constructed on environmentally contaminated grounds, thanks to the political machinations of Cagle's unscrupulous Uncle Sam. Thus with Asinof's last baseball novel (as with his very last non-baseball novel, *Final Judgment*), we come full circle to the prioritization of higher education in society. Cagle and Foxx's pathetic lack of opportunities in this regard stand in sharp contrast to Asinof's own superb, privileged training that he received during the 1930s New Deal era at institutions like Swarthmore College, Williams College, and Lawrence High School in Cedarhurst, Long Island.

To fully understand Asinof's attitude as an author on this subject, one must once again return to his seminal 1971 non-fiction work, *Craig and Joan*. Here, for the first time, he extensively explores the question of American public secondary education, since it applied so directly and decisively to his investigation at the time. One might expect a sympathetic or indulgent evaluation of the public school system in mostly white Blackwood, New Jersey, during the late 1960s (where Craig Badiali and Joan Fox attended), since

Asinof was himself a stellar product of all white public schools and private universities located only a few hours drive from the town. Any such notions, however, are quickly disabused in the opening chapters of the book. He begins with a withering critique, not only of Blackwood, but of all American secondary institutions, of which Blackwood is held up as a typical, albeit unfavorable, exemplar:

> It has been said of the American secondary school system that its primary—if unstated—purposes are to serve as a continued baby-sitter to keep overstimulated youngsters out of trouble, and to hold them out of the competitive job market for a few more years.[22]

This kind of environment, according to Asinof, lays the fundamental groundwork for the type of tragedy that he was reporting on. In terms of student graduates, the result then becomes, at best, those who try to rebel against the status quo in a constructive manner, or at worst (and far more typical), citizenry quite unequipped to function properly in a democratic republican society. Asinof summarizes the dilemma: "It would follow that civics is a difficult course to teach in the high schools. Inevitably, the kids are the victims who suffer the most, learning their first lessons in cynicism in the homes, followed by hypocrisy in the schools."[23] The root cause of the problem, suggests Asinof, is the affluent complacency of the privileged few, which is exactly the same malaise that Cagle suffers from at the beginning of the story in *Off-Season*.[24]

The only thing that such an ineffectual system excels at, argues Asinof, is producing underachievers. What few college graduates are turned out by these high schools, Asinof acerbically notes, will be of little use to the republic: "They will presumably learn to be teachers and return to perpetuate the very educational system that retarded them."[25] Asinof goes on to record the astounding factoid that, as of 1971, the suicide Vietnam protesters Craig Badiali and Joan Fox were the only former students from Blackwood to have achieved recognition outside of the town. Regarding Blackwood's failure to produce excellence, one unfazed student opined, "Well, *that* must be a distinction of some kind!"[26] Asinof reports that Blackwood cannot even excel outside of Blackwood with respect to extra curricular activities. By way of examples he gives a local boxing champion who is hurt badly when trying to compete professionally on a regional level, as well as the pitiful case of the high school marching band being reported winner of a national contest by the local press when in fact it did not even place.[27] As one of the dead couple's friends explained to Asinof, "I guess people only believe what they want to believe."[28]

All in all, *Craig and Joan* is the kind of close-up journalistic exposé in which Asinof excelled, and one that obviously became a springboard for many of his later major works. In *Off-Season* it is therefore no accident that the hero becomes the owner of a local newspaper and that the heroine is an investigative reporter. The nonfictional Craig and Joan's self-sacrifice, though perhaps futile and misguided, is presented by Asinof as being constructive in ways the adolescent couple never imagined. It may have not changed any minds in Blackwood about the war, but it at least proved that someone in that time and place knew not all was well with the country or its institutions. Returning to the world of fiction in Asinof's last novel, *Final Judgment*, the protest suicide of Anne Miner, though seemingly insane at its occurrence, does achieve its immediate objective (to halt a commencement speech) and later inspires those who witness it to live more useful and virtuous lives. Perhaps most extraordinary of all is that *Craig and Joan* was published in 1971 (four decades ago), at a time in which the funding crisis in public education was becoming acute but not nearly as critical as the situation is today.

Although there is no overt mention of public education in *Off-Season*, it looms over events in the novel as surely as if everything in Gandee, Missouri, ultimately depended upon its presence or lack thereof. As noted above, the public high school is a non-entity. Its most famous and financially successful graduate, Black Jack Cagle, is at first nothing more than an ignoramus, but gradually, painfully changes through experience. After Cagle has thoroughly vanquished all of his adversaries both on and off the playing field, he must still contend with himself. By the end of the tale, Cagle is well aware of his problem: "'You don't even know that you don't know,' Foxx had said. He had come to understand that. He now *knew* that he did not know, which of course frightened him all the more."[29] What had begun for Cagle as a personal quest to right a wrong in his home town ends with his realization that the true challenge will be reform his own behavior. Perhaps his inadequate education is even an advantage towards accomplishing this objective in that it strips him of all pretense and presumption. Returning to the seemingly unbridgeable racial divide in Gandee, the problem forcibly ties into public education through the issue of school integration. Corky and Ruby Coles are, respectively, a victim of and would-be martyr to racial injustice in Gandee. Both are warned well in advance of the consequences for their defiant actions, but proceed nonetheless out of pride and principle. Ruby is rescued in the end, and the murdered Cyrus becomes an inspiration, whose militant exhortation, "You gotta love it!" remains in Cagle's heart and mind, presumably for the rest of his life.[30]

Considering Asinof's unjustly bestowed reputation as a dour, angry, cynical, or pessimistic commentator on American history and culture, *Off-Season* is a surprisingly hopeful and optimistic novel in its future outlook. Cagle and Foxx succeed brilliantly in spite of all obstacles and in spite of all their personal handicaps. The axiological implication or lesson of the novelist is obvious: while good education may be crucial to any difficult endeavor, lack of education is not an insurmountable impediment, nor it is ever too late to start moving forward. In fact (and in a crunch), in Asinof's fiction, formal education is trumped almost every time by sound experience — this from an author who graduated cum laude from Swarthmore. On the other hand, Cagle and Foxx triumph, not only because they make a good team, but because Cagle learns how to effectively use his wealth and celebrity. Cagle may not have a bachelor's degree or even a high school diploma worth the paper it is written on, but he does have eyes and ears and is still young enough (age 27) to learn how to use them in new ways. He also has heart and soul; he can distinguish between right and wrong, plus has the physical and moral courage to risk self-sacrifice in an effort to change things, or at least not be mindlessly swept along with the tide. Above all, both Cagle and Foxx are able to continue their educations beyond their near-worthless formal schooling through pure force of will, which proves to be perhaps the most crucial and optimistic lesson of all.[31] It is not an easy task, however; aside from bruises and insults, Cagle must face disturbing truths about his own family, his erstwhile friends, and himself. In this endeavor, Foxx and Corky become his guides. Lastly, baseball is the storyteller's vehicle by which all of these things are accomplished.

Conclusion

Baseball is where youthful dreams begin, but it's also a test of character when the dream-come-true becomes a nightmare.

—Eliot Asinof[1]

Although the phrase is often overused, Eliot Asinof was a true American original. His published body of literary work, taken as a whole, stands totally apart from those of other writers and can barely be compared to anyone else's output. Those would-be critics who attempt to dismiss him as a one-note sportswriter, are missing the boat on at least three accounts. First, all five of his baseball books are among the very best of their kind, and three might be classified as great achievements. Second, his non-baseball and non-sports writings are consistently compelling—at least half a dozen of these works are wrongly neglected, in part because specialists within the outside areas that Asinof dared to successfully venture into have been unfairly dismissive. Third, and perhaps most importantly, many book lovers tend to forget that sports literature, when done well, has a lot to offer both in terms of pure entertainment and social commentary. Noam Chomsky, the closest thing to a mainstream radical that this country has ever produced, once quipped that among all the controversial things he has ever said or written, nothing caused him to take more criticism than a single remark to the effect that Americans should perhaps spend less time watching sports and more time doing other things. Into this explosive arena entered Eliot Asinof, a writer who dared to repeatedly challenge popular misconceptions and over-romanticized myths about the national pastime.

It is somewhat remarkable that Asinof, a native New Yorker to his very core, selected a Chicago-Midwestern theme for his best-known work, especially given his salty New Yorker outlook and world-weary perspective in almost all things.[2] Yes, there were strong New England connections to the scandal, and 1919 was a very important year for him personally—the year in which he was born; nevertheless, one would otherwise expect Asinof to view the distant historical events of flyover country (Chicago and Cincinnati) with limited curiosity, especially for such a sophisticated writer with a cosmopolitan outlook, added to his earlier workhorse experience in Hollywood, California. Perhaps it was the brief sojourns of his young manhood, first to Moultrie, Georgia (in 1940), then, for a longer period, to Wausau, Wisconsin (in 1941), that set the stage for this later fascination. It most certainly helped to lead him and gain admission into the Milwaukee home of the dying Happy Felsch (see Chapter 5), who proved to be his key source among the surviving Black Sox while breaking the true story behind the scandal.

The New Deal idealism spawned among the younger generation of Americans during the 1930s and 1940s under the presidency of FDR in turn gave rise to an extremely high conscious level of civic duty and national obligation that today is rarely seen in public life. Asinof was typical of his generation in this regard, and this devotion found ultimate expression in his writing. Perhaps the year 1941— the last year that a 21-year-old Asinof spent as a minor leaguer before the outbreak of World War II, represented the apex of this instilled idealism. The moment in Wausau during that summer as recorded by Asinof in *Bleeding Between the Lines* (see Chapter 14) is presented therein as if he was never happier with himself (and the game of baseball) than at that particular instant in time.[3] We suspect that Asinof's many famous acquaintances have never remarked upon his Wausau experience because it was considered insignificant in relation to his otherwise astoundingly eventful life. Wausonians have not remarked upon it perhaps because Asinof rarely talked or wrote about it, and when he did so, never glorified his adventure there nor presented the town in a strictly favorable light. Nevertheless, Wausau, in very real sense, represented the high-water mark of the future author's idealist New Deal youth. It also became the first in a long string of major disillusionments for Asinof; and yet, one cannot become disillusioned unless high ideals are strongly held to begin with. It is to the tremendous credit of Asinof as a literary artist that he maintained such a impressive, uncompromising level of idealism throughout his lengthy career, and long after his youthful aspirations had undergone a series of such brutal assaults and disappointments.

Most sports books are written by fans and for fans, a justifiable dynamic from a strictly commercial perspective in order to find the widest possible audience. To find a wide audience, one must write for the broadest demographic — the fans, since the United States is primarily a nation of sports spectators rather than sports participants. This is not necessarily the way things should be, but simply the way things are. The status quo is an exponent of our society's emphasis on competitiveness and winning. Victory is prized more than participation, therefore only winners generally get to participate at higher levels. For truly insightful analysis of a sport itself, however — one that is most likely to resonate with an actual or aspiring professional in that sport — a writer must have participated in the sport as an athlete. The more competitive this participation is, the better the writing is likely to be. Asinof's only writing competitor in this regard, if the term "competitor" is even appropriate, was the late George Plimpton (1927–2003), whose participatory multi-sport journalism will always make worthwhile reading. There are, however, several crucial differences between Plimpton and Asinof. For one, Asinof was paid to be a professional baseball player long before he became a writer and proved himself to be quite good at it. Later in life, his amateur golf skills were good enough for him to have turned pro, had he wanted to. In short, he was, by unanimous accounts, a fantastic and formidable athlete. Plimpton, in contrast, was a decent athlete with an adventuresome spirit, but one nonetheless indulged by his professional sports clients for the sake of publicity and novelty. While Plimpton, to his credit, fully recognized that a writer had to actually participate in a sport in order to get the true feel of it, his humorous, highly bankable "professional amateur" brand of journalism was aimed more at spectators and non-sports fans, rather than the athletes themselves.[4] Unlike Plimpton, Asinof knew all too well what it was like to seriously compete, excel, and triumph amongst his professional athletic peers.[5]

Asinof's own literary style of intermittent humor — dark, dry, and ironic — can be an acquired taste. As American essayist Gore Vidal once wrote, American audiences often confuse humor with youthful high spirits, and Asinof's brand of humor is the genuine article — as far away from cornball as can be — and therefore, not to everyone's liking. Far too often was he accused of being angry, overly serious, and humorless. It would be more accurate to characterize him as an author who preferred serious topics, sprinkled with doses of levity to make otherwise disturbing subject matter more palatable to a general audience. For example, even Asinof's most dour and pessimistic baseball novel, *The Bedfellow*, has episodes that bring a smile. One such moment comes when former major league slugger Mike Sorrell takes his first swing at a softball and hits, not a home run, but instead a squibbler down the foul line, followed by catcalls from the stands, then a genuine home run on his second swing, followed by (as he himself notes) mindless crowd adulation (see Chapter 9). Perhaps only former players can fully appreciate the absurd accuracy of a situation like this; then again, the scene could be interpreted as an allegory for Sorrell's post-retirement world of Madison Avenue advertising. After all, words like "pitch," "swing," and "home run" have multiple meanings in the English language. Beneath Asinof's subtle humor often lie serious undercurrents, and beyond his grave subject matter frequently can be found comedic material that no comedian could imagine, except to draw from real-life, actual experience.

Had Asinof never written the five baseball books that are the focus of this particular study, he still should be considered an American author of note. In fact, it is quite fair to say that the key to understanding all of his baseball works, including *Eight Men Out,* lies in examining his extensive non-baseball catalogue. There can be no question that appreciation for *Eight Men Out* is considerably enhanced by a read through of *1919: America's Loss of Innocence,* or, on a comedic-absurdist level, *Say It Ain't So, Gordon Littlefield,* or, for that matter, Asinof's gripping memoir, *Bleeding Between the Lines. The Bedfellow* might seem incomprehensible to any reader who has not seen Asinof's later journalistic productions such as *People vs. Blutcher, Craig and Joan,* or *The Fox Is Crazy Too.* Asinof merely used baseball as a convenient and efficient vehicle for telling difficult-to-accept truths about the world at large. For him, baseball was solely a medium to address larger issues in American society. He did not — and this is key — *did not* write about baseball for its own sake. And for this he paid a price. His is an amazing and cautionary case study in a professional writer trying to make a living by telling the public important things that they do not really want to hear. Is it a sign of our times that a writer of Asinof's caliber continues to go underappreciated and under-recognized?

This is not to say that Asinof's baseball observations are anything less than priceless. He was able to use the national pastime as a writing medium simply because he knew it so well from the standpoint of a former professional player. Writers should write what they know, and Asinof recognized this fundamental law of creativity. Accordingly, the many aspects of baseball making it unique as a sport shine through with perfect clarity in Asinof's works as in few other writers. Some of these aspects include, but are not limited to, the peculiar dominant left-handed advantage in the game, the relentless psychological battle between pitchers and hitters, the mystical absence of a clock, the intimate and often unpleasant verbal relationship between spectators and players, the acceptance and even expectation of fierce arguments with umpires, the unusual difficulty and indescribable joy of hitting a baseball, and (above all) a duplicitous sports culture in which cheating is openly tolerated, provided one can get away with it.[6] Although Asinof was never himself a pitcher, he fully appreciated, especially in his last baseball novel, the immeasurable role of an effective pitcher in a team's overall success, even by comparison to a football quarterback or hockey goalie.

Near the end of his life, Asinof tried to summarize and distill these elusive variables in words: "The magic of baseball is simply too loaded with hard-ass complexities, too subtle, too evasive."[7] This same idea — baseball's uniqueness and intricacy — had in fact been a recurring theme throughout his baseball writings over the years. In 1980 for *Sport* magazine, while writing about Willie Stargell's staggering clutch performance in the closely contested World Series of 1979, Asinof asserted that "as any manager can tell you, in a close pennant race it's the intangibles that makes winners."[8] Accordingly, he also had little patience with other writers, especially non-athletes, who attempted to be overly scientific with respect to analysis of the game. In reviewing one book that tried to statistically argue exactly at which point in a baseball contest pitchers should be changed, he complained that "the trouble with this idea is the trouble with the whole book: the human equation. Even if a manager didn't worry about all-important matters like a pitcher's pride, he would have, as one observer pointed out, 10 pitchers with sore arms by July 1."[9] The "human equation" is something that Asinof seems to return to over and over again in his baseball writings, not a surprising trait coming from an author with so thoroughly a humanistic educational background. For him, the unpredictable, indefinable human element in baseball is what makes the game so great and so distinctively American. One does not have to ponder too hard or too long to realize that other sports, while possessing their own fair share of uncertainties and individual heroics, do not have "intangibles" to the same degree as baseball, at least in the exact sense of the term that Asinof preferred to use.

Of all the bad raps that Asinof has received over the years as an author, perhaps the most inaccurate and distorting has been his frequently alleged pessimism and gloominess. After all, this was the man who first broke the true story behind the Black Sox, who first exposed the injustices of the Reserve Clause, and who proposed (tongue-in-cheek?) during the year 2000 that major league baseball should drop all of its absurd pretenses and re-segregate itself along racial lines (see Chapter 20). This was an author who passionately wrote about suicide protests (*Craig and Joan* and *Final Judgment*), inner-city police brutality (*People vs. Blutcher*), the amorality of Hollywood and television (*Bleeding Between the Lines*), and the abuse of the insanity defense within the criminal justice system (*The Fox Is Crazy Too*). Crustiness, however, should never be confused with cynicism. True political liberal that he was, Asinof essentially had a positive and hopeful view of human nature, one that invariably led him into personal and professional setbacks that would have crushed the spirit of many a lesser man. As part of his life's work, he deigned it his responsibility to candidly share these setbacks, as well as his triumphs, for the future benefit of readers everywhere. Among many useful lessons, Asinof teaches us that short-term monetary profit is not the most important thing in life, a rare and usual opinion to find articulated nowadays, but one badly needed nonetheless. And Asinof walked the walk in this regard, whatever his other personal shortcomings may have been. Great wealth and fame were not to be his during his lifetime. Those in the industry whose misdeeds and venalities he exposed labeled him a "troublemaker," as director John Sayles once ironically put it, but to those who appreciated his efforts Asinof the writer might be better described as a guardian of public decency.[10]

This brings us back to baseball, and finally, Asinof's legacy as a writer. When he wrote that the national pastime was a "test of character" for those who engaged in it, he was not referring to winning or losing, or even to how one played the game. It would be more accurate to say that he was remarking upon how the individual athlete-citizen responds under pressure and duress. Do we stay true to our ethical principles and ideals even when this means sacrifice and loss, or do we instead take whatever path offers the least resistance? When our dearest values are directly challenged, do we resist, or do we take the easy way out? When confronted with adversity, do we look and listen, or do we rush to defensive, self-righteous judgment? Baseball, in effect, becomes an adolescent testing ground, one in which athletes learn to face reality, whether they like it or not. Asinof was not so much "God's angry man," as screenwriter Walter Bernstein once tried to characterize him, but rather a sort of modern day, biblical Jeremiah, a voice telling us hard truths about ourselves as a society, even if we are in no mood to hear about it.[11] In retrospect, and in the final analysis, Eliot Asinof must be ranked as one of the great truth-tellers of our age, Jeremiah-like in stature, undervalued during his own day, but with a steadily-growing posthumous reputation.

Appendix: Timeline of the Life and Works of Eliot Asinof

1919	Eliot Tager Asinof born in New York City (July 13)
	Cincinnati Reds defeat heavily-favored Chicago White Sox in 1919 World Series, five games to three
	Boston Red Sox sell Babe Ruth to New York Yankees
1920	"Black Sox" Scandal breaks news
	Charles A. Comiskey suspends suspected players, costing Chicago the American League pennant
1921	Black Sox are found innocent by jury at public trial but banned from baseball for life by Commissioner Kenesaw Mountain Landis
1923	Yankee Stadium constructed ("the house that Ruth built")
1923–1934	Ruth-Gehrig era with New York Yankees; Yankees win seven American League pennants and four World Series; new baseball dynasty established
	At age seven, Asinof meets Babe Ruth, living in same neighborhood at Almanac Hotel; plays first sandlot game and hits grand slam home run
1925–1942	Branch Rickey general manager of St. Louis Cardinals; ascendancy of St. Louis National League franchise and establishment of modern minor league "farm" system
1927	New York Yankees' "Murderers' Row"; Ruth hits 60 home runs, Yankees win record 110 games and World Series in four-game sweep
1929	Stock market crash, beginning of Great Depression
1930–1947	Major League Baseball career of Hank Greenberg, future Hall of Famer and first Jewish American sports superstar
1932	Asinof family moves to Cedarhurst, Long Island
	FDR elected president, inaugurating New Deal
1933	First annual Major League Baseball All-Star game held at Comiskey Park in Chicago
1934	St. Louis "Gashouse Gang"; Cardinals win third World Series in nine years
1935	First Major League Baseball night game played at Crosley Field in Cincinnati

1936	Asinof graduates from Lawrence High School in Cedarhurst, where he captains baseball team
	Enters Williams College, Massachusetts; studies history under Frederick Schuman
	Reads original baseball poem to Robert Frost, who derisively calls it "a pop fly"
1936–1951	Joe DiMaggio era with the New York Yankees; 11 American League pennants and 10 World Series championships
1937	Asinof transfers to Swarthmore College, Pennsylvania
1937–1939	When not playing college baseball at Swarthmore, Asinof moonlights for various semipro teams in the northeast, including Chester, Pennsylvania, where he plays under alias "Johnny Elliot" to preserve college eligibility
1939	Asinof meets Swarthmore city fire chief and former Philadelphia Athletics star pitcher George Earnshaw, who recruits Asinof to play in amateur exhibition game at Doubleday Field for the recently dedicated Baseball Hall of Fame in Cooperstown, New York
1940	Asinof graduates with honors in history from Swarthmore College, where he captains baseball team; during senior year, studies Keynesian economics under Clair Wilcox, who takes class to see John Ford film *The Grapes of Wrath*, adapted from John Steinbeck novel
	Around this same time, Asinof meets future Major League (and Jewish) ballplayer Mickey Rutner, inspiration of his first novel
	That same summer, through influence of Earnshaw, Asinof given tryout with the Philadelphia Phillies, then briefly plays minor league baseball for the Moultrie (Georgia) Packers
1941	"Summer of '41": Asinof plays minor league baseball in the Philadelphia Phillies organization for the Wausau (Wisconsin) Lumberjacks
	Joe DiMaggio hits safely in 56 straight games, and Ted Williams bats .406
	The New York Yankees defeat Brooklyn Dodgers in World Series
	Asinof enlists in the army; meets journalist I.F. Stone
	Japanese attack Pearl Harbor (December 7)
	U.S. enters World War II
1942–1945	Through intervention of Hank Greenberg (in 1943), Asinof admitted to U.S. Air Force Officer Candidate School, where he graduates and is commissioned a Second Lieutenant; spends last two years of the war stationed on Adak Island in the Alaskan Aleutians, writing for base newspaper with Dashiell Hammett, who encourages Asinof's writing efforts
1945–1946	End of war; Asinof discharged from service; at Montpelier, Vermont, sustains leg injury during first minor league baseball tryout and subsequently discontinues regular playing career
1946–1947	Co-owns and manages Yonkers Indians, semipro team in New York Metropolitan Baseball Association, where he introduces league's first night lighting system; after league folds due to Major League competition from television, and unable to find work in

	journalism, Asinof enters family clothing business in New York as salesman
1947	Branch Rickey and Bill Veeck begin racial integration of Major League Baseball; Jackie Robinson plays with Brooklyn Dodgers and Larry Doby with Cleveland Indians
	House Committee on Un-American Activities begins "Hollywood" hearings
	Mickey Rutner plays 12 games in the Major Leagues with Philadelphia Athletics, then returns to minors
1948	Asinof meets future wife, actress Jocelyn Brando (sister of Marlon Brando) while she performs in Broadway production of *Mister Roberts*; at the same time, her brother stars in *A Streetcar Named Desire*
1949	Asinof among audience harassed by American Legion for attending Paul Robeson concert in Peekskill
1950–1953	Korean War
1950–1959	Asinof marries Jocelyn Brando (1950); son, Martin Asinof, born (in 1952); begins writing for television; first credit appears for live television series "Lights Out," for which he is paid $400 (circa 1950); among those fronting for blacklisted screenwriter Walter Bernstein, then Asinof is blacklisted himself (1952–1955), ostensibly for signing a petition at Yankee Stadium urging team to racially integrate (1951)
1953	Mickey Rutner retires from professional baseball; Asinof's short story "The Rookie" purchased for $125 and later (1955) published in literary anthology, *Discovery*, edited by Vance Bourjaily
1953–1962	Era of expansion and relocation for Major League baseball franchises; in 1957 the Milwaukee Braves, recently moved from Boston, defeat the New York Yankees in the World Series
1955	First novel *Man on Spikes* published by McGraw Hill; soon afterwards broadcast as one-hour live episode on NBC's Goodyear Television Playhouse
	Around this time, Asinof relocates to Hollywood
	Elston Howard becomes the first African American to play for the New York Yankees
1955–1959	Asinof in Hollywood writing uncredited scripts; around 1959, personally fired, first by Harry Cohn at Columbia Pictures for writer insubordination, then soon afterwards by Jack Warner at Warner Brothers for writing scenario in which projected John Wayne character in Western film *Yellowstone Kelly* punches a horse
1959	Asinof returns to New York City from Hollywood; credited with screenplay for 90-minute live adaptation of *Body and Soul*, broadcast on the DuPont Show of the Month for CBS
	Chicago White Sox defeated by Los Angeles Dodgers in World Series
	At the invitation of Fidel Castro, travels to Cuba as screenwriter for dramatization of Cuban Revolution, but finished product bears little resemblance to his work; also declines Castro's offer to be Cuban "Minister of Baseball"

1960	Offered $1,000 by David Susskind to write television screenplay on the Black Sox Scandal of 1919, but project cancelled immediately after Major League Baseball Commissioner Ford C. Frick applies pressure to show sponsor, the DuPont Company; *New York Times* reports incident, leading to Asinof receiving and accepting book advance for $1,250 from Howard Cady, then with G.P. Putnam Sons
1961–1962	Asinof conducts research and personally interviews many surviving participants of the Black Sox Scandal, including Abe Attell and Happy Felsch
1963	Book manuscript rejected by Putnam; Howard Cady, now with Holt, Rinehart, and Winston, persuades Holt to accept manuscript despite reservations and attempted editorial rewrites
	Eight Men Out: The Black Sox and the 1919 World Series published to critical praise and modest commercial success; book tour and numerous media appearances, including Chicago interviews with Irv Kupcinet, Robert Cromie and Studs Terkel
	Asinof sued by former Cincinnati pitcher Dutch Ruether and former Black Sox Chick Gandil for character defamation in book; charges are eventually dismissed by courts but initial Hollywood interest in work stifled as a result
	President Kennedy assassinated (November 22)
	Asinof among audience booing Bob Dylan speech at annual meeting of National Emergency Civil Liberties Committee
1965	Escalation of U.S. military involvement in Vietnam War
1966	Asinof and Clarence "Cito" Gaston meet in Batavia, NY
1967	*The Bedfellow* published by Simon & Schuster
1968	*Seven Days to Sunday: Crisis Week with the New York Giants* published by Simon & Schuster
1969	*The Name of the Game Is Murder: An Inner Sanctum Mystery* published by Simon & Schuster
1970	*People vs. Blutcher: Black Men and White Law in Bedford-Stuyvesant* published by Viking
1970–1972	*Flood vs. Kuhn* lawsuit eventually decided by U.S. Supreme Court, upholding professional baseball's reserve clause
1971	*Craig and Joan: Two Lives for Peace* published by Viking
1973	*The 10-Second Jailbreak: The Helicopter Escape of Joel David Kaplan* (with Warren Hinkle and William Turner) published by Holt, Rinehart and Winston
	American League adopts the Designated Hitter rule
1974	Richard Nixon resigns as president
1975	Professional baseball's reserve clause dismantled through legal arbitration; advent of free agency for players
	Film *Breakout*, loosely based on Asinof novel *The 10-Second Jailbreak*
	U.S. withdraws from southeast Asia; end of Vietnam War
1976	*The Fox Is Crazy Too: The True Story of Garret Trapnell, Adventurer, Skyjacker, Bank Robber, Con Man, Lover* published by William Morrow

Asinof declines $1,000,000 offer from gangster Frank Costello to write his story; Costello arrested by authorities soon afterwards

1976–1977 Asinof sued by David Susskind and Talent Associates for $1,750,000 over rights to *Eight Men Out*; suit is eventually dropped

1977 *Say It Ain't So, Gordon Littlefield* published by E.P. Dutton

1977–1987 Before directing his first feature film (in 1979) and before acquiring the movie rights, then-novelist John Sayles writes screenplay for *Eight Men Out* (1977); later (circa 1980) he purchases option on book (along with producers Midge Sanford and Sarah Pillsbury); following several initial rejections, project is sold to Orion Pictures after Sanford and Pillsbury produce hit film *Desperately Seeking Susan* (1985) plus numerous celebrity actors sign on to participate, including Charlie Sheen, D.B. Sweeney, and John Cusack; eight-week filming takes place (in October–November 1987), with baseball scenes at Bush Stadium in Indianapolis, Indiana, Sayles directing and cinematography by Robert Richardson (total budget $6,000,000); Asinof invited on set as consultant and plays a small role in film

1979 *Bleeding Between the Lines* published by Holt, Rinehart, and Winston

"The Secret Life of Rocky Perone" published by *Sports Illustrated*

1980 Rosie Ruiz claims to win Boston Marathon; Asinof negotiates to write story but instead exposes her fraud; interviews Willie Stargell for *Sport* cover story

1981 John Hinckley, Jr., attempts assassination of President Reagan and a copy of *The Fox Is Crazy Too* found among Hinckley's possessions; Asinof declines offer from Hinckley to write his story

1985 Asinof sells co-op in Manhattan; moves to Ancramdale, New York, where he builds house with help from son Martin

1988 John Sayles film *Eight Men Out* released to critical and popular acclaim

1990–1991 First Gulf War

1991 *1919: America's Loss of Innocence* published by Donald I. Fine

1992–1993 Toronto Blue Jays become first non–American baseball team to win World Series; Cito Gaston first African American to coach championship team

1994 *Strike Zone* (with Jim Bouton) published by Viking

Ken Burn's documentary *Baseball* is broadcast by PBS, with interviews and voiceovers by numerous participants from 1988 film *Eight Men Out*

Major League Baseball players go on strike, no World Series

1997 Appears on A&E History Channel's *In Search of History: World Series Fix! The Black Sox Scandal*

Major League Baseball begins interleague play

1998 Asinof shoots age (79) on the Taconic Golf Course near Williams College

Man on Spikes re-released by Southern Illinois University Press

1999 Delivers keynote address at annual Cooperstown Symposium

2000–2001 "The Dis-Integration of Baseball" and "Hey Joe: The Boocing of the Great DiMaggio" published by *Village Voice*

2000	*Off-Season* published by Southern Illinois University Press George W. Bush elected president
2001	Writes Foreword for Richard Peterson's book *Extra Innings*; appears on *ESPN Sports Center Flashback: The 1919 Black Sox Scandal* 9–11 Terrorist Attacks; U.S. invades Afghanistan
2002	Appears as character Silent Sam in John Sayles film *Sunshine State*
2003	U.S. invades Iraq
2005	Appears on ESPN's *The Top 5 Reasons You Can't Blame the 1919 Chicago White Sox for 'Throwing' the World Series*
2007	Writes Foreword for James T. Farrell's posthumous novel *Dreaming Baseball*
2008	Asinof dies (June 10) in Hudson, New York; numerous obituaries *Final Judgment* published by Bunim & Bannigan (September 1) Downfall of Lehman Brothers (September 15) and acceleration of economic downtown Demolition of old Yankee Stadium begins (September 22) Barack Obama elected president

Chapter Notes

Introduction

1. Eliot Asinof, "Turbulent Century of Swat: The Game Turns 101," *Life*, June 6, 1969.

2. Pronounced *Ay-zin-off* (first syllable rhymes with "way"). Tager was the maiden name of Asinof's mother, Rose.

3. In this respect, Asinof's work was typical of the time, comparable say, to the Civil War writings of Shelby Foote. One could even argue that lack of footnotes is making a comeback in current nonfiction literature.

4. Eliot Asinof, *Eight Men Out* (Austin, TX: Holt, Rinehart, and Winston, 1963; New York: Holt Paperbacks, 1987), 11.

5. This remarkable discovery was made by Jeff Kisseloff during the late 1970s. See Kisseloff, "Remembering Eliot Asinof," *The Nation*, June 24, 2008.

6. According to Kisseloff, the very last publication Asinof read on his deathbed (and not without offering criticism) was *The Nation*. See Kisseloff, "Remembering."

7. Ibid.

8. Like Asinof, I ended up just passing through Wausau, living there for about a year.

9. *Baseball-Reference.Com*, http://www.baseball-reference.com/.

10. Several other major Asinof works include large sections on baseball, especially his 1979 memoir *Bleeding Between the Lines* (Austin, TX: Holt, Rinehart and Winston), but these all deal mainly with larger, non-baseball topics; therefore, these will be quoted at length whenever appropriate in relation to his five baseball books.

11. These papers and manuscripts are currently held by the Dolph Briscoe Center for American History at the University of Texas at Austin. To be found among these are many unpublished works, including novels, short stories, screenplays, and articles, as well as earlier, quite different versions of his works from those eventually published.

12. For example, in Asinof's *The Bedfellow* (New York: Simon and Schuster, 1967), Mike Sorrell matter-of-factly relates how his knocking over an opposing catcher while scoring at home was countered with the ball being deliberately thrown at his head for several games afterwards (p. 94).

13. According to Asinof, this was a pioneering night game at Doubleday Field with a primitive lighting system which made everyone, especially batters, fearful for their safety. See Tom Wiles, "Asinof: A Baseball Life," *Ron Kaplan's Baseball Bookshelf*, http://www.ronkaplansbaseballbookshelf.com/2008/06/13/lest-we-forget-tim-wiles-on-asinof/ (accessed June 16, 2011).

14. See Kahn's comments at http://bronxbanter.baseballtoaster.com.

15. *Baseball-Reference.Com*.

16. Eliot Asinof, *Man on Spikes* (New York: McGraw-Hill, 1955; Carbondale: Southern Illinois University Press, 1998), ix.

17. Eliot Asinof, "Willie Stargell: Where I Come from, Where I Am Going," *Sport*, April 1980.

18. Asinof had fronted for blacklisted screenwriter Walter Bernstein during the 1950s (see Chapter 5). See also Clyde Haberman, "Recalling a Cheerful Man Made Angry by Hypocrisy," *The New York Times*, July 11, 2008.

19. To give just one example, I encountered small stacks of old newspaper clippings relating to Asinof's co-ownership and management of the Yonkers Indians in 1946–1947. These are rapidly disintegrating and need to be copied, otherwise the original source materials (if still extant) will have to be surveyed.

20. Obituary, *The Los Angeles Times*, June 12, 2008.

21. Interview with John Sayles.

Chapter 1

1. Asinof, *Man on Spikes*, xvi.

2. Ibid., xiii.

3. Asinof wrote that he never earned more than $100 per month while playing in the minor leagues. See Asinof, *Bleeding*, 62–63.

4. Some obituaries incorrectly stated that Asinof had been a first baseman, a position that he rarely played after turning professional. See *New York Times*, June 11, 2008, and *Washington Post*, June 12, 2008. The latest edition of *Man on Spikes* (published by SIU Press), has cover art showing a left-handed hitter wearing glasses (as does Mike Kutner in the novel); Kutner's real-life counterpart, Mickey Rutner, was right-handed both throwing and batting.

5. See *Baseball-Reference.Com*.

6. Asinof, *Bleeding*, 57.

7. Asinof's last reported playing appearance, amazingly enough, was in Cuba. See Asinof, *Bleeding*, 74.

8. Asinof, *Man on Spikes*, xv.

9. All of them went on to play professionally, including some in the majors, according to Asinof. See Asinof, *Bleeding*, 61–62.

10. Barrett reportedly nicknamed Rutner and Asinof "Hitler's Hebes." Asinof wrote that he was then "traded." See Asinof, *Man on Spikes*, xv. Rutner's version of events was similar: "The manager of the team [Barrett] ... said 'I can't have two Yids on my team,' so he released Eliot." See "World's Oldest Jewish ex-Major Leaguer Tells All," *New Jersey Jewish News*, September 27, 2007, accessed June 17, 2011, at http://www.ronkaplansbaseballbookshelf.com/2007/10/02/mickey-rutner-as-muse/.

11. See *Baseball-Reference.Com*. See also "World's Oldest Jewish ex–Major."

12. Kutner, in the novel, is an outfielder, as was Asinof in real life.

13. See *Baseball-Reference.Com*. Interestingly, Rutner's minor league lifetime batting average was almost identical to Asinof's (.296), albeit over a much longer time span.

14. Asinof wrote: "Was there anti–Semitism in front office decisions? ... Does a bear dump in the woods?" See *Man on Spikes*, xvi.

15. See Asinof, *Man on Spikes*, xv. See also Asinof, *Bleeding*, 130–131.

16. It was through the influence of Greenberg, a lifelong acquaintance and commissioned officer in the U.S. Air Force, that Asinof was himself admitted to officer's school, eventually leading to the writer-to-be crossing paths with Hammett in the Aleutians. Greenberg's father and Asinof's uncle had once played pinochle together. After Greenberg became a major league star, Asinof knew him on a more personal level both as a fan and fellow Jewish professional athlete. See Asinof, *Bleeding*, 125–126.

17. The professor called Asinof's effort "an abomination." See Asinof, *Bleeding*, 132.

18. Asinof, *Bleeding*, 122–123. The poem is reprinted there. Retelling this story, according to Asinof, also helped him to persuade skeptical executives at Holt, Rinehart, and Winston to publish *Eight Men Out* in 1963. If true, thank you, Robert Frost. Read closely in retrospect, Frost's dismissal of Asinof's juvenilia comes across as very sly, constructive criticism.

19. Schuman is quoted in Asinof's Foreword to *1919: America's Loss of Innocence* (New York: Donald I. Fine, 1990), 11. The writings of Keynes are repeatedly cited throughout the work with approval as well (see pp. 80–81, 84, 97, 108–109).

20. Jeffrey Lott, "Eliot Asinof," *Swarthmore College Bulletin*, 2000.

21. Asinof, *Bleeding*, 128–129.

22. Asinof's son, Martin, stated that his father was the first team owner in this league to install a night lighting system for the its home playing field. This no doubt increased expense overhead while revenues were declining. See also Asinof, *Bleeding*, 129–131.

23. Ibid., 131.

24. Wallace was a candidate for the Progressive Party. See Asinof, *Bleeding*, 131. Asinof family lore tells a slightly different version of the couple's meeting. According to Martin Asinof, his father was on a date with Rita Moreno when they encountered the Brando siblings. Before the evening was over, Marlon paired off with Rita, while Eliot and Jocelyn stayed together. The story was retold in numerous obituaries for Asinof, including those for the *New York Times* (June 11, 2008), *Washington Post* (June 11, 2008), and *Guardian* (June 28, 2008). The two versions can be easily reconciled if Eliot and Jocelyn first met at the Henry Wallace rally, but had their first date after this later chance (?) meeting.

25. Asinof, *Bleeding*, 131–132. Asinof had also reportedly been in a previous relationship with the actress Kim Hunter. See Kisselhoff's website, *Eliot Asinof*, http://eliotasinof.com.

26. Asinof, *Bleeding*, 132. Asinof's son, Martin, stated that his father's permanent break with the family clothing business in fact came after he had experienced an unpleasant anti–Semitic incident in the South as a traveling salesman. "He [Eliot] told my mother he

wanted to be a writer, and she said 'Fine, be a writer.'"

27. Asinof, *Bleeding*, 133.

28. Ibid., 134.

29. Ibid., 135–137.

30. During an interview, Asinof's son, Martin, stated that "I always admired my father's work ethic. The anecdote about Vance Bourjaily [who passed away two days after this interview] making him do a complete rewrite of 'The Rookie' was typical. Eliot would always say that a writer must give it his very best effort, then rewrite the piece over and over until it was satisfactory. It's worth the effort, he would add, because a writer will be remembered and judged by what he produces."

31. Asinof, *Bleeding*, 134–135. In 1979, Asinof co-dedicated *Bleeding Between the Lines* to Bourjaily and Mickey Rutner. "The Rookie" was purchased by *Discovery* in late 1953 but not published in the multi-volume series until early 1955. The postscript noted that the story was appearing concurrent with Asinof's first novel, *Man on Spikes*.

32. Notably, one of the benign antagonists in the story is named Red Schalk, a possible allusion to Ray Schalk, Baseball Hall of Famer and one of the uncorrupted members of the 1919 Chicago White Sox team. Years later (during the 1960s), Schalk would give Asinof some rough treatment, both before and after the release of *Eight Men Out*. Perhaps Schalk was upset about this unsympathetic character in Asinof's tale. When Asinof wrote it in the early 1950s, he had no known reason to portray Schalk harshly, although Schalk was on the verge of being elected to the Hall of Fame in 1955. This may have provoked Asinof the writer to use his name as antithesis to the more worthy character of Kutner, just as several of the Black Sox may have been viewed as more worthy than Schalk to be elected into Cooperstown.

33. One is reminded of an anecdote from the late Shelby Foote, who reportedly remarked that he had been in over 30 fist fights during his life and had won almost all of them, but it was the few he lost that he remembered with absolute clarity.

34. Asinof, *Bleeding*, 137–139.

35. Asinof, *Man on Spikes*, xvi.

36. Asinof, *Bleeding*, 139. The original proof, dated December 9, 1954, was dedicated "To my wife, Jocelyn." See Asinof papers at the University of Texas at Austin. Later, the novel was dedicated to Mickey Rutner. See Asinof, *Man on Spikes*, xvii.

37. Asinof, *Bleeding*, 138. Harris went on to produce a tetralogy of baseball novels, the best known of which is probably *Bang the Drum Slowly* (New York: Kopf, 1956), later made into a movie in 1973.

38. The novel ends with the line, "For a while, they [Kutner and his wife] were unable to control the wonderful laughter that poured out of them." See Asinof, *Man on Spikes*, 276.

39. Ibid., 274.

40. Ibid., 170.

41. Curiously, Asinof has Kutner playing in the farm system of the "fictional" Chicago Lions, a thinly disguised representation of the Chicago Cubs, while the multi-generational Lions team owners, the Mellon family, recall the Wrigley family, long-time owners of the Cubs. The climactic game in the final chapter is played in Chicago against Philadelphia, presumably the Phillies. Asinof would return to a match up of these two clubs in his collaborative (with Jim Bouton) 1994 novel *Strike Zone* (New York: Viking), see Chapter 13. The Cubs vs. Phillies would also later figure improbably in Asinof's 1963 classic, *Eight Men Out*, with allegations of gambling corruption in contests between the two National League teams unexpectedly leading to exposure of the Black Sox. Asinof himself, it should be recalled, played two years in the Phillies' farm system.

42. Rutner as a professional player was registered at 5'11," 190 lbs., while Asinof was listed at 5'10," 180 lbs. See *Baseball-Reference.Com*.

43. Asinof, *Man on Spikes*, 262. See also Eliot Asinof, *Strike Zone*, 142; *Final Judgment*, 195.

44. Asinof, *Bleeding*, 63.

45. Like Mickey Rutner's promising baseball career in real life, the fictional Mike Kutner's pursuit of a major league dream is interrupted by World War II. Like Asinof in real life, the fictional Kutner is stationed in the Aleutian Islands. See Asinof, *Man on Spikes*, Chapter 6 ("The Sergeant").

46. The classic Japanese-language movie of this title by Akira Kurosawa was released in 1950, a few years before Asinof wrote *Man on Spikes*.

47. Richard Peterson, *Extra Innings: Writing on Baseball* (Champaign: University of Illinois Press, 2001), 115.

48. Asinof also later complained that in Ken Burns' acclaimed baseball documentary, "the gentle articulate sweetness of the black Buck O'Neal ... denied the rage of his colleagues." See Peterson, *Extra Innings*, x.

49. Asinof, *Man on Spikes*, 160, 172. There

is also a similar near mishap anticipating these collisions in Chapter 5 ("The Clown"), 113.

50. Incident reported in the *Wausau Daily Record-Herald*, June 26, 1941.

51. Similar to Kutner in the novel, Asinof (according to previous box scores) had been shifted from the centerfield position to right field only two days prior to the collision. See *Wausau Daily Record-Herald*, June 23–24, 1941. In the book, Kutner is shifted to left field, making room for Ben Franks, the new African American player, in centerfield. See Asinof, *Man on Spikes*, 154.

Chapter 2

1. Asinof, *Bleeding*, 133–134.

2. Asinof, *Man on Spikes*, back jacket cover.

3. Asinof, *Bleeding*, 140. One cannot help but wonder if this high praise from the son of a leading journalist who exposed the Black Sox resulted in Asinof acquiring his first serious interest in the 1919 scandal.

4. Asinof, *Bleeding*, 140.

5. Asinof, *Man on Spikes*, back jacket cover.

6. Asinof, *Bleeding*, 140.

7. Asinof, *Man on Spikes*, back jacket cover.

8. Peterson, *Extra Innings*, 107, 111, 143.

9. Asinof, *Man on Spikes*, iii–ix.

10. Asinof, *Bleeding*, 140.

11. Asinof papers at University of Texas at Austin.

12. Interview with Martin Asinof.

13. Asinof, in addition to being a writer, was a good musician (a pianist).

14. The broadcast is listed as Season 4, Episode 21. See *The Internet Movie Database*, http://www.imdb.com/title/tt0591166/. It received a positive preview from *Time* magazine, where the reviewer judged it the "most interesting of the teleplays." The review added that "the play had moments of power and persuasiveness" and "seemed on the verge of saying something important not merely about baseball, but about big enterprise in general and the enterprise of life itself. Unfortunately, the idea was never rounded out." See http://rks-baseballbookshelf.wordpress.com (cites a posting from www.bronxbanter.com dated November 6, 2008). A copy of the screenplay, complete with a "happier" ending attached in which Kutner steals home to win the crucial game, then blackmails the owner into giving him his release, can be found among Asinof's papers at the University of Texas at Austin.

15. Asinof, *Bleeding*, 140.

16. Jeff Kisseloff also noted that Gene Kelly was preliminarily slated to play the lead role in *Man on Spikes*. See *Eliot Asinof*, http://eliotasinof.com.

17. This film was based on another book from 1955 (the same year as *Man on Spikes*), titled *Fear Strikes Out: The Jimmy Piersall Story* (Boston: Little, Brown & Co.), co-written by Piersall and prolific author Al Hirschberg.

18. *The Richard Boone Show* won a Golden Globe award in 1964. It featured a fine revolving cast of then up-and-coming acting and writing talent. Coincidentally (or not?), one of the staff writers for this program was named J. R. Littlefield, calling to mind Asinof's eponymous antihero by the same last name in his 1977 novelette, *Say It Ain't So, Gordon Littlefield* (New York: E. P. Dutton) (see Chapter 7). Asinof prepared two separate versions of *Man on Spikes* for the show in 1963 and 1964, both with an alternative "happier" ending than the original, one in which Kutner gets his revenge on everyone by intentionally (!) blowing the crucial game of the season. See Asinof papers at the University of Texas at Austin.

19. Two versions of the screenplay are on file, one under the sole authorship of Asinof and one co-authored with Spano. Both versions, once again, have "happier" endings than the original, one in which Kutner is the hero of the crucial game, but is not eligible for the playoffs and succeeds in getting his release from the team owner. This scenario has overtones of *Strike Zone*, which Asinof was co-authoring with Jim Bouton around the same time (see Chapter 13). It also reflects Asinof's continuing preoccupation with creating more palatable endings for a screen version of his first novel. See Asinof papers at the University of Texas at Austin.

20. Asinof, *Bleeding*, 141.

21. *The Internet Movie Database*, http://www.imdb.com/title/tt0538644/. Channing is the name of the fictional college around which all episodes in this series were written.

22. Frank Gerstle played Eddie Martin and Ralph Meeker played Frank Martin. Ibid.

23. The screenplay, though broadcast in early 1964, is dated late 1962. Earlier drafts or others episodes written by Asinof not used in the series are titled *The Ordeal of Eddie Martin* and *The Man Most Likely*. See Asinof papers at the University of Texas at Austin.

24. "I got out of LA by luck," Asinof is quoted as saying. See Lott, "Eliot Asinof."

25. Asinof implies that the prelude to this dismissal by Columbia came with his parental refusal to allow his young son, Martin, an Uncle Marlon Brando look-alike, to be cast by Columbia in *Dennis the Menace.* See Asinof, *Bleeding*, 143–146.

26. Asinof, *Bleeding*, 147–149.

27. In the 1956 classic Warner Brothers-John Ford Western *The Searchers*, John Wayne's demon-chased character is faced with a similar situation — the scalp of a loved one decorating a hostile Indian's horse. He keeps his cool during negotiation, but only to better wreak havoc later against all Native Americans in general. Finally, in the 1974 Mel Brooks anti–Western satire, *Blazing Saddles*, movie audiences were treated to the sight of a horse being felled by an angry human fist.

28. Asinof, *Bleeding*, 149.

29. "I returned to New York to try and become a writer again," wrote Asinof. See Asinof, *Bleeding*, 149. Obviously, for this artist, "writing" in Hollywood did not qualify.

30. Castro's passion for the game is well documented, as is Cuba's reputation for producing star-quality major league ballplayers. According to Martin Asinof, Castro at one point offered his father a job as Cuba's "Minister of Baseball." The offer was declined.

31. The year 1961 also marked the Bay of Pigs invasion along with long-term hostile relations between Cuba and the U.S. The then recently divorced Asinof added in his memoir that while in Cuba, he found time to play some baseball (to the delight of the locals) and received a marriage proposal from a wealthy Cuban widow. See Asinof, *Bleeding*, 71–75. According to http://www.imdb.com/title/tt0055362/, the director of *Rebellion in Cuba* (originally titled *Barbudos*, or "Bearded Ones") was one Albert C. Gannaway, and the cast, in addition to Chaney, featured former boxing champion turned aspiring movie actor, Jake LaMotta, later the subject of Martin Scorcese's acclaimed film *Raging Bull* (1980).

32. Asinof, in the immediate wake of *Eight Men Out*'s 1963 publication, wrote a barely fictionalized short story titled "A Gambler's World Series," for *The Saturday Evening Post*, November 30, 1963, highlighting the then-current nebulous betting activities of a pseudonymous Abe Attell (see also Chapter 5). Rockwell, however, did not paint for the cover of this particular issue.

33. The central figure in Rockwell's *The Rookie* was reportedly modeled by a local high school player.

34. Wiles, "Asinof."

35. Martin Asinof noted that the new edition of *Man on Spikes* was honorably admitted to the Baseball Hall of Fame Library as part of this same event.

Chapter 3

1. This widespread resentment was surely a major factor in the fans turning against the players' union during the 1994 major league baseball strike.

2. Asinof wrote, "There are no more dynasties in the age of free agents." See "New York Manager Dallas Green: On the Spot," *New York Times Magazine*, March 26, 1989. It should be added that the Toronto Blue Jays under coach Cito Gaston (see Chapter 9) were denied the chance to achieve this feat in 1994 when major league baseball players went on strike.

3. At that time, the Athletics were in Philadelphia and owned by Connie Mack. The 1972–1974 Athletics were in Oakland and owned by Charles O. Finley.

4. Coincidentally, actor D. B. Sweeny, who would later play the role of Shoeless Joe Jackson in the film adaptation of *Eight Men Out*, also once played baseball in Australia.

5. Asinof, *Bleeding*, 105, 109.

6. According to *Baseball-Reference.Com*, the aging Pohle aka Perone did succeed shortly thereafter in 1980 to make a one game comeback appearance with the Salem (Oregon) Senators, going 0–1 at the plate. He now runs a baseball camp (Richard Pohle Baseball Development) to unapologetically help others get their shot at the big time by any means necessary. Pohle's namesake son, Richard, later played several seasons of minor league baseball.

7. Asinof, *Man on Spikes*, 5.

8. Asinof prepared no fewer than five screen adaptations, treatments, or outlines for "The Secret Life of Rocky Perone," *Sports Illustrated*, June 18, 1979. These are variously titled *How About That!*, *Baseball Joe*, *All Riiiight!*, *You Could Look It Up*, and *From Richie to Rocky to Rodney*. See Asinof papers at the University of Texas at Austin. Co-writing credit for the film short of *Rocky Perone* is given to Richard Pohle himself, who also plays an acting role.

9. Rickey's first baseball masterpiece as a general manager, a direct product of his own farm system and player development methods, was the 1934 World Series champions, the

"Gashouse Gang" St. Louis Cardinals. After World War II, Rickey went on to lead the charge for racial integration of major league baseball while general manager for the Brooklyn Dodgers. Race relations in America (and in baseball) would then become another one of Asinof's major themes as a writer.

10. Asinof, *Man on Spikes*, 200.

11. Ebbets Field had last hosted a World Series in 1920 for the Brooklyn Robins. Before 1941, the Brooklyn Dodgers had been, in a certain sense, every baseball fan's favorite loser, similar to today's Chicago Cubs. The Dodgers, despite seven World Series appearances over the next 15 years, would not succeed in winning the Series (or defeating the Yankees) until 1955, the same year that Asinof's *Man on Spikes* was published.

12. Asinof pays brief tribute to his fond memory of Gilbert in *Bleeding Between the Lines*, 63–64, and pays brief homage to Gilbert's baseball talents in "Journey Back to Bushville," *New York Times Magazine*, July 24, 1966. Gilbert, who formerly played in the Dodgers organization (the team which won the National League pennant in 1941), also is given a favorable cameo appearance in Asinof's uncredited teleplay from 1964, *Channing: Swing for the Moon* (see Chapter 2). Gilbert seems to have liked Asinof and played him regularly before Asinof's 1941 season was cut abruptly short, allegedly by team ownership (see Chapter 13). Herman Cruller plays for the fictional St. Clair team.

13. In the novel, the unsavory Phipps is player-manager of Kutner's team in the fictional town of Maldeen, Mississippi, which may be a thinly disguised representation of Moultrie, Georgia. Asinof's 1940 brief stint at Moultrie was cut very short due to his failure in adjusting to deep–South, prewar racism and possibly anti–Semitism as well (see Chapter 9).

14. Asinof, *Man on Spikes*, 7.

15. A good, short encapsulation of Asinof's baseball values as a player, told in the first person, can be found in *Bleeding*, 62–63. Elements of it reappear later in *Strike Zone*, 130; and *Off-Season* (Carbondale: Southern Illinois University Press, 2000), 148.

16. Earnshaw happened to play his last year of professional baseball with Branch Rickey's St. Louis Cardinals in 1936.

17. Asinof, *Man on Spikes*, 4.

18. Ibid., 6–7.

19. Ibid., 5. This passage foreshadows the shallow media adulation surrounding the 1998 home run derby contest between Mark McGuire and Sammy Sosa, as well as the later revealed scandal involving prior steroid use that so clearly set the stage for this popular rivalry.

20. Surprisingly few baseball fans seem aware that Babe Ruth, long before crowned "Sultan of Swat" by sportswriters, was a terrific all-round player — pitcher, batter, base runner — and World Series champion with the Boston Red Sox in 1918, prior to his contract being sold to the Yankees.

21. Asinof was fond of recalling how he, at age seven (around 1926 or 1927), met Ruth outside the Almanac Hotel in New York, not far from where the Asinof family lived. Ruth was apparently intrigued by the young Eliot, who, unlike other boys in the crowd, seemed genuinely star-struck and did not ask for Ruth's autograph. See Asinof, *Man on Spikes*, xv. Asinof's son, Martin, added that Eliot was patted on the head by the Babe, then refused to have his hair washed for a week.

22. Asinof, *Man on Spikes*, 253. This passage is also found in the "The Rookie," which constitutes the final chapter of the novel in its revised form. Schalk, the narrator tells us, hails from Georgia (p. 255), again recalling Asinof's unpleasant experiences there as a player.

Chapter 4

1. Asinof, *Man on Spikes*, 11.

2. I was most fortunately given a baseball scholarship to help pay my way through college, but ended up being mostly a bench warmer. In retrospect, I believe this was primarily due to my own lack of motivation, since baseball ceased to be the most important thing in my life by that time. Amazingly, I also learned (in my own case, at least) that playing baseball for money was a lot less fun than playing it to defy my father, who disapproved of baseball until I received money for it, after which he became a great supporter. There was also a serious personality conflict with my college coach, and I must admit that nothing was ever done in his presence to change his low opinion of my playing abilities.

3. Like myself, Al was a left-hander who could pitch, but liked hitting better. In a competitive amateur league, he remained a long-ball threat at the plate well into his late 40s.

4. *Baseball-Reference.Com*.

5. Peterson also makes this remark in reference to Eric Rolfe Greenberg's 1983 novel *The Celebrant* (New York: Everest House),

itself partly inspired by Asinof's next work, *Eight Men Out*. See Peterson, *Extra Innings*, 111.

6. Dr. Wilcox is remembered for, in addition to being a long-time faculty member at Swarthmore, chairing the International Trade Conference of 1949, which produced the General Agreement on Tariffs and Trades, as well as authoring the book *Public Policies Toward Business* (Homewood, IL: R. D. Irwin, 1975).

7. John Ford won an Oscar in 1940 as best director for this film.

8. Lott, "Eliot Asinof."

9. Asinof, *Bleeding*, 127.

10. *Eliot Asinof*, http://eliotasinof.com.

11. In Asinof's last novel, narrator Kenneth Flear remarks in relation to his son Ted and his own father (Ted's grandfather): "I had once described my own father as a man never seen not wearing a necktie. This had intrigued Ted who claimed to be equally hard put ever to see me *with* one." See Asinof, *Final Judgment*, 7.

12. Lott, "Eliot Asinof."

13. Interview with Martin Asinof.

14. Interview with John Sayles.

15. Asinof, *Man on Spikes*, 173.

16. Cobb must certainly be ranked as the most successful player of the dead-ball era in the statistical sense. As for those who maintain that modern athletes are generally better at all things, I would counter that the best way to rank performance of any kind is strictly within the historical context of its own time and place.

17. During an interview, Asinof's son, Martin, stated that "I always admired my father's work ethic."

18. Stump's original article was published by *True Magazine* in July, 1961 (the same month as Cobb's passing), titled "Ty Cobb's Wild 10-Month Fight to Live." Stump also co-wrote Cobb's authorized (and sanitized) autobiography *My Life in Baseball: The True Record* (Garden City, NY: Doubleday, 1961).

19. As a player, Asinof also tried to model aspects of his own playing style after that of Cobb, such as his bunting skills. See Asinof, *Bleeding*, 60.

20. Asinof wrote that Cobb was "brilliantly portrayed" by Stump. He also wrote that the Hollywood executive to whom he pitched the project had no intention of doing it, but was attempting to get to Joe DiMaggio through Asinof for a tell-all biopic on his brief, stormy marriage to Marilyn Monroe. See Asinof, *Bleeding*, 189. Asinof did, however, draft an outline on the Cobb story. See Asinof papers at the University of Texas at Austin.

21. Even within baseball, Cobb stood accused of gambling abuses and dirty tactics, of which he was most likely on both accounts quite guilty.

22. If there be truth in the story, then the famous photograph of Hank Greenberg, Babe Ruth, Charlie Gehringer, and Lou Gehrig kneeling together on the edge of a dugout, with Greenberg and Gehrig as far apart from each other as possible, takes on new and troubling poignancy.

23. See Kisseloff, "Remembering." On the *Eliot Asinof* website, Kisseloff elaborates that "Greenberg, who knew something about Jew-baiting (he later told Eliot that Lou Gehrig was a master at it), interceded on Eliot's behalf and got him into OCS [Officer Candidate School]." See *Eliot Asinof*, http://eliotasinof.com.

24. The rivalry between Greenberg and Gehrig was legendary. Both were native–New York, hard-hitting, All-Star MVP first basemen playing for perennial American League pennant and World Series contenders. It is still debated which of the two was the greater athlete.

25. By another strange coincidence, Gehrig passed away on June 2, 1941, not long before Asinof's minor league playing career would come to an abrupt halt in Wausau, Wisconsin (see Chapter 15).

26. The film, directed by Sam Wood and produced by Samuel Goldwyn, also featured an all-star team of writers, including Herman Mankiewicz and Jo Swerling.

27. Asinof, *Man on Spikes*, 9. This sequence also calls to mind an early scene from the film version of *Eight Men Out*, in which Happy Felsch (played by Charlie Sheen) makes a similar outstanding catch before colliding with the centerfield fence.

28. Asinof, *Bleeding*, 138. Bernard Malamud's *The Natural* (New York: Harcourt, Brace, 1952) was also made into a very good motion picture by Barry Levinson in 1984, starring Robert Redford, Robert Duvall, Glenn Close, and Kim Basinger. This was four years before *Eight Men Out* became a movie in 1988.

Chapter 5

1. Harry Reutlinger was a news reporter covering the Black Sox Scandal in 1920 for *The Chicago American*. See Asinof, *Eight Men Out*, 192. This probably represents Asinof's own reaction to Felsch's confession during their personal interview some 40 years later.

2. Asinof, *Eight Men Out*, 121.

3. Journalists who originally broke the scandal (such as Hugh Fullerton and Ring Lardner) were restricted by, among other factors, a more limited media and lack of historical distance.

4. Asinof, *Eight Men Out*, 197.

5. The work has remained continually in print since its initial 1963 publication.

6. Ernest Hemingway, it should be remembered, committed suicide in 1961, the same period during which Asinof was writing *Eight Men Out* between 1960 and 1963.

7. Asinof, *Eight Men Out*, xiii.

8. One is compelled to ask whether the scandal would have ever gone public without double-crossed gamblers stepping forward.

9. The Dodgers had fought hard to win the National League pennant that year, defeating the Milwaukee Braves, another relocated franchise, in a post-season playoff match.

10. Later, Asinof became critical of this trend: "The tradition of great ball clubs in historic relationships with their communities ... has all but dissolved with the maddening city jumping of money-hungry club owners." See Eliot Asinof, "The World Series," *The New York Times*, September 30, 1967.

11. The 1959 Series was filled with odd incongruities, such as two pinch hit home runs by Dodger journeyman Chuck Essegian, who otherwise had an undistinguished career and, like Larry Sherry, never played in Brooklyn.

12. Asinof, *Bleeding*, 147–149. See also Lott, "Eliot Asinof," and Haberman, "Recalling a Cheerful Man."

13. Jeffrey Lott, among countless others who have read *Eight Men Out*, perceptively observed that "Asinof's sympathy lies with the players." See Lott, "Eliot Asinof."

14. Asinof, *Bleeding*, 62.

15. Wiles, "Asinof." For further discussion of this incident, see Chapter 16.

16. Asinof played under the pseudonym Johnny Elliott for a semiprofessional team in Chester, PA, while still attending Swarthmore College. See Lott, "Eliot Asinof."

17. After winning their only league title in 1941 with a regular season record of 71–40, Wausau was defeated in the playoffs by another team that had finished behind them in regular season standings of the Northern League, the Duluth Dukes. See *Wausau Daily Record-Herald*, September 17, 1941. The fourth place Eau Claire Bears went on to win the league title that year. See http://www.usfamily.net/web/trombleyd/NorthernstandingsbyyearTable.htm#1941, 5–6.

18. Ibid., 4. Although Kerr was not one of the eight original Black Sox, he was their pitching teammate (number three in the starting rotation) who won praise for winning two games in 1919 Series and not taking any bribes. Later, however, Kerr was suspended for one year by Commissioner Kenesaw Mountain Landis for consorting with the outlawed Black Sox, playing exhibition games with them. See Asinof, *Eight Men Out*, 282–283.

19. This statement should be qualified with a reminder that Asinof, as a New York native, was a lifelong Yankees fan who grew up hero worshiping Ruth during the 1920s and 1930s. Nevertheless, the scathing indictment of the long-ball game in *Man on Spikes* (see Chapter 3) strongly suggests an authorial point of view, as well as the fact that Asinof, as a player, was not a long-ball hitter.

20. Asinof's attempted minor league comeback came to a halt in 1946 at Montpelier, Vermont, where he pulled a hamstring during tryouts. Here, he was able, however, to meet manager Ray Fisher, who had pitched for the Cincinnati Reds against the Chicago White Sox in the 1919 World Series. See Asinof, *Bleeding*, 129.

21. One documented example of Asinof's loyalty to friends was his agreeing to front or blacklisted Hollywood screenwriter Walter Bernstein. As a side note, Bernstein was the credited screenwriter for Woody Allen's film *The Front* (1976), based on Bernstein's own story. See Asinof, *Bleeding*, 48. See also Haberman, "Recalling a Cheerful Man."

22. Jackson hailed from South Carolina and Williams from southern Missouri.

23. In his memoir, Asinof wrote of having mentioned to Felsch at the time that he too had "played some pro ball." See Asinof, *Bleeding*, 115.

24. Gandil and Risberg were uncooperative when interviewed by Asinof. Gandil also later sued Asinof for character defamation. See Asinof, *Bleeding*, 162.

25. Consider Collins, a graduate of Columbia University, and the illiterate Joe Jackson. Have two individuals more different from each other in terms of background and education ever stood on the same playing field together as teammates?

26. See *Saturday Evening Post*, November 30, 1963, published less than a month after the Kennedy assassination, which some have hypothesized was initiated by organized crime.

27. Lott, "Eliot Asinof."

28. These same outstanding qualities are to be found in almost all of Asinof's writings, both sports-related and otherwise.

29. The original 1960 research report compiled by Asinof for Susskind was also titled "The Witness." See Asinof papers at University of Texas at Austin.

30. The working title, *Say It Ain't So, Joe,* would later during the 1970s be co-opted by other writers hired by Susskind in order to bypass Asinof's strong-opinioned involvement in the project. See Asinof papers at University of Texas at Austin.

31. Asinof, *Bleeding*, 12.

32. Ibid., 86–88, 119–120. See also Lott, "Eliot Asinof."

33. Asinof, *Bleeding*, 86–88. See also Asinof papers at University of Texas at Austin.

34. See Asinof papers at University of Texas at Austin.

35. Asinof, *Bleeding*, 119–123.

36. The Aleutian Islands were also the wartime post of another great American writer to-be, Gore Vidal.

37. Asinof, *Bleeding*, 127–128. See also Haberman, "Recalling a Cheerful Man."

Chapter 6

1. Asinof, *Bleeding*, 48–49. Asinof had once fronted for Bernstein as a screenwriter after the latter had been blacklisted by Hollywood during the early 1950s.

2. Asinof, *Bleeding*, 151.

3. Ibid., 118.

4. Ibid., 151–152. According to the *International Movie Data Base*, Asinof would again appear as a guest on The Irv Kupcinet Show in July, 1971, following the publication of *Craig and Joan* (New York: Viking Press, 1971). Terkel would later portray journalist Hugh Fullerton in the film version of *Eight Men Out.*

5. Asinof, *Bleeding*, 155.

6. Walter Bernstein, in his memoir *Inside Out,* also wrote that Asinof "did not suffer fools gladly." See obituary by Stephen Bowie at *The Classic TV History Blog*, http://classictvhistory.wordpress.com/2008/06/26/obituary-eliot-asinof-1919–2008/ (accessed June 20, 2011).

7. Asinof, *Bleeding*, 153–154.

8. For example, in 2001, respected baseball literary critic Richard Peterson listed *Eight Men Out* as one of the best nine baseball books ever written. He labels *Eight Men Out* "the seminal work on the scandal and, with its rich detail and compelling story, one of baseball's most impressive narratives, a history written as a novel." See Peterson, *Extra Innings*, 145. Such praise is typical.

9. Victor Luhr's *The Great Baseball Mystery: The 1919 World Series* (New York: A. S. Barnes, 1966) was perhaps the first major effort representing the trend of renewed interest in the scandal, appearing shortly after Asinof's exposé.

10. One example is the long-debated question of whether Eddie Cicotte was in fact unjustly denied a bonus by Comiskey in 1917. Such issues appear insignificant when viewed as part of the big picture. No one can deny that Cicotte, like several of his teammates, was obscenely underpaid in relation to his outstanding performance and key role in Chicago's 1919 pennant drive. More importantly, no one to date has proven the story of Cicotte's unpaid bonus to be untrue. Another example is whether an anxious kid on the streets really implored Shoeless Joe Jackson, "Say it ain't so, Joe." Late in life Asinof cited James T. Farrell (who was in a good position to know) as an alleged eyewitness to the event. See James T. Farrell, *Dreaming Baseball* (OH: Kent State University Press, 2007), vi. Even if the incident never really occurred, could any story better sum up the tragedy in poetic terms?

11. Asinof, near the end of his life, pretty much summarized this same persuasive argument in succinct fashion. See Farrell, *Dreaming Baseball*, vi. I would further argue (the conventional wisdom) that in no other sport is a team's success as dependent on one individual as a baseball team's success depends on its pitcher.

12. From the Cincinnati point of view, another notable recent book is *Red Legs and Black Sox: Edd Roush and the Untold Story of the 1919 World Series* (Cincinnati, OH: Emmis, 2006) by Susan Dellinger, the granddaughter of Roush. Among several, Dellinger reveals the priceless nugget that Roush believed Cincinnati star pitcher and local boy hero Dutch Ruether (who later sued Asinof for character defamation) may have been involved with gamblers as well during the 1919 Series, affecting his dismal performance in game seven.

13. The true beginning of a more nuanced and comprehensive view of the Black Sox Scandal began with Asinof's own book in 1963.

14. This was Lancaster's last film appearance.

15. The most famous line from the movie, "build it and they will come," has nowadays been turned into a bad joke by the sagging American real estate industry. In fairness to Kinsella, he is among those who have praised *Eight Men Out*, reportedly saying "that fellow Asinof already proved the real story is better than fiction." See Peterson, *Extra Innings*, 153. Given recent criticisms against Asinof for allegedly departing from facts of the scandal, Kinsella's remark takes on special poignancy. Asinof wrote that *Field of Dreams* was "enjoyable," but criticized Kinsella's later work, *The Iowa Baseball Confederacy*. See Eliot Asinof, "Did Leonardo Invent the Home Run?," *The New York Times Book Review*, April 20, 1986.

16. Perhaps a more praiseworthy example of this more imaginative genre is *The Celebrant* by Eric Rolfe Greenberg, a book partially inspired by Asinof's work and highly praised by baseball literary critics such as Richard Peterson.

17. Asinof's son, Martin, recently related that *Bleeding Between the Lines* represented his father's effort to "bare his soul, talk about his personal feelings, and try to say something about the world."

18. Surprisingly, this monumental feud goes unmentioned in the lauded new biography by Stephen Battaglio, *David Susskind: A Televised Life* (New York: St. Martin's Press, 2010). This omission is akin to writing a biography of Mark Twain without mentioning Twain's controversial views on the Shakespeare authorship question.

19. Asinof wrote later that he was aware of only one other instance in which a writer did not jump at the chance to see his work made into a movie: J. D. Salinger's absolute refusal to allow filming of his novel *Catcher in the Rye*. See Asinof, *Bleeding*, 159–160.

20. Susskind died in early 1987 shortly before *Eight Men Out* finally went into film production with another company (Orion Pictures). Arguably, one epitaph might be: "Had it not been for him...."

21. Asinof, *Bleeding*, 203. No known legal action was taken by Susskind against Asinof after the memoir was published by Holt in 1979. Early drafts of the manuscript for *Bleeding Between the Lines* date from 1978 and have litigious working titles such as *Say It Ain't So, David Susskind*, and *Up Yours, David Susskind*. See Asinof papers at the University of Texas at Austin.

22. See Daniel J. Voelker and Paul A. Duffy, "Black Sox: 'It ain't so, kid, it just ain't so,'" *Chicago Lawyer*, September 1, 2009, 47–50.

23. Asinof wrote that "many of the sources spoke in complete privacy and choose to remain anonymous." See Asinof, *Eight Men Out*, xiii. He also admitted using some fictional characters in order to identify plagiarists. See Asinof, *Bleeding*, 42.

24. The article authors in fact cite *Field of Dreams* as if it were an accurate portrayal of Jackson.

25. This writer, it should be disclosed, is a member of the Illinois bar as well. To make any outlandish argument, one occasionally effective method is to discredit your opponent by pretending that he disagrees with widely accepted facts (when in fact the opponent actually agrees), then, after cumulative repetition, tell the jury something they really *want* to hear ("It ain't so, kid, it ain't so").

26. Whatever happened to critical thinking? To simply say that Jackson must have been innocent because he batted .375 during the Series is similar to saying that Fred McMullin must have been innocent because he went 1–2 at the plate during the same playoff. To repeat: *statistics only tell part of the story*.

27. The absurd claim is made in the article that Asinof should be singled out for preventing Jackson being elected to the Hall of Fame. Asinof himself went on record to say that Jackson should be admitted; for him, lily-white innocence was not a prerequisite. Asinof's condensed biography of Jackson written for *Encyclopædia Britannica*, 15th edition, is probably a better apology for the great slugger than the article in *Chicago Lawyer*. (Note: Asinof's name is misspelled "Asinov" by the encyclopædia.)

28. Asinof, *Bleeding*, 156.

29. The first sign of trouble appeared when Fox executives wanted *Eight Men Out* to be a serious sports movie "[l]ike the *Grapes of Wrath* was a Western" (sic). See Asinof, *Bleeding*, 156–157. Mistakenly referring to the John Ford classic as belonging to the Western genre was particularly galling, given this film's cherished place in Asinof's memory as a 1940 college student at Swarthmore (see Chapter 4).

30. Asinof, *Bleeding*, 164–165.

31. Ibid., 161–163. Curiously, in *Eight Men Out*, Ruether's name is consistently misspelled as "Reuther."

32. Asinof's last baseball book utilizing the sports gambling theme, *Strike Zone*, will be examined in Part IV of this study.

33. Asinof wrote that *Breakout* was "a terrible movie" and "disastrous multimillion-dollar flop." See Asinof, *Bleeding*, 14.

34. "Let's do it right or not at all," Asinof told incredulous NBC executives in 1976. See Asinof, *Bleeding*, 56.

35. Sayles stated in an interview that he first encountered Asinof's novel during the early 1970s, thanks to a footnote in a poem by Nelson Algren. Sayles was impressed not only by the story's movie potential, but also by its labor angle and the broad scope of Asinof's journalistic research.

36. Coincidentally, Sayles' sample screenplay on the Black Sox was first sent to Evarts Ziegler, who was Asinof's literary agent at the time of *Eight Men Out*'s release in 1963. Ziegler, who had fallen out with Asinof years before, told Sayles that his screenplay was impressive but a movie on the subject would never be made.

37. Sayles recalled a total acquisition price of $100,000, with himself contributing $75,000.

38. Sweeney later co-authored with Asinof a spec script titled *Fire in the Sky*, an action drama about forest fire fighters. See Asinof papers at University of Texas at Austin.

39. Mike Medavoy was Orion's head of production at that time, according to Sayles.

40. Orion required the film to clock in under two hours, which it does, barely.

41. Sayles and Asinof had many points in common as reputed iconoclasts within their respective fields. They had also both attended William College in Massachusetts. Reportedly, when they first met, Sayles opened with, "You're on the rumor mill, El. Everybody in the movie business thinks you're a troublemaker." "Why did you hire me, then?" Asinof retorted. "I hired you because of it," responded Sayles. See Lott, "Eliot Asinof." According to Sayles, Asinof was given a role in the movie at the suggestion of Maggie Renzi after they had met. Asinof also happened to be friends with Studs Terkel and Cliff James, both of whom had significant character roles in *Eight Men Out*, as reporter Hugh Fullerton and owner Charles A. Comiskey, respectively.

42. The original 1963 edition of *Eight Men Out* had been co-dedicated to Asinof's stepson and son, respectively, "Gahan and Marty."

43. "The Black Sox Scandal Is Forever," unpublished draft article. Asinof also sketched an undated stage play titled *The Year of the Cynic*, perhaps hoping to capitalize on the film's success. See Asinof papers at University of Texas at Austin.

44. Former Chicago White Sox star outfielder Ken Berry was hired to coach the actors in the finer points of the game, as well as to memorably play a heckler taunting Shoeless Joe Jackson in the movie. Charlie Sheen (as Happy Felsch) was said to have professional playing ability and shows it in the film, while Sweeney (as Jackson) played at the collegiate level and later professionally in Australia. Sweeny prepared for the role by working out with the Class A Kenosha (Wisconsin) Twins of the Midwest League. He appropriately described the story as "a loss of false innocence." Sayles' regular leading man, David Straithairn, turns in a memorable performance as the sympathetic Eddie Cicotte, also displaying an athletic adaptability that he had always possessed. See "Special Features," *Eight Men Out* (20th Anniversary Edition), DVD, directed by John Sayles (1988; Los Angeles: MGM/UA Video, 2008). Director Sayles is himself an athlete and played baseball in high school.

45. Sayles stated that he wrote the role of Silent Sam for Asinof in *Sunshine State* because he remembered Asinof's golf prowess, still formidable at age 83. He also added that, by that time, Sayles, Maggie Renzi, Asinof, and David Straithorn's family had all become friends and neighbors in upstate New York.

Chapter 7

1. Asinof, *Say It Ain't So*, 182.

2. The problem, identified by Asinof during the 1960s, is that "the real source of baseball's inevitable demise lies in the lamentable fact that American boys are no longer *playing* the game." See Asinof, "Turbulent Century."

3. In his fine introduction to the latest edition of *Eight Men Out*, Stephen Jay Gould makes this point as well, citing the influential *Historical Baseball Abstract* (New York, Villard, 1985), xv, by Bill James, one chapter of which is titled "22 Men Out" in homage to Asinof's work.

4. The Chicago White Sox impressively defeated John McGraw's formerly-dominant New York Giants in the 1917 World Series, four games to two; the Sox pennant win that same year, however, was tainted by reliable reports that Chick Gandil organized a team payoff of the rival Detroit Tigers to play poorly during the last week of the regular season (which they proceeded to do). One could well argue the

Black Sox both won and lost championships through illicit bribery.

5. There were also unsubstantiated rumors that individual performances in the 1918 World Series (with the Boston Red Sox defeating the Chicago Cubs) had been influenced by gambling payoffs as well.

6. A great "what if" in sports history asks whether a healthy Red Faber pitching for Chicago in the 1919 World Series would have changed the outcome. Many have observed that it may have well prevented the scandal, limiting tainted pitchers Eddie Cicotte and Lefty Williams to perhaps as few as four starts, rather than six. Asinof also made this point in *Eight Men Out*, 115.

7. This famous remark was made to a Chicago Grand Jury in 1921 by Shoeless Joe Jackson, who claimed that Risberg threatened to kill him if he talked, a claim Risberg later denied and vocally resented. Jackson and Risberg later played outlaw baseball together in Louisiana. See Asinof, *Eight Men Out*, 178, 208, 288.

8. Ironies abound. Felsch, the rebellious son of a hardworking, pro-union, Milwaukee German socialist family (see Asinof, *America's Loss*, 323), becomes a victimized pawn in one of the most infamous scams caused by unregulated commerce in American history.

9. "I did it for the wife and kids," confessed Cicotte. See Asinof, *America's Loss*, 293. Indeed, Cicotte's children were able to go to college, a family farm mortgage was paid off, and Cicotte himself, intelligent person that he was, later was able to find a second career in forestry. Cicotte, unlike most of the other Black Sox, also had the good sense to demand full payment in advance from the gamblers.

10. For example, Jackson supposedly asked manager Kid Gleason to bench him before the first game, presumably because he did not want to participate in the fix. His request was refused and Jackson played. See Asinof, *Eight Men Out*, 58–59. It should be added, however, that the sources for this alleged incident are obscure.

11. Farrell, *Dreaming Baseball*, vii.

12. Asinof was often known to friends as El (short for Eliot), "L" also being the first letter in Littlefield's last name, a name that otherwise speaks for itself. Regarding the first name Gordon, one is tempted to think of the campy Flash Gordon comic book and film character so popular during Asinof's formative years in the 1930s. Obviously, this is all conjecture.

13. Asinof, *Say It Ain't So*, 1.

14. Anyone doubting this quality in Asinof need only read a few pages of *Bleeding Between the Lines* as the author calmly details his expensive and acrimonious legal battle with David Susskind.

15. Asinof, *Say It Ain't So*, 50.

16. Ibid., 4. Asinof's parents and grandparents were Russian Jewish immigrants. My own maternal heritage includes Mayflower descent, which gives me some degree of insight into the often preposterous overvalue assigned to this distinction.

17. Ibid., 20.

18. Ibid., 53

19. Ibid., 4, 45–46, 182.

20. Ibid., 73.

21. Ibid., 73, 114, 169.

22. Ibid., 122.

23. Other minor biographical parallels with Asinof's life are sprinkled throughout *Say It Ain't So, Gordon Littlefield*, such as the New York Bull's Willie Jones originally hailing from Moultrie, Georgia, where Asinof briefly played minor league baseball in 1940. See Asinof, *Say It Ain't So*, 135.

24. This, according to the *Internet Movie Database* (IMDb). See also the Asinof papers at University of Texas at Austin.

25. Asinof makes an obvious allusion to the John Garfield film in his profile of Denny McLain, as "a mod version of those old John Garfield movies you see on *The Late Show*: the tough, talented kid who is his own worst enemy but is virtually indestructible." See "Denny McLain: I Snap Back Real Quick," *Sport*, June 1970.

26. Asinof, *Bleeding*, 48. Blogger Stephen Bowie has suggested that Bernstein may have been the true scriptwriter for "Body and Soul," with Asinof acting as a front (see http://classictvhistory.wordpress.com/2008/06/26/obituary-eliot-asinof-1919–2008/). I am inclined to accept things at face value, since Asinof stated that he had done several scripts for Susskind's Talent Associates in the past (see Asinof, *Bleeding*, 12). Moreover, television script quality, however dismal it may have been, has little to do with authorship attribution. Asinof may have been neither particularly proud of it, nor eager to highlight his long, previous association with Susskind any more than necessary, especially in light of the bitter litigation between the two that would later emerge.

27. "Did you ever take a dive, Champ?" Asinof asked a cagey Attell, who responded

"Well, a coupla times I held up bums for a few extra rounds." According to Asinof, Attell was still trying to stack the odds in sports betting to his dying day, sometimes brazenly hitting up on Asinof for bet money, presumably in return for past services as an interviewee. See Asinof, *Bleeding*, 108.

28. Asinof makes a similar point in *Eight Men Out*, 284–285.

29. See Gould introduction to *Eight Men Out*, xviii.

30. Not long before Rose's fall from public grace, Asinof wrote a profile of him. See Eliot Asinof, "Pete Rose Can't Lose," *Sport*, April 1989.

31. Following *Eight Men Out*'s publication, Eddie Cicotte's reported willingness to open up and share more information about the scandal was frustrated by death before Asinof could reach him. It is likely that he took many a secret to the grave. For Asinof, in this sense, Cicotte was perhaps "the big one that got away." See Asinof, *Bleeding*, 118.

Chapter 8

1. Asinof, *Bleeding*, 128.

2. In 1967 (when I was 11 years old) was Ken Berry's best season as a player, in which he was selected to the American League All-Star team; and his team, the Chicago White Sox, made a compelling, but ultimately failed, pennant run.

3. We include Buck Weaver in this group (who hailed from Pennsylvania) only because he was one of the eight players banned. Weaver had nothing else to do with the fix except being made privy to its conception, for which failing to expose he was excessively punished in a manner equal to the other seven Black Sox (see Chapter 7).

4. Asinof, *Eight Men Out*, xiv.

5. Asinof, *Bleeding*, 127. Hammett was author of, among other well-known works, *The Red Harvest* (1929), *The Maltese Falcon* (1930), *The Glass Key* (1931), and *The Thin Man* (1934).

6. Asinof, *Bleeding*, 126.

7. Ibid., 127.

8. Citing Plato's *Laws*, the Renaissance humanist Montaigne makes a similar point in his well-known essay, "On Some Lines of Virgil."

9. The title of the film is taken from the work of British Victorian poet William Ernest Henley, with the title itself later coined by his publisher, Arthur Quiller-Couch. The word is Latin, meaning "Undefeated." The film itself has been critically and commercially well-received, far more so the latter in fact, than *Eight Men Out* the movie ever was.

10. The title of John Carlin's book was *Playing the Enemy: Nelson Mandela and the Game that Changed A Nation* (New York: Penguin, 2008), dealing with Mandela's encouragement and support of South Africa's nearly all white championship Rugby team during the 1995 World Cup tournament.

11. Asinof, *Bleeding*, 105.

12. Asinof, *America's Loss*, 317.

13. Asinof, *Bleeding*, 116. "We was scared," Felsch pointedly told Asinof. See Asinof, *America's Loss*, 324.

14. At the time, Stone worked for *PM Magazine*. Among other things, Stone impressed upon Asinof that the impending war against Fascism was a just one, and needed to be pursued regardless of outcome for its own righteous sake. See Asinof, *America's Loss*, 14–15.

15. "History is the record of man's struggle to survive his own venality," eloquently wrote Schuman. See Asinof, *America's Loss*, 11. Asinof also thanked the Williams College Library for its assistance in his acknowledgments. See also p. 15.

16. Asinof's son, Martin, related that "*1919: America's Loss of Innocence* was an important statement for him [Eliot], and it's a well written book, but quite honestly, many people (including myself) cannot get past the first hundred pages because the events it portrays makes us so angry." My response was, "Welcome to American history."

17. Asinof, *America's Loss*, 346.

18. Ibid., 14.

19. Ibid., 13.

20. Ibid., 348–349.

21. Curiously, in addition to his dramatic journalistic breakthrough with Happy Felsch of Milwaukee, Asinof had yet another Wisconsin association that had led to an earlier, big impact on his writing career. This was Senator Joseph McCarthy, who led the blacklisting efforts which smeared Asinof and his friends. Asinof later referred to McCarthy as a "snarling tarantula." See Asinof, *Bleeding*, 12[illegible].

22. Asinof, *America's Loss*, 298–299.

23. Ibid., 323.

24. Asinof, *Eight Men Out*, 192–193.

25. Asinof was incredulous. See Asinof, *America's Loss*, 322–324.

26. Ibid., 341–342.

27. Within the context of the then-recent Pete Rose scandal, Asinof wrote, "It is as if all of history demands its own repetition regardless of ever-changing circumstances." See Asinof, *America's Loss*, 347.

28. Asinof, *Eight Men Out*, xviii.

29. Wiles, "Asinof."

30. Asinof, *America's Loss*, 341. Asinof writes in the past tense presumably because he was referring to the views of F. Scott Fitzgerald and Walt Whitman, as well as his own; nevertheless, one is tempted to ask: Would Asinof still consider these things to be true today?

31. Director John Sayles perhaps put it best when he remarked that the year 1919 and the Black Sox Scandal represented America's passage as a nation into a period of "stormy adolescence." See "Special Features," *Eight Men Out*, DVD.

Chapter 9

1. Asinof, *Bedfellow*, 61.

2. Asinof's *People vs. Blutcher: Black Men and White Law in Bedford-Stuyvesant* (New York: Viking, 1970), with events also set in New York, could arguably be considered part of this same group; however, close examination suggests otherwise. *Blutcher* was a totally non-sports related work of investigation journalism, ushered in a new decade for its author, and was released by his new publisher (Viking).

3. Asinof's *Final Judgment* (2008) and *Craig and Joan* (1971) begin with withering quotes from Camus' *The Fall* (New York: Knopf, 1957).

4. Asinof, *Bedfellow*, 65.

5. Ibid., 20.

6. The Mets' name was presumably omitted to avoid copyright infringement.

7. The "Amazing Miracle Mets" of 1969 were still several years in the future and even then shocked the conventional wisdom of baseball by winning the World Series over the highly favored Baltimore Orioles.

8. One might consider the Washington Senators as such. By this time (the 1960s) both the Dodgers and Giants had relocated to California.

9. See Asinof, *Bedfellow*, 49. The character of Eric Lopert, "Negro playwright and novelist, essayist and short-story writer," possibly represents James Baldwin (1924–1987), friend of Asinof's former brother-in-law, Marlon Brando.

10. Asinof, *Bedfellow*, 29. Asinof also read Fitzgerald, as evidenced by opening quote from *Eight Men Out*.

11. Asinof, *Bedfellow*, 98, 213.

12. Asinof would have been about eight years old when *The Jazz Singer* premiered in 1927 as the first full-length feature film with sound.

13. Asinof, *Bedfellow*, 40.

14. Ibid., 185. Sutton Place is an exclusive address located on Midtown Manhattan's East Side.

15. Asinof, *Bedfellow*, 50.

16. Ibid., 58.

17. Martin Asinof confirmed that his father had been working on *The Bedfellow* for many years prior to its 1967 publication.

18. See Asinof papers at University of Texas at Austin.

19. "Cloud Nine" was written by Norman Whitfield and Barrett Strong, and reportedly recorded and released by the Temptations in October 1968. It is therefore unlikely that Asinof knew of the song before writing the novel; more likely, he was familiar with the phrase as urban street lingo. The song won for Motown Records its first Grammy Award in 1968.

20. Asinof, *Bedfellow*, 23.

21. Asinof signed on to play with Moultrie as part of the Philadelphia Phillies farm system. See Asinof, *Bleeding*, 93–94. The Phillies organization of the mid–20th century was notorious for its resistance to racial integration, both on and off the playing field.

22. Asinof, *Bedfellow*, 147.

23. See ibid., 123–124; and Asinof, *Off-Season*, 8.

24. Asinof, *Bleeding*, 58. Anyone who has ever experienced any kind of success in baseball will vividly remember hitting his first home run.

25. Asinof, *Bedfellow*, 118. Asinof, somewhat in contempt, referred to softball as "an abridged version of the real thing." See Asinof, *Bleeding*, 102–103.

26. See Asinof, *Bedfellow*, 123; and Asinof, *Man on Spikes*, 5.

27. This version of the story comes from an interview with Asinof's son, Martin. See also Wiles, "Asinof."

28. Interestingly, the records do not reflect Asinof having ever hit a triple. He did, however, hit two doubles. It is possible that he reached third on an error or fielder's choice, or that the records are incorrect. See *Baseball-Reference.Com*.

29. Asinof, *America's Loss*, 154–155, 310, 348.

30. Asinof, *Bleeding*, 129–130.

31. Kisseloff, "Remembering."

32. Asinof, *Bleeding*, 151.

33. Asinof, like Gaston, played outfield as a professional.

34. An example of differences between the two is that Sorrell emphatically does not play golf (Asinof, *Bedfellow*, 186), whereas Asinof was a terrific golfer (see Chapter 11).

35. "It has class," notes Sorrell, who in the novel was originally named George Henry Johnson Jr., after his hated father. See Asinof, *Bedfellow*, 11. In the American South outside of Louisiana, Gaston's last name is more often pronounced with the accent on the first syllable. Canadians, especially French Canadians, more typically pronounce it with the accent on the last syllable.

36. Sorrell states that he is six feet, 194 pounds (see Asinof, *Bedfellow*, 11), while Gaston as a minor league player was listed at six feet, three inches, 190 pounds (see *Baseball-Reference.Com*).

37. During their interview, Gaston complained to Asinof that in Batavia "I can't get an apartment so as to bring my wife," thus hinting at tensions within his first marriage. See Asinof, "Journey Back to Bushville."

38. For details of Gaston's life and career, see the on-line Society for American Baseball Research, Alfonso L. Tusa C, "Cito Gaston," *The Baseball Biography Project*, http://bioproj.sabr.org/bioproj.cfm?a=v&v=1&bid=2629&pid=4966 (accessed June 20, 2011).

39. Sorrell's father-in-law bellows at him: "People do things for you. Then, maybe, you do things for them." See Asinof, *Bedfellow*, 111.

Chapter 10

1. As a qualifier to this statement, it should be added that Asinof during his earlier screenwriting career and been very involved with the crime thriller genre. See Asinof papers at University of Texas at Austin.

2. The murder victim in Asinof's *The Name of the Game Is Murder: An Inner Sanctum Mystery* (New York: Simon and Schuster, 1969) is coach Bart Fain, a name obviously reminiscent of Asinof's old scout from *Man on Spikes*, Durkin Fain.

3. More likely, Asinof was well aware of this noncommercial aspect of the work, but, true to his reputation, wrote it anyway because the subject matter interested him.

4. In this regard, *The Name of the Game Is Murder* is appropriately subtitled *An Inner Sanctum Mystery*. All three books in Asinof's New York trilogy deal with the hidden elements of big business which touch upon and decisively influence professional sport franchises.

5. Asinof had himself been a military Second Lieutenant in the U.S. Air Force during World War II. The Mike Ogden character from *Name of the Game* is precursor to Ernie Kolacka from *Strike Zone* (see Part IV if this study), a former athlete whose ambitions are thwarted by a war wound and who is nursed back to health by his future wife.

6. In *The Bedfellow*, Sorrell originally comes from Watts, as does former star running back (and murder suspect) John "Scot" Johnson. All of the murder suspects from the fictional New York Bulls football team seem to later reappear in slightly different incarnations for Asinof's 1977 novel, *Say It Ain't So, Gordon Littlefield*. See Asinof, *Name of the Game*, 84. In an eerie manner, Asinof anticipates both the South Central L.A. riots of 1992 and the O. J. Simpson trial of 1995.

7. Asinof, *Name of the Game*, 84.

8. Peterson, *Extra Innings*, 117.

9. Within the pages of Book Review Index, Asinof's *The Bedfellow* attracted a grand total of three notices, despite its author having written *Eight Men Out* and *Man and Spikes* as his last two previous books. Tellingly, the total combined number of reviews garnered by *The Bedfellow* and *The Name of the Game Is Murder* were fewer than those attracted by Asinof's *Seven Days to Sunday: Crisis Week with the New York Giants* (New York: Simon and Schuster, 1968), which was generally well received by the critics, being essentially a sports book. The Index, however, only includes a sampling of these reviews.

10. *Publishers Weekly* 192, no 19 (November 6, 1967): 45.

11. *Kirkus Reviews* 35 (January–December, 1967).

12. *Library Journal* 92, no. 15 (1967): 4521.

13. See Margot Siegel, "Black and White Novel," *Minneapolis Tribune*, February 18, 1968.

14. See Asinof papers at University of Texas at Austin.

15. Asinof's earlier baseball novel, *Strike Zone*, co-written with Jim Bouton (see Part IV of this study), though told in a realistic manner by both authors, only hints at racial tensions within the game. For example, when umpire Ernie Kolacka (the voice of Asinof) unfairly calls a third strike on African American batter Leon Banks, it provokes a

major eruption of tempers both on and off the playing field. See Asinof, *Strike Zone*, 205–206.

16. Asinof's son, Martin, stated that his father took on the project while "while the bruises were still there," which would have been in the immediate aftermath of The Bedfellow's 1967 publication. He added that his father felt *People vs. Blutcher* "was an important book." We agree with this assessment.

17. These broader, more forward-looking cultural themes are established from the outset of Asinof's study. See Asinof, *People vs. Blutcher*, xiii.

18. Asinof, *Bedfellow*, 127.

19. Asinof, *People vs. Blutcher*, ix. *The Autobiography of Malcolm X* (New York: Penguin, 1973) was co-written with journalist Alex Haley. I am inclined to believe that the turn of phrase came directly from Malcolm. This famous quotation packs an extra punch for those of us who claim Mayflower descent.

20. Asinof, *People vs. Blutcher*, 121–131, 141–143.

21. These unflattering traits also sometimes appear in Asinof's depiction of the New York City Police Department in *The Name of the Game Is Murder*, the third book in the same trilogy as *The Bedfellow*.

22. Asinof, People vs. Blutcher, xi.

23. Ibid., xii. Asinof's comparison to "escape from prison" calls to mind his 1973 nonfiction work, (co-authored with Warren Hinkle, and William Turner) *The 10-Second Jailbreak: The Helicopter Escape of Joel David Kaplan* (New York: Holt, Rinehart, and Winston), later made into a stinker of an action movie, *Breakout* (1975), starring Charles Bronson. The escape referred to in People vs. Blutcher is, of course, considered far more difficult to achieve than breaking out of a Mexican prison. The fictional Sorrell in *The Bedfellow* appears to accomplish it (his escape from the Watts ghetto of his childhood), but at the cost of personal integrity.

24. Asinof, *People vs. Blutcher*, xii.

25. "And now it keeps you a nigger," counters Fuchs. See Asinof, *Bedfellow*, 65.

26. An unpublished novel about the Yukon by Asinof from the late 1990s probably grew out his exposure to the poetry of Service. See Asinof papers at the University of Texas at Austin.

27. Eliot Asinof, http://eliotasinof.com.

28. Eliot Asinof, *The Fox Is Crazy Too: The True Story of Garrett Trapnell, Adventurer, Skyjacker, Bank Robber, Con Man, Lover* (New York: William Morrow, 1976), 300. By extension, the same could be said for all professional expert opinion witnesses.

29. Asinof, *Bedfellow*, 95.

30. Fuchs, almost boasting, tells Sorrell , "I'm saying all these things to you because I'm getting paid to do it." Asinof, *Bedfellow*, 213–214.

31. This is taken from an interview with Martin Asinof. His father had earlier made similar refusals to lucrative offers from gangster Frank Costello and fraudulent Boston Marathon winner Rosie Ruiz. See Kisseloff, "Remembering."

32. Asinof, *Fox Is Crazy*, 306–307.

33. This well-known descriptor for Asinof is originally attributed to Walter Bernstein, for whom Asinof once fronted as a screenwriter after Bernstein had been blacklisted. Asinof's literary executor Jeff Kisseloff better described him as "a man of good cheer." See Haberman, "Recalling a Cheerful Man."

Chapter 11

1. It is worth pointing out that the stated (and accomplished) objective of Rocky Perone (aka Richard Pohle) was not necessarily to be a major league ballplayer, but rather a professional or minor league player who, as such, would make it into the permanent record books as having once played professionally.

2. Asinof, *Bedfellow*, 62. Unspoken is Janet's Carr's similar fear of Southern anti-Semitism. Note: Jews have always lived in Atlanta, albeit with their ethnic identity submerged ala *Driving Miss Daisy*. My own late mother, who was from Atlanta and of the same generation as Asinof, claimed never to have knowingly met a Jew face-to-face until coming North married after the war.

3. Asinof, *Bedfellow*, 62.

4. Perhaps by coincidence, the Moultrie Packers were part of the Philadelphia Phillies farm system, the same organization to which Curt Flood was traded in 1969. Flood alleged, among other things and with some justification, that the Phillies franchise at that time had a reputation for racism both in the front office and in its fan base.

5. *People vs. Blutcher* would be published the same year (1970) that Curt Flood filed his historic lawsuit against major league baseball.

6. Asinof, *People vs. Blutcher*, 211.

7. Had the catch not been made, I probably would have been pulled. First I had been

nearly ejected from the game, and then almost knocked out. I went on to pitch a complete game and our team won the contest. Asinof, as a former ballplayer himself, would have well understood how unpredictably such things can play out.

8. Asinof, *People vs. Blutcher*, 164–165.

9. Branch Rickey was also, for all practical purposes, the inventor of the modern baseball farm system, in which the young Eliot Asinof was a minor league player during the 1940–1941 seasons. These experiences forever shaped his view of the game in his writings, as the pages of this study hopefully demonstrate.

10. Asinof, *Bedfellow*, 200.

11. Sorrell's comment is made in response to a challenge from another man's nervous joke that he was willing to share his golf clubs, but not (it is implied) his wife, who has been flirting with Sorrell at a party hosted by a former African American teammate. See Asinof, *Bedfellow*, 186.

12. These details are from an interview with Martin Asinof.

13. Martin Asinof also said that his father learned to golf right-handed because right-handed clubs were the only ones he had access to at the time.

14. Most of these articles were written for *Golf Illustrated*, plus several proposals for a golf-related novel. See Asinof papers at the University of Texas at Austin.

15. Asinof, *Bedfellow*, 212.

16. Ibid., 123.

17. Asinof, *Bleeding*, 63–64.

18. Ibid., 129. Asinof's phrase "on spikes" naturally recalls the title of his first novel.

19. Asinof, *Bleeding*, 74.

20. Ibid., 103.

21. This came in response to a compliment from Rizutto, who remarked that Asinof could "still take a fine cut at it [the ball]." See Asinof, *Bleeding*, 103.

22. For example, right up to the year of his death, Asinof was offering interview commentaries on the Black Sox Scandal. See "Special Features," *Eight Men Out*, DVD.

Chapter 12

1. Asinof, *People vs. Blutcher*, xi.

2. The old Comiskey Park in Chicago, named after the controversial owner of the 1919 Black Sox, had been demolished in 1991 and replaced across 35th Street with U.S. Cellular Field.

3. Hence patient readers are presented with my own diverse writings, which attempt (in vain, perhaps) to meaningfully explore various specialized areas of knowledge from a layman's perspective.

4. Incredibly, Sorrell's powerful father-in-law scolds him at length for objecting to this arrangement. See Asinof, *Bedfellow*, 110–113.

5. None of Asinof's numerous obituaries (with the exception of UK's *Guardian*) mention *The Bedfellow* as one of his works, which is unfortunate.

6. In the final paragraph of *The Bedfellow*, 223, Sorrell takes up smoking for the first time, a symbol of his moral surrender. Fans of *Mad Men* might recall that the fictional firm of Sterling Cooper represents, with no apologies, the marketing interests of cigarette companies. This is but one parallel between the television series and Asinof's realistic, forward-looking work of fiction.

7. Asinof, *Final Judgment*, 64. In this novel, Anne Miner, though 21 years of age, is described as having the "dissolute appearance of twenty-seven or more." Twenty-seven is the same age as Mike Sorrel in *The Bedfellow*; for Asinof, late-twenties in age seems to symbolize a certain loss of innocence (see p. 31).

8. Asinof, *Final Judgment*, 205.

9. Asinof, *Bedfellow*, 108.

10. Ibid., 104.

11. Asinof, *Man on Spikes*, 161.

12. Peterson, *Extra Innings*, x.

13. This ambivalence is also alluded to in *Strike Zone*, in which African American ballplayers are represented as still being (in 1994) a rather separate group within the larger team structure (see Part IV of this study).

14. Consider, for example, that Asinof was born in 1919, a period in which the Ku Klux Klan was highly visible and Jim Crow segregation laws were still whole-heartedly supported by the majority of Americans. By the year of his death, an African American had become President-elect. Asinof makes repeated reference to a resurgent Klan in his post–World War I, U.S. history volume, *1919: America's Loss of Innocence*, 30, 50, 69, 150, 152, 155, 246.

15. Thirty-eight years earlier, Asinof had written, "If it is true that any citizen can become President of the United States — or the wealthiest entertainer in Hollywood — the odds are not likely to influence many [African Americans] to give their lives to it." See Asinof, *People vs. Blutcher*, xii. Note: Asinof's Hollywood reference was made a decade before the Reagan administration.

16. In the novel, as Obama leaves the green room for his interview, Asinof adds, "He didn't need any makeup." See Asinof, *Final Judgment*, 196–197.

17. Asinof, *Bedfellow*, 95.

18. Consider, for example, Asinof's non-fiction Garrett Brock Trapnell from *Fox Is Crazy*, whose numerous misdeeds are underscored in the books subtitle.

19. For Asinof, the often porous divide between sanity and insanity would also be explored in his final baseball novel, *Off-Season* (see Part V of this study).

20. Asinof, *Bedfellow*, 95.

21. Ibid., 202.

22. Asinof, *Name of the Game*, 38.

23. Ibid., 145.

24. Ibid., 188.

25. Interestingly, Asinof's profile of embattled star pitcher Denny McLain identified the early death of McLain's father during his teenage years as a source of McLain's tough resilience. See Asinof, "Denny McLain."

26. Interview with Martin Asinof. In *Man on Spikes*, Mike Kutner's grandfather is portrayed as having been a German immigrant miner. The father is a coal miner in Kentucky (p. 13).

27. Interview with Martin Asinof.

28. Asinof, *People vs. Blutcher*, xii.

Chapter 13

1. Asinof, *Strike Zone*, 61.

2. Ibid., 77.

3. It was also during this period (1985) that Asinof moved from Manhattan to Ancramdale in upstate New York, building his retirement home there with help from his son, Martin.

4. For the charming story of Asinof's boyhood encounter with the Bambino, see Asinof, *Man on Spikes*, xv.

5. Coincidentally, 1959 was the same season the Chicago "Go-Go" White Sox won the American League pennant, only to lose to the underdog Los Angeles Dodgers in the World Series, causing some to believe that Chicago was still cursed because of the Black Sox. Asinof was at this time returning to New York from Hollywood (see Chapter 5). Brosnan went on to play his last major league game with the White Sox in 1963, the same year that *Eight Men Out* was published.

6. Asinof, for his part, had a high opinion of Brosnan's *The Long Season* (New York: Harper, 1960), "a sparkling, intelligent account of what it was like in the biggies." See Eliot Asinof's Book Review of *The Bronx Zoo* by Sparky Lyle and Peter Golenbock, *New York Times*, July 4, 1979.

7. Bouton's well-publicized comebacks and attempted comebacks as a professional player included stints with Bill Veeck's Chicago White Sox, where he played in the minors during the 1977 season, then later with Ted Turner's Atlanta Braves, where he finally made it back to the majors in 1978. Bouton's writing career has been prolific by baseball standards as well, producing numerous sequels to and variations on *Ball Four* (New York: World, 1970), including *I'm Glad You Didn't Take It Personally* (1971), *I Managed Good, But Boy Did They Play Bad* (1973), *Ball Four: The Final Pitch* (2000), and *Foul Ball* (2003).

8. Bouton also had a Chi-town connection, attending high school in suburban Chicago Heights, where he was reportedly somewhat of a benchwarmer. Not until later did he show the devastating fastball-curveball combination that made him a standout with the championship Yankee teams of the early 1960s.

9. Asinof, *Bleeding*, 64.

10. Asinof, *Strike Zone*, 61.

11. The work was specifically dedicated to Mara Wellington and Allie Sherman. Asinof wrote, "I have moved freely through the inner sanctums." See Asinof, *Seven Days*, 9. The phrase echoes the title of 1969's *The Name of the Game: An Inner Sanctum Mystery*, the third entry in Asinof's New York trilogy.

12. Asinof, *Seven Days*, 9. Interestingly, Giants quarterback Fran Tarkenton, whom Asinof interviewed at length in *Seven Days*, later co-wrote (with Herb Resnicow) his own novel, *Murder at the Super Bowl* (New York: Morrow, 1986).

13. These accolades come from the cover jacket of Asinof, *Seven Days*.

14. Asinof, *Seven Days*, 8.

15. Interview with Jim Bouton. The working title for the proposed novel was *Against the Wall*. See Asinof papers at University of Texas at Austin.

16. Okrent, like Asinof, is the well-known author of several baseball and non-baseball books, including *The Ultimate Baseball Book* (Boston: Houghton Mifflin, 1979). Okrent has praised Asinof's *Man on Spikes* as "perhaps the truest baseball novel ever written." See Alex Belth, "The Professional," *Bronx Banter*, http://bronxbanter.baseballtoaster.com/archives/1015739.html, quoting Okrent from the *New York Times*.

17. Interview with Jim Bouton.

18. At the time of Bouton's playing career with the Yankees, Asinof did an even-handed profile of Yankees manger Johnny Keane, of whom Bouton was sometimes critical in his memoir. See Eliot Asinof, "The Word for Johnny Keane Is Patience," *New York Times Magazine*, May 30, 1965.

19. See Haberman, "Recalling a Cheerful Man."

20. Interview with Jim Bouton.

21. Interview with Martin Asinof. Presumably, the mutual sportswriter acquaintance was Leonard Schecter, editor of *Ball Four*. Everyone interviewed agrees that Bouton and Asinof split a $90,000 advance from Viking, who never recouped their investment through sales.

22. Bouton also stated that he negotiated a larger advance from Viking for both writers than Asinof would have been able to get on his own, notwithstanding Asinof's high reputation as a writer. Given Bouton's marketable celebrity status, this account seems likely.

23. One suspects the analogy also applies to the virtue of patience, one for which Asinof was not personally known, although he likely would have found a better way of expressing it as a writer.

24. Interestingly, in the novel, the son of Ward (Bouton) is also named Martin, while the son of Kolacka (Asinof) is named Joe. Kolacka also has a daughter, Amy.

25. Asinof, *Eight Men Out*, 149–150. By coincidence, the owner of the Chicago Cubs in 1920, and the person who initiated the investigation, was William Veeck, father of the same Bill Veeck who would later own the Chicago White Sox and become a friend of Asinof's. Another, possibly unrelated, coincidence is that five years before co-writing *Strike Zone*, Asinof wrote a cover-story profile of Yankees manager Dallas Green, who had previously managed both the Cubs and the Phillies with some success. Asinof noted that "Green ran the Phillies the way Captain Bligh ran the Bounty." See Asinof, "New York Manager Dallas Green."

26. Asinof, *Strike Zone*, 99.

27. Asinof, *Bleeding*, 105.

28. Asinof, *Strike Zone*, 76.

29. Ibid., 109.

30. Ibid., 203.

31. At one point, Kolacka compares an umpire-colleague's delusions of grandeur to a bad golfer playing a good round. At another, he equates a favorable turn of events in the game to the effect of making a very good golf shot. See Asinof, *Strike Zone*, 142, 158.

32. Kolacka's playing career is ended by a Korean War injury, similar to the manner in which Asinof's playing career was permanently disrupted by World War II and playing injuries sustained soon afterwards.

33. Kolacka states that he is 60 years old and a 38-year veteran. See Asinof, *Strike Zone*, 10. When the novel was being written, Asinof was approximately 75 years old and it had been roughly 38 years since his first novel *Man on Spikes*, had been published.

34. Kolacka and Asinof also have, as one would expect, some interesting differences. For example, Kolacka is born on April 27, whereas Asinof's birthday was July 13. Curiously, April 27 is also the birthday of Civil War hero Ulysses S. Grant, but this is not mentioned. Like William Shakespeare and other April-born noteworthies, Kolacka identifies himself as a Taurus birth sign. See Asinof, *Strike Zone*, 56.

35. The uncounted, total number of rewrites for *Strike Zone* appears to have been daunting. See Asinof papers at University of Texas at Austin.

Chapter 14

1. Asinof's last two novels would be released respectively by an academic publisher, Southern Illinois University Press (*Off-Season*), and a small independent, Bunim and Bannigan (*Final Judgment*).

2. Many widely-read authors are not skilled at marketing, of course. Those who are not, however, and wish to enjoy short-term commercial success within their own lifetime, must either develop these skills or hire someone else to do the job. Otherwise, the best that can be hoped for is posthumous recognition.

3. *Publishers Weekly* 241, no. 19 (May 9, 1994): 62.

4. *Library Journal* 119, no. 7 (April 15, 1994): 110.

5. *Booklist* 90, no. 15 (April 1, 1994): 1404.

6. See belated book review of *Strike Zone* by Joe Gray dated October 9, 2010, *BaseballBG*, http://www.baseballgb.co.uk/?p=9360, quoting an earlier post from *Baseball Think Factory*.

7. Interview with Jim Bouton.

8. This was the 11th annual Symposium on Baseball and American Culture held at Cooperstown. Strictly speaking in mathematical terms, the 20th century ended in the year 2000, but this is not accepted by popular culture, which prefers the year 1999.

9. According to Asinof's son, Martin, his father was also invited to this event in con-

junction with the 1998 reissue his classic novel *Man on Spikes* being admitted into the Hall of Fame library. It also anticipated the 2000 release of Asinof's last baseball novel, *Off-Season*.

10. Reprinted in Tim Wiles, "Asinof: A Baseball Life," *Ron Kaplan's Bookshelf*, http://www.ronkaplansbaseballbookshelf.com/2008/06/13/lest-we-forget-tim-wiles-on-asinof/ (accessed June 20, 2011).

11. Wiles, "Asinof."

12. Wiles adds that "even her attention is unrequited [by Asinof], as was the case, there were some things we just couldn't tolerate back then." See Wiles, "Asinof."

13. This Shakespeare quote is from Act II of *The Tempest*, the same play (and act) from which Asinof took the title of his third baseball novel, *The Bedfellow* (see Part III of this study).

14. Asinof, *Bleeding*, 62.

15. Ibid., 63–64. Asinof, in addition to having used Gilbert favorably as a cameo character in his screenplay *Channing: Swing for the Moon* (see Chapter 2), fondly praised Gilbert's playing and strategic baseball skills when writing a piece on the minor leagues. See Asinof, "Journey Back to Bushville."

16. Asinof, *Bleeding*, 64.

17. Asinof graduated cum-laude (in history) from Swarthmore College in 1940. He also captained the Swarthmore baseball team.

18. The nearest geographic minor league franchise to Wausau is currently the (Appleton) Wisconsin Timber Rattlers, a Class A team affiliated with the Seattle Mariners. Wausau itself has not hosted a minor league affiliate since 1990.

19. I, too, played high school and semipro ball in a WPA-built stadium, the old Ames Field (now demolished) in Michigan City, Indiana, long-time home of (among many other teams) the Michigan City Stars, owned and managed by former minor league player Al Shinn (see Chapter 4).

20. As an indication of its quality, the Northern League in future years would groom major league players the caliber of Henry Aaron, Bob Feller, Lou Brock, Roger Maris, and Minnie Minoso, to name just a few.

21. *Wausau Daily-Record Herald*, May 7, 1941. Asinof's name is misspelled "Alsenof." The name was variously misspelled as "Asinde" (April 28), "Alsnof" (May 5), and "Alsenof" (again) on May 9, before local reporters finally got it right on May 10 with "Asinof." By this time, he had become a fixture in the Lumberjacks' starting lineup. Asinof, being left-handed, could also play first base on occasion. See box score on April 28 (for game played on April 27).

22. *Wausau Daily-Record Herald*, June 6 and June 17, 1941.

23. In Kolacka's case, it is the Korean War. See Asinof, *Strike Zone*, 75.

24. *Wausau Daily-Record Herald*, June 3, 1941.

25. Asinof, *Man on Spikes*, 10.

26. *Wausau Daily-Record Herald*, May 10 and June 4, 1941.

27. Today, it is still astounding to see how many major leaguers, especially among good hitters, do not know how to bunt and refuse to learn. Asinof recalled with pride perfecting his bunting skills by emulating Ty Cobb's reported drills. See Asinof, *Bleeding*, 60.

28. *Wausau Daily-Record Herald*, June 20, 1941.

29. Interview with Martin Asinof.

30. Asinof, *Bedfellow*, 121.

31. *Wausau Daily-Record Herald*, June 24, 1941.

32. Asinof, *Man on Spikes*, 145.

33. *Wausau Daily-Record Herald*, June 26, 1941.

34. In the novel, Kutner diffuses tension among teammates by admitting that the mishap was his own fault. See Asinof, *Man on Spikes*, 173.

35. Asinof, *Bedfellow*, 32–33.

36. Asinof, *Strike Zone*, 177–178.

37. *Baseball-Reference.Com*.

38. Asinof, *Strike Zone*, 241.

Chapter 15

1. Asinof, *Strike Zone*, 127.

2. Interview with Jim Bouton.

3. In one intentional violation of baseball etiquette, Kolacka shows his contempt for fans by dusting home plate with his backside facing the nearest stands. See Asinof, *Strike Zone*, 202.

4. Ibid., 158–159.

5. Ibid., 76.

6. Ibid., 115.

7. Ibid., 140–141.

8. Ibid., 204–206.

9. Ibid., 158.

10. Ibid., 205.

11. Ibid., 127.

12. Ibid., 159–160.

13. During an interview with Asinof's son, Martin, he recalled a story from his father about receiving the exact same kind of anti–

Semitic treatment as a batter from an umpire named "Reagan." The called strikes were so outlandish that fans began yelling, "Jew," not at Asinof, but rather at the umpire, an uncomplimentary reference to, presumably, his dishonest calls. This may have been Asinof's remembrance of umpire "Irish" Bob O'Regan, possibly active in the Northern League at that time.

14. Asinof, *Strike Zone*, 186.

15. No one understands this dynamic better than left-handed pitchers (as I was in my youth) who have developed skillful pick-off moves to first base. It is an invaluable defensive tool, if done well it usually violates the balk rule, but is rarely called a balk by umpires, particularly at the professional level. This is because professional umpires understand the difficulty in detection and do not wish to expend their credibility on violations that are not clear-cut. Consequently, opposing teams also tend to accept good left-handed pick off moves without argument. What other sport has such a compromise?

16. With the third baseman and first baseman both charging for the sacrifice bunt, the usual safe play would be to throw to first base, being covered by the second baseman.

17. Asinof, *Strike Zone*, 139.

18. Asinof, *Bleeding*, 63–64.

19. Asinof, *Strike Zone*, 175.

20. Ibid., 202.

21. Ibid., 215.

22. Asinof, *Bedfellow*, 32.

23. Asinof, *Bleeding*, 62–63.

24. Ibid., 62. Asinof would later (in 2000) quote the very quotable Berra in the opening to his last baseball novel, *Off Season* (see Chapter 17).

25. In self-appraisal, Asinof wrote, "Though I was a good ballplayer, I knew I would never be good enough." See Asinof, *Bleeding*, 63.

26. Ted Williams was more articulate and probably more accurate when he said that hitting was fifty percent "from the neck on up."

27. Asinof, *Bedfellow*, 32–33.

28. Asinof, *Man on Spikes*, 157.

29. Ibid., 157–160.

Chapter 16

1. Kolacka's less-than-adoring twin children, now grown and married, live in Boston and Richmond, respectively — both sizeable Eastern cities but still definitely second tier by New York City standards. See Asinof, *Strike Zone*, 33

2. Descendents of German, Scandinavian, and Polish immigrants have always been the dominant ethnic groups in Wausau.

3. Today, the only active mosque in Central Wisconsin is also located in nearby Marshfield, Wisconsin. This, of course, did not exist in 1941.

4. Wausau still has its own separate Jewish cemetery, a bygone reminder of the racial and religious segregation that once existed there. Wausau was far from being alone in this regard, both in primarily German-American towns and those that were not.

5. The photo is to be found in the special collections of the Marathon County Historical Society.

6. *Wausau Daily-Record Herald*, May 7, 1941.

7. Asinof, *Strike Zone*, 45.

8. Ibid., 87.

9. Ibid., 47, 56.

10. Ibid., 86–87. To his chagrin, Enid also wants Kolacka to be more like his hated rival, Sirotta, who, unlike Kolacka, elects to be a strikebreaker for higher pay. See p. 146.

11. Asinof, *Strike Zone*, 188.

12. Ibid., 33.

13. Ibid., 88.

14. Asinof, *Name of the Game*, 36–38.

15. Asinof, *Off-Season*, 17.

16. See 1930 U.S. Census for Wausau, Wisconsin.

17. In the earlier drafts, Enid is presented as the sister of Kolacka's best friend from the war, the same man who attempts to bribe him in the story. In what appears to be the original draft, the last line written by Asinof is: "I never faced the fact that I didn't love her." See Asinof papers at University of Texas at Austin.

18. In an interview with Asinof's son, Martin, he stressed that appropriate identity protection was always a major concern in his father's writings and speeches. This is not a surprising quality for a writer who first succeeded in breaking the true story behind the Black Sox Scandal.

19. Asinof, *Strike Zone*, 163.

20. In presenting the extramarital affair between Kolacka and Trisha, the novelist goes out of his way to avoid all sordid stereotypes, and instead seems to rely more on the courtly tradition of romantic literature. See Asinof, *Strike Zone*, 163.

21. Ibid., 189.

22. Asinof, *Bleeding*, 16.

23. Asinof, *Strike Zone*, 146.

24. Ibid., 99–100.

Chapter 17

1. Asinof, *Off-Season*, 82.

2. Since 1962, the Baseball Hall of Fame has given the J. G. Spink Award for excellence in baseball writing, a distinction that surprisingly was never given to Asinof; then again, this might be appropriate in that the award seems to be intended for sportswriters, and, as this study as tried to emphasize, Eliot Asinof was far more than a sportswriter in his professional writing career.

3. Both the re-release of *Man on Spikes* in 1998 and the new release of *Off-Season* in 2000 were featured as part of the SIU Press "Writing Baseball" series.

4. Asinof's prominent appearance on A&E partly compensated for his inexcusable exclusion from Ken Burns' 1994 documentary, *Baseball*, reportedly due to a producer refusal to work with Asinof. Many of the participants from the 1988 movie version of *Eight Men Out*, however, were invited to take part.

5. Berra quotes: "You've got to be careful if you don't know where you're going, because you might not get there," and, "If you come to a fork in the road, take it."

6. Hannibal was of course also the home town of Mark Twain. Ron Powers is perhaps best known for his collaboration with James Bradley on *Flags of Our Fathers* (New York: Random House, 2000) the memoir of Bradley's father at Iwo Jima during World War II, later (2006) made into a successful motion picture by director Clint Eastwood. The book appeared the same year as Asinof's *Off-Season*.

7. Koenig was a long-time friend of Asinof's who co-owned with him the Yonkers Indians semiprofessional baseball team in 1946–1947.

8. The original working titles of the novel were *Free Agent* and *Hero*, the former an oblique reference to Cagle's enviable status as a professional ballplayer unbound by the old reserve clause (see Chapter 19), and the latter a direct reference to Cagle himself. Asinof's original proposal for the novel has different character names and a different setting. Publisher rejection letters for the proposal date from 1993. See Asinof papers at University of Texas at Austin.

9. Asinof, *Off-Season*, 148.

10. Kutner admits to coaching and umpiring baseball out of love for the game, after he had retired as a player. See ibid., 148.

11. Ibid., 149.

12. Ibid., 45.

13. When Cagle and Kutner meet, the latter is described as "maybe eighty years old," the same age as Asinof at the time of the novel's publication. See ibid., 148.

14. Asinof, "Willie Stargell."

15. Asinof, *Off-Season*, 76.

16. Ibid., 128.

17. The dedication reads, "For my friend, the late Dashiell Hammett." See Asinof, *Name of the Game*, 5.

18. Ibid., 13, 150.

19. Ibid., 113.

20. Hinkle was an independent magazine editor championing Kaplan's cause for some time previous. Turner was also an editor and former FBI agent familiar with the case. Asinof was brought on board with the project no doubt because of his investigative writing abilities combined with a proven willingness to take on controversial or unpopular subject matter.

21. Asinof, *10-Second Jailbreak*, 253.

22. Ibid., xi.

23. Ibid., 15.

24. Some of these families included the Gores, the Bouviers, and the Vidals. Another distant relative was the distinguished American author, Gore Vidal, who, like Asinof, served in the Aleutian Islands during World War II. See Asinof, *10-Second Jailbreak*, 11. Skyjacker Garrett Brock Trapnell, subject of Asinof's unsettling 1976 character study, *The Fox Is Crazy Too*, also came from a famous American family.

25. For clarification, Hershner was a Vietnam War veteran while the much older Asinof was in the U.S. Air Force during World War II.

Chapter 18

1. *Publishers Weekly* 247, no. 11 (March 13, 2000): 63.

2. *Library Journal* 125, no. 3 (February 15, 2000): 194.

3. For Asinof's baseball writing of this more popular descriptive type, his best exemplars are *Man on Spikes* and *Strike Zone*, not *Eight Men Out* or *Off-Season*.

4. *NINE: A Journal of Baseball History and Culture* 10, no. 2 (Spring 2000): 157–159.

5. *Booklist* 96, no. 15 (April 1, 2000): 1437.

6. Interview with John Sayles.

7. Asinof, *Craig and Joan*, vii.

8. Interview with Martin Asinof.

9. Asinof was told by the local high school administration that he was "an upsetting influence" and "politely but firmly asked to leave." See Asinof, *Craig and Joan*, ix.

10. Kisseloff, *The Nation.*
11. In the novel, the would-be martyr Ruby Coles addresses Cagle as "J. C." See Asinof, *Off-Season*, 55–58.
12. Ibid., 18.
13. A friend of the doomed couple told Asinof that "they wanted to be martyrs. She [Joan] used that word." See Asinof, *Craig and Joan*, 177–178.
14. Asinof, *Craig and Joan*, 146. The modern church condemned such acts as suicide, and (it is implied) because most churches had yet to officially oppose the war which motivated the acts. The theological issue of legitimate religious martyrdom versus proscribed suicide was in fact a very early topic of debate in Christian church. Augustine, among others, wrote extensively on the subject.
15. Asinof, *Craig and Joan*, 238.
16. Asinof, *Off-Season*, 2.
17. Ibid., 25.
18. Ibid., 89.
19. Ibid., 115.
20. The very fictional name of Gandee itself sounds like a small-town caricature of the martyred Indian political leader, Mahatma Gandhi (1869–1948), one of the great world leaders in Asinof's lifetime.
21. Various working titles for *Final Judgment* in its (many) earlier drafts include *Flear*, *Anne in Full Color*, and *End Over End*. The gestation period for the novel was clearly a long one, dating back over 20 years during a time in which Asinof was beginning to write again after having taken significant time off. See Asinof papers at University of Texas at Austin.
22. Asinof, *Final Judgment*, 33.
23. The martyrdom theme, along with its political (versus religious) associations, was explored in my earlier study, *Perpetua of Carthage: Portrait of a Third Century Martyr* (Jefferson, NC: McFarland, 2009). One wonders if the very well-read Asinof was familiar with the famous prison diary of Saint Perpetua.
24. Asinof, *Final Judgment*, 19.
25. By 1999, Asinof was 80 years old.

Chapter 19

1. Asinof, *Name of the Game*, 17. Writing a book review, Asinof criticizes another author for equating baseball with poker playing. See Eliot Asinof's book review of *Percentage Baseball* by Earnshaw Cook, "Don't Bunt, the Gizmo Says Hit!" *Life*, April 15, 1966.
2. Asinof, *Off-Season*, 148.
3. Eliot Asinof, "Hey Joe: The Booing of the Great DiMaggio." *Village Voice*, February 6, 2001.
4. According to Asinof's article, DiMaggio in 1938 was paid an annual salary of $25,000 by Rupert.
5. Asinof added that it was his first baseball novel which in turn led to his initial meeting with DiMaggio. See Asinof, "Hey Joe." (See Chapter 2.)
6. The story is also recalled in Asinof's memoir *Bleeding Between the Lines*, 189–190. See also Asinof, "Hey Joe."
7. Asinof alludes to Colonel Rupert's cutting remark made against DiMaggio at the time, "I hope the young man has learned his lesson." See Asinof, "Hey Joe." Asinof's abortive screenplay project on the last year of Ty Cobb (later made into a movie by Ron Shelton) was also, according to him, merely a ruse by the producer to snag a DiMaggio film project through Asinof. See Asinof, *Bleeding*, 189. (See also Chapter 4.)
8. See Asinof papers at the University of Texas at Austin.
9. Asinof, *Off-Season*, 4.
10. Ibid., 8.
11. Asinof, *Bedfellow*, 123–124. In Asinof, *Off-Season*, 33, the novelist seems to evoke Sorrell, the former fictional New York Mets outfielder, with a reference to old Shea Stadium, where Cagle the National Leaguer (Los Angeles Dodgers) plays whenever he is in New York. The same passage also mentions the Roosevelt Hotel where Cagle chooses to stay in town, and where Asinof cemented his final publishing deal for *Eight Men Out* during the early 1960s. See Asinof, *Bleeding*, 122–123.
12. Asinof, *Bleeding*, 58.
13. One wonders if Asinof's decision to have a pitcher-hero in his last novel was inspired or instigated by his earlier thorny collaboration with pitcher Jim Bouton on *Strike Zone* (see Part IV of this study).
14. Asinof, *Off-Season*, 1.
15. Ibid., 8.
16. Cagle successfully finishes his perfect game nonetheless, but is rightfully annoyed at his father's behavior. See ibid., 14.
17. Ibid., 87.
18. Ibid., 8, 10.
19. See ibid., 84; and Asinof, *Strike Zone*, 176.
20. Asinof, *Off-Season*, 95.
21. Ibid., 149.
22. Ibid., 148.

23. Asinof, *Strike Zone*, 130.
24. Asinof, *Man on Spikes*, 3.
25. Asinof, *Off-Season*, 148.
26. During the newly-established era of free agency in baseball, Asinof wrote: "Now players are giving up games with lackadaisical attitudes rooted in financial security." See Asinof, "Pete Rose."
27. Asinof, *Off-Season*, 3.
28. Ibid., 2–3.
29. Ibid., 99–100.
30. Asinof, *Man on Spikes*, 133.
31. See Eliot Asinof, "The Dis-Integration of Baseball: A Modest Proposal for the Great Game," *Village Voice*, January 11, 2000.
32. This is yet another recurring theme in Asinof's baseball works. See Asinof, "Hey Joe." In *Bleeding Between the Lines*, 115, Asinof shared how, at the beginning of their interview, former Black Sox Happy Felsch challenged him with the very same observation. Two years later, in 2003, Asinof reiterated his contempt for commentators who focused on numbers: "Statistics have always been the sportswriters' measure of a ballplayer." See Eliot Asinof, "Ferguson Jenkins: King of the Mound," *Time International*, Canada ed., June 30, 2003.
33. In contrast, Asinof poignantly recalled how the dying DiMaggio requested from him an autographed copy of *Man on Spikes*. See Asinof, "Hey Joe."
34. During his numerous interviews with survivors of the 1919 team, both crooked and honest, most expressed initial hostility towards writers. Examples: "You writers are always feeding on the players," Chick Gandil; "I don't cotton much to writers," Ray Schalk; "All company men [sportswriters]," Happy Felsch. See Asinof, *Bleeding*, 91, 95, 115.
35. Asinof, *Off-Season*, 120.
36. Three years after the novel's publication, Asinof wrote: "Pitchers are a breed apart. They work every few days, and everything depends on them. They are special, and they know it." See Asinof, "Ferguson Jenkins."

Chapter 20

1. Asinof, "Dis-Integration." By the late 1960s, Asinof consistently and correctly maintained that baseball was no longer the most popular sport in America — an honor which since belongs to football. Some of his comments include: "Baseball, sad to report, has gone out of universal fashion" (see Asinof, "World Series"), and, "It may be that America has changed too much for baseball" (see Asinof, "Turbulent Century").
2. Asinof wrote: "As the nation goes, so goes the national pastime." See Asinof's Book Review of *The Bronx Zoo*.
3. Asinof, *Off-Season*, 9.
4. Asinof also acknowledged as one of his influences the works of Ron Powers who is originally from Hannibal, Missouri, as was Mark Twain.
5. Asinof, *Off-Season*, 97.
6. Cagle's immediate reaction is that black baseball teams would simply win all the games, thereby defeating the drama of the event. Corky protests that whites would counter by doing whatever was necessary to become competitive again. See Asinof, *Off-Season*, 79–98.
7. Asinof, *Bedfellow*, 58.
8. Asinof, *People vs. Blutcher*, xiii.
9. Asinof, "Dis-Integration."
10. Asinof also takes a quick jabs at sportcasters (see Chapter 19) and "high-powered representatives" of players, immediately calling to mind his unflattering portrayal of Cagle's agent Gordon Stanley in *Off-Season*. See Asinof, "Dis-Integration."
11. Asinof, *Off-Season*, 40–43.
12. Asinof, "Dis-Integration."
13. Jenkins could qualify as African American, however, based on his ownership of an Oklahoma horse ranch. See Asinof, "Ferguson Jenkins."
14. Jenkins' best years as a major league pitcher, however, came mostly with the Chicago Cubs during the late 1960s and early 1970s.
15. Asinof, it would seem, was incapable of writing an ordinary puff piece at this point in his career. See Asinof, "Ferguson Jenkins."
16. Asinof, *Off-Season*, 29. This anticipates Mike Kutner's similar criticism of modern baseball in general during the final pages of the novel (see Chapter 19).
17. Asinof, *Off-Season*, 31.
18. Ibid., 44.
19. Asinof, *Bedfellow*, 223.
20. Asinof, *Strike Zone*, 241.
21. Asinof, *Off-Season*, 149.
22. Asinof, *Craig and Joan*, 81–82.
23. Ibid., 138.
24. Writing in the early 1970s, Asinof refers to these defenders of the status quo in Nixonian terms as the so-called "Great Silent Majority." See Asinof, *Craig and Joan*, 139. Today, it is arguable whether any such electoral majority is motivated more by self-satisfaction or profound fear of losing what little they have left.

25. Asinof, *Craig and Joan*, 141.
26. Ibid., 139.
27. Ibid., 141–142, 243.
28. Ibid., 243.
29. Asinof, *Off-Season*, 144.
30. Ibid., 149.
31. Asinof, it should be recalled, was able to do the same, even though he was given an outstanding formal education in his youth.

Conclusion

1. Asinof attributes this viewpoint to James T. Farrell, but writes as though he is in complete agreement. See Farrell, *Dreaming Baseball*, vii.
2. Asinof's lifelong fan loyalty to the New York Yankees and New York football Giants represent only two small examples of this within a professional sports context.
3. Asinof, *Bleeding*, 63–64.
4. Plimpton's first work along these lines was *Out of My League* (New York: Harper, 1961), recounting his being allowed to pitch batting practice before a major league baseball All-Star Game. It may have been partially inspired by the ground-breaking realism of Asinof's 1955 novel, *Man on Spikes*.
5. In comparison to Plimpton's high-profile amateur forays in professional playing circles, Asinof described how during his first tryout with the Philadelphia Phillies, he suited up in uniform with little notice, took batting practice, and played first base during infield warm-up, a position less familiar to him than centerfield. He promptly blended right in with the other professionals and was offered a contract with the Phillies soon afterwards. See Asinof, *Bleeding*, 62.
6. As noted earlier, one is reminded of the ancient Spartans, in which stealing was punishable, not for the intrinsic act of stealing, but for the thief's carelessness in being caught.
7. Peterson, *Extra Innings*, xi.
8. Asinof, "Willie Stargell."
9. Asinof, "Don't Bunt."
10. Asinof, normally a tough judge of character, referred to Sayles as "a first-class guy who surrounds himself with first-class people." See Lott, "Eliot Asinof."
11. Haberman, "Recalling a Cheerful Man."

Asinof Bibliography

Published Books

Asinof, Eliot. 1955. *Man on Spikes.* New York: McGraw-Hill. Reprint, Carbondale: Southern Illinois University Press, 1998.

_____. 1963. *Eight Men Out.* Austin, TX: Holt, Rinehart, and Winston. Reprint, New York: Holt Paperbacks, 1987.

_____. 1967. *The Bedfellow.* New York: Simon and Schuster.

_____. 1968. *Seven Days to Sunday: Crisis Week with the New York Giants.* New York: Simon and Schuster.

_____. 1969. *The Name of the Game Is Murder: An Inner Sanctum Mystery.* New York: Simon and Schuster.

_____. 1970. *People vs. Blutcher: Black Men and White Law in Bedford-Stuyvesant.* New York: Viking Press.

_____. 1971. *Craig and Joan: Two Lives for Peace.* New York: Viking Press.

_____, Warren Hinkle, and William Turner. 1973. *The 10-Second Jailbreak: The Helicopter Escape of Joel David Kaplan.* Austin, TX: Holt, Rinehart, and Winston.

_____. 1976. *The Fox Is Crazy Too: The True Story of Garrett Trapnell, Adventurer, Skyjacker, Bank Robber, Con Man, Lover.* New York: William Morrow.

_____. 1977. *Say It Ain't So, Gordon Littlefield.* New York: E. P. Dutton.

_____. 1979. *Bleeding Between the Lines.* Austin, TX: Holt, Rinehart and Winston.

_____. 1990. *1919: America's Loss of Innocence.* New York: Donald I. Fine.

_____. 2000. *Off-Season.* Carbondale: Southern Illinois University Press.

_____. 2008. *Final Judgment.* New York: Bunim and Bannigan.

Asinof, Eliot, and Jim Bouton. 1994. *Strike Zone.* New York: Viking.

Other Selected Baseball Writings

Eliot Asinof. 1955. "The Rookie." In *Discovery No. 6.* New York: Cardinal Pocket Books.

_____. 1963. "A Gambler's World Series." *The Saturday Evening Post,* November 30.

_____. 1965. "The Word for Johnny Keane Is: Patience." *The New York Times Magazine,* May 30.

_____. 1966. "Journey Back to Bushville." *The New York Times Magazine,* July 24.

_____. 1966. "Don't Bunt, the Gizmo Says Hit!" Book review of *Percentage Baseball* by Earnshaw Cook. *Life,* April 15.

_____. 1967. "The World Series Is No Autumn Classic." *The New York Times,* September 30.

_____. 1969. "Turbulent Century of Swat: The Game Turns 101." Book review of *Baseball* by Douglas Wallop. *Life,* June 6.

_____. 1970. "Denny McLain: I Snap Back Real Quick." *Sport,* June.

_____. 1979. "The Secret Life of Rocky Perone." *Sports Illustrated,* June 18.

_____. 1979. Book Review of *The Bronx Zoo* by Sparky Lyle and Peter Golenbock. *The New York Times,* July 4.

_____. 1980. "Willie Stargell: Where I Come from, Where I Am Going." *Sport,* April.

_____. 1985. "Jackson, Shoeless Joe." In *Encyclopædia Britannica.* 15th ed.

_____. 1986. "Did Leonardo Invent the

Home Run?" Book review of *The Iowa Baseball Confederacy* by W. P. Kinsella. *The New York Times Book Review*, April 20.

_____. 1989. "New York Manager Dallas Green: On the Spot." *The New York Times Magazine*, March 26.

_____. 1989. "Pete Rose Can't Lose." *Sport*, April.

_____. 2000. "The Dis-Integration of Baseball: A Modest Proposal for the Great Game." *Village Voice*, January 11.

_____. 2001. "Hey Joe: The Booing of the Great DiMaggio." *Village Voice*, February 6.

_____. 2001. Foreword. In *Extra Innings: Writing on Baseball* by Richard Peterson. Champaign: University of Illinois Press.

_____. 2003. "Ferguson Jenkins: King of the Mound." *Time International*, Canada ed., June 30.

_____. 2007. Foreword. In *Dreaming Baseball* by James T. Farrell. Edited by Ron Briley, Margaret Davidson, and James Barbour. OH: Kent State University Press.

Secondary Sources

Other than excerpts from *Extra Innings: Writing on Baseball* by Professor Peterson's book (see above, 2001), there are to date no known published studies focusing on Asinof's work.

Asinof's literary executor, Jeff Kisseloff, currently maintains a website under construction, *Elliot Asinof*, at http://eliot asinof.com, which includes a very good short biography through 2000 by Jeffrey Lott, "Eliot Asinof," published in the *Swarthmore College Bulletin* in 2000.

Kisseloff also wrote a tribute, "Remembering Eliot Asinof," for *The Nation*, June 24, 2008.

A summary of Asinof's 1999 Cooperstown Symposium speech can be found in "Asinof: A Baseball Life" by Tim Wiles, *Ron Kaplan's Bookshelf*, http://www.ronkaplans-baseballbookshelf.com/2008/06/13/lest-we-forget-tim-wiles-on-asinof/.

Following Asinof's death in 2008, numerous obituaries appeared. *The New York Times*, July 11, 2008, printed "Recalling a Cheerful Man Made Angry by Hypocrisy" by Clyde Haberman and "Eliot Asinof, 'Eight Men Out' Author, Is Dead at 88" by Bruce Weber.

Other obituaries were in *The Washington Post*, June 12, 2008, by Joe Holley; *The Los Angeles Times*, June 12, 2008, by anonymous staff; and *The Guardian*, June 26, 2008, by Michael Carlson.

Some of the more informative internet postings include those by Stephen Bowie at http://classictvhistory.wordpress.com, the John Sayles Stock Company website at http://www.ericenders.com, and "The Professional" by Alex Belth at http://bronx banter.baseballtoaster.com.

Other isolated references to Asinof's life and works are cited in the footnotes.

Index

www.ingramcontent.com/pod-product-compliance
Lightning Source LLC
Chambersburg PA
CBHW021650110726
47902CB00007B/1906

* 9 7 8 0 7 8 6 4 6 3 0 2 2 *